# GATE OF THE MULTIVERSE

## WOLVES OF THE TESSERACT BOOK 2

### CHRISTOPHER D. SCHMITZ

TREESHAKER BOOKS

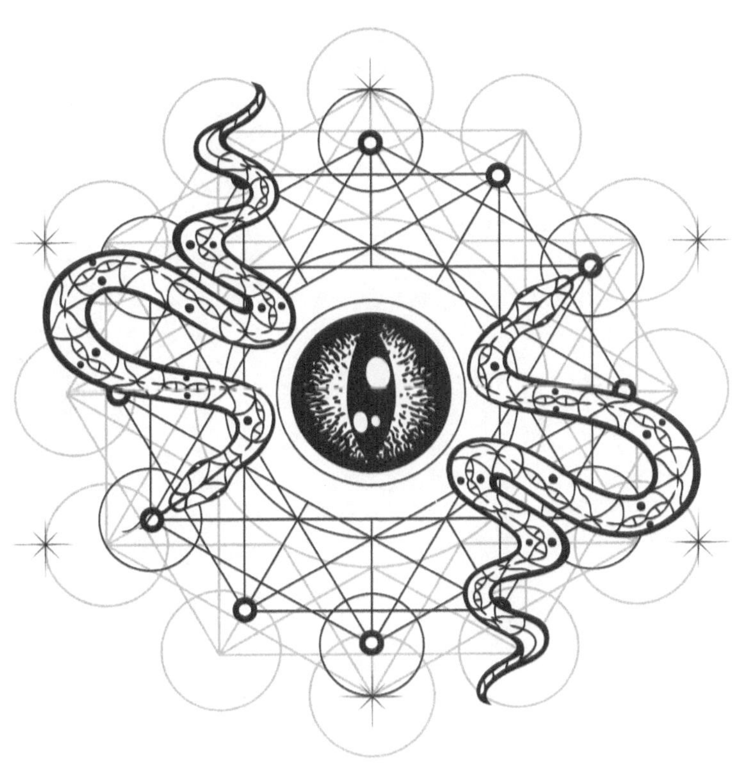

# CONTENTS

# SPECIAL OFFER!

Stay up to date on the world of Wolves of the Tesseract... you'll get access to a bunch of special freebies, bonus content, and the author's newsletter. You can unsubscribe at any time.
To get access to this exclusive group, just follow this link:
https://www.subscribepage.com/wolvesofthetesseract
and add your email to be added immediatley!

# PROLOGUE

*Ancient Times... Straruck... in the Desolation Realm*

"I know all about the different dimensions of the multiverse!" The vagabond howled secret information from the front of the writhing, pulsing crowd that gathered at the edge of campus. Security personnel held the line and made way for several reptilian guests as they approached the shrine at the college. This dissenter was the only one protesting and had been largely ignored—the remainder of the vyrm people buzzed with excitement—none responded to this person's trepidation.

He continued shouting with a kind of manic fervor, demanding an audience. "You don't understand! Even if you don't care about *their residents,* don't you remember the prophecies of Maetha?"

The forbidden name caught the attention of a soldier from the priest class. A lithe and agile vyrm, he looked like a member of the Black caste as he approached. He wore a different frock than the rest of the Thousand Elders, who paraded behind him on their way to the temple for the ceremony. Questioning the security officer who held the protester back, he asked, "Do you know this one?"

The guard nodded and responded in the vyrmic holy tongue out of respect. [Yes. He is Professor Karin-Ja.]

[He teaches here?]

The guard nodded an affirmation.

Karin-Ja tilted his head inquisitively. By the sigils on his robe's cuffs, he recognized the man as a personal assistant to one of the leaders. "If you would allow me to speak to the elders, please," he persisted.

"Greetings, Karin-Ja. My name is Keldric." He motioned to him and the sentry let him pass. "Please, walk with me."

They left the processional throng behind at the campus and headed for the outskirts of Straruck. Karin-Ja's scowl protested. "Where are you taking me?"

"We cannot disrupt the Elders. They are in the middle of the Great Ceremony. Perhaps there will be time later for you to make your case, whatever that may be. In the meantime, I want to show you something. On the way, please tell me everything you know of Maetha; I have always been interested in the prophecies."

Karin-Ja smoothed the itching scales on his neck where a wisp of sand had gotten beneath them. He flicked the detritus away. "Prophecy is not as much of a what—it is more of a *whom*." He excitedly prattled on about the ancient legend of Maetha—the vyrm savior.

Keldric smiled as they arrived on a grassy knoll just outside the city. He waved his hands at the glory of the expansive fields. The fruitful Plains of Neggath spread out before them. [The grandeur of the architect is our glory,] he quoted an ancient proverb from the holy texts of early Mae'le-ggath: an ancient, purer version of the vyrm religion which predated the devotion to the annihilator god, Sh'logath.

Karin-Ja bobbed his head in agreement.

"Do you believe in Maetha?" Keldric noted, "There has been something of a recent renaissance in his belief, you know."

"This is true. And yes! I believe in him as more than a myth."

Keldric grinned. "Who do you say Maetha is?"

Karin-Ja looked confused. "We cannot know *who* he is. Not until he reveals himself."

"But some say that it was Rasthakka; others say it was Kadrist. Of course, the upper caste claims it was King Chirasq or his brother, Pharaoh Akroth. *But I like this new movement...* people say it is one of these travelers: the brothers from the Prime dimension. Perhaps *one of them* is Maetha."

"What?" Karin-Ja was taken aback by the premise.

"But they've done so much to help stabilize the faith and the Elders are quite taken with them."

Karin-Ja shrugged. "I'm more interested in truth than with inter-caste politics."

Keldric narrowed his eyes to slits as he regarded him. "Are you *caste-less*?" His voice carried a hint of scoff. He chuckled, "You *are*—you follow Krakkath!"

The topic of caste was unfriendly and certainly taboo, given Karin-Ja's appointment as a professor. The Followers of Krakkath were outlawed—and the professor could truthfully spit on the ideas of Krakkath; he had proven untrustworthy and even now sat on the high council. Of the two prongs of belief held by the caste-less, Krakkathian ideas were as anathema as the other, nihilistic perversions of the old ways.

Karin-Ja merely glowered in response. "What did you bring me to see?" He motioned to the verdant plains. "I already know the glory of Edenya... I teach on this. What more can you show me?"

"Something *greater*."

Karin-Ja cocked his head.

Keldric flashed a wicked grin. [*I am Maetha!*] He snatched a ceremonial blade from his hip and plunged it deep into Karin-Ja's chest.

Karin-Ja tried to scream, but Keldric clamped his mouth shut with one powerful hand. With the second, he jerked the dagger up and through the torso until his victim finally stopped struggling and fell limp.

Letting the body tumble to the ground, Keldric shook his head disapprovingly. "We mustn't disturb the important work of the Elders—not when the Birthing of Sh'logath is so close at hand."

He wiped the bloody blade across the grass until it was clean and then returned to the ceremony.

On his return, Keldric noticed that the doors still hung open to the great temple. He breathed a sigh of relief; he'd already given so much in service of the agod that he dreaded not being present when the Thousand Elders performed the sacrifice.

He poked his head inside and looked around for his master—the High Priest and leader of their faith. Keldric stopped one of the elders who ambled nearby and asked after his master, using his ceremonial title. "Where is The Voice?"

The aged vyrm pointed a talon towards a distant antechamber.

Keldric hurried to find him. He stepped into the room and found The Voice standing with the two human travelers from the Prime—former servants of the Architect King.

Basilisk held a darquematter amulet in his hand. It glimmered and strained against the fine chain as it hovered in the air, pointing to the bound and gagged tarkhūn: a member of the vyrm's highest genetic line. The man dragged his blade across the tarkhūn's neck and ended him while The Voice instructed him on the final parts of completing the ritual of Dunnischkte.

The elderly Voice watched with rapt interest as the tarkhūn's glowing life force was ripped from the reptilian prisoner and sucked into the Dunnischktet foreigner. Keldric stood and stared, wide-eyed. The ritual had never actually been performed, to his knowledge.

Basilisk groaned and shuddered at first. His skin burst into the scaly features of the vyrm and then receded to something of a hybrid state and Basilisk seemed able to control and shift which he was in.

The Voice glared over at his servant and caught him frowning. "Is there a problem, Keldric?"

"No. I'm sorry, I just… shouldn't we concentrate on the Sacrifice?"

Croaking with laughter, the saggy old vyrm grinned and rested in his chair. "But what comes *after* the Birthing?"

"Sh'logath rises and stabilizes all with the peace of his glorious destruction! When he exists and all else is set right, everything will be nothing and nothing will be everything!"

The Voice regarded him skeptically. "It will not be as simple as that," he insisted. "The Birthing will not establish the Devourer's presence—not until Sh'logath's Heralds awaken him." The Voice flicked his eyes towards the foreigners.

Keldric frowned again.

"Don't worry. I have prophesied a great many things and have one more to make before I give my power to the Brothers of the Apocalypse: the Dunnischktets." He took the forlorn vyrm into his hands and looked Keldric in the eyes. "Something deep within tells me that *you will be alive to see the Awakening.*"

Keldric smiled at that, but still glared at the interlopers with apprehension. Only the older brother could pass for vyrm.

"I understand your reluctance," The Voice comforted him. "You have always been my most zealous adherent. But take comfort—if the Dunnischktets fail, the Brothers of the Winnowing will arise and initiate the final Awakening."

Keldric stared at the old vyrm, tight-lipped. Long ago, the aged crone had gone by the name Krakkath—and he had been alive to know the ancients before they passed. He had been steeped in the aroma of the old ways. In his youth, Krakkath revered the seven demigods who nearly destroyed the vyrm race in an effort to build a bridge to Nihil for their long-forgotten purpose.

"Few know the legend," he replied, also drawing Nitthogr and Basilisk into the conversation. The older brother handed the amulet to the younger one, and The Voice continued. "It is a long-lost prophecy etched into the Tablet of Rasthakka—recorded long before we understood the nature of reality—the Tesseract—or knew about the Lurking Devourer beyond the veil. Rasthakka, the High-Priest of the pre-Sh'logath cult, knew about realms beyond the Tesseract, even, and personally knew the Seven Brothers of the Winnowing." He sighed, thinking of days long past.

"Rasthakka's works were largely destroyed, but a copy of them remains in the temple of Koth... presumably Kith, too. It indicates treachery in the ranks of the Brothers. The Awakening will happen—either by the Brothers of the Apocalypse or the Brothers of Winnowing. That much is assured." His eyes gleamed as if he had some secret insight that he would not share.

Keldric looked down and saw Nitthogr holding the chain.

The jewel-like artifact pointed directly at him while Nitthogr anchored it around one finger. Keldric reconfirmed his prophecy with the old priest. "And I will be alive to see it?"

"You will be... of sorts." The Voice nodded and Nitthogr slashed his blade across Keldric's neck, completing the second Dunnischkte.

# CHAPTER ONE

*E*arth…

Claire squeezed Zabe's hand. He'd been confined to the hospital bed for several days, even after regaining consciousness following the incident in Nebraska, when he and the rest of Claire's friends had come to her rescue.

The sorcerer, Nitthogr, had used her like a game piece to try to assume ultimate control over reality. His insane cultists, the heptobscurantum, had been promised the spell caster would destroy all of reality. When that hadn't proved the case, they got their own wizard and battle ensued, with Claire caught in the middle.

Jackie, Zabe, and his cousin Wulftone had come to her rescue. But it had been Zabe's direct confrontation with Nitthogr and the Great Devourer, the nega-god Sh'logath, which had almost proved too much for Zabe. In the end, Sh'logath had been the one to destroy his own. Nitthogr's betrayal of him had proved too much to tolerate, and Sh'logath sucked him into the nether realms, unmaking him.

Zabe tended to heal much faster than most, but that rule didn't apply so much to show-downs with cosmic horrors of godly proportions.

For their part, the hospital had taken Zabe in and begun the work, registering him as a John Doe at first. And eventually, Zabe's fingerprints came back as belonging to Robert Schaeffer.

Rob was Earth's copy of Zabe. But Zabe was a Prime: a resident of the Prime dimension, a kind of alternate, master reality which he'd taken Claire to in order to save a princess—who was the Prime version of Claire, Princess Bithia.

Claire studied the charts and documents on a clipboard which Jackie had swiped from just outside the door. The only logical explanation for Zabe's identity was that he was Rob, a former classmate of both Claire and Jackie—a man who was now an over the road trucker in his adult life and who had kidnapped Claire and offered her up to the cultists.

"Serves you right," Claire mumbled.

"What's that?" Jackie asked.

She turned the chart over to her friend. Jackie chuckled. "They think Zabe is Rob... and mister Schaeffer is going to get one expensive hospital bill sent to him." She quirked her mouth into a grin. "You're right. It *does* serve him right. But more importantly, do you suppose this joint has room service? Can we bill some fancy steaks to the room?"

Claire smiled, wishing it worked exactly like that.

Zabe stirred and opened his eyes with a blink and a yawn. "I think I must have dozed off."

Deep within, Claire felt Bithia's emotions stirring. She yearned to return home. The Prime had to be rebuilt, and the princess was critical to those efforts. Since Bithia's death had occurred with Claire present, Claire's body had absorbed Bithia's mind and Claire now shared head space with her, which was an odd sensation, and made all the more peculiar by the fact that only *she* could hear or feel Bithia. But the two personalities had come to a sort of understanding while they fled the cultists for weeks on end after their return to Earth.

Zabe looked at Claire and furrowed a brow, as if he could tell something bothered her. "What's up?"

"Bithia is eager to get back to the Prime and begin rebuilding efforts," she said. "I mean, *I am* eager. I guess we are one and the same now."

Zabe nodded and took Claire by the hand. "There is no worry. Those efforts are already underway. They were already beginning before I got my cousin. Where is Wulftone?"

Jackie's eyes sparkled at the mention of his name. They'd only known each other a few weeks, but had seemed to get on well. "He went back to the Prime for that very reason."

"Okay," Zabe said, but that hadn't seemed to help put Claire at ease.

"I'm not ready to go back. Not yet. Not until we find my father," she insisted.

Zabe nodded as he threw off the sheet that covered his body. "Alright then. Let's go find him."

"Wait," Claire said as the man from another dimension yanked tubes and wires from his body where monitors had been affixed. "We can't just leave. You haven't been properly discharged."

Zabe raised an eyebrow. "Is that going to be a serious problem?"

Jackie laughed and shook her head. "Not for *you*. But it might be for Rob. He's going to get the bill for your stay."

Claire had already told him about Rob's betrayal when he delivered her to the cultists. Zabe threw a jacket over his form. "That tool? Good."

Zabe looked at a defibrillator set mounted on the wall. They'd used a more economy version of one so long ago at Professor Jecima's when they'd restarted Zabe's heart after the first altercation with vyrm agents. "Is that thing expensive?"

Claire nodded.

Zabe chuckled. "Then thank you, Rob." He ripped it off the wall and stuck it into the folds of his coat and then led the group out of the room and away from the hospital in search of Sam Jones, Claire's father.

Idrakka stalked through the silent halls of the abandoned building. The dry, Texan air tasted like iron and blood to the undersized tarkhūn. Someone, several someones, had died nearby—and recently—he'd bet his scales on it.

His master had tasked the vyrm with monitoring the earth realm to locate and isolate a certain paranormal event that had been prophesied millennia before the rise of the Sh'logath cult. The weird happenings in Pecos had been kept mostly under wraps by the reclusive group of occult dabblers he'd been watching—they loosely fit the description.

Idrakka had long meant to look into their activities, but so many other leads appeared to hold more promise—until he stumbled onto a freshly published book during his research. *Black Goat* was a poorly written and terribly reviewed piece of fiction by some unheard of indie author—but the trashy, pulp novel seemed to bleed facts about an ancient prophecy Idrakka had been watching for.

The author had recently been found dead—gripped by a madness that drove him to murder—and practically on the other side of the United States. He'd even kidnapped and murdered a reader, according to a report one of his sources had sent him.

A psychotic author wasn't a good lead. Idrakka figured that *all writers* were at least a little bit mentally unhinged, but the author had become obsessed with a seven-pointed star, a sigil, and it was a big clue.

Idrakka quickly consulted the paperback to double check the details. His vyrm eyes had little problem reading in the dark. Idrakka's home realm had long become accustomed to low light environments.

A photo of the author's crime scene and a seven-pointed star drawn on the nearby door matched the second paper. Wedged inside the cover was a printed copy of an old carbon rubbing from the etchings of Rasthakka—an identical seven-pointed star.

Idrakka stepped through a door in the recently abandoned facility and walked into the central antechamber. He licked his lips; the smell of old blood nearly overpowered his other senses.

The tarkhūn detective took in the scene. Bodies littered the stone floor, dead for weeks now in all likelihood. Idrakka paced through the area, shining a flashlight through the darkness to make sure he didn't miss any details.

He expected the coroner would arrive in the morning to take the bodies to the morgue. The man was a contact of the heptobscurantum and so it did not take much effort to convince him to delay long enough for the vyrm agent to examine the scene.

Inset at the room's center rose a stone slab. A seven-pointed star was barely visible in the rock, engraved in ancient days and eroded by eons of weather before some builder had integrated it into the architecture. Encircling the macabre scene, a larger engraving shaped another mystic sigil.

He rubbed a finger on the crevasse and touched it to his tongue. Blood. Idrakka traced the circumference until his forefinger caught the fine chain of a necklace nearest a dead woman. A large handgun lay nearby where her body had fallen.

The vyrm lifted the charm and squinted at it. "A hierophanticus?" Idrakka was pretty sure it was one of the darquematter amulets stolen long ago before the Veritas or the Guardian Corps could sequester them all away within the massive vaults of the Prime.

Glancing at the grisly scene, Idrakka knew he'd finally found what he had been looking for. The tarkhūn pulled out a hand-sized piece of glass encircled with a high-tech frame.

He activated the communicator and set it on the ground. Several seconds passed before Basilisk finally answered the beacon. A three-dimensional, life-sized image sprang from the focusing gem.

"You have something to report?"

"Yes," Idrakka told his master. He dangled the amulet so that Basilisk could see it clearly. "The Darque has been breached." He noted the second sigil's shape. "It appears as if Akko Soggathoth has awakened."

The leader of the tarkhūn sat back in surprise. "Interesting," he said with a grin. He paused for several long moments while Idrakka waited patiently.

Idrakka knew his master was calculating the next move, planning for several steps in the future and guessing his opponents' responses to each potential chain of actions.

"I have a new task for you, ice-lord. I need you to act as one of my spies. I assume you have been keeping an eye on Caivev as well?"

"Yes Lord, but I am a frostmancer, not a shade. My brother Jarkara would be of better service as a spy."

Basilisk cocked his head and regarded Idrakka callously.

"Forgive me," he begged. "I have kept up to date with her as much as possible. What are your orders?"

"This will take much time," Idrakka said, more to convince himself that he was capable than to inform Basilisk of facts he was already aware of. "Years most likely. Akko Soggathoth will be unable to locate until he is ready to reveal himself—unless the myths of the Brothers of the Winnowing are incorrect."

The vyrm ruler turned his communicator to show a close-up image of a game piece. "I have considered moving this pawn for months now. It may be months longer before I decide... and *this* game is far more important than the game tables in my garden. I am patient, Idrakka, so long as the pawns remain diligent."

"I understand," he reported.

"Find her," Basilisk ordered. "Become indispensable to her purposes. *Your cover must be absolute.* You know how to proceed."

Idrakka nodded and then cocked his head when he heard the sirens in the distance. The time had come for him to move.

He pocketed the amulet and saluted his master. Finally, he slipped the communicator into a cloth bag and smashed it before he slid away into the hot Texas night time air.

Idrakka scattered the smashed debris that had been his only link to his home and headed deep into the cover of his enemies' forces. Somewhere, somehow, he'd find The Black—Caivev—and make himself indispensable to her.

"Pack it all up!" Vivian howled. She stormed through the door to Bruce Cannon's underground facility in a flurry of urgency. With her entourage in tow, she stomped through so quickly that she nearly knocked the scrappy Cerci Heiderscheidt off her feet.

Heiderscheidt glared daggers at the woman who she only knew as Nitthogr's assistant. A massive man put his hand on her and gave her a terrifying glance. As she stared into his horrible face, she spotted the telltale scales under his makeup disguise. He was vyrm.

"Skrom!" Vivian barked. "Stay close."

"Miss Vivian," Doctor Pietro Walther greeted amidst the confusion. "What is going on here?"

She bristled at her pseudonym. "Plan B. And call me Caivev from now on," she ordered. The ruse was over: Claire Jones knew she had been an imposter.

"Plan B?" Walther stammered, "But... Sisyphus has surely got it all under control, whatever it is your comrades have planned for Nebraska, that is." The scientist refused to give up hope in his personal hero, Jacob Sisyphus.

Caivev only flashed him a skeptical look. "World domination can't be left up to guys like that," she retorted. "Besides, that traitor

Nitthogr might still have some nasty surprises in store for the great Sisyphus." She spat the former herald's name like a spurned lover. Once she would've welcomed any such advances, but not after the fallen hybrid's betrayal.

"I'm here to make sure that we retain an option to rebuild if everything goes to crap!" She pointed her tarkhūn guard, Skrom, towards Walther's giant contraption which they'd used to breach the barriers between the realms.

Skrom nodded and snapped off the bloody catheter tubes that powered the device before dragging it towards the exit. In a whirlwind of movement, others in her private vyrm force boxed up whatever items and research looked important.

"But... but all my research," Walther protested. "What I'm doing is groundbreaking—revolutionary work! It must continue. *Did the Seven pull my funding even after all my results?*" He fluttered around the lab in a tizzy, and his eyes searched desperately for the woman he'd met only a few times prior. Walther only knew his billionaire benefactors were wary of Caivev's lethality... but regardless, she'd somehow gained their total trust.

The big guy, Skrom, rumbled in a low baritone, "Don't worry, Doc. She's got a plan. You won't ever hafta worry about resources again."

Heiderscheidt and Walther's eyes met. Everything suddenly felt different—quiet. The gentle, mechanical hum of the above ground business that hid the laboratory suddenly stopped. Everything switched off in huge banks as the grid shut down. They had no choice but to go with Caivev, whether they believed in the promises of an outsider or not.

"Where are we going?" Walther glanced over to where their blood-donor prisoners remained tied down and unconscious. Remaining alive was only one captive; he'd been daisy chained to the blood bank used to fuel the dimensional breaching device. Caivev had delivered him personally to the facility.

Caivev stepped around the corner and looked at the man briefly but discounted any value in keeping Sam Jones in her care—he'd only drain their resources and cause potential confusion and delay. As little regard as a nihilistic death cultist had for life, she was not inclined to kill the man. But neither did she plan to make an effort to preserve him. "Leave him here to die in the dark."

She grinned at the doctor and then leered at Walther's porcelain-skinned assistant, Mizz Cerci Heiderscheidt. "I hope you have some sunscreen around here."

Heiderscheidt gave their hosts an inquisitive look.

Caivev told her, "You're going to need it where we're going."

Charobv and Kreephast stalked through the murky gloom of the old temple. Thick tangles of spider webs parted before them as Charobv used a stick to clear the path. The stale scent of an old world and humid earth spilled into their heightened vyrm senses.

Bright LEDs lit their way as their beams washed the ancient corridors with visibility. No person, man or vyrm, had passed this way for millennia.

"The hopeful Dunnischktet was right. It *is* the Lost Temple," Kreephast whispered reverently.

Charobv cleared a huge swath of webbing and the sudden, sterile light sent a horde of insects and spiders scurrying for cover. He revealed an ancient vyrm symbol engraved into the Central American stonework.

Kreephast shimmied with excitement and encouraged his counterpart to activate the ancient technology.

After tracing the symbols with an anxious finger, Charobv pressed his palm to the panel, and it powered up. A bioluminescent light glowed through the cracks and seams between stones throughout the halls. It warmed up and intensified until the vyrm scouts no longer needed their LEDs.

They walked through the tunnels between the ancient chambers, mouths agape with wonder at the ancient site they'd only known through myth and folktale. A stack of dusty manuscripts lay piled atop a stone table in a kind of narthex area adjoined to a room with two opposite doors and a central hallway. An engraved slab lay between the sheaves of parchments.

Kreephast bent over the stone tablet and whispered reverently, "The Tablet of Rasthakka." He gently caressed the carving with a deep reverence. "Do you know how rare a find this is—and on Earth, of all places?" Next to that was a kind of ancient binder containing the mad scribblings of Kadrist, Rasthakka's contemporary.

"How do you know?" Charobv asked. The language was an early and dead version of the vyrm holy language. "Can you actually read it?"

"No," he admitted. "But I recognize some of the symbols from copies saved by the religious caste. There are tools available to help us translate."

Charobv held up a hand for silence. "Do you hear that?"

Kreephast nodded. "It sounds like... singing?"

Lilts from a barely audible voice emanated from within one of the doors. They crept close and eavesdropped as best as they could.

"It's an older song. I recognize it from somewhere," Charobv stated. "It was popular on the Prime many years ago."

Kreephast nodded, but he did not open the door. "I think I know what is inside... if rumors are true. But we will wait for Caivev before exploring it further. First, we must prepare the temple for her arrival. She will want everything ready."

Vikrum Wiltshire looked back at his partner, Atticus Sexton, to make sure the man was still with him. Sexton had already puked his guts out at the sight of the macabre scene.

Bodies laid dead. Some had been dismembered and others were cut open in ritualistic fashion. None of them had survived, although there had been bloody footprints departing the scene, but they vanished two steps into the parking lot. A CCTV feed on a nearby gas station and an ATM confirmed that nobody had driven in to give the mysterious survivor a lift.

"Oh, this is bad," Sexton mumbled, and not for the first time. He wiped the remaining dampness from the corner of his mouth.

Wiltshire frowned and nodded. "Help me find the body," he groused.

"Which one?" Sexton scanned the floor and the abundance of corpses.

The two investigators worked for The Red Order, a secret society of paranormal detectives who were funded and sponsored by the Vatican. The Order had pulled some strings to get them access to something that set off all the red flags with the group's brass.

"Hall," said Wiltshire. "It all ties back to Quintin Hall."

Sexton set his jaw and got to work. The two men diligently checked over each of the corpses, with the local police hovering nearby to make sure that nothing was done by the third party to contaminate the scene of the massacre.

Quintin Hall had been a long-time acquaintance of Wiltshire and Sexton. He had been a former Brother of the Order and had gotten Wiltshire entry into their ranks.

After a thorough search, they found no sign of Hall. That fact made Wiltshire's stomach sink. Russo had first alerted them to the disruption in Texas with an emergency signal that was reserved for apocalyptic-level threats: a code sixteen sixteen, the biblical reference noting demons gathering for Armageddon.

Though they did not find Hall, they spotted any number of occult documents. Much of them were hand written and appeared to be the only editions.

Sexton carefully handled them, careful not to smear a blood spatter that marred a sheaf of papers. "Auto-writing?" he asked.

"Almost certainly," Wiltshire said, looking them over. Auto-writing was a form of communion when a vassal allowed a terrifying power from beyond to take control of the vassal's hand—kind of a dear-diary form of ouija.

"I don't recognize it," said Wiltshire as his partner took a few photos and sent them to their director for any additional insight.

Moments later, Sexton's phone jingled with a tone far happier than their surroundings suggested as appropriate. Then another jingle, and another.

"Russo's hot about whatever this is," Sexton said.

And then Wiltshire's phone also chirped. The sender was from an unknown number.

*I am aware of the situation in Pecos, Texas,* the message read. *I would like to contract you to send me a digital edition of your findings... I fear your Praetor's "Armageddon" code may not be for your people, but for mine.*

Wiltshire scoffed and thumbed his device. *Yeah, right, it'll cost you a brick of gold, buddy.*

A few moments passed before a reply. *Your terms are acceptable.*

*Who are you?* Wiltshire asked in disbelief.

*What you do with the Order, I also do... only I am somewhere else,* came the response.

Wiltshire's brows knit together and he texted furiously. *The Red Order is worldwide. There is nowhere else.*

His phone buzzed with another message.

*You and I both know that is not true. You have met a wolf, I've heard.*

"Damn it, Grandfather," Wiltshire growled, getting Sexton's attention.

"What's up?" his partner asked, dealing with his own furious text exchange. Sexton dealt with Praetor Russo, his and Wiltshire's boss. Wiltshire and Russo did not get along and so Sexton ran interference and was usually the one to communicate with the praetor.

"Bigfoot's got loose lips," Wiltshire mumbled.

Sexton cocked his head. "Do I want to know?"

Wiltshire shook his head and turned away, leaving Sexton to deal with their superior. "It's nothing. Really. More one of my private cases than Order business."

After a nasty argument with the Praetor, Wiltshire did more and more private work, following much in Quintin Hall's footsteps. Except that Wiltshire was not as frequently hard up for cash like Hall had been. He'd extorted a ranking member of The Seven, the ruling body of the Heptobscurantum cult, into gifting him a one percent stake in the cult's holdings, effectively making Wiltshire wealthy.

But though he didn't need the paycheck from the Order, he *did* need its connections. Connections to assets and folk like Grandfather Tlugv. *Bigfoot.*

Grandfather was the only creature outside of Sexton and Wiltshire who knew of a previous encounter with a werewolf. But not just *any* wolf. There were a number of types of werewolves in the paranormal community—but this kind was unlike the Order was familiar with—it was from some extra-dimensional community.

"Whoever this guy is," Wiltshire mumbled at his phone, "He's connected if he's been able to raise Grandfather Tlugv and get him to chat. Connected... *or sincere.*

*I don't even know what this document is,* Wiltshire wrote.

*I will share my findings with you... in private.* A moment passed before a followup message. *Praetor Russo is something of a difficult person to work with. If I can translate and share, I will.*

"Finally, someone I can get behind," Wiltshire mumbled.

*We shall communicate again soon*, came the final message on Wiltshire's phone.

Sexton's voice startled Wiltshire. It took on a booming quality he was unused to hearing from his partner. "Pack it up, guys. The Order is taking all of these documents back with us."

One of the local policemen scoffed. "Oh yeah? Under who's orders?"

Sexton fixed him with a level gaze. "Officer. Check your personal bank account."

The cop gave him a skeptical look, but he took a smartphone from his pocket. Another officer did the same. One by one they logged in to check their account balances and looked back up googley eyed. And then, as if on cue, the police stacked up the documents and whatever other occult materials they could find and headed towards the exit of the old warehouse building.

"Russo?" Wiltshire asked.

Sexton nodded. "Whatever this is, it's significant. A moving truck and the cleaners will be here within half an hour."

Victor Adams shifted in the uncomfortable, sticky heat. Tourists used to visit the area, but they'd stopped going to the northern Panamanian region ever since Chiriquí declared independence. Economic instability and violence made it uncharacteristically hostile for foreigners. That fact made the hospitality eager to serve and earn a piece of the shrinking, foreign supply of tourism income.

The Persian mobster didn't care for the humidity; it made his prosthetic chafe and stick. He rubbed under the itchy hook where his ring-studded hand used to be and stared across the table.

A copy of the New York Times he'd brought lay on the table. Caivev's likeness, barely discernable in the edge of the photo, had been captured on camera as she watched over the larger-than-life leader of this third world country. Chiriquí had finally begun to stabilize under the charismatic rebel leader General Nyagittari's leadership.

Bringing over a tray of drinks and a hookah, a low-caste and obsequious vyrm named Theera left the glassware on the table. Those at the table barely made eye contact with him; they were each familiar enough with the Black to understand that Theera was a scut—a servile vyrm and barely a person as far as their culture was concerned.

Bruce Cannon and Jacob Sisyphus sat on either side of the bronze-skinned Persian in the dim lounge and faced Caivev. Sisyphus shifted uncomfortably within his overly starched shirt that struggled to absorb his sweat and bunched up at his massive shoulders. He'd bulked back up to his pro-wrestling size in the months since the Nebraska incident. Perhaps he'd even surpassed his former glory.

Caivev could feel the changed attitudes in what remained of the Seven. They'd finally been blooded by real, cosmic conflict and became more dangerous now than they ever were, even under the guidance of the powerful Nitthogr.

"Where is the fourth?" she asked. None had escaped the failed Awakening unscathed and not all injuries were physical. She looked back to the door where one of her trusted vyrm generals, Charobv, stood guard.

Charobv shook his head to indicate no others would come.

Adams pulled the hookah closer with his hook and took a deep draw on the pipe. "Thornton's become something of a recluse since his recovery—if you can call it that. He would not answer the call."

Cannon nodded measuredly. "I've heard he hasn't left his estate and will not see anyone."

Caivev grimaced as she regarded the wealthy museum mogul. Bruce Cannon seemed somehow different, though each of the survivors had been changed. She assumed they each resented her for abandoning them before the Awakening, but she wasn't surprised that they answered her call. Men like this craved power, and she could offer it to them.

"What is the state of the Heptobscurantum?"

The men traded reluctant glances around the table. It was a sore spot for them.

"We are rebuilding," Adams said through his thick accent. "But it will take time. Most of our remnant is from the lower ranking proletariat who were not ready for an invitation to the Awakening. The battle in Mullen wiped out most of our high-ranking members. It will take a couple of years to rebuild—*but we will overcome*."

Sisyphus scowled at Caivev. "Why should we even consult with this outsider? She is allied with the Black—and it was the vyrm of the Black that tore through our forces and prevented the Awakening of Sh'logath. If not for them, we may have succeeded."

She accepted his criticism and nodded. "I suspected a backup plan would be prudent... and those vyrm in question acted on the orders of a traitor. They died faithful to the cause—they just didn't know of the sorcerer's betrayal. Besides, how would the outcome have been different if I had been *there* instead of *here*?" She stabbed her finger down into the newspaper and pointed to Nyagittari. "This is what I've been doing."

"Stabilizing war-torn tropical countries is a poor excuse," Sisyphus scoffed.

"It's not the politics I'm after," she hissed. "It's access to certain resources of unimaginable power." She glared across the table and her eyes flashed with zealous flame. "The Awakening ritual is not the only way to summon Sh'logath."

The three men leaned across the table inquisitively.

"There is an ancient, cosmic gate built eons before Nitthogr and Basilisk were ever born. It can open the way to Nihil and invite the Devourer in... and we don't need the blood of Claire Jones to activate it. It's not even within the realms of the multiverse. It will only be a matter of time before I can access it."

Sisyphus blinked wistfully. He and his companions hung on every word. Caivev knew she had them exactly where she wanted them.

"It is true that de facto leadership of the Black has fallen to me since Nebraska. I only want to know," she asked seductively, "when I call, will the Heptobscurantum answer and come to my aid in service of the Great Devourer?"

"We'll be ready," Sisyphus murmured and slid a paper across the table to her. "Meanwhile, in the interest of a quid pro quo, help me locate something that *I* desire."

Loud rumbling noises from the industrial generators echoed through the dank hallways of the temple. Cerci Heiderscheidt stepped over a pile of massive cables and power conduits that snaked through the corridors. Doctor Walther had the operation well in hand as he puttered about the nearby chamber where they'd set up their machines deep inside the jungle lab.

Before she could step out to do some exploring, the contraption they'd assembled split the veil between dimensions with unnerving power. A pained gasp escaped the lips of a kidnapped local woman as the machine bled her energies and life essence as it powered the device. The hostage's eyes traced the blood-darkened intravenous lines that attached her to the apparatus.

Cerci spared a glance backward to watch as the triangular door widened and opened a portal into a different location. She grinned as a trio of Caivev's masked vyrm leapt through the breach and into the bank vault in a different hemisphere and began pitching gold bricks back through the portal.

She wouldn't be needed until later. The scientist walked the dimly lit halls of what the vyrm had called the *Lost Temple*. In her spare time, she'd begun recording and unraveling some of the ancient hieroglyphics with the help of some old lexicons Skrom had supplied her with. The huge tarkhūn wasn't smart, but he sometimes proved handy.

Veering a direction she hadn't gone before, Cerci explored a winding stair that emptied into a massive, pillared room. At the far end, an immense set of double doors stretched from floor to ceiling, leaving only enough gap for a plaque that she paused to translate as "*to Koth*." She assumed Koth was a name.

Whatever the gates were made of, it was not something that Cerci was familiar with, and it was not likely of Earth. She touched the doors with her hand and shuddered with excitement—some new mystery to solve. The alien metal felt cold to the touch, even in the wretched, persistent heat of the tropical environment.

Turning to head back, Cerci took a round-a-bout way and walked through a passage until she came to the central narthex she'd passed through earlier without a second thought. This time, a faint song caught her ear, and she tilted her head to listen. Following the sound, she stalked through the anteroom until she came to a locked door at one side.

She leaned her ear up against an old door and listened. A haunted sounding baritone floated through the barrier singing in a foreign tongue. The voice was beautiful and decidedly male, though young.

A thump on the door startled her, as if the owner of the voice had leaned against the locked entry. "Is someone there?" she asked. "What's your name?"

"My name is Zurrah," he replied. "They *will* come for me."

# Chapter Two

Claire and Jackie had rented a car which now bumbled along through the country highways that lay between Nebraska and Minnesota. Zabe sat in the back, munching on a gas station roller dog. As Jackie drove through the middle of Iowa, Claire reflected on how she'd stayed off her enemy's radar by moving from one rural town to the next.

Before falling for Robert Schaeffer's trickery, she'd only just learned of her father's disappearance. He had been working to unearth a new archaeological wonder at a dig site in the Chiriqui region of Panama, which was currently undergoing a dramatic war as some new party rose to power. News outlets reported that he'd been kidnapped in the turmoil of political upheaval.

"How come nobody has reached out for a ransom?" Claire asked, thinking about where they should begin their search.

Jackie shot her a look. "Well, you've obviously been a little out of touch lately," she said.

Claire's brows pinched.

Jackie explained. "You've been missing and presumed insane for months while being chased through a network of inter-dimensional portals by apocalypse cultists. So, yeah... foreign warlords probably didn't have your forwarding address for a ransom note."

Claire set her jaw. She knew Jackie was probably right.

"Maybe I could reach out to a consulate or an American embassy or something? Maybe they'll have information on the situation?" Claire hoped. "If I told them who I am..."

Zabe leaned forward. "No," he interjected seriously. "We can't let them know you're around. The heptobscurantum may have been defeated—and it may take them time to recover, but they are still out there and they have great influence."

Claire crossed her arms. "So our best bet is to just sit and wait?"

Jackie shook her head. "No. We go back to where it all started for us."

"Minnesota... Duluth?" Claire noted.

"Specifically, we go back to visit Professor Jecima," said Jackie. "You don't have any family that they'd likely call if there was a ransom demand, but your dad and Jecima were close. Maybe he's heard something?"

Claire nodded. "I suppose that makes sense. Plus, they worked together, so if any of their coworkers had news, Jecima would have heard of it."

Zabe nodded his approval of the plan. "We need all the help we can get right now. There aren't a lot of local allies that we can trust." He looked at Jackie. "Besides, we have to go back there, anyway. You used that magic to send the mystic blade to Jecima."

Claire gave Jackie an odd look. "Magic? I thought you said you used Fedex?"

"Magic was maybe the only way to explain it to Zabe. But he's right. We had to go back for it, anyway."

She suddenly seemed to have an epiphany. "Oh. What was that guy's name?" Jackie gripped the steering wheel and slapped it as they passed a truck stop. "You told me about some detective guy who claimed he was friends with bigfoot or something like that."

"Vikrum Wiltshire," Claire said as if there was a sour taste in her mouth. He had been who she was running from when Rob had picked her up on a very similar patch of Iowan highway. Wiltshire had claimed he wanted to help, and he seemed sincere—but over the last few months, Claire had learned exactly how much appearances could deceive. "I'd much prefer to leave him as a last resort. I don't know if I can trust him. He's in bed with the cultists after doing a job for one of their leaders."

"Alright," Jackie said. "Duluth it is." She reached for the radio's tuner band and turned it on. "Looks like it's oldies, country, or religious music," she said after a few moments scanning the waves.

With the dreadful twang of resonator guitar backing a crooning voice, both girls looked at Zabe, who was unfamiliar with Earth's music. He cringed at the country music after a few seconds.

"If silence is not an option, is it too late to side with the heptobscurantum?" he asked.

Wiltshire walked away from his partner and towards the coffee shop inside the El Paso airport, where they waited for connecting flights. The airport in Pecos had barely been large enough to hire a shuttle out of.

"I told you that it's a private matter," Wiltshire insisted. "You're more than capable of escorting all the Praetor's shiny new loot back to New York."

"While you head back to Minnesota?" Sexton asked. But it hadn't been a question. "Vikrum, don't take this the wrong way, but whenever you get much past earshot of me, you tend to get in over your head."

One edge of Wiltshire's mouth upturned playfully. "So it's not just me, then? Listen, it's no big deal. I just want to follow up on a private lead about the girl. And I did just fine while I was on vacation."

"You literally joined the annihilationist cult we've been spending so much time fighting against," Sexton accused.

"Details, details," Wiltshire laughed. "I'm on their payroll because I own a lot of stock in their public holdings. That's different. Plus, I'm going to Michigan, not Minnesota."

"But you're still chasing the girl?"

Wiltshire accepted a cup of black coffee from the girl behind the counter and sipped slowly. He nodded seriously. Claire Jones, and her father, had proved to be extremely elusive. "Actually, I'm looking for her father, Sam. I was down in Panama right before Texas. Something happened to him, but I got a long-shot lead that he might have been transported to Detroit."

Sexton blinked at him. "It's hard to see what Detroit and war-torn Chiriqui have in common."

"Well, they're both dumps, and it's easy to get shot in either one," Wiltshire quipped.

Sexton shrugged, acquiescing the point.

"I'm just going to check it out quickly and then hop a commercial plane back to the Big Apple," he promised. "You know, unless there's an apocalypse or something. Obviously, I'll stop that first and then hop on the next flight. Cross my heart." Wiltshire grew silent for a moment. "Based on my intel... I'm not confident my findings will be happy ones."

Sexton gave him a melancholy look and said nothing. There hadn't been much happiness for either of them lately. Plus, it had been hard for both of them to forget what had happened in New Orleans when a demon had pronounced a curse on Wiltshire... or maybe it had been on everyone else connected to him. The curse was uncertain and overly vague—though members of the supernatural community seemed to know about it more than any members of the Red Order and it had come up on several occasions.

"I promise. Simply checking in," Wiltshire reiterated.

"Fine," Sexton said in a tone usually reserved for angry housewives to indicate that things were *definitely not* fine. He ordered a cup of coffee for himself and paid the barista.

They sat opposite each other for a few minutes, silently sipping coffee.

"What do you think the mess in Pecos is all about—what does it mean?" Sexton wondered.

"Whatever it is, it's connected to the rest of the weirdness. This goes far beyond Quintin Hall getting mixed up with some girl who turned out to be a psycho cultist."

"Weirdness?" Sexton asked.

Wiltshire nodded. "Think about it. It's like someone cranked up the planet's paranormal dial all the way to eleven. I mean, there is always stuff for us to look into, but come on... the sheer volume of craziness in the supernatural world has ramped up like an explosion. There are so many jammed together lately that I'm running frazzled. That alone is a worth investigating."

Sexton furrowed his brow as he thought it over. "Come to think of it, you may be right." His eyes darted back and forth, but seemed to look right through Wiltshire, who assumed he was doing some mental math. "There have always been ongoing incidents, but they have been increasing exponentially lately. I'll bring it up with Russo. It's got to mean something—there's got to be something big coming."

Wiltshire grunted his approval over another sip.

"But let's not call this anything other than what it is," Sexton said, gathering his things as a voice announced flight times over the speaker system.

Wiltshire cocked his head.

"You're turning into a softie, Vikrum Wiltshire. You have a soft spot for the girl."

"I'm not some smitten, creepy old stalker," he defended.

"No. Not like that," Sexton laughed. "It's *all* girls. You're a little soft wherever a damsel in distress is concerned."

Wiltshire chuckled as his partner stood and headed for his flight's gate. "Well, maybe the girl's got some weird supernatural juju."

"You think there's something supernatural in the Jones family?" Sexton asked.

"It's easier a safer assumption than that. I've gone soft," Wiltshire said.

The voice on the speaker reminded them again that Sexton had to report to his gate.

"Whatever, you old hard-ass," Sexton said with a grin. He turned to leave.

"Hey Atticus. Stay safe, and be careful," he said. "I'll see you in New York."

Pain scratched at Doctor Sam Jones' throat. It had been days since he'd had anything to drink, and even longer since he'd eaten. A blindfold covered his eyes, but he could sense the deep darkness even beyond the blinders; there was no light to see by, anyway.

A few hours ago, at least Sam assumed his internal clock still remained consistent. The last homeless man chained up near him gasped with a little shudder and died. There was no sound any longer except for his own breathing.

His wrists ached. *Everything ached.* And he felt weak.

Over the last several days, whatever drugs he and the others in the room had been on wore off. Sam had been in and out of consciousness throughout the whole ordeal and he'd been able to understand the voices who mostly spoke English. Whatever was going on was not related to the political upheaval in Chiriqui. The drugs must have been related to constitution or some other physical factor; the men and women who were restrained nearby must have been mentally ill, homeless, or addicts with severe problems. As they had come to consciousness, they'd all spoken only nonsense, if at all, before they expired. Judging from the sounds in the dark, few had made much of an attempt to break free.

Sam growled his defiance in the dark. *I am not going to simply give up and die here.*

He relaxed and tensed his hands, discovering there was some play in the restraints due to the dehydration. He repeated the motion a few times and each time, his hand slipped further through the loop that held him in place, and then it came free.

Sam gasped at the sensation. His arms had gone mostly numb from hanging vertical for so long. His shoulder screamed at him as the arm dangled limply and blinding pain washed over him for several seconds. Finally, Sam shook himself from the sensation and grasped at his other arm.

Still weak, he couldn't quite reach his other wrist and grabbed onto his arm instead, finding a medical tube affixed to him. He yanked it free from his skin and heard a splatter on the floor. He felt something warm trickle down to his armpit. Touching the wetness, he put it to his lips. *Blood. No wonder I'm all shriveled up... they were draining me like some kind of giant spider.*

He tried reaching again and grabbed a hold of his wrist and found a velcro strap. He yanked it free with a gasp and then doubled over, practically spent from the effort. Crumpled on the ground, he was able to release his feet from the straps at his ankles.

After several minutes spent on the cold floor, painful tingles washed over his body as the restored blood flow felt like he was being assaulted by pins and needles. "Just lucky I got anything left," he groused into the darkness. His voice was cracked and split like baked mud and it hurt his parched throat to speak aloud. He did it anyway, in defiance of what his captors had intended. "Bastards nearly bled me dry... barely anything left in the tank."

Once the sensation of static and white noise coursing through his veins had subsided, Sam crawled to his feet and explored his surroundings. It was too dark to see much, but he found the bodies of the other victims, strapped into vertically tilted medical beds much as he had been and similarly drained. He barely remembered why—some kind of mad experiments where his captors opened gates between dimensions... or tried to, anyway. Sam had been blindfolded and drugged so he wasn't sure about many details other than that the machine ran on blood.

He glanced back at the husks of the other victims. They all looked local. "Strange that they'd go to all the trouble to get me down in Central America if they could use anybody. Unless... Claire..."

Sam knew he had to get out of there and find his daughter. He shuffled through room after room and found the entire place in disarray. It had been raided of anything of value before being abandoned wholesale. Equipment lay strewn all over. Wastebaskets were overturned and, in some spots, charred where certain piles of items were simply destroyed rather than taken.

He stumbled into a room that had been a small commissary. A sink lay nestled between a small economy refrigerator and a coffee pot. There were no cups in the cupboard and so Sam used the glass pot to collect water. The tap's water came out weakly and with barely any pressure. What there was quickly dissipated to nothing, but it was enough to get Sam a couple cups of water, which he greedily drank before checking the fridge.

The fridge was mostly empty. It, too, was off. There was nothing inside of any use or value. He peeled open a tupperware container with some kind of noodle and vegetable dish that had long been abandoned. A fuzzy growth had developed a top layer on it.

Sam scowled and continued rummaging through the contents, finding only baking soda, old scientific samples, a container of coffee grounds. Nothing else was edible. Starving, he stormed out of the room, paused at the door, and then returned and scarfed down the rotten noodle mix, moldy fur and all. He could barely taste its contents, and he was thankful for that.

Eventually, he found a stairwell that led upward. The sounds of his feet clanging on steel treads felt vaguely familiar as he climbed. *I think they took me in this way?*

The nearer the top he rose, the more he smelled smoke. *Old smoke... this was several days ago. They must have set it ablaze on their way out.*

Sam pressed against the steel door, but it might as well have been a wall. There was some kind of machinery blocking it. The fire had caused a deep crack nearby, however, and Sam was able to widen it by knocking a few bricks free, and then he squeezed through, tumbling through the soot and then floundering to his knees.

He tried to dust off the blackened detritus, but only smeared it around himself, worsening it and caking more ash onto his body. Sam looked up and locked eyes with a strange man who looked just as surprised as he was.

The man held a hand gun at the ready as he looked Sam over. Finally satisfied, he lowered the gun and then holstered it. "Are you Doctor Jones?"

Too exhausted to question the man's motives or to attempt a lie, Sam merely nodded. He figured the man probably recognized him anyway, so there wasn't much sense in resisting.

The man held out a hand and helped him to his feet. "My name's Vikrum. I'm just passing through, but heard I might find you here."

Sam gave him a hesitant look.

"Don't worry. I've got a tight time line, but let me buy you a steak and a plane ticket home. You look like you've been through the wringer," the man said.

"And a shower?"

"Obviously."

Sam smiled. "I've got to find my daughter."

"Good luck with that one," Vikrum said. "She's hard to get at, but if anyone can make her stop running, it's probably you."

Vikrum helped shoulder some of Sam's weight as they headed out of the factory building, which looked ready to collapse at any moment. "Whew. You weren't kidding. You really *do* need a shower."

Jackie's rental car finished squeezing between two cars near where Claire's apartment was and where her favorite local coffee shop was. Her eyes were bleary and red with fatigue.

"I could have driven that final leg, you know?" Claire said.

Jackie turned and smiled with annoyance. "Dear... you know I love you, but it would take you two hours to get this think parallel parked, and I'm desperate for caffeine."

Claire shrugged sheepishly. Jackie was one hundred percent correct on that score.

She looked up at the place where her apartment had been. "Do you suppose it's still there?" Claire asked. "My apartment... my stuff?"

"Probably not," Jackie said. "It's been months, and there's no shortage of college students needing housing here in Duluth."

Claire looked up at what used to be her balcony, noticing someone else's patio furniture. "It's just stuff," she sighed. "We're just swinging by on our way to Jecima's, after all."

Jackie and Zabe both nodded at her.

"You're still on the lam," Jackie said, "so we'll bring you your coffee. You stay here where nobody will notice you and call the cops."

Claire nodded and gave them a coffee order when a police car stopped directly opposite them in the street and boxed them in. The patrol car's lights turned on halting traffic.

"Ohmygodohmygodohmygod—" Jackie began hyperventilating. Zabe stiffened. Claire slouched way down in her seat, trying to make herself small.

Traffic driving by came to a halt and the police officer in the front got out and moved to the back of the car. Jackie looked like she was ready to bolt, but Zabe urged her to relax with a hand on her shoulder.

The cop had barely given them any of his attention. Instead, he opened the back door and released his passenger.

Sam Jones stepped out onto the street and looked directly at the same balcony patio the others had been.

"Dad?" Claire asked, sitting up. She felt a sudden wave of emotion flowing off of Bithia. A yearning and a longing for her own father: the Architect King who had sacrificed himself so long ago. None of that made sense to Claire. She knew that time functioned differently in the Prime and she'd long since given up trying to figure out how it worked.

Before anyone could stop her, Claire flung her door open. "Dad?" she called.

Sam nearly jumped out of his skin at the sound of her voice. He turned to meet her gaze and practically broke. He ran to her and they embraced.

Zabe and Jackie leapt out of the car, ready to intervene if there was some sort of vyrm trickery involved, or if the officer planned to call in the presence of a fugitive. Instead, the policeman leaned against the side of his cruiser with his arms crossed. He caught sight of Claire's friends and held up a hand.

"No worries. This is all off the books—I'm just repaying a favor and was told not to ask any questions," the cop said. In fact, he barely paid any of them more than half a glance, as if he knew better than to ask questions, or even look too closely.

Sam squeezed his daughter tightly. He looked haggard and underfed.

"I've been trying to call this whole way," he said.

Claire leaned into the embrace. "Yeah. I've been... a little out of cell range."

He laughed. "You and me, both."

The cop turned to them. "I was supposed to make sure that you're okay from here. I know your kidnappers were never caught. Will you be alright?"

Sam nodded and released his escort, who returned to his car, turned off his lights, and drove away.

"How did you get up here so quickly if you were kidnapped?" Claire asked. "We figured you'd be the hostage of some Panamanian warlord."

He scowled and shook his head. "Whoever was in charge of it, she sounded like that girl—your fiance's sister."

Claire's nostrils flared. "Vivian."

Zabe placed a hand on Claire's shoulder. "Maybe let's get our coffee and then get off the street?"

Claire nodded. "This is Zabe. He's protecting me... and getting coffee, evidently. Let's get in the car and I'll tell you everything on the way to the professor's. Jecima is holding something for us."

"Jecima? You got the old man involved?"

"There was nobody else," Claire said as her friends went to order the coffee, but barely traveling beyond sight lines. "He's holding something we picked up... in another dimension. And we've got to get it back to the Prime."

The words didn't seem to phase her scientist father.

"You already know about it?" she asked.

"Only bits and pieces, really. Things I gleaned from overhearing Vivian and her cronies."

"I want to know everything," Claire insisted.

"And so do I," Sam said. "Tell me all about the Prime."

"I will," promised Claire. "We're headed there soon. We'll show it to you as soon as we can get there."

Sam hugged his daughter again. "There was another guy who was looking for you. Suddenly can't remember his name. Had a slight English accent and a funny name."

"Yeah. I know. He'll be looking for a long time. The Prime isn't on Earth, or anywhere close."

"Then let's get going. What are we waiting for?" Sam asked.

"Coffee," said Claire. "We're just waiting on coffee."

# Chapter Three



***The Prime...***

Zabe had brought Claire and her father to the Prime several days prior. His life had been a whirlwind of activity since.

Since his return to the Prime, Zabe had officially assumed the Master at Arm's position of the Guardian Corps—he'd taken his father's job, and his grandfather's before him. His cousin Wulftone came on as his second in command, a much deserved appointment after fighting valiantly in the battle at Earth's Worldgate in Nebraska.

Zabe walked in and stood at the raised dais in the center of the training hall, where the new recruits stood at attention, waiting for his speech. He stretched and rolled his stiff shoulder in the socket; it still ached from the recent battle in Nebraska. Zabe nodded to Wulftone, who walked a meandering circle through the clusters of hopeful troops.

During the reclamation of the Prime, a promising young soldier named Harken became an easy favorite to command the Royal military. His efforts to overthrow the vyrm during Shardai's last-ditch efforts became the stuff of legend.

Zabe glanced at the handsome man. He didn't know if it was luck or fate, but everything Harken set his mind to seemed successful and he'd hurdled over many soldiers in the exams who had far more military experience.

He adjusted the leather cuff on his wrist and looked over the crowd. Zabe recognized several of the faces from headshots he'd seen on enrollment applications.

While he was happy about the influx of new recruits, it was still far too few. Nitthogr's attack had proved wickedly devastating. In times past, Zahaben had turned away applicants, only taking the best and brightest. Now, they accepted all who were willing into the academy.

The once-proud armies of the Prime might not fully recover for an entire generation, and the realm would long remain in desperate need of soldiers to guard the dimensional gates and protect against future threats. This first class of troops was largely symbolic; more trainees would come along as the Prime recovered from the devastation, but this one was special—it proved their peoples' resilience and dedication to all they held dear.

Wulftone paused in front of a girl. She stood a full head shorter than everyone else and had notched her belt so it would fit. "How old are you? Are you even old enough to join the military, recruit?"

"By one day, sir," she replied.

"Are your parents around to verify that?"

"All my family was killed by the vyrm, sir."

Wulftone looked hesitantly at Zabe. Zabe nodded his approval, hoping she might make up in zeal what she lacked in stature.

Just as he poised himself to address the hall of new recruits, a door opened in the back and Claire entered. She wore the royal robes and a tiara-like crown that were appropriate; everyone kneeled as she walked. Jackie followed at a slight distance.

Nobody else noticed, but Zabe could see the awkward smile on Claire's face and the slight kilter in her gait—as much as she was a melding of Bithia and Claire's minds and personalities, she still wasn't quite used to her royal role.

Her eyes twinkled as they met Zabe's. "I have a request." She leaned in and half-whispered, "I can do that, right?"

Zabe chuckled and hid his smile from the trainees before nodding. His eyes caught Wulftone's. His cousin stared at Jackie with a similar twinkle... and so did Harken.

"Jackie wants to join the military."

Zabe grimaced slightly at the thought of putting their friend in harm's way. "Neither the military nor the Guardian Corps is a safe place, you know—and nonprimes have never been allowed to join before."

Jackie grimaced at him.

"That's why I made a royal request," Claire noted.

Zabe asked Jackie, "Why do you want to join?"

"I just want to help," she said. "You've seen how I roll, Zabe. I might even have more experience fighting vyrm than many of these other recruits. And you know my loyalty is unwavering."

Zabe reluctantly bobbed his head. "This won't be easy, you know."

"Oh good," she said playfully. "I needed a new challenge. I've already watched more soap operas than the normal human psyche can handle and I was looking for my next mountain to conquer."

Zabe merely shook his head and shrugged. He pointed to a spot in the nearest group. Jackie stood next to the short orphan Wulftone questioned.

"Thank you," Claire whispered before giving him a peck on the cheek and departing.

Jackie looked down at her smaller neighbor, who watched her, enamored. She'd gotten accustomed to her novelty that came with a foreign heritage, even though she couldn't see any difference.

The girl was still staring at her. "Um, hello."

"I'm Gita," she whispered enthusiastically. "Can I touch your skin? You smell good. Does everyone from Earth smell like that?"

"Only fellow Cinnabon junkies," she responded sardonically.

"I don't know what either of those is. Can you make me a junkie?"

"Deal." Jackie shook Gita's hand.

Zabe rolled his eyes and Wulftone merely grinned.

Wulftone handed Zabe an envelope sealed with the wax stamp of Shjikara, the high cleric of the Veritas. Zabe broke the seal, scanned the document, and dropped the form in his trash bin with a scowl.

"Good news?" Wulftone asked sarcastically as he raised his eyebrows.

Zabe grimaced. "The Veritas must've gotten wind that we were recruiting again. They want to know if we will recommend soldiers for service." He stood in a huff; Zabe and the few remaining officers had been on their way to an observation where they planned to grade their students, in fact, and select the elite or especially skilled to invite into the Guardian Corps. "We'll barely have enough troops to adequately guard the dimensional gates and Royal City the way it is. Now, this guy wants his cut?"

The Veritas was a monastic order and possessed a stronghold in the nearby mountains. They were mystics, scholars, and pacifists... despite the fact that they had their own army. They were the sect of magicians and psychics from which Nitthogr and Basilisk had come from. And they'd done nothing to help during Nitthogr's invasion: a fact that chaffed most of those military members who'd survived the vyrm's most recent incursion.

Wulftone followed Zabe as he strolled towards the training grounds to watch the exercises. "They did save our family's bacon during Nitthogr's invasion," he reminded him.

"If you can call it that," Zabe sighed. "They let Shardai and a few resistance members hide out in the catacombs. I understand they are a reclusive sect from the old ways of the Guardian Corps, but anyone who won't fight in such a conflict isn't truly worthy of that name."

Shrugging, Wulftone noted, "Maybe that's why they go by the name Veritas, instead."

Zabe frowned at his cousin's attempt to play devil's advocate. "If they're only meant to be priests, why carry any weapons at all, or form their brotherhood out of the warrior class?"

Wulftone shrugged. He knew it was more than political resentment that bothered his cousin—the war cost Zabe his father. Zahaben died when the sorcerer stormed the castle. If the Veritas had come down from the mountainside abbey and fought, Zahaben might still be alive... and Bithia, too.

"Will Claire join us to watch the exercise and watch Jackie in action for the first time?"

Zabe frowned. He'd seen far too little of her since returning to the Prime. "She is busy with Pollando, one of the other clerics. Claire may have Bithia's memories and the important parts of her mind, but they are still tutoring her with a crash course in royal diplomacy and Prime theology."

The men arrived at the edge of the training fields: a large garden maze hundreds of meters across and set up with a number of traps, obstacles, and barriers. "Remember this?" Wulftone smiled at his cousin as they ascended the observation tower. They'd gone through training together, in fact, and the maze was something of a rite of passage. Before Nitthogr, it wasn't uncommon for the children of corpsmen to receive waivers and go through the maze trials as teenagers.

"My father was so excited to watch me and..." Zabe trailed off. He never talked about his brother. He'd closed off that part of him. "He was so proud when my team took the flag for the win."

Wulftone smiled warmly—he'd been on that team. Together, they stared at the center of the maze and spotted the prized object guarded by a gauntlet of obstacles. "Just like old times."

Harken stood in the preparations area and addressed the gathered trainees. His unamplified voice boomed across the deck where the recruits stood at attention.

"Remember that today counts. This is the day you've been waiting for—and I haven't invested these last several months' worth of intense training into you for nothing! You will be graded on your performance in these trials, like usual, but there will be more eyes on you.

"General Zabe and Lieutenant General Wulftone will be watching to see whom they might extend an offer of Guardian Corps armor sets to. Remember, the GC are specialists, elite, but they don't always make selections based on cumulative skill—so don't worry if you wind up staying in my ranks at the Royal Military. I trained you. I know what you can each do, and I'll be glad to retain you."

He stood straight and tall, then gave his class of recruits a salute. They returned the gesture and broke into their four assigned factions.

"Everyone perform weapons checks and get to your assigned positions," Harken ordered.

Hands clattered against weapons as the troops double checked and verified that their weapons had been set to stun, rather than the default kill setting.

"The games begin in fifteen minutes—you all know the drill! Live fire with stun blasts." His voice echoed a few decibels above the footsteps as they hurried off towards their starting corners at the edges of the maze while he barked a quick rules primer for the modified capture the flag exercise. "Points awarded for the first team to capture the device inside the gauntlet; points awarded for every enemy you put down; points awarded for every second your team holds the trophy; points awarded at the Generals' pleasure for feats of bravery or skill—be at your best—and remember that we're all on the same side at the end of the day."

Harken paced the perimeter of the maze and glanced back to where team Beta huddled together, scrambling to form a quick game plan. He smiled and managed to pull his eyes off of Jackie and her friends. Beta team wasn't the strongest or most talented, but they had the most heart as far as he was concerned, and he was rooting for them.

Jackie poked around the hedge corner of the maze and ducked back as the crack of blaster fire tore up her cover. "Gita, you're up." She didn't know how she'd feel about sending in a friend to play bait in a deadly fire situation, but everyone was set to stun and Jackie was willing to press her luck.

Jenner nodded to the short girl. "You got this." They'd worked in a team of three and moved their way through the grounds as they covered each other's backs.

Gita steeled herself and tried to shake out the nerves that nearly crippled her. She really hated being shot, but she was the smallest target and so it made sense... she just hoped she could be as small of a target as possible.

The tiny soldier leapt into the open and rolled into a prone position as she fired. None of her shots went anywhere near the enemy targets, but the move drew out the gunners on the far side of the corridor.

Jackie and Jenner leaned out and picked off the enemies. Blue energy jolts smacked into their chests and crackled with crippling lightning.

Jenner charged ahead impetuously and turned a corner deeper into the maze. Jackie rolled her eyes and ran after him. "Hold up," she yelled, trying to catch him. She hadn't figured out just yet if his impulsivity was because of his age and status as the youngest recruit of the batch or if he was just trying to impress Gita.

They caught up with him just in time to rescue him from an outgunned firefight. His rash actions may have exposed him to gunfire, but it also distracted the enemies who thought they'd caught him alone. Gita and Jackie cut them down and then cleared the way to the central contraption. Their goal lay at the center of the rotating machine of punishment.

"I can do this," Jenner said, as if he had something to prove. He launched his body towards the moving obstacle course that made up the automated gauntlet. The first few obstacles were only moderately difficult, but they got progressively harder when anyone ventured deeper; knocker bars and swinging weights promised to punish anyone who ventured too far.

"Ah crap," Jackie said, realizing that the device her team was after laid in the middle of a four-way intersection at the center of the gauntlet.

Jenner rushed ahead and got most of the way through before a heavy pylon smashed into him, knocking him back with bone-crunching force. He jumped to his feet and took another blow to his spine from a spinning, weighted pendulum that sent him reeling back towards the pylon, which hit him again, this time leveling him.

"Crap, crap, crap," Jackie muttered, raising her weapon and bracing herself against the edge-wall of the maze. She watched Gita sprint towards the pain-laced hall of the gauntlet.

Wulftone and Zabe both cringed as Jenner took a beating at the hands of the obstacle-laden machine. Beta team had been the first to locate the pathway in the center where their primary objective lay. Alpha team's scouts were not far off, however, and they could see them approach from the observation area.

Harken watched nearby and commented, "I thought it might be either Alpha or Beta team that found the center first."

Zabe grunted an acknowledgment.

Suddenly, the tiniest member of the Beta trio darted forward. She slipped past the first few impediments and then surged forward, headfirst, and skidded below the pylons that pummeled Jenner. Her small stature let her slide below the threat range of the smashing arms and the gauntlet's pendulums and knocker bars—but barely.

Wulftone arched his brows and turned to Zabe. "Woah. Isn't that the same move used by your..."

"Yes," Zabe stated, stone-faced.

Wulftone turned back to the action. He knew it couldn't be easy to watch old memories replayed before him.

Gita skidded to a stop with barely a centimeter left to skootch until she could grab hold of the trophy. She shouted triumphantly to her teammates. As soon as she got her hands on it and scored points for her team, a scout from Alpha group cleared the mouth of the corridor.

Jackie braced against the wall to improve her steadiness. She fired two shots; both found their marks at a range well beyond the weapon's normal accuracy rating. Both Wulftone and Harken beamed with pride at their friend's success.

Zabe turned to Harken. "Was that just luck?"

"I don't think so. She did mention something about first-person shooter games from Earth."

A second scout jumped up he fired and tagged Gita who howled with pain. The shot jolted her in the arm, numbing that limb, but she remained conscious.

Jackie took aim again and put another long-distance shot into the scout, disabling him in a clutch situation.

Zabe whistled at her skill. "Congratulations on your training," he said. "That's definitely not mere luck."

"I think she's just a natural." Harken refused to take credit for it.

Gita screamed in pain only seconds after the giddy screams of success when she took the flag. She scooted herself around to face Jenner. "Catch!" She slid the prize along the ground where Jenner snatched it up before executing a deliberate retreat. Behind him, Gita pushed herself forward on her toes, staying below the ranged of the obstacle course's painful, clockwork appendages.

Jackie laid down some cover fire as her friends extricated themselves with the objective in hand. Jenner wouldn't be able to fire his weapon as long as he carried it—the device's signal deactivated his pistol. "The clock's running—we're in the lead for points," Jackie cheered them on as they cleared the last few hurdles.

Jenner and Gita scrambled to their feet, and the threesome ducked around the corner, heading back into the maze and in search of the rest of their teammates.

"Good," Gita said, shaking the tingling numbness from her arm. "Now we've just got to hold on to the lead."

"By now, Alpha, Gamma, and Delta teams ought to be mostly inside the winding maze and looking for us—let's risk a direct route back," Jackie suggested.

She, Jenner, and Gita rounded a corner and entered a section of the labyrinth composed of old ruins. The long, straight hall exposed them on the stretching straightaways, but they knew it provided the fastest, most direct routes back towards their team.

In the distance, another group from Beta popped out and beckoned for them excitedly as they held the position. Jackie made a break for them, carrying the package to safety amid the larger numbers. Jenner and Gita brought up the rear.

They planted a hundred meters back to provide a safety buffer in case any opposition came from the rear while the rest of Beta group protected the game's primary goal.

A few long seconds passed, and the area grew quiet as their teammates moved further towards the fortified areas close to their staging zone. Suddenly, a gunman from Gamma broke into the lengthy, walled path, firing wildly.

Gita and Jenner sprinted away and jumped over some broken ruins for cover—Gita on one side, Jenner on the other. Their opponent fired relentlessly, barely pausing to aim. The cacophony nearly deafened them. The shots seemed louder than normal, with a distinct crack of the air as he fired.

Jenner looked worriedly to Gita from behind the chunk of the massive, toppled pillar. Gita was pinned down behind a tiny retaining wall and couldn't move a muscle without exposing herself. Busted fragments of rock spat skyward as the zealous enemy tried to tag her with his crimson laser bursts.

"Those are lethal blasts!" Jenner yelled, telling her to stay down.

Gita's eyes widened as she understood. Somehow, the soldier from Gamma had either failed to perform his weapons test or accidentally switched it over without realizing it.

Jenner leaned into the opening, screaming for him to stop, but only drew a burst of deadly energy. Between the tunnel vision rush of adrenaline and the aura of blood in the water he felt with his prey pinned down, the Gamma soldier wasn't about to let up.

Red rotating lights spun every hundred meters atop the wall, signaling an emergency end to the event. Jenner leaned out enough to get an eye on the observation deck and saw the generals scrambling as they rushed towards them—they'd seen the malfunction, too... but they would never get there in time and the soldier who pinned them down was too enthralled by the excitement to notice the signal.

Jenner yanked his head back behind his cover before the gunner could blow it off.

Gita's eyes filled with panic. Her terror filled Jenner with rage. He spat a bunch of curses and broke a piece off of his weapon. Jenner had plenty of reason to be angry. Bottling his rage up had become his norm in the wake of personal disaster after disaster. He was sick of it. Jenner channeled that rage and used it to keep him going as he concentrated on a solution—he didn't want to kill the idiotic recruit from Gamma if he didn't have to—but there was little chance he could get a drop on the jumpy triggerman, anyway.

Jenner had read up on a few obscure combat tricks and gritted his teeth as he tried one of them. He rammed the broken metal piece into the tangs of the weapon's charging ports, making the device into a makeshift bomb.

He threw the gun over his barricade where the remainder of his busted pillar towered precariously like a granite stump. The weapon cycled up and emitted a shrill whine as it reached critical levels.

"I have an idea," Jenner shouted. "Throw your gun over."

"Are you crazy? He'll kill us—he thinks he's set to stun!"

"Trust me."

Gita tossed the pistol. Sure enough, the recruit charged at them, gun still blazing, thinking he could disable the enemy with a few quick stun shots. A split second later and he would nearly have a critical angle on the two—but Jenner's blaster exploded in a ball of concussive fire that leveled a section of the wall and toppled the chunk of the freestanding pillar.

The bewildered soldier reeled away from the blast and hopped out of the path of the tumbling pillar, barely avoiding the crushing blow. Jenner leapt out from his cover and tackled the enemy, using the element of surprise to easily wrestle the gun away from him.

Zabe, Wulftone, and Harken arrived a few moments later.

As the dust settled, the rest of the troops trickled their way over and received an impromptu debriefing. Everyone was relieved, especially the accidental gunman, that nobody had been killed.

Harken pulled Jenner aside. "That was some quick thinking," he told him. "But I'm afraid you're not going to be in my military unit."

Jenner's face flashed with a pang of worry.

"That sort of swift reaction is the kind of thing General Zabe looks for in troops he wants for his Guardian Corps."

The boy smiled and then glanced back at Gita. "I hope so. And I hope that Gita makes the cut too."

Harken smiled placidly, fully recognizing that twinkle in his eye. He stole a glance of his own towards Jackie. "Just don't get too crazy trying to protect your own—the mission always comes first. But here, take this as something to remember today by. You never know when you need an extra boost." He pressed a large bullet into the youth's fist.

Jenner turned it over in his hand. "An explosive round? Aren't these illegal?"

Harken shrugged. "Not *exactly*. But they are rare and expensive—so just call it a keepsake and don't ask questions," he laughed. "But they're definitely not safe. Just like every romance I've ever had. Be cautious and wise, my friend."

Jenner bobbed his head thankfully as his superior clapped him on the shoulders with congratulations.

"You probably saved his life," Harken reiterated, indicating the opponent from Gamma. "And you definitely saved hers," he motioned to Gita.

Jenner stared at Gita longer than politeness allowed for.

"Remember," Harken cautioned, "there's nothing quite so fiery as girls or bullets. Keep your head down. Both can be cruel mistresses."

Zabe knew he was dreaming, but he didn't have any control over the events happening to him. He wouldn't have changed it if he did, anyway.

He held his bleeding side where he'd been gored by a feral talon-beast in the wilderness. He didn't bother to check for weapons. This had all happened to the teenage Zabe once before and he knew they'd been lost in the fight to drive back one of the sorcerer's incursions; he'd gotten separated from his unit as they fought the vyrm back to their source.

Young Zabe wiped the mud off his name badge and rank marker affixed to the breastplate over his heart. He didn't do it to check that this was his memory, but rather because it was important. The insignia marked him as a freshly minted soldier with only a few skirmishes under his belt, earning him the honor of a name badge—General Zahaben had not opted for any special privileges to be awarded to his sons.

He held his side to keep the blood flow staunched as he slogged through the marsh. Zabe felt light headed with the loss of blood and he knew that the creature still stalked him through the bogs—the smell of fresh blood let the beast know exactly where its prey was and how badly wounded it remained.

He could've stopped it, but his brother was a skilled tracker. While Zurrah was still too young for the trials, he'd honed his skills on hunting trips.

Zabe crawled out of the slough and into the bracken of the fen. He had less fear this time. He knew the outcome already.

Just as the talonbeast charged through the underbrush, Zurrah leapt out from the trees and plunged a sharpened pike into the ravenous, felinoid beast, saving Zabe's life.

A few years his junior, Zurrah wore the freshly minted Guardian Corps armor he'd only just earned. Before they even left the fens, Zabe took Zurrah's knife and etched his brother's name into the metal of the chest plate.

"I haven't earned it yet," Zurrah argued.

Zabe argued, "As long as I'm concerned, you've earned both name *and* rank."

The Master at Arms awoke in his bed. He hadn't spoken about his brother in years, though he thought about him often. Something about watching the new recruits had conjured up the memories.

He only hoped that he could do better by this new crop of trainees. The threat of Nitthogr had finally been averted, but the Prime was in dire need of warriors as committed as his brother Zurrah. He needed more than heart and commitment, however; Zabe needed men and woman of skill and tenacity. Zurrah hadn't survived—and Zabe was committed to ensuring that his trainees fared better.

# Chapter Four



*Three Years Later...*
*The Prime.*

Zabe held Claire tightly as they stood outside the apartment door to the suite she shared with her father and Jackie. Three years had slipped away like grains of sand in an hourglass, barely noticed as the Prime rebuilt from the vyrmic incursion.

Daylight had barely begun to creep through the arched windows in the long hallway of the royal citadel. Claire stifled a yawn.

The couple's all-nighter had been too-long in coming. Ever since beginning the rebuilding efforts to repair Nitthogr's damage, they'd barely managed any time together. They'd finally begun stealing it from other areas—chiefly during their late, sleeping hours.

He squeezed her again. "I've got to go," Zabe whispered.

Claire pouted slightly. Zabe's new position demanded much of him. The Guardian Corps still needed constant rebuilding, and the Prime needed to remain vigilant against any new threats. They knew there were many. "Fine," she sighed, relinquishing her hold on him. She had her own duties to attend to.

Zabe held her hand for a second longer. "Will you tell your father soon?"

She nodded. "Soon."

Zabe grinned, let her hand go, and went to work.

Claire watched him go before slipping quietly into her living quarters. She hoped to sneak inside before anyone realized she'd been out all night.

The aromatic scent of strong coffee hit her as soon as she cleared the door and Claire knew she'd been busted. Sam Jones, her father, nodded to her as she closed the door sheepishly behind. He lifted the carafe and poured her a cup.

"Late night?" he asked.

Claire shrugged and embraced the warm mug. She chugged half the cup and then refilled it as the caffeine slapped her brain into some semblance of wakefulness.

"You and Zabe... things are getting pretty serious?"

Claire laid her head on the table as if defeated. "Yes," she sighed. She'd never been good at hiding anything from him.

"*Real* serious?"

"Uh-huh," she agreed from below the cascade of falling hair.

"Are you still worried he's in love with Bithia instead of Claire Jones?"

She looked up at her father and gushed all of her emotions. They spilled out as barely coherent, rapid-fire sentence fragments. "We're the same. I think we've merged more fully. Bithia and me—Claire and me. I don't know. Yes. We—I love him. Responsibilities, you know, Princess of the Prime, and stuff. Argh! Relationships are so hard!"

Claire put her face back down on the table.

Sam grinned. "Believe it or not, I've felt all those same things before... when your mother was—before she..."

"You felt the pressures of being some kind of inter-dimensional princess, *too*?"

He chuckled. "You don't know the half of it."

An awkward silence passed between them. Claire finally picked herself back up and sipped her coffee again.

"I'd do anything to get back to that nervous, angsty tension... that swelling, eager sense of hope and love. Relationships are *good*. Trust me. This is how we were made to *be*." He smiled warmly.

The door slammed open and then shut with a bang as Jackie stormed through, exasperated. "Relationships suck!" she exclaimed.

Jackie joined them at the table and slumped into a heap in a spare chair, dumping a bundle of newspapers and other sundries as she collapsed. She laid her head on the table, just like Claire had done, and pouted.

Claire cocked an eyebrow at her disheveled friend. She still wore the clothes she'd been wearing the previous evening, and her hair was a matted mess.

"Late night?"

Jackie blew a raspberry and glared at her friend while Doctor Jones sorted through the materials she'd dropped on the floor, including a few weeks of old newspapers from Earth. He liked keeping up with events from their home realm. "You could say that. I know I used to want guys to like me, but I take back everything I ever wished for."

Claire patted her friend on the head playfully. "Boy trouble?"

"Remember when I couldn't find a date for your wedding that never happened? Now I can hardly keep them off me! I was out with Wulftone and accidentally called him Harken in the middle of the conversation!" She hung her head again. "Things were simpler before coming to some weird alternate universe where I've somehow become an exotic sex-symbol. But at this rate, I'm going to make both guys so mad at me I'll wind up going as your *dad's* plus one to your next wedding."

Sam piped up. "Excuse me. Wedding?"

Claire shot her closest friend a warning look. "She's talking hypothetically, Dad."

Sam shrugged nonchalantly, but his eyes indicated he might suspect more than he'd let on.

"Ugh," Jackie continued, "And I've got more drills and training this morning, too. *Both* of them are going to be there. My life is over."

"So just pick one," Claire laughed.

"*Could you?* That's like picking to give up ice cream or chocolate forever. You can't just *pick one*. Which do you choose?"

"Chocolate," Claire and her father both said simultaneously.

Jackie scowled while they laughed and high-fived each other.

"You guys are too weird." She rolled her eyes and hung her head again.

Claire grinned and shrugged. She knew it was a compliment.

"Speaking of weird," Sam flipped to the back page of the news article to continue reading. The front page-page story listed strange accounts of high profile robberies. Witnesses claimed seeing an odd, triangular projection at the heists. One major diamond theft threatened to bankrupt an entire Central-American country. "I've seen this before!" He flashed them an artist's rendering of the triangle.

"So have I." Claire peeled off the front page and began reading in greater detail. "A story about a kidnapping during Nitthogr's invasion in the Prime came to me a while back. One of my subjects told a story about his family's slaughter by other people—not vyrm. It was Professor Jarfig's family; Jarfig was the head of the Prime Museum. One of his children survived the attack. Jenner was just a teen... barely old enough to enter the Royal Army for training with a special exemption, which I granted in lieu of his circumstances."

Sam looked at her inquisitively.

Claire glanced at Jackie, who also looked at her oddly. "You're doing it again."

Claire's cheeks flushed slightly. She sometimes slipped into a different kind of voice, making it obvious when Bithia's side came through more overtly than Claire's.

Sam gave her an out and changed the subject. He slid a different section of the newspaper across the table and nodded at the headline. *Local Philanthropist Teaches Orphans to Sail.* "Didn't you know her in college?"

Claire skimmed through the article about Holly Wainsmith, a rich girl she'd had a few classes with at the U. She'd trained a group of parentless children to sail; it detailed their plans to sail from Florida to Bermuda on something of a dream vacation for the underprivileged. "She was always championing some new project or cause," Claire nodded as she tapped Holly's family photo.

"She must get it from her mother, who was an absolute saint. I only met her father once. I got a real sleazeball vibe from him." Claire did a double take and then pressed the paper close to her face for a better view. "Oh. No wonder," she mumbled as she identified what appeared to be a familiar, seven-pointed star pinned to the lapel of Holly's father, Percival Wainsmith.

"Leave us," Basilisk ordered his guards away from his sanctum while he abused his victim. The other captured vyrm remained bound in chains and on their knees. Their eyes shone with defiance.

He stepped on the neck of the vyrm interloper. "I already know who you work for," he said calmly. "You are members of the Black and you have been planted here in order to spy on the tarkhūn—to spy on *me*." He applied more pressure until the scaly vyrm cried out.

The pained yelp echoed through the hybrid warlord's sculpture garden. Grimacing as he crushed the poor captive's skull, the trio of shackled prisoners watched for any opportunity.

Finally, with Basilisk's back turned, one of the vyrm pulled a shiv from his boot and leapt for the leader with a howl. "For the Black!"

Within a split second, five of the statues sprang to life with weapons drawn. One of them tackled the assassin, and the others executed his three companions with cold precision, cutting their necks without a moment's thought.

Basilisk turned and grinned at the vyrm he'd baited into action. "You must be Chartarra," he greeted warmly.

"Shades," Chartarra hissed at the perfectly camouflaged soldiers. The skill was one of the two more common ones given to the gifted tarkhūn. He hissed again, this time chiding himself for not anticipating such protective measures.

"It must be true," Basilisk absentmindedly combed his fingers through a long lock of hair which hung neatly from his head. "The chiefs from the five tribes of the Black must've arranged this attempt independent of Caivev. She would not have been so sloppy in its execution. But don't worry—I'm taking steps to ensure that they won't continue undermining their rightful leader, my brother's successor."

Chartarra stared ahead blankly. He refused the give his tarkhūn captors anything useful.

Basilisk continued, "I knew that the son of Charobv was among the Black's assassination attempt. I also knew that the first attack was a ruse in order to get some of my would-be murderers close enough to strike."

"I don't know who Charobv is," the young one hissed.

"Of course you do... and of course you'd have to say that," Basilisk retorted calmly. "You and I both know that your father is one of Caivev's primary generals on Earth. He is intimately involved in her affairs and is one of a few trusted soldiers capable of running her newest campaign."

The haughty leader glared down at the restrained captive, who wasn't yet convinced. "I could name other names to show you exactly how much I know. Kreephast is your father's partner, along with a newer one named Idrakka and a race traitor named Skrom... another of my wayward tarkhūn committed to walking in Regorik's footsteps."

Chartarra looked into Basilisk's eyes. He could tell the man knew every detail. "Then what do you need with me? I will never betray the Black."

Basilisk stooped to one knee and met Chartarra's gaze. "I would never expect you to." He nodded to his shades, who released the prisoner. "You stand at a crossroads, son of Charobv... will you help negotiate a peace between the Tarkhūn and the Black? I want only to unify our peoples once more—to bring an alliance such as we had during the Syzygyc War. Only then can we finally fulfill the destiny of our great race." He took Chartarra's face into his hands. "I have foreseen our fate, and it is glorious!"

Chartarra looked into his eyes and believed him. "What do you need from me?"

"Just information. Caivev is vital to my plan, but she will not answer my summons."

"I can do nothing against the leader of my people. Such a thing is too great a—"

"I would never ask it," Basilisk feigned shock. "I only ask what portal she meets the other leaders of the Black through, and on which plane, so that I may pass on an invitation for palaver." He paused and then reinforced his position. "Even if I meant for some nefarious ends to fall upon Caivev, the Black is far too resilient for a mere assassination to topple them. We have an ideological conflict that can only be resolved through conversation—not with bloodshed."

The young vyrm muttered a curse under his breath and gave up a location.

Basilisk stared into his face while his new friend listed the few possible locations for the meeting. He gazed into Chartarra's eyes and believed him.

Quick as a flash, he raked his claws across the throat of the general's son.

Chartarra grasped his neck and collapsed. He gurgled once in protest and then bled out next to one of Basilisk's gaming tables in the statue garden.

"We finally have a location," he said and signaled one of his shades to fetch his own battle planners and astrologers in order to draw up a plan.

Sam smiled as he entered his spacious office while holding his thermos full of coffee. He grinned and took a sip of the brew. Perhaps he couldn't help his daughter with her romantic woes, but at least he'd been able to pass on a love of caffeine. He was sure she'd turn out fine.

Motion sensors picked up his presence on entry and everything in his historical research lab activated. The archaeologist slid into his seat and marveled at the advanced technology of the Prime. True, he sometimes missed Earth, but working in the Prime gave him a whole new set of mysteries to uncover, and quite honestly, discoveries made in this dimension unraveled so many of the questions asked after on Earth—plus he never had to worry about funding, limitations, or red tape. Claire's high position had ensured that.

The massive computer screen awoke to display the ancient religious and mystic texts that he'd been researching last night. He still had trouble reconciling the dual nature of reality that residents from the Prime so readily embraced: natural and supernatural coexistence as different aspects of science. His earthly upbringing hadn't prepared his mind to accept the fact that both forces were merely different faces of the same coin—each with its own approach and method of understanding.

Sliding over to the table at the center of the room, he pinched the bridge of his nose and massaged away the headache gained by pouring over the historical texts he'd been working with. He'd immersed himself in the uncomfortable flip-side of reality yesterday; today he could give himself a break and deal with the more empirical side of things, the parts he was more at ease with.

Sam took another sip of coffee and leafed through the pages as he recalled his early conversation. He was quite familiar with Professor Jarfig. In fact, his surviving son, Jenner, had met with him to pass on his father's work before he entered the Royal Military Academy.

Jenner seemed like such a driven young man—conducting himself as if he'd grown up far too quickly. Witnessing your family's murder would certainly do that. Jarfig had seen it as his obligation to the historical record to chronicle the vyrm's taking of the Prime; Jenner made sure to honor his father's memory by delivering those fastidious notes to those who could put them into the annals of history.

The doors eventually slid open again and his lab-mate entered. Wearing his ever-present Guardian Corps armor, Tay-lore crossed the room in perfect human fashion, even giving a cordial nod to Sam, who nodded back.

Tay-lore stopped at the far side of the room. "How did I do, Sam Jones?"

Sam chuckled and nodded. "You're getting better every day."

With a slightly robotic voice, Tay-lore confessed, "I have been practicing."

"I can tell." He'd been helping Tay-lore try to become more human—or at least appear that way.

The android tilted his torso to peer at his friend's documents. "Have you learned all you had hoped to about the supernatural nature of the universe?"

Sam sighed. "It's not quite so simple for us," he reminded the automaton. Tay-lore had always been a little too human for his own robotic species, making him too glitchy for his own kind. That had likely been what preserved him as the sole survivor of the uprising many centuries prior when the Guardian Corps spared him. However, his glitchy forgetfulness was often inconvenient.

"Then perhaps it is good that Shandra is waiting for you outside." The construct took his seat at a neighboring console, where he resumed monitoring a million sources of data from across the planes as only the android could. "I think I meant to say that when I came in."

Sam opened the door for the cleric of Veritas and welcomed her in. "Sorry about the wait," he told her.

The middle-aged blonde woman tried not to look perturbed, although Sam always felt a little intimidated by clerical uniforms and robes like the ones she wore. Shandra pushed through with a smile, recognizing the irony of the situation. "I'm partly to blame. I was supposed to come yesterday to help you work through some of your research."

He nodded, figuring that today would now be another, filled with arcane research, instead. Shandra was responsible for cataloging, managing, and sometimes responding to crises involving arcane artifacts. If something needed collecting by the Guardian Corps so that it could be hidden within the Chamber of Mysteries, she was one of the people making that decision.

"I was really hoping that you could help bring me up to speed on things."

"Things?" She raised an eyebrow inquisitively.

"So many things," he laughed. "I must admit that I am so poorly versed in the arcane that I might need some serious tutoring. I'm especially trying to make sense of pre-Sh'logath cult beliefs of the people of Edenya—before it became known as Desolation."

Shandra bobbed her head measuredly. "I can help somewhat—the old Mae'le-ggath can be confusing and there is much we don't know," she told him. "First, let me show you something that might interest you specifically. It is in the tower."

"Ooooh," Tay-lore said luridly.

He turned to address them in the awkward silence that followed. "My apologies. I have been working on humor. Perhaps Sam Jones is not the only one requiring a tutor."

*You are lovely, my child, and I know you've been inside my home.*

Caivev whirled around the sweaty marketplace at the edge of Changuinola. In one fluid motion, she'd drawn her concealed vyrm disruptor pistol and waved it at the whispers behind her.

The locals yelped and dove for cover. Vendors snapped up handles on their rickshaws and carted away their goods as fast as possible. People shielded their face from her as a sign that they wouldn't be able to recognize her if the policia came: an unspoken request to spare them.

She spun around again as the whisper laughed at her. The marketplace cleared out within seconds, leaving only the confused Caivev.

Residents of the war-torn country of Chiriquí didn't mess around when it came to violence. Too many of their loved ones had fallen into the civil war that followed the secession of the Chiriquí and Bosca Del Toro provinces when they'd declared their independence under the brilliant leadership of General Nyagittari's guerillas.

Caivev understood their fragile state more than any could realize. Her vyrm generals had been largely responsible for the war. Retaining control over the Lost Temple was her number one priority at the moment—that and locating the source of the voice that she was so sure she'd heard.

"Show yourself," she demanded to the empty air.

*You've seen my house, daughter. I've watched you from afar.*

"Ya-rawr!" she yelled, spinning again and firing her alien blaster. Her bolt of energy struck an abandoned chicken coop; it exploded in flaming debris.

*You are a true believer, and I've marked you for a special purpose.*

She turned again, this time under more control. Caivev was certain she'd pinpointed his direction, but the voice grew fainter.

"Purpose? What purpose?"

The voice grew quieter, but didn't change direction.

*You know. The purpose—the only purpose.*

Caivev dashed forward and found a rickety door left half ajar near a retaining wall. She peeked inside and found a low-ceilinged hovel with a floor covered in used straw. Based on the animals tied outside, she could only assume the room was a shelter for a local farmer's goats.

"Come in, come in," an elderly woman crooned from her seat behind a badly distressed table. She beckoned widely with her hands, obviously unable to exactly locate the guest with her milky white eyes. "*He said you would come.*"

"Who said I would come?"

"He refused to tell me his name. But I know how he whispers."

The old crone beckoned for her to take a seat.

Out of curiosity, Caivev complied. She glanced down at the rune-marked bones the old woman had been recently using for some arcane purpose. They lay arranged haphazardly upon a poorly carved image of a skull.

"You are a fortune teller?"

She nodded, slowly. "That is what *some* have called me."

"Then tell me my future, old woman."

The blind mystic dropped a handful of bones as she breathed laboriously. Using her hands and fingers, she touched the arrangement of her tools and traced the edges of the engraved skull to get a sense of their location.

"You do not have a future." She grumbled, confusedly under her breath. "Not you... *there is no future in you?*"

"What do you mean?"

The old woman looked suddenly frightened. "All future ends with you!"

Caivev stared at her while she suddenly began to convulse and the woman's white eyes began to cloud and turn red. Her voice dropped several octaves.

"Through you, there is no future!"

Caivev met the hag's gaze and grinned. "Who are you?"

The old woman shuddered violently enough that her neck snapped and she collapsed, falling utterly still.

Behind Caivev, she heard the voice again. "I am Akko Soggathoth."

Caivev spun and found a hovering mass of blackness. The writhing pool of inky, ethereal tentacles and bubbles pulsed as it spoke, shimmering and quasi-transparent.

She could only see him from the corner of her eyes as if he were the shadow beast from some child's nightmare vision, only visible in the blind the spots of the eye—elusively disappearing under any scrutiny. And yet he certainly existed somewhere between seeing and non-seeing.

"I am the true Herald of Sh'logath," he said. "We have a common goal, you and I." The inky mass laughed as his voice took a tone of mirth. "I am the first of my kind to awaken: the first of the seven brothers."

"The Seven Brothers of the Winnowing?" Caivev asked breathlessly.

"Very good. We must awaken the others," he said.

"How? So much of your prophecy was hidden by Nitthogr after he proclaimed himself the Herald of Sh'logath."

Akko Soggathoth laughed again. "The pretender did not destroy everything—he kept many things hidden away within the Temple and its twin—I even know about the boy. Everything you need is inside my house. Well, almost everything."

Caivev felt inexplicably drawn to the dead woman's pile of bones. One of her nine ivory carvings was not a bone at all, but something else entirely.

It felt metallic to Caivev as she picked it up. She could feel the innate power of the weird charm; the carving had a lead-like sheen and bore a certain resemblance to Bithia's dimensional inversion pendant.

"Darquematter?" she asked. Caivev only knew scraps of the legend, but she was sure she could locate more details with little effort. "Is this a hierophanticus?" The seven keys could each open the prison doors to the fractured realms of the Darque dimension, where the brothers slumbered.

"Correct. But you will need more than just elements from my world to complete your task."

The door swung open as a goat walked inside. Caivev watched it for a second, and then she caught movement from the corner of her eye as something leapt from the shadows at the edge of the room.

A black creature snarled from its tentacled face. It crouched to pounce with heavy scales bunching up like flexible scale-mail. It snatched up the prey and, with its clawed feet and powerful mandibular appendages, the dog-sized beast ripped the goat to shreds in seconds.

"The abyssal auraphage is native to the Darque dimension. It will help you find a sacrifice appropriate to awaken each brother."

Sticking a tongue-like proboscis through its tentacles, the auraphage sampled the air. It gave a kind of growling whine and retreat backward into the shadow.

A man burst through the door wildly. "You! Do you speak English? The monsters—they took me! Please, you've got to help me," he raved.

"I speak English," she responded.

"Oh thank God! It's after me! The thing—the goatman! I don't even know how I got here—the last thing I remember was infiltrating a cult in Pecos, Texas—is this Mexico?"

Caivev only regarded him coolly.

"My name is Quintin Hall and I'm a paranormal investigator. You've got to believe me!" He caught a glance of the dead bone-thrower and then spotted the hierophanticus in Caivev's hand. "No! Not again."

Caivev glanced down at the auraphage as it growled from nearby. She just barely caught sight of the twisting mass of black that was Akko Soggathoth as it snatched Hall around the neck with a squid-like arm.

The man shrieked, "No!"

She looked back up to find Quintin Hall standing, completely calm.

"I have my vessel," he said. With a grin, a sudden shadow came over his body and the man transformed into a fiendish goatman—like some necrotic, decaying faun. Smiling devilishly, he transformed back into a humanoid appearance and took a leash from his pocket.

The auraphage had also transformed. It was every bit of a Rottweiler and it obediently sat for its master, who hooked a leash to its collar.

"Now please, we should get going. We have so much to do before we can awaken my brother. Once I bring you up to speed, my little pet and I will go in search of the next sacrifice: the person whose blood tastes right to open the gates. "

Tay-lore peeked through the threshold of the door and fidgeted nervously. He glanced at the princess and at Zabe, who appeared to enjoy some much needed time together. For all his humanistic defects, he couldn't stop being either a human or a robot.

He knew he was deeply flawed. The fact that he was pacing anxiously reminded him of how flawed he was as a robot—the cold hard logic of his programming should have insisted that he interrupt whatever moment they'd finally stolen for themselves. But it would sadden him to intrude. The fact that he felt emotions, or had friends, or went by the pronoun *"he,"* were all facts to him and their implications ran deep. Tay-lore did not know how to be anything else than what he was: something more than either human or automaton.

Finally, he readied himself to interrupt. If he had lungs, he might've sighed, even if that would've only been a learned trait meant to demonstrate solidarity with his human peers.

"Tay-lore," Zabe called from the adjacent room. "I see you—come in here. What's on your mind?"

He stepped into the room. "Pardon me. I do not mean to intrude, but I found news of our enemies while going about my usual surveillance."

Claire asked worriedly, "Good news or bad news?"

"Neither, I suppose. But it is of interest, I am sure. The tarkhūn seem to be at war with different factions of the vyrm again."

"The Black," asked Zabe.

"They are always at odds with the Black, it seems, but this is more than that. The tarkhūn have been targeting different rogue cults operating within the species."

"You mean the factionless?"

"It appears to be more than that," Tay-lore paused insightfully. "They have been trying to locate the Followers of Krakkath and also eradicate something called the Seekers of Maetha."

"You mean the Rovers?" Claire asked.

Zabe shook his head. The topic had long been an area of interest for him, and seeing the unaligned vyrm in the wastelands of Desolation had been the highlight of their last joint trip to the realm.

"Both predate the Sh'logath cult founded at the Plains of Neggath. They are older than Nitthogr and Basilisk and have been around for eons."

Claire looked hopeful. "Could this be an indicator that the vyrms' hearts and minds might be changing—turning away from the Devourer?"

Zabe grimaced and shook his head. "No. The religion has always been about Sh'logath, but there existed an earlier version that was slightly altered by the revelations of the Thousand Elders. Think about Earth's long history with Judaism and their whole cultus before the arrival of the Christ and the emergence of his followers and church as they moved the religion forward."

Claire nodded, though she could feel that Bithia had so many questions about that particular segment of history. She didn't have many answers, but had always intended to delve more seriously into a study of faith, but she'd never made it a high enough priority to sufficiently answer those questions that her Prime mind yearned for answers to.

"Do you think this means they could be mobilizing for war? Are we in any danger?" she asked Tay-lore.

"No. I do not believe so," he stated. "I just thought you would want to know. There are indications that some tarkhūn have visited your home realm. Nitthogr was clever and knew how to disguise his activity enough that we have difficulty detecting any of the movement or communication from the Black. The tarkhūn are less adept. I would not dare to guess at what is happening within the factions—I only know that there is activity, and much of it is hostile."

"Thank you, Tay-lore," Claire said.

He did his best attempt to nod appreciatively and returned to his station. Deep down, he knew that he could have sent the information remotely, but deep down he craved contact and his station was lonely whenever Sam Jones was gone.

Shandra led the way through the topmost section of the tower. A newly installed metal door barred their path, and she touched her thumb to the sensor. It clicked and unlocked, allowing them access to the room. "All members of the royal family and certain members of the military and councils have programmed access," she promised, although her tone of voice didn't seem to indicate it was a fact that pleased her. "This is why I was late yesterday. I got so caught up in our work and I quite lost track of time."

Sam walked in a loop and examined the ancient set of mirrors. "I didn't think vanity would be welcomed amongst the Veritas... I mean, you're pretty and all, but..." He trailed off and watched her try to conceal a slight blush.

"These are a set of very powerful artifacts," Shandra replied. "From this room, and with these mirrors, one could access any of the known portals through the Tesseract."

He raised his eyebrows and gave them a second look. "You mean during the right lunar or solar alignments?"

She shook her head. "No. These can send a traveler through to anywhere. It is a one-way trip, but it defies the normal requirements of portal travel."

Sam examined the different engravings on the different mirrors and arrived at one with no glass. "So I can return to Earth whenever I want?"

Shandra nodded slowly. "Yes, but return would still follow the regular astronomical requirements." She indicated the glassless mirror. "We took measurements for a new cutting and the Earth mirror will be fully repaired by this afternoon. Are you eager to return?"

He wrinkled his nose. "Not really. Everything that's important to me now is in the Prime. I guess I have a few friends back there, but my life is here now."

"Good. Earth is important and planeswalking is more dangerous than people realize. Some clerics have long believed it was the constant travel that corrupted Nitthogr and Basilisk prior to their great fall. Earth has always been relatively off-limits because of the will of the Architect King. The mirrors shouldn't be used lightly."

Shandra's face softened when she looked at the Earth-man. "The Prime would hate to see you return to Earth... I mean, I don't know much about history, but I'm sure your research is important. Maybe our paths will continue to cross as you remain in your studies?"

Sam nodded. He looked at the blonde cleric, who was so passionate about her work. It seemed like every month he had fewer and fewer reasons to ever return.

# CHAPTER FIVE

Caivev crept down the steep bank of The Crag, a deep ravine a few clicks from the Hidden Temple where she could translate from one destination to the next. She stepped onto the platform and activated the portal that would allow her to planeswalk to the sylvan realm where her allies waited. She glanced around and tried to shake the uneasy feeling that plagued her.

Chalking it up to nerves, she ventured on ahead. She'd already used a two step-portal transition and shifted between two other dimensions in order to obfuscate her true destination in case any enemies followed.

Caivev activated the intermediate portal with a drop of her own blood and stepped through. Immediately following the piercing agony of her body disintegrating and rematerializing on another plane, she was finally greeted by the warm smells of the heavily wooded realm. From her spot on the giant stone disk protruding from the dirt of the forest glen, she could see vyrm forces leaving their wooded havens to greet her: the five members of the Black's council approached and a huge contingent of vyrm soldiers following behind.

About halfway through the clearing, she slowed her gait. An odd noise caught her attention, and she turned back towards the old ceremonial site where she'd arrived. Some kind of barely audible whine emitted nearby, as if it came from a power supply.

With her hackles suddenly raised, she caught sight of her contact in the distance. Mumbling every curse word she knew beneath her breath, Caivev raised her disruptor at them and watched them through the magnification of her scope. The five paused, understanding that she was checking them out.

Caivev raised an arm in salute to test them. Her welcome party each raised a return arm of salute. She cursed again and noted that they'd walked past some sort of painted line in the grass meant to mark a location. They were supposed to raise two arms in double salute to verify their identity.

"Shades," she whispered, knowing her meeting had been compromised. Caivev sprang to her feet and dashed back towards the portal location. Her assailants scrambled after her.

The shrill noise grew louder as she approached. Before she could get to the gate, a crackling blue orb of energy zapped her and flung the woman back in the dirt.

She suddenly recognized the noise: a force field generator. Caivev snapped her disruptor to attention and fired off a few shots at her pursuit. The shots flew wide except for one, which blasted the dirty tarkhūn into a steaming pile of meat.

The shrill whine grew exponentially louder and a burst of static echoed around her. Finally recognizing that their leader was under attack, the nearby members of the Black leapt into position and fired at the remaining four shades, but a larger protective dome that popped up on the paint markers turned back their blaster fire. Ricochets flung wide and some wild bolts fragged their own troops.

Caivev cursed again and dove for cover, trying to find her remaining attackers in her sights. She suddenly felt out of sorts—like she'd been drugged while someone screamed into her ear. The pain in her brain made her vision seem to shudder. Every fear and failing in her memory suddenly drilled its way into the forefront of her mind.

"Get out of my head, lich," she cursed at the tarkhūn psychic. Caivev groaned and then turned her thoughts inward and mentally thrust them at the vyrm telepath who she assumed hid nearby.

Her head cleared immediately as the psychic hold crumbled. The lich obviously didn't expect an opponent who possessed training to resist psionic attacks.

The four enemies were on her in a flash, regardless, even as the larger of the two barriers overloaded and crackled, winking out of existence under the barrage of heavy blaster fire. The remaining shades deactivated the last force field, dragged their captive onto the platform, and then leapt into a different dimension with their victim in tow.

Jackie flung the cold, wet towel overhead as she collapsed into a heap outside the Guardian Corps' training gym. Every part of her ached, but the training made her happy—even if it meant she had to face her gaffes and work with Harken and Wulftone.

She'd pretended like nothing had happened, and Wulftone, to his credit, played along. Jackie bit her lip in consternation. That little kindness tore her up even more! How could she not just fall into the guy's arms?

Glancing over her shoulder, she caught sight of Harken heading towards her. Harken with his stupid, handsome dimpled chin. From the corner of her other eye, she saw Wulftone also headed her direction.

"Dear Lord," she whispered. "This is how my life ends."

Walking up ahead in the distance, she spotted Claire and Zabe wearing some goofy looking getups and harnesses. They could've been rolled in butter and wearing breadcrumbs for all she cared!

Jackie sprang to her feet and jogged towards them, pretending not to notice either of her two suitors.

She waved to Claire and Zabe as she closed the distance. "Hey! What are you guys doin? Where ya goin?"

Jackie rocked eagerly on the balls of her feet while Claire turned to greet her. Her friend immediately caught the look on Jackie's face and the way she refused to turn and see if either Harken or Wulftone had followed told her everything.

Claire tried to signal her friend that it was safe, but the two guys watched from a distance. "We were just headed spelunking," she said.

"Is that like snorkeling? Can I come—I've got to get out and do something outside of the gym. You know, expand my horizons."

"It's cave exploration," Zabe said.

"Of course you can come," Claire interjected, looking over her friend's shoulder and throwing an arm around her to give her an excuse her watchers would accept. "We're headed this way."

"But I thought it was going to be a..." Zabe stopped when Claire gave him a sharp look. He didn't quite know what it meant, except that he'd been overruled and any argument would be futile.

"Right this way, I guess?"

Caivev quickly realized her captors didn't intend her any ill will, but neither did they relax their hold on her. With her familiarity of planeswalking, it seemed obvious within a few quick trips between the dimensional gates that they headed for a gate that would take them to Limbus.

The shades made perfect abductors. They used their camouflaging and disguise abilities to perfectly blend in with the surrounding populations as they ferried their captive between different portal locations. They were not, however, good conversationalists and switched into obscure languages when they chose to communicate so that Caivev could not eavesdrop on them.

When they finally arrived at Basilisk's city, a seed of dread lodged in her belly. The journey took two days, and the sudden thought of a confrontation and conversation with the tarkhūn leader unnerved her greatly. She sighed and began the long trek up the winding hillside as her "guides" forced her along the trail that would end in their leader's sanctum—and possibly her death or imprisonment within a case of living stone if he chose to petrify her.

The shades did not parade her as a trophy, but Caivev couldn't help but feel as if she was one. As they passed through the city, thousands of sets of eyes peered out at her from the darkness of vyrm dwellings.

She grimaced as they reached the edge of the sculpture garden. Several new acquisitions ringed the edge of his collection and she paused to take it in. A completely normal family from the Prime stood locked in stony repose; their clothing indicated they were commoners and nothing indicated anything special about them. Chuckling and shaking her head, she knew it was difficult to understand why the eccentric tarkhūn leader did the things he did—or whom chose to imprison and for what purpose.

Caivev could see her enemy in the distance where he hunched over one of his high-tabled games. She hadn't conversed with him in years—since prior to Nitthogr's final push to take the Prime. Before that, relations had been tense, but hadn't yet bubbled up into war again.

Basilisk called to her and beckoned. The shades departed and left them alone.

Caivev knew that would hardly be the case and assumed he had at least a dozen bodyguards hidden among the stone figures. She hardened her heart and proceeded through the maze of statues with her head held high and her dignity intact.

Basilisk leaned over a nearby place-setting of food and wine and motioned for his guest to move closer. "You and I have much to discuss," Basilisk stated warmly.

Caivev kept her temperament cool and slid onto a high stool. She adjusted her place setting and served herself. Basilisk did likewise.

"There were easier ways to call me to a diplomatic parley, you know."

Basilisk raised an eyebrow mischievously and sipped from his goblet. "I hardly think so. Especially not after I had all your tribal chiefs killed."

Caivev paused mid-bite and glared at him. Her piercing look demanded more information.

"They exercised too much autonomy. You might not have known that they'd begun running their own operations against me, independent of your authorization. In fact, they'd just recently tried to kill me on three separate occasions." He touched his chest with mock indignation.

She wore her best poker-face, but this was new information to her. Caivev didn't reward him with any response. Instead, she ate a few bite-sized pieces of fruit. "These rousch-berries are certainly ripe for this time of year."

Basilisk grinned. He enjoyed playing this game with her; she was better at it than she gave herself credit. "I couldn't let them entertain the idea that they might be able to survive without you, my dear. Or worse, that a coup might be a good idea." He sipped deeply from his cup.

"What is it that you brought me here to discuss?"

"So many things, Caivev. Primarily, I'm concerned that the Black felt they could operate in such independence of their leader."

Caivev watched him over the rim of her cup as she took a deep draught. It was obvious he wouldn't give up on this topic.

Basilisk leaned across the table and refilled her cup from the table's pitcher. "It seems to indicate that your attention is greatly diverted to something else." He folded his hands and waited for an answer.

She sipped from her glass again; glad to be finally heading towards the real topic. "There was no question in there," Caivev stated coyly.

Basilisk grinned. "You know how deeply my curiosity runs. What are you up to?"

This time Caivev grinned. "Don't your spies know everything?"

"Humor me."

"To what end?" she toyed with him. "What is in it for the Black?"

He stood and motioned for her to join him at a nearby gaming table. Basilisk reset the pieces to the strategy game and moved his piece first. Caivev faced him and moved a piece. Another move. A move. A countermove. They positioned pieces quickly, decisively. And almost as quickly as it began, Basilisk ended it. "You are mated."

Caivev frowned, but she had expected nothing less from the master gamesman.

"Again." Basilisk did not ask. He commanded and reset his pieces.

Move. Move. Move. Move. Again, his knights captured her queen.

"You play too disciplined," he said, resetting the game again.

Move. Move. Over and over. He won again.

"Predictable. Since when has Caivev, a potential Dunnischktet, ever played the game so safely?"

Caivev growled with frustration and reset the pieces. She moved her pieces quickly and furiously, nearly slamming them down on the tiled squares.

Move. Move. Loss.

She glowered and grumbled, resetting again—silently cursing Basilisk's smug, gloating smile.

Move. Move. Move. Counter-move. Move. Faster and faster, they acted and reacted. She recklessly challenged his openings and sacrificed pieces. Move. Move. Stop... the table was cleared of pieces except for the two most powerful units on either side. The game had stalemated.

Basilisk grinned and leaned close. "There is the risk-taking zealot I knew you were."

Caivev glared across the completed set. Her original question still lingered in the air. *Why should she share any information with him?* She bent over and batted his piece off the table anyway, despite the tie.

"Alright. I will tell you why I brought you here." Basilisk chuckled with genuine mirth.

"The Black lives in diaspora, scattered through the multiverse. What I wish for the Black is the same thing that I desire for the Tarkhūn. I would like to arrange an armistice of sorts—no, a true peace. My ultimate goal is the reunification of the vyrm peoples. Restoration to their ancestral lands here in Desolation."

His idea intrigued her, but still, Caivev balked at such a grandiose proposal. "They would never go for it. I know the Black," she said. "And besides, that *project* I am so preoccupied with makes the entire idea useless."

Basilisk grinned. "Do tell."

Zabe rolled his eyes as he tossed the length of rope down the old mineshaft on the outskirts of the military facility near the Prime's training academy. The girls' high pitched prattling nearly drove him nuts... not because of the noise, but because he couldn't make sense of it. For the life of him, he couldn't follow whatever their words meant—like they had some kind of highly advanced secret girl-language his brain couldn't comprehend.

He merely sighed and stuck to the original plan: an afternoon with Claire that would hopefully give them both privacy, plus a romantic setting. Zabe glanced back at Jackie and then at the carved symbol. It had been etched into stone inside the mouth of a newly unearthed hole.

If his plans for romance turned out to be a bust, he'd at least be able to do some exploring. The engraved sigil bore too much resemblance to his family crest to be mere coincidence and nobody had yet been inside this cave that construction crews had discovered during the post-Nitthogr repairs.

"You girls are still coming, right?"

Claire nodded and cinched up her friend's harness properly. She didn't miss a beat, nodding to Zabe and keeping step with Jackie's worried conversation... boy drama.

Zabe didn't pay it much attention because he already had everything he ever wanted—or almost did. He felt certain that would all change soon. He grinned as he swung a leg over the lip of the descent and dropped in.

They kept discussing who Jackie should date. Zabe was certainly rooting for his cousin to come out on top.

"Are they still watching us? They're watching us, aren't they?"

Claire resisted the urge to look. "How should I know—but don't turn around!"

"I can't not! I can feel their eyes. They're *both* watching me." Jackie nearly wept like some kind of junior high drama queen. "I always wanted to be treated like a side of beef and now the universe is finally getting me what I want and it's awful! Why? Oh God—why have I been doing all those crunches? This is what happens!"

"You do look great, by the way," Claire interrupted. "Don't think I haven't noticed."

"Aww. Thanks," she responded, momentarily pulled out of her self-pity—she'd worked hard and the military made her into something of a beefcake. "But seriously! I've got to look!"

"Don't you dare! You'll only encourage them both. You have to talk to them one at a time."

Jackie grimaced and stared down the hole where Zabe had already begun his descent. "Yeah. I'm sure you're right. But it's crazy hard!"

Wulftone and Harken walked towards each other and met in the middle, where Jackie had just fled from them to join Claire and Zabe.

"Harken," Wulftone greeted the man.

"Wulftone."

Jackie floundered to catch up with the two, and both of her suitors chuckled at the absurdity of it. They watched her suit up and could tell she'd intentionally ignored them... as if men from the Prime suffered the same kind of petty and jealous rivalries that Earth boys were prone to.

"Earth girls," Wulftone chuckled.

Harken joined his laugh.

Jackie suddenly turned and looked back at them.

Harken stuck his chest out slightly, trying to play it cool.

Wulftone sighed at his rival's hubris. When he tried to wave, Jackie startled as if she hadn't realized she'd even turned back—and then she flung herself into the chasm, perhaps with too much vigor.

Already at the bottom of the cavern, Zabe waited for Claire to finish rappelling and decided that now was the best time he was going to get. The constant interruptions would never quit—and he wanted to make his intentions official.

High above them, Jackie still floundered with the momentum that she'd dropped into the pit with and her flashlight played all across the deep grotto, splashing the whole chamber with light that caught in the luster of crystals embedded in the substratum. The entire cavern danced with illumination.

Claire, only a few feet from the bottom, quipped, "We just need some music. It's like a disco ball down here, or something." She focused on disconnecting from her rigging as Jackie called back down.

"I got you covered!" The light show intensified as the clumsy climber momentarily fidgeted with a mp3 player. A second later, music flooded the shaft, reverberating off the walls.

Claire turned around and found Zabe kneeling and holding an engagement ring. The lights flashed off of that gem, too.

"I asked your father this morning," he said. "I would very much like to set a date and marry you, Claire Jones."

"Ohmygodyes!" she practically leapt into his arms and held him tight. In the back of her mind, she felt a foreign sense of confusion. Regret. Betrayal? Remorse. The duality in her mind that was Bithia's presence retreated slightly. Claire couldn't interpret the feeling—but it scared her. She held Zabe tighter because of it.

Jackie practically screamed as she watched her friends below. "Did you just pop the question?"

Claire turned and wiped the tears that she assumed were from joy and gave her a thumbs-up. Something in the dancing lights caught her eye.

"Zabe, Isn't that your family crest?" she pointed to a large, bound tome lying haphazardly against the wall amongst some other random items from antiquity.

Basilisk steepled his fingers and watched Caivev with rapt interest as she explained her discovery of the Lost Temple of Koth and her meeting with Akko Soggathoth. The demigod claimed he would awaken his brothers, trapped in their Darque Dimension prisons, and then call Sh'logath out of the nether—through the mythic Nihil Bridge.

"Perhaps it was always this way? The Thousand Elders could have been wrong," Caivev wondered aloud. "Maybe it was always destiny that the Seven Brothers of the Winnowing herald the agod's arrival."

The tarkhūn leader shrugged. "Perhaps. It is possible that there was some error—a forgotten prophecy perhaps, or maybe the clashes between the followers of Rasthakka and Kadrist were so blinded by their allegiances that they overlooked or reinterpreted the old writings."

Caivev toyed with him. "Then perhaps they were all wrong, and the Rovers were right." She grinned with delight as Basilisk wrinkled his face in disgust.

"Maetha is a lie," he spat and then calmed himself. "I'm sure that the tarkhūn and the Black can all agree that there is no truth outside of Sh'logath."

Caivev tilted her brow in measured agreement.

"Do you really believe that Akko Soggathoth will bring about the Awakening?"

"I think it is my duty to try."

Basilisk looked at the stalemated game board. He knew that Sh'logath was peace—it was central to the entire theology of the vyrm's cult—and he had struggled to come to any concrete conclusions ever since that day the Syzygyc war ended so long ago. But he'd recently felt his own awakening. He'd finally begun to make decisions and recognized that peace's definition might be more subjective. Looking at the tentative Dunnischktet he'd finally begun to understand what he really wanted out of life.

"I will make you a deal, Caivev. You and I will reach a concrete deal for a coexistence between the Black and the tarkhūn. As a show of good faith, I will return to you every member of your caste which we hold in captivity so that you are at your best when you present our alliance deal to the tribal heads. I will even lend you some of my own highly valued soldiers whom I will send to your temple in short time. But when Akko Soggathoth's plan fails, you will serve me and I will lead the vyrm into their glorious destiny."

"What makes you so sure I will fail?"

Basilisk stepped to another game table and moved the pieces back and forth while he talked, playing both sides as he so often had in the past. "Your pieces are in motion. You certainly have all the pieces that you need in order to win... but I know the opponents that you face."

"Claire Jones," Caivev muttered under her breath.

"No, dear Caivev. It is not Claire Jones you face but the power of the Architect King, which has marked her with destiny." He stood in silence for several long moments as he stared at the table. Finally, he stated, "You are free to go. You have free rein in the Desolation and your prisoners will be returned before you depart."

Caivev bowed low and accepted his deal. She felt certain that whoever the tribes installed as the new chiefs following the assassinations leading up to her capture would be amenable to an accord—especially if it meant the return of thousands of their lost kinsmen.

"One more thing," Basilisk said. He snapped his fingers and a recognizable figure stepped out of the shadows. "I have someone to introduce you to."

Zabe, the son of Zahaben, walked towards them in his monstrous, lycan form. Caivev's face fell with sudden betrayal, and then the werewolf's form melted down into that of a regular vyrm of the Black.

"Take Jarkara with you. He is perhaps the most gifted shade I've employed in some time; he's capable of shapeshifting so well that he can even phase out his tattoo. Few shades can do that without the added help of makeup. I'm sure you will find him useful. In fact," he glanced at a nearby game board as if he'd predicted some future move, "he might just save your life."

Claire returned home. Her smile gleamed almost as brightly as the ring on her finger. She found her father sulking at the table.

He brightened when she walked in—though it was somewhat forced. "Do you have important news for me?" he asked.

She hid her ring hand behind her back. "Not until you tell me what's bothering you. Spit it out and stop bottling it up."

He laid his head down on the table in faux-defeat. "Lady troubles," he groaned pitifully and laughed.

Claire laughed at the reversal of situations. "You want to talk about it?"

"I tried talking to Tay-lore."

"How'd *that* go?" she giggled.

"About how you'd expect. I'm not sure if he's mastered humor and was messing with me or if the android is *that bad* at understanding human emotions... he described relationships with some kind of analogy about downloads and gigawatts. It was weird and creepy." He sulked like a teenage girl.

Claire chuckled again. "So, do I know her?"

"You know everyone, Claire," Sam kissed his daughter's forehead, "and Bithia."

She gave him a lopsided hug. "Well, tell me who she is."

"The Cleric who has been working with me on my research into the nature and history of the Prime. You know, blonde—gorgeous. Green eyes that sparkle and see through you at the same time?"

"Shandra," Claire said as her father nodded. "But she's never looked at *me* like that. I mean Bithia. And we've known her a long time. You're on the verge of reciting poetry, though, so you must have it bad."

"It's so strange," Sam said honestly and with less humor. "I have so little in common with her—like we're almost opposites, but being with her is like..."

"Electricity," Claire interrupted him. "Like you're from two opposite planets but drawn together by something stronger than either of you?" She sighed wistfully. "I'll brew the coffee while we stew in all the feels."

Sam grinned and nodded. He grabbed his daughter by the wrist. "First, show me that ring."

Jackie stood still as a stone as she hid in the women's locker room. She held her breath and tried to remain as silent as possible, even though she melted inside as she listened to Gita answer the rap at the door around the corner. For all Jackie's bravery, she sent a tiny girl to answer the door so she could avoid her crush.

"I'm sorry," Gita said. "You must've been mistaken. I'm the only one in the locker room."

"That's weird," Harken said from the other side of the door. "I could've sworn I saw her duck in here." He chuckled knowingly.

"Nope," the pint-sized female member of the Guardian Corps responded. "You want me to tell her anything?"

Jackie's ears prickled as she leaned slightly closer to hear him best.

"Well," Harken mock-sighed, "I was going to ask to see her later, but I suppose that will have to wait. I had this made for her—that Earth recipe she likes so much."

"I'll take that," Gita said as she swiped the paper sack from his hands.

"Alright. But you're sure that—"

Gita slammed the door shut. "I'm changing—don't open up!" she hollered at the door while she walked deeper into the locker room and greedily pulled the pastries from the sack. She shoved a whole one into her mouth and moaned with pleasure as the flavors hit.

Jackie snatched one from the bag and did likewise. Her cheeks puffed out like a squirrel at a nut stash. She mumbled through her mouthful, "Hashtag: blessed."

Gita raised an eyebrow.

"It's something they say on earth when they're excited and want people to know."

"Hashtag: I wish someone gave *me* the Krispy Kreams."

Jackie busted a gut with laughter. "That's not quite how it works—you sound like you need to see a doctor for personal problems."

Both girls laughed for a moment.

"Still, I can't believe you're not jumping at Harken," Gita rolled her eyes as she took another doughnut. "I mean, he went to all the trouble to have these made for you—plus he's soooo hot!"

Sighing, Jackie eyed the remaining stash of crullers. "I don't know what to tell ya, kid. I don't know how I feel... but these things sure are good."

Gita nodded.

"Besides, he's not the only hottie around here. How about that Jenner—eh?"

Gita shrugged and chomped another mouthful.

"I can't get these guys to take it down a notch. I don't think that even overdosing on doughnuts would make them leave me alone! Especially with the Guardian Corps' workout regimen... a fat lot of good it's doing me now. I mean, look at me." Jackie stood up and pointed to her body.

"You look normal to me," Gita said, confused.

"Exactly! I lost like thirty pounds since Zabe upped the preparedness drills! I'm *too good looking*—how will I know when someone likes me for who I am instead of how I look? Honestly, *even I* want a piece of this," she joked.

"*General* Zabe," Gita said, fearing protocol. She'd tried so hard to get into the Corps that she played as close to the rules as possible... at least when it came to Zabe and Claire.

Jackie waved the comment away. "Whatever. He's engaged to my best friend. As long as I'm not in a sensitive crowd, I could call him General Doodie-head if I wanted... I think."

"Best friend?" Gita looked confused. It wasn't a common term in the Prime.

"Someone you're very close to."

"Are we best friends?"

Jackie's face softened towards the younger girl. "Of course," she said. "People can have a few best friends."

Gita smiled and lay back on the locker room bench. "You know, I think Wulftone has been sweet on you since before you ever even met Harken."

"Argh!" Jackie growled, feigning rage. "I don't want to talk about this anymore!" She jammed a pastry into Gita's mouth and then stuffed one into her own.

She mumbled her words through her full mouth. "Tell me about your family. What was it like growing up in the Prime? Where are they now?"

Gita went quiet. She barely even made a chewing sound. "They are all gone—it was horrible... I'd prefer not to talk about it."

# Chapter Six

With a flash of eldritch power, Caivev and Jarkara materialized at the portal site deep in the Central American jungle. The ozone sizzle in the air dissipated quickly and yielded to the humid, heavy air laced with the odor of thick vegetation.

She put up her hands and turned a slow circle when she heard the distinct sounds of cocking guns all around The Crag. "It's me, you idiots."

Jarkara, plain and ordinary as any vyrm could be, did likewise and faded towards the back of the confrontation.

The vyrm guards she'd set to watch the location lowered their weapons and slinked towards her from behind the mounds of carved ceremonial bones the natives had piled nearby for generations. They didn't even bother with human disguises and they let their scales show. Nobody was supposed to be here except the forces of the Black, the fictional General Nyagittari had seen to that.

"They reported that you were taken by the tarkhūn," one stated as he eyed her up and down.

"The new tribal chiefs are already arguing over who will lead following your capture."

Caivev glared at them both. "The rumors are obviously greatly exaggerated."

"How do we know you're not a shade?" One guard asked astutely, readjusting his grip on the weapon.

"Ashes of Roanoke," Caivev gave him the pass phrase to prove her identity.

The other guard raised his gun. "They could've had a lich siphon that out of her mind!"

Both Caivev and the other guard glowered at the zealous sentry. "I've had psychic training," she spat. "It would take more than a mere lich to break into my mind and pull out anything useful."

He lowered the weapon sheepishly.

"Keys," she demanded. A few moments later, she bounced through the jungle trails in the old jeep, traveling the handful of klicks between the portal and the Lost Temple.

She found her generals in complete disarray. The man and his dog sat bored against the wall, flipping his hands back and forth. Caivev nodded to the imposter who she knew to be Akko Soggathoth.

The demigod looked slightly comical, wearing an incredibly thick pair of oven mitts; he returned the greeting. He looked much the same as before, but he held a small hierophanticus which looked far eastern in origin and carved of the foreign darquematter in the shape of an idol. His dog rested next to him.

Caivev's forces stopped mid-stride when they saw her enter. Idrakka tipped his head ever so slightly in greeting to Jarkara, who didn't dare return a nod.

She pointed at her supernatural partner, who stood in response, curling his lip in a delighted sneer.

"What's going on?" the beefy Skrom asked.

"It's time to show them what we're onto," Caivev said. "Enough games. Let's show the Black who you really are."

Akko Soggathoth nodded. A split second later his form melted into the decaying half-goat, half-man form he truly was.

"Is that the hierophanticus you sought to awaken your first brother?"

Soggathoth nodded. "It is the key that will open to Akko Nuggezeth."

Idrakka, Skrom, Charobv, and Kreephast stood in silence. They knew just enough of their own mythology to understand that the shapeshifter was an alternate Sh'logathian herald of prophecy. Their silence allowed enough of a lull for the banging on the door to be heard. Only Jarkara was startled by it.

Caivev felt a twinge of guilt as she glanced at the mystic chamber where time refused to advance. Nitthogr's kidnapping of Zabe's brother Zurrah had been one of her first missions when she'd secretly fed intelligence to the sorcerer after he'd captured her heart... before his eventual betrayal. She didn't envy the boy's eternal imprisonment—still, she couldn't exactly free such a valuable asset without any personal gain.

Kreephast, half made up in his fake diplomat costume, leaned in and whispered. "Caivev. A word in private? Just you and your trusted leaders?" He nodded slightly to indicate Akko Soggathoth.

Idrakka intoned, "Is there anywhere we could go that he could not hear if he chose?"

Caivev shot him a nervous, sidelong glance. The scrawny vyrm had climbed into the top ranks quickly. He wasn't particularly skilled—but his loyalty was paramount. She trusted his instincts, and it worried her if Idrakka was wary of him.

Kreephast pointed to the door opposite of Zurrah's. The others followed him in, and Akko Soggathoth watched them curiously as he stroked the tentacles of his abyssal auraphage. They left Jarkara, still an outsider, and Akko Soggathoth to stare at each other across the room while they held a meeting.

As soon as the door latched shut, it opened again and the party exited. In the second chamber, time continued to pass while it did not in the real world—the reverse of the other time-locked prison.

Caivev had much to think about. Though a second had passed, she'd held council with her generals for hours in the stasis chamber and Kreephast had proved his extensive knowledge of history and atheology after she laid out their plan for them: awaken the Seven Brothers and release Sh'logath independent of Basilisk, the remaining Herald. She'd also brought them up to speed on the truce between the tarkhūn and the Black and Basilisk's insistence that Jarkara accompany them to ensure the lasting peace.

They were in agreement to pursue an alternative Awakening. Still, Kreephast's warning ringed in Caivev's ears. "We cannot put too much trust in Akko Soggathoth; he is a fickle trickster of legend. Be on guard in case this is no more than a game to him."

"Is there a problem?" Akko Soggathoth asked as they returned.

"No problem," Caivev promised.

In response, her four generals bowed and pledged their service to the demigod's plan.

"No problem at all." Where Nitthogr had failed, Caivev swore she would succeed.

Sam skootched closer to Shandra as they bent over the book Zabe had brought them. Zabe watched them work while Tay-lore analyzed the data from the scanners.

"This book is old," he said with his mechanical monotone. "Very old."

Shandra gingerly turned a page and looked at it with intrigue. The spine and cover had been embossed with an emblem similar to that of Zabe's family crest—perhaps an earlier precursor to what it eventually became.

Sam consulted the lexicon to verify the translation. "It's titled the Lineage and History of Vangandra."

Zabe raised an eyebrow while Shandra tugged at her lip thoughtfully. "What does that mean?"

"There is an old legend about Vangandra," she responded. "He was an ancient hero: the first defender of the Tesseract."

"It is very obscure," Tay-lore agreed. "His guardianship supposedly took place before the creation of the Chamber of Mysteries. I've only encountered snippets of it from one source in the archives of the Veritas."

Shandra nodded.

"But what does it have to do with my family?" Zabe pointed to the crest.

"Vangandra and King Leolon were the only survivors of an attack by the vyrm—the first attack they ever made, actually," she explained. "They were after the tesseract. Vangandra slaughtered all but four of the vyrm who escaped, and he and his children, the 'Wolf Folk,' went on to protect the tesseract as the original Guardian Corps."

"Almost," stated Sam as he leaned over the book and his lexical resources.

"That is the legend," Tay-lore said.

"I mean that this book offers some corrections to that," the archaeologist responded. "It claims to have been written by Vangandra's descendants who were told a slightly different account." He quoted a loose translation.

"When the scaly men attacked, they killed without mercy or remorse, heading directly for the Tesseract which remained with the royal line at all times—as directed by the Architect King and the priests. Their champions wore armor and rings of strange elements which reacted violently to the power of the Great Gem.

"Men of the Prime rallied around King Leolon and when the invading champions drew too close, they vibrated with unexpected resistance—the weaker ones withdrew to safety but the champions persisted. Within a hand-span of the sacred jewel, the vibrations disintegrated nearly every man and enemy nearby, crumbling them to dust—reducing them to atomic content. Only Vangandra and the King remained for us.

"The champions' armor exploded into fragments. Most pieces dug deep within the enemy. It liquefied and burned deep inside and was absorbed. They burst out with different powers—as did Vangandra, who had shifted into the first lycan hybrid and fiercely defended his friend and king to safeguard the tesseract and Leolon's honor.

"Repelled by the ferocity of the lycan, the scaled ones displayed symptoms of madness. They retreated and in their frenzied bloodlust slaughtered their own, leaving the hillside littered with reptilian corpses before they winked out of existence in full retreat.

"When they'd exploded, pieces of their armor were flung into the distance as if from a trebuchet. One of these shards of alien material was recovered and great care was taken to keep it a far enough distance to prevent another, similar reaction. Artisans crafted a totem from the wreckage as a reminder of this day."

"Here is their example." Sam flipped a page and turned the book to show them a crude drawing of a very distinct artifact resulting from that incursion. *The Dimensional Inversion pendant.*

Zabe stared dumbfounded by the book—as did Shandra. The implications were as far-reaching as they were mysterious.

Shandra looked very uncomfortable. "I have someone under the protection of the Veritas who should see this." She looked at Zabe apologetically as he cocked his head.

"We have something of an expert on the vyrm in our care: someone who has an intimate knowledge of their fanatical religion." She bit her lip sheepishly. "This is all *very* confidential."

The leader of the Guardian Corps could see it in her eyes: they were harboring a vyrm. He did not like it one bit that they had kept one of their enemy hidden and without his knowledge—it directly contradicted his mandate as leader of the corps and he was sure that Claire would've told him if she had known. Zabe demanded gruffly, "Is he Black or Tarkhūn?"

"Neither," she said, surprising him. "Trenzlr came to the Prime quite accidentally and identifies himself as a Seeker of Maetha—a rover—part of a religious movement that predates the Sh'logath cult. I will make introductions."

"Do you want some food?" Cerci Heiderscheidt asked through the door. She'd occasionally visited the narthex and had conversations with the prisoner on the other side.

"No thank you," the young voice responded. "I just ate a little while ago, before leaving with my father, General Zahaben. We were separated. My brother fought off the wizard's forces, but they still got me. That was not so long ago... my father is coming, you know."

"But it's been days since I last talked to you," she said.

"Days? Has it been that long?"

Heiderscheidt scrambled to her feet when she saw Doctor Walther and Caivev approach. She distanced herself from the forbidden door.

Using the old lexicons borrowed from Caivev's generals, she'd translated almost everything she could get her hands on. Heiderscheidt had a pretty good idea what their sponsor's plans were about—and she'd hoped to eventually get out before things got too ugly. She was always looking for the next adventure, the next great mystery to unravel. Maybe the boy behind this door was it.

"There you are," Walther said. "Our benefactor has been looking for us. We have a new assignment," he stated, eagerly wringing his hands.

"Not that I haven't enjoyed using our machine to rob the world blind, but I will be grateful to push the boundaries of science again," she said. Only Heiderscheidt knew she lied—the thrill of the heist as she and Walther raided caches of diamonds and pillaged vaults of refined gold and platinum had been the most exhilarating thing she'd ever done. She'd needed the excitement, not for the fact that it pursued some kind of ideological ends like propping up the newly formed Chiriquí country, or funded their scientific endeavors.

Heiderscheidt knew that Walther, to some degree, had channeled funds to his own causes. He'd given several gifts to his friend Sisyphus, the former pro wrestler, and helped reinvigorate some clandestine organization. They'd also worked on some kind of joint experiment in the past, which she knew very little about, except that it involved cloning blood cells. But recently, Cerci Heiderscheidt's drug of choice had switched from the rush of knowledge to the surge of adrenaline.

"What are we studying?" She asked as she followed Caivev to the massive double door that towered deeper within the pyramid-like temple.

Caivev pointed to the door, which had already been identified as a gate to the Temple of Koth. Akko Soggathoth stepped out of the shadows, nearly startling the poor scientists who'd come to accept undead fauns, lizard people, and alternate dimensions as part of a reality that had long been hidden from their eyes. Little shocked them anymore.

"Have you practiced the signs?" The goatman's voice hissed like a viper's.

The scientists watched Caivev nod. Akko Soggathoth grinned as she held up a fist and flashed a series of very specific hand motions. They each noted that the man-beast had six digits on his hands and so he could not accurately make the hand symbols.

"Good. Make the first sign: middle fingers down, thumb tucked."

Caivev made something like the "horns" symbol that people raised up at rock concerts.

"The second."

Heiderscheidt grinned as Caivev struggled to transition between them. She enjoyed watching important people fail.

Caivev lifted the middle finger and flared her thumb wide. The scientist memorized the transitions, wondering if she could perform them if pressed.

"The third and fourth?"

The third came easy. All four digits stretched out, and the thumb crossed, like a command to halt. The fourth merely tucked the pinky down to meet the thumb.

"Excellent," Akko Soggathoth said. "It is time to prove that you can do them by awakening the eye and opening the door." His appearance shimmered for a second, and he transformed back into the human shape.

The man looked confused as a black kind of mist pulled away from him, as if shadowy ether evaporated off of him. Heiderscheidt guessed the fiend must've relinquished his host.

"What... where... you again!" he reeled wild-eyed from Caivev who snatched him by the wrist.

"Hold still," she commanded as she reached for a knife.

"No!" He struggled and wriggled free of her grasp. Turning a wide circle, he called out, "Victoria! It's Quintin—where are you, Victoria?"

"Fine," Caivev spat, grabbing him again with both hands. "Have it your way." She bit off half of his pinky finger and dragged the bleeding man towards the door. He howled in pain but remained too disoriented to continue fighting her physically. She used his bleeding stump to paint an oval with a line on it, much like a crude eye. Caivev dragged his bloody hand in a pattern around the eye which resulted in a seven-pointed star.

Quintin staggered back when Caivev released him but howled in terror again, only seconds later, as the blackness re-enveloped him. The decaying goatman returned to her side as she performed the hand motions in front of the sigil scrawled with blood.

He bent low and retrieved the severed finger as Caivev struggled through the first transition. She completed the sequence and nothing happened.

"Again," Akko Soggathoth commanded. With a giggle, he popped the finger into his mouth and chewed it to paste.

Caivev growled, and this time succeeded with the proper hand shapes. The door clicked with a loud groan and a sucking sound, as if from a leaky airlock. She held the herald in her gaze, wordlessly asking for the next step.

"Now you may enter the Darque," he stated menacingly. "I will go and make preparations to release my brother. There is one more thing I need first. Retrieve the book you find on the other side."

"Where will I find it?"

Akko Soggathoth shrugged playfully. "I'm certain that you will." He turned and departed.

Slightly unnerved and more than a little wary, Caivev pushed open the doors to the gateway, and the scientists followed her within; they left the door ajar for good measure. Inside, Koth looked like a mirror image of their temple; the door read Kith from this side.

Akko Soggathoth's book lay irreverently on the floor, as if it had been flung inside from the other temple door. Caivev retrieved the old tome, which had been inlaid with some kind of darquematter filigree and latched shut with a clasp of the same material.

She tucked it under her arm and led them past a ceremonial chamber and through the winding corridors before coming to the pyramid-like structure's entrance in the hallway tied to the mirrored structure's narthex. Koth's layout was the exact opposite of the sister temple.

They gazed at the blasted glassine and obsidian landscape, which took their breath away. There appeared to be no sky—only an empty blackness spilling into the void. Iridescent, shimmering seams of energy cracked reality in the distance, like solidified lightning. "It is just as Akko Soggathoth described it," Caivev said reverently.

"It is marvelous," Walther whispered, equally impressed. "And it's obviously well outside of the thirty-three dimensions we've been able to open with my machine."

The sky flashed with an even darker flare, as if an electrical storm in the nether burned with darkness beyond the color spectrum's black. The otherworldly energies sent shudders down the spines of the trio, calling their attention upwards.

Venturing only a little beyond the yawning entrance, they looked skyward. The Temple of Koth was crowned by a set of curving, obsidian spires at its flat top; far above that, a massive ring hung in the sky, terrible and dark like a concrete funnel cloud churning with slow malice. The Nihil Bridge.

Caivev turned to her madcap scientists and said very seriously, "Whatever it takes, you must find a way to access this location from your machine. Unless given another immediate task, this is your primary mission."

Walther hesitated. "I don't know that it will be possible." He looked around fretfully, almost overwhelmed by her request. "I will have to take some readings."

"Whatever it takes," she repeated. "I'm sending you two to Germany soon. General Nyagittari—Kreephast—has built up an embassy there. Your equipment will arrive soon. Remember, *whatever it takes*."

# CHAPTER SEVEN

"Thank you so much for this opportunity," said Respan, as Zabe unsheathed the Stone Glaive from behind his back. The long-hafted, massive sword might have actually belonged to Claire, but it had been Zabe's trademark since his triumph over the sorcerer Nitthogr.

"It's in good hands," Wulftone told his cousin. "I've known Respan since before the invasion."

Jenner stood on his tiptoes in order to get a better peek at the mythic Stone Glaive. The son of the missing historian had become something of a page to Wulftone who'd helped mentor the young man.

"He's as good of a scientist as there is," Wulftone stated of the researcher whose expertise crossed the realms of both mechanical and supernatural sciences.

Respan laughed nervously as he laid the huge blade upon his examination table with due caution. "I'm just trying to not turn myself to stone here."

Jenner stated the obvious, "The ability to turn all our kin trapped in the Desolation back to flesh would give us an instant army. The Prime could finally have its revenge."

"Well, that's only if I can figure out the blade's secrets, much as Basilisk has done." Respan made charcoal rubbings of the sigils engraved upon the ancient blade. "Reverse engineering the blade's powers will prove no small task."

Zabe nodded at Wulftone. "This is surely a weapon we'd want—even if deploying it offensively seems unlikely. Not much makes me want to revisit my time in the Desolation." He watched Wulftone's overeager study of the sword. "Is this maybe a distraction for you?"

Wulftone pretended he didn't know what his cousin implied.

"You're using this project to put your focus on something other than Jackie?" Zabe poked him in the ribs and lowered his voice.

Wulftone bit his lip. "I'm trying really hard not to hate that charismatic tool," he muttered quietly—even *he* didn't really dislike the guy... but he privately resented the competition.

Zabe patted him on the shoulder while he vented the rest of his frustrations—most of them came out as newly invented curse words he'd created specifically for Harken. "Hey. He's a hero, you know—a real people's champion and a good soldier." Zabe rapped Wulftone on the chest. "But you're a *better man*. Jackie will see that. Stay the course."

He sighed. "I hope you're right. I'm playing it cool, but it's my experience that nice guys usually lose to cute dimples... stupid, cute dimples."

The entire room flashed with red lights and ear-splitting klaxons. Everyone in the lab immediately sprang into action; the military alert signaled invasion.

Zabe snatched up the Stone Glaive, ready to fly into action. The other soldiers in the room prepared to dutifully follow him to battle stations, but he paused and looked down at the weapon. "You need all the time you can get to unravel the blade's secrets, Respan. Make this your highest priority. We have no idea when a solution might be absolutely necessary."

Basilisk stood as regal and proud as if he were a welcomed and invited diplomat. He stood upon the immense stone slab that was the Prime's central world-gate. Behind him, some inanimate object, covered by a sheet, had been brought through the rift with him.

Members of the Royal Army, plus the highly specialized Guardian Corps, formed a thick ring of opposition around the tarkhūn leader where he stood on the dais; thousands of guns remained steadily trained on him. The portal point lay just outside the military base and only a few klicks from the walls of the royal city.

Zabe and Wulftone, with Jenner in tow, hopped off the anti-grav sled they'd raced to the gate. They picked their way through the formation and found the command unit.

"Good work, Harken." Zabe rapped the soldier on the shoulder as they arrived. He'd performed perfectly and detained the intruder as protocol dictated.

Harken nodded and saluted.

Zabe gestured back. Even Wulftone gave an obligatory return salute.

"What does he want?"

"We don't know," Harken replied. "He came through and has just been waiting there patiently."

Basilisk picked Zabe out of the crowd and his face brightened. He waved to get the commander's attention.

Zabe grimaced and then joined the reptilian leader on the platform. "Basilisk." He greeted him with a tight-lipped, curt bow.

Basilisk responded with a stiff-backed, formal bow. "Commander Zabe of the Guardian Corps." He winked. "I wondered if you might have been wearing that marvelous sword you acquired the last time you toured my home. And where is Bithia Claire Jones?" He rattled off the names as if they were one word. "She really ought to be here."

"You're going to have to deal with me for now."

Basilisk raised his eyebrows and then a voice called out.

"I am here," Claire yelled as she glided through the air on an anti-grav sled of her own. She quickly parked the unit and then joined them. Her presence obviously unnerved Zabe, who flashed her nonverbal warnings to try to keep back. She pretended not to understand it.

The vyrm leader grinned broadly. "Words are a far more dangerous weapon than any invention of man, don't you think? However, I'd hate to see a nervous finger ruin a diplomatic mission."

Zabe turned and gave a hand signal to the troops. They lowered their guns but kept them at the ready.

"I've come to sue for peace," Basilisk stated.

Zabe stifled a laugh.

Basilisk cocked his head at the man, not understanding what was so funny.

"I have arranged for a true cessation of hostilities with the Black," he said proudly. "I am nearly in total control of them, entirely, as it always should have been. In the meantime, the tarkhūn plan to pursue peace with our neighbors."

Claire's face softened towards the scaly leader. "You have finally made your choice? You know how your game plays out?"

Basilisk smiled through his snake-like mouth. "I have decided how this ends."

Zabe eyed him skeptically. "How can there be peace? You will never gain control of all the vyrm."

"I have assurances from the Black that in a short time, they will come under my yoke."

"But there are more than the two factions. What about the rovers that you call the Followers of Krakkath or the Seekers of Maetha?"

Basilisk wore a visibly upset face. "You have my assurance that those renegades will have soon disappeared entirely. They are a candle in the wind and their light is all but faded." He kept his voice low, not wanting to lose his composure. Basilisk turned to Claire. "I was pleased to learn that I'd heard wrong about your father."

Claire nodded graciously, although the depths of the tarkhūn leader's knowledge always unsettled her. "We ought to discuss the terms of our truce," she said in a very Bithia-like tone.

"Agreed. But first, I wanted to bring a gift I have no right to keep." Basilisk yanked the sheet away from the nearby statue and revealed a defiant-looking Zahaben. Every detail had been preserved in stone.

Zabe reeled back in surprise. "Father!" he rushed to the figure. "What have you done with him? Turn him back this instant!"

"I'm sorry," Basilisk stated. "There is no way to undo the effects, at least none that I'm aware of."

Zabe whirled to face him. His eyes flashed with danger and his skin seemed to bristle, as if he might shapeshift into his lycan form and tear his enemy to pieces. "Why have you done this?"

Claire looked into his eyes with a pained look of apology. They begged him not to blow what might be the Prime's first opportunity at true peace.

"I am sorry for his condition," Basilisk said. "I have many spies in the ranks of the Black. One of them whisked away Zahaben before my brother could take him alive."

"But I saw him die!"

"Did you see him actually expire? Did you check to see if his body still drew breath as he battled the invading armies?"

Zabe merely growled in response.

"He did not cooperate with me in the least. This was almost four years ago, before I had the revelation that inspired me to seek peace—before you and Claire came to me in Limbus. I can only apologize for it, but I felt it wrong to keep him hidden while I hold palaver with his son and soon-to-be daughter-in-law."

Zabe could only nod slowly, diplomatically, and accept Basilisk's story. But he didn't have to like it, *or believe it*. From what he understood of the petrified condition, he hoped that Respan was up to the task.

Jarkara adjusted his knit wool cap and walked the long decks of the cargo ship as it plowed through the choppy Atlantic waters. He kept to himself as he'd done since entering the oceanic region. Just a day and a half ago, the shade killed a sailor and assumed his place on the barge specifically for his mission; he knew he'd find his target soon.

He watched over the waters in the failing light with keen vyrm eyes, knowing exactly what to search for. Finally, he saw it: the wreckage of a sailboat and its marooned passengers. Jarkara sprinted for the captain so that they'd be able to stop the massive craft in time make a rescue.

"I don't know how you could even see them that far away," Captain Woodson congratulated the shade as the slowing cargo ship drew closer and he dispatched a rescue crew to pick up the marooned sailors. Woodson greedily rubbed his hands. "I'm pretty sure that's the Wainsmith girl! I read about her sailing out this way in the newspapers—some kind of charity project."

"I know who she is," Jarkara grinned and Woodson clapped him on the shoulder, mistaking his humor for an expectation of an extra payday.

"Funny that she didn't radio for help from the Coast Guard," he noted. "Maybe her equipment malfunctioned?"

"Or maybe it's ours?" Jarkara suggested. "I suppose we might not be receiving if they'd tried to alert any nearby vessels."

Woodson furrowed his brow. He didn't like that thought and tossed the imposter his key to the bridge. "Run up and do a radio check for me? I'd like to be here when we bring them aboard."

Jarkara nodded and headed towards the radio room with every intention of sabotage.

Woodson had just finished wrapping his guests in warm, dry blankets and begun an unsolicited tour of his craft when gunfire erupted. The captain nodded to the six young teens that accompanied the young woman. "Go back that way and you'll be safe." He unsnapped the strap that held his sidearm fast and muttered, "Out of the frying pan and into the fire."

"Is it pirates?" Holly Wainsmith asked.

"I'm not sure," Woodson said. "They'd be pretty brave to attack so close to the U.S." One second later, a bullet tore through his head and he collapsed.

Holly screamed and fled with the teenagers in her care. They rounded the edge of the main superstructure. Shipping containers made a confusing maze of chaos, where surprised sailors fought an impromptu battle against hordes of green-skinned, reptilian humanoids.

Blood splattered the decks and small arms fire peppered the atmosphere. Loud blasts cracked the air as the invaders fired some kind of hand-held laser cannons that fried her unwary rescuers.

"Where did they come from?" one of the teenagers shrieked.

Holly pulled the girl to her side and then slid back the way they'd come. "I have no idea—but we've got to find someplace to hide!" She looked up to the windowed command bridge but could see the silhouette of someone smashing equipment—she assumed that was the radio. Her own had mysteriously malfunctioned after some kind of micro-explosion disabled her craft, slowly sinking them into the ocean with no alternative but to limp towards a shipping lane.

"There," Holly pointed to a forty foot cargo container with her father's company name on it. The door hung slightly ajar, and she noticed a crudely spray-painted star near the handle as she heaved it open.

A massive reptilian man stood within, holding an armload of strange equipment beneath each bicep. He set down the sci-fi props and grinned at the girl through his carnivore teeth and snatched her up in a flash, covering her mouth to prevent her from calling for help.

The woman nearby looked into Holly's eyes and laughed at her fear. She stepped aside so that she could see the decaying goatman, who lurked nearby with his mischievous yet vacant eyes and a large book held under his arm. His oven mitts made the scene go beyond terrifying to absurd.

Holly Wainsmith thrashed and struggled as the behemoth cinched her wrists and ankles with cable ties. The woman gagged her mouth with a strip of duct tape when a line of teenagers stepped inside, looking for their chaperone.

As soon as the first one's eyesight adjusted to the dark, she shrieked in terror.

"What should I do, boss?"

"Do your thing, Skrom. Throw all the kids overboard for all I care."

Zabe nodded to Respan as his crew of movers finished transporting the statue of Zahaben into the research facility. He'd made sure they took the greatest care possible with the figure trapped in stone.

With weary steps, he left the scientist to his work in his segment of the laboratory building and walked down a hall to a different wing where Sam Jones and Tay-lore requested his presence before a different meeting. He grumbled to himself over how the duties of Master at Arms of the Guardian Corps included a lot more meetings and diplomacy than he realized he'd signed on for.

He raked his hands through his scruffy hair and arrived at his next appointment. Finding the Prime's most prominent enemy suddenly on their doorstep had been unnerving enough—but something about how he conducted himself during their "peace talks" deeply bothered Zabe. Basilisk knew too much—too many specifics of their recent inner workings. His spy network was legendary, but how could the tarkhūn leader know about things like Respan's attempts to reverse engineer the Stone Glaive unless he had a mole?

Sam greeted him with a sympathetic tone as he entered. Tay-lore tried to show compassion in an admirable attempt and awkwardly tried to hug Zabe. Behind him, Sam tried to wave the automaton off from the maneuver, but failed.

"I'm so sorry for your loss," Tay-lore said in an overly weepy inflection as he nearly strangled the Captain of the Guard in a bear-hug. "I have a number of sympathy poems memorized. Would you like me to recite one?"

Zabe broke and burst out laughing at the ridiculousness of it all. "With friends like you, Tay-lore, it's a wonder that the vyrm ever thought they could make me miserable."

Tay-lore recoiled. "I'm not sure what you mean. Did I not do it right? Should we hug again?"

"No." Zabe held up a hand. "I'm fine. Respan will eventually find the cure. I'll be okay until then. Tell me what you guys discovered."

Sam turned the old book towards his soon-to-be son-in-law. "The Veritas, mostly Shandra, helped us finish translating the text from the story of Vangandra."

Zabe nodded, familiar with Sam's growing affinity for the cleric. His next appointment was with her, in fact.

"Yes, that too," interjected Tay-lore. "I also wanted to bring up some of my recent findings—massive fluctuations in the Tesseract's energies."

"First, your thing," Zabe said to Sam. "What did you find?"

He pointed to Zabe's wrist cuff, where the family crest of his line had been embossed. "There is no special significance to your father's bracelet—at least, nothing more than sentimentality. I'm sure that previous scans revealed nothing because that has always been the case. Your shapeshifting ability does not come from any special, outside force or arcane artifact. It comes from within. According to your ancestors, all of Vangandra's lineage had this ability—they just needed to learn how to focus and draw it out. Your father's bracer merely gave you something to focus on before you knew how it worked."

Idrakka watched Jarkara closely as they held the bound woman between them on the forecastle of the ship. She was far too precious to let escape.

The remainder of Caivev's helpers dropped their modified buoys into the icy water at precise points determined by their global positioning devices. Nearby, an immense console that looked as if Doctor Walther might've designed it stood affixed to a network of cords and cables connecting to wireless units that communicated with the floating devices.

Moments later, handheld radios squawked as the teams reported in that they were all green lights. Charobv flipped a switch on the mysterious console.

Pulsing energy beams shot vertically from each of the floating contraptions that formed a large ring in the frothy water. Within seconds, the high-tech laser grid borrowed from a foreign dimension bored a hole through the water and created a dry tunnel that dropped to the surface far below.

Idrakka and Jarkara scooped up their prisoner and met Caivev at the motorized lifeboat where she waited with the fiendish Akko Soggathoth and his pet. The tentacle creature sniffed excitedly at Holly Wainsmith, who writhed with horror. Grinning, the herald commanded the abyssal auraphage to stay while they piloted the craft to the first buoy and latched the boat to it, cautious not to let it slip over the edge, which dropped more than three miles to the bottom of the vertical shaft.

Using a mechanical winch system Caivev's crew had strung between two of the floating stations, they rode a modified elevator into the depths. Skrom, Idrakka, and Jarkara repeatedly lit and tossed flares over the edge of the lift to provide light. As they finally drew nearer to the bottom, the illumination revealed the ruins of an underground city, both ravaged and preserved by the pressures of the deep.

With the exception of Holly Wainsmith, Akko Soggathoth put a different hierophanticus into the pockets of each one on the journey. It would protect them from certain evils, he promised.

Ancient buildings stood in a variety of states of decay, and broken pillars littered the landscape. The elevator stopped and Akko Soggathoth led the way, as if he possessed intimate familiarity with the location. Skrom carried the weeping prisoner as if she were no more than a light burden.

"It is there," Akko Soggathoth pointed to the temple near the center of the drop zone. "This is the source of those strange energies the native race has long been mythologized in the Bermuda Triangle region. My brother lies within."

They gathered outside the door and paused to examine the strange hieroglyphics carved into the doors. They appeared too similar to Egyptian logographic characters to be coincidental.

Skrom kicked in the door with a fierce boot. "We don't have time to look at the pretty pictures. The laser grid only has so much power before it fails—and I ain't getting crushed by the ocean because of some ancient poetry."

Akko Soggathoth giggled in agreement and led the way through the dark. His companions lit a number of flares and followed until they came to a central chamber.

Skrom dragged the prisoner forward and laid her upon a thick slab of stone that resembled an altar; the central groove terminated in a small hole in the middle of the altar. Akko Soggathoth anxiously skittered around the room, using his talons to clean the slime and gunk out of the carvings etched within the nearby rock. He meticulously cleaned a large cube of plain granite with a single alcove hollowed out.

"We are ready," the fiend said in his raspy voice and took out the ancient statue from its protective case, handling it carefully with his thick mittens. "Make the sacrifice." Akko Soggathoth positioned the darquematter idol in the alcove and nodded to the vyrm who used a knife to cut open the victim.

The Wainsmith girl's eyes jolted wide with panic and pain, and then all feeling slowly faded as she died on the Atlantean table.

He watched greedily as her blood drained into a bucket, which he used to splash across the stone block where he playfully drew a smiling face in the dripping splatter of blood before tracing a large square shape around the edges.

"My dear Caivev," he asked. "Please open the gate."

Caivev made the series of hand motions she'd practiced under the beast's tutelage. The edges where he'd drawn with blood seemed to ignite with supernatural flame and the center ruptured the lines of reality as it collapsed in on itself with a swirling pool of void.

Akko Soggathoth handed Caivev the book that he'd been toting with him since she found it in Koth. "Hold this until I return." He stepped through the murky portal and disappeared.

Just enough time passed for them to feel nervous about their time limit before the goatman returned. Behind him, the portal burped out a shadowy blob like a writhing pool of ethereal, black and bubbling tentacles. An ethereal line of smoke trailed after where unbreakable fetters tied him to some arcane anchor within the Darque. His chains shimmered in the air, keeping the bound evil in check.

"My brother, the next youngest," Akko Soggathoth announced. "This is Akko Nuggezeth."

A palpable sense of doom filled the room and none could seem to locate the shadow with their eyes—only catch glimpses of him from the edges of their vision. The inky mass flitted through the party before returning.

[You have no body for me, brother,] it said in a disembodied, ancient dialect that each somehow understood in his or her mind.

"Correct," Soggathoth hissed. "You must rest to regain a portion of your cosmic energies... I've already had that luxury. A suitable host will be located soon." He took the tome from Caivev and un-locked the book's darquematter lock before unfurling the pages. He took great care not to touch the mystic material inlaid at the book's edges. "Until then, I will keep you safe in the ancient book. You know how I mean."

The two heralds held a brief argument in their screeching tongue. This time, the mortal minds did not interpret.

"You must act soon. The portal closes promptly and then the waters will cover the old city once again, entombing you. If you don't have a host, the Darque will reclaim you before you could hope to take a body."

Even though they could not directly see him, the vyrm and Caivev could feel the begrudging tension roll off Nuggezeth as his younger brother forced him into the pages of the grimoire.

Akko Soggathoth held the book open. "Make your mark and write your name."

A dark tentacle burned its sign into the parchment, and the dire presence seemed to dissipate, sealed inside the pages of the locked grimoire. The beast disintegrated as the pages pulled him within and the eldritch chains released the creature and slowly retreated back within the tear between worlds.

Within a few more minutes, the team rode the winch system to the surface. Moments later, the salty waters reclaimed the ancient location.

Sam had just finished explaining to Zabe what the ancient Vangandrans wrote about the transformation when the laboratory doors opened. Shandra entered with a figure cloaked in dark monk's robes that concealed his face. She wore a similar cloak, which she tossed aside to reveal shiny battle armor, not unlike the Guardian Corps' battle suits.

"Expecting trouble?" Sam asked with a hint of worry in his voice.

"Uncertain," she responded. "Basilisk was recently on our plane and so I will take no chances with the safety of my ward."

Zabe glared suspiciously at the hooded figure. He shared Shandra's misgivings but knew that someone had been funneling the tarkhūn information; any vyrm under the protection of the secretive monastic caste automatically had his suspicion. He already harbored a great deal of resentment for the Veritas who refused to engage the Black during Nitthogr's invasion, even if he was grateful for them when they lent his Grandfather Shardai access to their tunnels.

Tay-lore slumped as a sign of disappointment that his turn to share had been skipped. He had a lot to learn about sympathy, but his disappointed and pouty mannerisms proved accurate.

Shandra nodded to her guest. "This is Trenzlr."

The vyrm pulled his cloak back and revealed his scaly, green face. He bowed in a sign of respect, but even that made Zabe's hackles bristle; he'd been fighting this race his entire life and recognized that giving Trenzlr any benefit of the doubt would prove a difficult task.

Zabe bit his lip during the introductions and bowed diplomatically. He silently uttered a few choice curses for his position again. "I thought I was supposed to find you at the monastery?"

Shandra nodded measuredly and checked the clock nearby. "Yes, a short while from now. Trenzlr has not been out of the cloister since he arrived here years ago. Much like Doctor Jones, he is a foreigner in our lands and wished to see the Prime—and also to meet Sam."

Zabe raised an eyebrow. "How long has he been here?"

Shandra realized from his tone that she may have over shared. She wordlessly worked her mouth in fear that his anger might bubble over if the Guardian Corps learned Trenzlr had been on the Prime since before Nitthogr's assault.

"What's more important is how he got here," Sam deflected, coming to Shandra's aid. "Tell us that story, Trenzlr."

Shandra locked eyes with Sam and silently thanked him.

"I was with my people, my tribe, when it happened." He spoke sincerely and Zabe's interest in history and the vyrm rovers won out over his ire. Zabe crossed his arms and bid Trenzlr continue.

"We were traveling like we often did. Rovers are nomadic and victimized by both the Black and the tarkhūn wherever they find us. They usually leave us alone as long as we don't get too close to any of their communities, but this time, they came out of nowhere, like they were hunting us. They slaughtered my people, my family. We scattered and fled; there was so much blood... I remember running, and then I was suddenly here. I don't quite know how. I wandered for a few days until I was discovered by the Veritas who took me in."

Shandra interjected, "We believe that between the blood and all the activity, a dormant gate might have been activated by pure coincidence and Trenzlr was whisked away... either by accident or by divine providence. I suppose that it is entirely up to a person's perspective and how sincerely you adhere to faith."

Sam asked, "What kind of rover are you?"

"A good one," he responded.

"I meant, are you a Follower of Krakkath or a Seeker of Maetha?"

Trenzlr smiled through his scaly lips. "I would answer the same, but add that my tribe is loyal to Maetha: the promised one who will bring about peace and restore us to the Tesseract as an adopted lineage."

"How is that different from Krakkath?" Sam asked. "Very little information is available to us about the rover tribes."

"That is probably because forces have been systematically destroying our people since before the Thousand Elders' Sacrifice—ever since the Great Schism when Rasthakka and Kadrist set a new tone in religion and deviated from the earliest cult teachings by focusing more on Sh'logath instead of on his Templars and chosen ones, the children of the void who sowed systematic destruction: the Seven Brothers of the Winnowing.

"Rasthakka spoke in conjecture and Sh'logathian devotion during a sort of cultic renaissance. Kadrist took a more liberal approach and ignored almost all the old legends, twisting them into myths with less literal meaning—at least inasmuch as the Seven Brothers were concerned. While Rasthakka taught a kind of peace and began to drift from Sh'logath—and perhaps even advocated for Maetha, Kadrist taught that *peace was destruction*.

"While Rasthakka is remembered fondly for helping defray the first war that brewed between the first tarkhūn king Chirasq I and his brother Akroth who posed as an Earth Pharaoh during her people's infancy, people often mistake him as the Maetha—the great restorer."

"I thought the Seven Brothers of the Winnowing were a vyrm fairy tale," Zabe finally spoke up. "They have almost nothing to do with the Sh'logath cult."

"That's because they were a part of Sh'logath worship long before Rasthakka came on the scene, when it was called Mae'le-ggath—but Maetha is older than that, even. Also, because their origins come from the Darque dimension. Very few vyrm know about the Darque anymore—the cult has downplayed it for years because if there is a Darque, then there is a need for Maetha, and if Maetha is real, then Sh'logath is a force of evil, not of peace."

Zabe's head spun as if he'd begun the conversation at the wrong point. He had no context for Maetha or the myriad of other names Trenzlr had mentioned. He finally knew how Claire must've felt when he first told her about the Prime. "The Darque?"

The vyrm winked at him. "Not all things, in reality, come from the Tesseract or were designed by the Architect King. Where do you think the vyrm originally came from?"

Dumbfounded, the group could do nothing except blink. Such a radical idea had never entered any of their minds before.

"Is that true?" Tay-lore asked. "There is nothing in my data banks to corroborate your claim."

Trenzlr shrugged. "It is a theory—*my theory*. I've been studying ancient texts for as long as I've been alive, forbidden texts from Edenya..."

Zabe traded confused glances with Sam. "Desolation," Shandra quietly clarified for them.

"...I've developed my thoughts free of encumbrance by the teachings of the Sh'logath cult, and the archives of the Veritas have helped me a great deal. I truly wish to be a resource for the Prime—the royal family and the Veritas. I believe that Maetha is tied to the fate of the Prime."

Zabe nodded politely, although he had no intention of letting Trenzlr, the least threatening vyrm he'd ever met, meet his betrothed. The risks were too great.

Tay-lore held up his hand to beg a question. "You are well versed in the myth of the Seven Brothers of the Winnowing?"

Trenzlr nodded.

"We have scarce data on them. Can you write down everything you know for our records?"

The vyrm nodded curiously. "I can. Is there anything specific you want to know?"

An alert chimed behind the android, who accessed the warning remotely and called its information to the large flat-panel view screen. "I've been monitoring news from Earth and lately some troubling information has come up. The name Sh'logath has appeared in a number of texts and other places I monitor, which is not uncommon and indicates that the Heptobscurantum has rebuilt more quickly than expected."

This time, Trenzlr cocked his head inquisitively.

"The human branch of the Sh'logath cult," Zabe informed him.

Tay-lore continued. "I've found another name alongside his lately. Do you know anything about the Akko Soggathoth?" He pointed to the display and a spike in power alongside data readings from the Tesseract. "Amid a flurry of his references, I recorded this anomaly's energy signature." He turned back to the chirping noise and overlaid another, similar reading. "This new event just occurred."

Trenzlr looked at them all very seriously. "If Akko Soggathoth is at work, I think we may have a very real and serious problem."

# Chapter Eight

S am Jones stood in front of the newly repaired glass in the Hall of Mirrors. His daughter and Zabe stood by his side.

"I really do wish that you'd take a small escort along with you," Zabe said.

Claire vigorously nodded her agreement.

"I said it already," Sam stubbornly stated. "It's just a short visit to a small city in Minnesota. There's hardly any chance something could go wrong."

Claire raised an eyebrow. "Like three years ago with the Heptobscurantum and mad scientists?"

Sam batted the notion away. "It's not like that—and besides, I'm not important enough to target anymore."

His words hung in the air. He hadn't been a significant player in the war before, either, but he was a leverage piece because of who he *was* important to. Sam hugged his daughter. "I'll be careful," he promised, "but Miles is on his deathbed and I don't think he could take explanations of interdimensional bodyguards at face value."

Claire surrendered the battle and let her father go. "You'd be surprised. All the same, give Professor Jecima my regards. Tell him I'm still thankful for how he helped me years ago... Tell him my cheek still hurts," she laughed. "He'll know what it means."

Sam nodded as his daughter activated the mirror. He smiled at her and then a moment later disappeared through the looking glass.

Tay-lore clutched the ream of print-outs that quantified and supported his assumptions regarding the strange readings he'd collected. He felt certain that the power spikes rippling through the dimensions were not natural—and had drawn the only logical conclusion.

He entered the royal throne room and hoped that his friends would see it the same way. The android felt an odd sort of trepidation as he approached the Prime's throne. Tay-lore's awe was partly due to the massive, locked doors to the Chamber of Mysteries which towered several paces behind the seats. The other part was his affinity for Claire and Bithia before her.

With no one in the room, he retreated and began the trek towards the Guardian Corps' keep: a walled partition where they kept their barracks, offices, and a few other specialized rooms. Tay-lore caught Jenner in the hallway.

"Excuse me. Do you know where I can find Commander Zabe?"

Jenner bit his lip. "That depends on how important it is."

"Quite," Tay-lore replied. "Is he on a mission of some secrecy?"

"You might say that." Jenner shrugged. "He's stealing a few hours away with the Princess at the Old Keep ruins, so I wouldn't intrude unless it's a matter of life and death."

Tay-lore nodded. His conversation could wait a couple hours... he hoped. It was time sensitive, but the android knew Zabe and Claire needed regular breaks to recharge, just as he sometimes required a power cycle of his own. He turned to leave, thinking about how odd it was that a low-ranking corpsman knew the secret location of the Prime's princess and highest military commander. He nearly bumped into Shandra.

He bent with a short bow for respect. "Cleric Shandra."

She jabbed him in the chest, where he held his notes. "Is this true?"

Tay-lore cocked his head in confusion.

"Your recommendations for response measures?" She clarified her ire while they walked down the corridor and towards a more secure location. "I don't like it."

"You read my report," Tay-lore sounded impressed, "so soon? I just sent it very recently."

Shandra shrugged. "With Sam away for a few days, I feel like I've got a little more free time than I've had of late." Her voice conveyed confusion and uncertainty over what that meant. "It came as a welcome distraction to my thoughts."

"Did you have trouble understanding the scan data? It is a very complex process that..."

She held up her hand. "I trust *how* you collected the data. The Veritas have also been monitoring power emanations from the Tesseract—but by a different process. We agree with you; there's something happening across the dimensions—something new and scary."

Tay-lore pressed the issue. "Similar readings have been noted before—when artifacts of power came into close proximity to the royal gem."

"Similar or identical?"

"*Very* similar. Items such as the dimensional inversion pendant or other mystic items containing the darquematter substance... it's almost as if darquematter readings have increased in strength and number."

"Where did you hear those words?" Shandra snapped at him, pulling him aside and looking around to make sure nobody else had overheard. "The existence of such an element is not one of public knowledge."

Tay-lore felt a kind of nervousness in his emotion circuits. "I first encountered it in the old book—Zabe's book, which I translated, *The History of Vangandra*, it was titled." He trailed off and felt a little guilty that he didn't tell her he'd also accessed the Veritas's secure library without permission and corroborated what the book said against the Order's records. "Trenzlr was also a wealth of information regarding my research. He provided me with many translation keys that helped unlock ancient vyrm texts never before decoded. Many of them seemed written as Edenyaic myths: a series of folktales about the ancient days and the Brothers of the Winnowing—long before they were trapped in the Darque when the vyrm race translated their existence and abandoned their own reality in favor of Edenya... the Desolation realm of the Tesseract."

Shandra eyed him suspiciously, suspecting that he'd delved into forbidden libraries and collections to uncover the texts he would have needed. Without any proof, she let it slide and concentrated on her primary concern. "'*Very* similar,' you said. Explain the differences."

"Minute frequency and pitch shifts in ambient waves if you compile the emanations versus the regular sine wave pattern of the..."

Shandra held up a hand to stop him. "Explain it in a relatable way to humans."

Tay-lore played a pleasant musical scale up and down through his audio box. He played that same scale again except on the middle and last notes he played the note flat.

The cleric scowled, but she understood; they arrived at Tay-lore's lab. As an expert on mystic artifacts, she knew exactly what had caused the disruptions, and it was time to come clean. "It is hypothesized within the Veritas that all darquematter reacts violently with the Tesseract... What I'm about to tell you is absolutely confidential." She stared at him sternly. "We've not even shared this with the Royal family."

Tay-lore had no doubt that she would have him dismantled if he ever leaked sensitive information.

"The pieces that reacted to the Tesseract and exploded during the vyrm's first encounter, thousands of years ago, seemed to be imbued with special properties—fragments of their champion's broken armor. There are other pieces of darquematter from other sources. They have a different sort of ability. Could these readings you've detected be from those sorts of objects?"

Tay-lore nodded. "I suspected that very thing. One of the vyrm myths was called *The Seven Keys*. It is a particularly wicked fairy tale about a vyrm child who found a hierophanticus that unlocked a gate to where Akko Sxkakzacros, the vilest of the brothers, slumbered in the Darque.

"The seven Darque hierophanticese—*the seven keys*—each open a portal into the prisons where the Brothers of the Winnowing sleep. Each one is specifically set to open via a special key and by sacrifice."

"How much of that is legend, and how much do you suspect is true?" she asked.

Her statement confused him—her vocation was centered on faith. Tay-ore had assumed she'd immediately reach the same conclusion he did. "I think it's *all true*... except for the vyrm child in the story who is a sort of 'everyman,' or in their case 'everyvyrm.'"

The religious woman muttered a bunch of curses typically unbecoming of her position. "I've seen the texts you mentioned, but we haven't had them fully translated yet. We've only begun to work backward through old texts with the information Trenzlr has provided." She sighed and looked upward as if in apology for breaking sacred rules. "The Architect King was quite specific when he set Earth apart and told us to leave it alone. We've already bent so many rules for the sake of the Jones family."

Tay-lore watched her coldly. His findings led him to only one course of action: intervention. "We must collect the hierophanticese and prevent the opening of any more portals into the Darque. I believe Akko Soggathoth is the one at work and I think he's awakened one more already—probably Akko Nuggezeth, according to a gematriac sequence clearly encoded in the text."

"So we can predict his plan?"

"Perhaps. Perhaps not. But there is an old end-game written within vyrm prophecy. We know this demigod's ultimate goal."

Shandra swallowed hard and nodded. Enough texts had been translated for her to know that. "The rise of Sh'logath."

Tay-lore nodded slowly. "I think that Akko Hormundlyr is next. Time might be critical."

"I said that I didn't like your plan; it makes me uncomfortable to planeswalk at all, let alone into Earth. But I did not say that I disagreed with it. It may be necessary to intervene in the affairs of the Earth realm—the fate of the Tesseract may rest on collecting these hierophanticese and preventing our enemy from piercing the Darque."

Caivev strolled through the dim corridors in the Lost Temple of Kith's belly. She kept a wary eye out and eventually found Akko Soggathoth in the large chamber where the Koth gate had closed.

He glowered at the barrier which he was incapable of opening on his own and stroked the heavy tome. The Darque denizen heard her approach but paid her no mind.

"It won't open with you just staring at it."

The goatman chuffed animalistically. "I am aware, child." He mumbled a few choice curses and then grinned manically with a giggle. "The enemy thought he could wreck, imprison, and even lock us from our home realm." He drummed his fingers on the clasped book. "I guess we shall see who has the last laugh in the end, the so-called 'Architect King.'"

"You miss your home?"

Akko Soggathoth looked at her incredulously. "Never. There is far too much fun to be had here to yearn for that broken place." He smirked at her confusion and then turned back to the door.

Caivev thought better than to try to figure out the twisted fiend. "My agents have reported in. They are close to finding the next hierophanticus. Others from the Heptobscurantum are seeking the rest of the artifacts. It will take some time to arrange for all the bribes to fall into place and get us access to the hidden places so we can access the Darquegate with minimal interference. We don't want any prying eyes ferreting out what we're up to until it's too late. As soon as the Prime realizes our plans, they will attempt to stop us."

Akko Soggathoth nodded but didn't look back at her. "You have the sacrifice secured?"

She nodded. "Your pet found one, as promised, though it did eat its handler in the end."

He smiled cruelly. "Don't worry about the Prime. I have been masking us from their weaker psychics. They would be hard-pressed to find someone skilled enough who could pierce my veil from their plane. Even if they do, they won't understand until it is too late."

Caivev waited and watched him for a few minutes, but Akko Soggathoth had no more to say. With her skin prickling from his disconcerting aura, she retreated back towards more familiar parts of the structure.

Zabe walked towards the broken, crumbling wall of the Old Keep. The previous home of the Guardian Corps had been entombed within creeping vines and flowering tendrils of greenery.

Wulftone kept step with him. "I haven't been here since..."

Zabe nodded solemnly. "That was the first time I ever saw my father shift—when he'd been so hard pressed to get back to us. I'd only ever seen Shardai turn lycan before that."

"We both lost family that day," Wulftone said. "My father... your brother." He spat and cursed Nitthogr's memory for the repeated invasions.

"It was the first time Zahaben had worn this," Zabe pointed to his leather wrist-cuff, which indicated he was the leader of his house. "I'd always thought that it was what made him lycan."

Wulftone raised his eyebrows with intrigue. "Then what is it?"

Zabe held out his book, *The History of Vangandra*. Dozens of cards with written translations had been tucked between the pages so that it could be read. "It's family... something far more important that brings on the change. Wearing Zahaben's crest only meant that I understood the depths of what I was fighting for at a deep level."

They stood for a silent moment at a spot and both looked down. Both men understood the significance of the location.

"This was where it happened."

Zabe nodded. He handed his wrist cuff to his cousin, who'd been like a brother all of these years—a surrogate brother for the one he'd lost that day. "Try it on. Perhaps it will inspire you to reach deep down and harness the hunter within."

Wulftone looked back to the grassy slope where Claire and Jackie sat on a blanket, chatting in the sun with a picnic basket and a bottle of fine djat-berry wine. "I think I understand that deep yearning to protect and to fight for my own."

"I'm so glad you two could come," Claire bumped her shoulder against Jackie's playfully. "So... you and Wulftone, then?"

She grinned. "I dunno. I'm taking it slow and still kinda splitting the time between him and Harken. I still haven't made up my mind—but I've made up my mind to make up my mind."

Claire grinned lopsidedly. She understood and couldn't help but envy her friend—but not for the romance side of things. Jackie's problems were a lot more tangible than wrestling with a fractured psyche, ruling the galaxy, and planning a wedding.

"I'm just so happy to get away for a few hours," Jackie groaned as she over-filled another glass of wine. She nodded towards where the two men seemed to be paying their respects to something. "Do you suppose that's where it happened?"

"Where what happened?"

Jackie's jaw almost dropped. "You don't know?"

Claire thought back. She even accessed Bithia's memories, but came up blank. "I know there was a huge battle that destroyed the old keep. That was like a decade ago... Zabe's never talked about it Bithia was... otherwise indisposed."

"I read about it in a book on the Guardian Corps' history. It was actually collected by Professor Jarfig, Jenner's father. Zabe lost his little brother in that battle. It was really bad from what I read. They never found him."

Claire furrowed her brow and remembered the small Guardian Corps armor she'd worn that day they broke into the throne room through the secret tunnels below the castle. She knew there was more to that story, but didn't want to push Zabe on it. Claire wanted him to open up on his own.

They watched their guys for a few minutes as they started pushing each other around a little. All of the sudden, Wulftone stretched and shifted into a lycan form similar to Zabe's.

"What the crap!" Jackie spilled her wine in surprise. "Since when can he do that?"

The two returned to the picnic. Wulftone, in his werewolf form, sauntered triumphantly. He scooped Jackie up effortlessly as a test of his strength.

Jackie blushed. She'd quite forgotten how hot a lycan's furry skin was. Her cheeks flushed as she leaned into his rigid muscles and she wondered if she might've made some internal choices between Wulftone and Harken.

Claire looked at Zabe and Wulftone incredulously. "Can you still shapeshift even without your crest?" she asked.

"I believe so," Zabe said. He closed his eyes as if concentrating. A few seconds later, he changed, too. Grinning, he also scooped up Claire, and the four collapsed on their picnic blanket in a heap with the women curled up on their lycan's chests as if they'd been victorious conquerors.

Simultaneously, the guys' lycan ears perked up. Hypersensitive hearing caught sounds that only they could hear. A moment later, an anti-grav sled crested the hill and settled nearby, ruining their remote get-away. Tay-lore and Shandra got out; Harken had accompanied them.

Wulftone growled low with feral frustration on a register that only Zabe could hear.

"It must be important," Zabe said as his bestial form melted away into his human one. "I don't even know how they found us."

# CHAPTER NINE

Z abe and Claire sat at the head of the long table in the meeting room. Wulftone and Jackie sat nearby—they were already in the loop because of the android's info dump. Wulftone sat unnecessarily close to Jackie as Harken took a seat opposite them. Shandra escorted Trenzlr into the room and Tay-lore presided over the stack of information he'd put together.

"So what are we looking at here?" Zabe asked as he leafed through the sheaves of paper and focused on the highlighted portions.

"We've got to go to Earth and stop the release of Akko Hormundlyr," Shandra stated.

Claire and Zabe stared at her blankly. The fact that a *Veritas* advocated planeswalking to *Earth* did not go unnoticed.

Tay-lore guided the brief discussion on Akko Soggathoth's release and the Herald's ultimate plan to release Sh'logath and accomplish where Nitthogr had failed. "Princess, may I borrow the Dimension Inversion Pendant—the necklace your father gave you?"

Claire removed it and handed it over; it no longer wielded mystic properties over her since Claire Jones was the last of her versions spread across the multiverse—although it still provided her some modicum of protection versus magic attacks. Tay-lore passed it around the room.

Shandra introduced them to the material. "This item is made of a material known as 'darquematter.' It is the same stuff that our targets will be made out of—these items are also mystic artifacts and may or may not have special properties, but each will probably be regarded as a powerful or special object. A hierophanticus, like this one," she indicated the pendant, "is imbued with power so it can fulfill a specific task—the seven Darque hierophanticese are keys to a realm beyond the reach of the Tesseract. It is where the legendary Brothers of the Winnowing are trapped... two have already been released."

"We have deduced that the next brother to be pulled from the Darque is Akko Hormundlyr. It is probable that the brothers are being awakened in a specific pattern, per the numerology Tay-lore discovered in the ancient legends."

Zabe held up a hand. "So the recommended course of action is a smash and grab? Identify and steal the hierophanticese before the bad guys can get them?"

Shandra nodded.

"That sounds simple enough—though with high stakes," Zabe said.

Harken interjected, "I'm not quite sure who these bad guys are? Akko Hormundlyr and Akko Soggathoth—they're demigods. They've got to be working with someone... the Heptobscurantum, maybe, since so much of this activity revolves around Earth?"

"The Heptobscurantum may be involved," Tay-lore agreed. "I have surveillance in the Earth realm. It appears that the vyrm are also involved—the Black, at least."

Harken spat, "It figures." His hatred for the Black was well known—his rise to popular position had been bought with the blood of his friends, relatives, and many of the senior military officers who preceded him. "That dirty tarkhūn lied to us in our home."

Claire leaned forward and spoke diplomatically. "Basilisk may have been sincere. He said the Black were coming under his rule—not that it was yet absolute... and besides, there are bound to be splinter cells of rogue vyrm all across the planes for some time, even if he has been truthful."

"Do you trust him?" Harken asked.

She laughed, "Not even close. But that doesn't mean we should blow a major diplomatic victory over our suspicions."

Harken shrugged with compromise. "So, where does this leave us?"

"Expect to see vyrm on Earth," Wulftone said matter-of-factly. "Always expect them—and shoot as soon as you see scales."

Trenzlr cringed at the statement, but ultimately nodded. "Given what is at stake, that might be a fair characterization."

"What if we fail?" Zabe asked. "What's our backup plan? After all, the vyrm have a head-start on us."

"I'm certain a clairvoyant as powerful as Bithia would've been able to locate the portal locations that lead to the Darque. *She could probably find the access points where they will pull Akko Hormundlyr through.*"

All eyes turned to face Claire. She swallowed her reluctance to give her mind over to her Prime version. Claire looked at Zabe and felt dark emotions well up in her gut—*is this just proof that I'm not good enough for him? I'll never be* her. *Could Bithia ever betray me and take over my body completely, forcing me out? ...we've been somewhat less cohesive since Zabe proposed. Is that* my *jealousy or is that* hers?

Claire sighed and her eyelids fluttered as she momentarily surrendered control to Bithia. She eventually opened her eyes. "I am sorry, but I can't detect anything. I wish I could help—maybe if I was on Earth?"

Everyone at the table gave her worried looks. Bringing the last descendant of the Architect King away from the protections they'd built around her seemed like the definition of a bad idea.

Zabe reached across and held her hand. "It's okay. We'll just make sure we get the hierophanticus first. What does it look like, Trenzlr?"

"I believe I've found a link in ancient lore," the vyrm responded. "Your ancient Earth was once ruled by a wicked ruler named Akroth. He and his brother were partly to blame for the beginning of the modern Sh'logath cult—they brought it one step closer to its current incarnation."

Tay-lore projected an image onto the wall nearby with depictions of Akroth, an early Egyptian pharaoh. He cycled a few images, some of which were museum artifacts on a traveling display. One in particular depicted a grisly scene of Akroth executing prisoners by scaphism—a torture where victims were force-fed and then stuffed inside confined containers so that they were devoured alive by insects. The plate caption read, *Akroth was notoriously known for executing anyone accused of touching his royal scepter—even including his wives.*

"It seems most likely that his scepter is the hierophanticus we seek," Trenzlr said. "But that's not a guarantee."

"You noted that these items give off some kind of reading you can detect?" Claire asked Tay-lore.

"Yes, Princess. I could create a sensor—Respan invented one already that I'm sure I can miniaturize. It would only be accurate within a thirty-foot radius or so, but that should be sufficient."

"Do it," she said. "We can send one team to Akroth's tomb to search with the sensor and send another team to collect the museum's scepter." Claire looked around the room and did not find any disagreement on their faces.

"We'll get you all as close as we can via the Hall of Mirrors," Shandra said, "but you will have to make your way back here through the portals' normal operation. I trust you each have a basic knowledge of how to locate and use them to planeswalk?"

Nods circulated the room. They'd all either become familiar with the anathema chapter of the Grimmorium Nitthogr or personally experienced it.

"Good," Claire stated. "You will all leave as soon as Tay-lore can put together his device. Go steal me a scepter."

Sam flipped through the newspaper as he glanced out of the eighth-floor window of Jecima's recovery room in the New York City surgical ward. His elderly friend remained in an induced coma following his extensive surgery, but was expected to make a recovery.

*Unlike Claire's friend*, he thought, scanning the headlines where he read about Holly Wainsmith. They'd found wreckage from her boat as well as a destroyed container ship, which appeared to have been blown up by pirates or terrorists; ironically, both boats had been owned by the Wainsmith Holdings, adding financial injury to the distraught family.

Sam looked up when he heard a knock on the door. Jenner, dressed in a poorly assembled tourist outfit, stepped into the room and greeted the archaeologist. Sam looked at him, confused.

"Jenner? How did you get here? Is everything alright—is Claire okay?"

"Yes. Yes, she's fine." Jenner handed Sam a wrapped bundle of documents.

"What's this?"

"Tay-lore sent me. He wanted to get your insights on this and bring you up to speed, even though you're out of touch for the foreseeable feature. Is this your friend?"

Sam nodded even as he began plowing through the documents at an unbelievable pace. He was a well-practiced speed reader and nearly finished the stack of papers by the time Jenner finally grew tired of examining the Earth technology. He pulled the sheets closer to his tired eyes on the last packet that detailed their pending plans and read it in greater detail.

"When are they leaving to try and grab this... hierophanticus?"

Jenner checked his timepiece. "They've already left by now, for sure. A few hours ago, most likely. It took some time to find you."

Sam sprang to his feet and hurried Jenner out the door while he scrawled on a piece of paper. "I need you to get this to Shandra as soon as possible," he stuffed the paper into the young soldier's hand as he pulled up an astronomical chart on his smartphone. "You know where the nearest portal location is that will get you back to the Prime?"

Jenner nodded.

"Saint Patrick's Cathedral," he told him anyway. "My lunar chart says it will be open until midnight. After that, it will either take a week for it to reopen or else we'll have to travel half-way down the coast to find a connecting portal. Now go—and bring Shandra to that address as soon as possible!"

"But, Dr. Jones... *why?*"

"Because you guys are all after the wrong thing!"

Harken caught up to Jackie as they walked through the hallways. The corridors led to the mirror room where their team awaited. Harken walked close enough that their arms brushed against each other and he smiled, revealing his deep, gorgeous dimples.

Jackie smiled and looked away. She felt a twinge of shame well up within her at the thought that Wulftone might notice.

The muscular soldier grinned when he spotted her reaction—and her guilty response. "Am I intruding? I mean... are you and Wulftone together now?"

Jackie blushed. Not all the men in the Prime were as romantically reluctant as Zabe. "No," she said. "Well, I mean, kind of—but we haven't really talked about it. Like, are we exclusive?" she asked herself aloud.

Harken smiled and playfully pushed her into the wall; her armor clacked against the brick. "Then you can have dinner with me after this mission?"

She pushed him back. "Maybe I will, then."

He grinned boyishly and with a nod, they turned back to their duty.

A moment later, the door opened to let them into the Hall of Mirrors. Wulftone stood in the entry and they both hurried inside, where a small cadre of troops waited composed of a handful of soldiers under Harken's command and a few Guardian Corpsmen under Wulftone's charge.

Gita surreptitiously winked at Jackie as she entered with beau number two.

Tay-lore stood in the center of the room, holding a small, hand-held device with a tiny display screen. It looked like a miniature radar. "Glad you two could finally make it." His voice dripped with so much sarcasm that Jackie cringed.

"Too much?" the android asked in his more natural and serious tone.

Jackie nodded as her apprehensive look finally began melting away.

"My apologies. I had read that humor and sarcasm can sometimes take the edge off of tense situations... I will keep trying."

Wulftone interjected, "Maybe just tell us how to use the locator instead?"

Tay-lore seemed off-put, even for an artificial being, but shrugged and demonstrated the power toggle. It operated almost exactly like a radar, in fact. "You can see the approximate location of artifacts imbued with arcane power." He put it into Wulftone's hand.

The display screen showed they were surrounded by a cluster of thirty-two little blips. "You can see it's registering the mirrors," he continued. "They do not contain any darquematter, however. They were crafted by the Veritas during the time of exploration by The Brothers—before their corruption was discovered and the Grimmorium Nitthogr was confiscated." He toggled the second switch with two clicks, and the mirrors stopped displaying.

"This mode isolates the reading to only darquematter pieces—specifically the darquegate keys."

"Thanks," Wulftone said before turning to his troops. Tay-lore nodded and ducked out. He had more important places to be at the moment.

Zabe stood on the rooftop of the museum with five other soldiers. They'd left for earth some time before the others and needed the extra time to get into position; the portal gate in New York City lay quite a distance away from their target. The team also needed an opportunity to buy supplies for their heist—they didn't want to look conspicuous walking through the city carrying tools specific to thievery.

He did feel naked, however, without the Stone Glaive strapped across his back. The huge sword would have made walking the earth streets difficult in daylight; the police would surely stop them if he openly carried a giant sword through the urban setting. Zabe also felt it best to leave it with Respan for now—perhaps he would have a scientific breakthrough with him away.

The Guardian Corps commander signaled the others to keep the noise to a minimum. Stealth was their highest priority.

He watched over the edge of the building and consulted his timepiece. Zabe nodded as the security guard walked by; they'd spent the last four hours mapping on-site security movements.

A few minutes after the lonely patroller left, the intruders dropped their coils of cord over the rooftop and repelled the side of the building. On the floor, one of Zabe's men disabled the sensors on the sliding, transparent doors and disengaged the lock.

Clad head to toe in black, they slipped within the building like a collection of wraiths. Zabe paused near a junction leading to different exhibition wings and consulted his map. He was no stranger to museum raids, but hadn't needed to avoid security before. He had no desire to harm any humans tasked with protecting the historical artifacts.

He slid the directions back into his pocket and led his crew down the proper hall. Minutes later, they emerged in an ancient Egyptian world staged by the traveling exhibit staff.

They fanned out and filtered through the displays, each keeping their eyes trained on Zabe, ready to receive silent instructions. The display pieces descended backward through time, arranged chronologically according to the rule of different ancient leaders of the era.

Zabe held up a clenched fist as they crept past a series of dioramas depicting slaves and the building of a temple dedicated to the worship of Set. An adjacent graphic displayed a replica of the god defeating Apophis. Set, a giant snake, represented the ancient Egyptian force of chaos. Everything Trenzlr told him about the civil war between the tarkhūn shade, who became Pharaoh Akroth, and his brother Chirasq I, ancient ruler of the tarkhūn, suddenly made sense.

Whispers broke the silence. Someone else had entered the room.

Zabe motioned to his troops, and they crouched as low as possible. Someone else had infiltrated the Egyptian wing at the same time, only they didn't have the same sense of remaining silent.

Jackie picked herself up off of the hot sand and turned in time to see Gita fly through the portal, bursting into existence as she did a somersault and rolled into a crouch beside her friend in the desert sands. The portal location was nothing more than a broken, obsidian foundation, which might have once been the base of an obelisk or some other magnificent architectural achievement. Now, only rubble remained.

Harken and Wulftone both reached for Jackie to help her up. Gita intercepted Wulftone's hand and stood, thanking him.

It was barely nine in the morning, but already the morning sun baked the ground and dried up any evening moisture that might have clung to the sand. Gita and Jackie pulled sand-hued camouflaged hoods over their heads to block the fiercely hot sun and to obfuscate their presence.

Wulftone pointed to the deep grooves in the sand and waved Jackie closer.

"Tire tracks," she confirmed.

The leader nodded. "Desert winds should've filled these back in if they were more than a few days old."

Even Harken agreed. "We ought to proceed as if the enemy is already here."

Gita, the most diminutive of the force that invaded the Egyptian landscape, crawled up the shoulders of a tall soldier. She turned a slow arc with a handheld ocular scouter pressed to her face. Dropping the binocs, she pointed into the distance.

"Over there," Gita called out to Wulftone and Harken, but not too loud. "There's some sort of excavation that way." She patted the soldier on the shoulder and then slid back to the ground. "Thanks, Murdo."

The party moved out swiftly, but cautiously. Jackie shot Gita a worried glance as Harken and Wulftone each walked closely on either side of her. Gita merely grinned, but something about the way they hovered during the build-up to potential conflict irked her.

Jackie spotted a stone outcropping and intentionally struck her foot on it as if it might trip her up. Instead, she reeled backward and watched Harken and Wulftone each lunge forward to steady her; they accidentally grabbed each other's hands instead.

With her arms folded, she shook her head chidingly. They looked back. Each wore an embarrassed look on his face, but took the hint and afforded her more room to operate in.

A few minutes later, they crested the edge of an illicit excavation zone hidden among the desert sands. Trenches and deep rows cut through the dunes had been dug haphazardly until the tomb raiders found what they'd been looking for. A shallow basin opened around a central structure, unearthed by the equipment and vehicles parked nearby under the tan camo netting.

The forces strategically moved through the dig site with weapons drawn and ready until they surrounded the small building. Murdo, the tall soldier Gita had ridden atop of earlier, ducked inside to scout the area. He returned a few seconds after.

"It's a stair. It goes deep below ground; all seems quiet."

Wulftone nodded. "Let's go exploring, then."

Tay-lore stood next to Claire in the throne room, discussing the nature of what he'd learned of the Mae'le-ggath and how it might've changed over the course of the religion's bloody history. It had undoubtedly evolved through a number of iterations before solidifying into the current cult. His conversations with Trenzlr had proved very informative.

"You're hovering—and you're stalling," the princess accused. He stood nearby while she trained with Pollando. The leader of the Mystic branch of the Veritas, he tried to help hone Claire's skills on the psychic and eldritch planes. Bithia had been immensely talented, and Claire's weaker abilities left the throne in a comparative vacuum.

Pollando had just finished with her daily instruction. He bowed and departed for the monastery in silence.

"What? I never..." Tay-lore couldn't believe he'd been quite so transparent.

"It's okay," she laughed. "I understand."

Tay-lore relaxed, glad he hadn't offended the princess. He *had* been hovering. Something worried him on a deep level: her father and fiancé were both away, as were many of the most skilled warriors in the Prime.

He glanced at Claire. Something about her connected to him on a deep level and made him fiercely protective. Tay-lore wondered if that was what love felt like; he would certainly die for her were that ever required.

"Princess, can I ask you for a favor?"

She looked at him funny. "How can I help?"

He'd never had to ask for something before, but he had a plan that required some resources. "I need a large sum of gold."

Claire laughed audibly. "Whatever does an android need gold for?"

"You'll see... if my hunch pays off."

She chuckled again at the notion the artificial intelligence had a hunch. "Of course. Requisition whatever you think you need from the vault."

The android suddenly whirled around. His sensors picked up a potential threat; footsteps sprinted towards the throne room doors. Tay-lore tensed and a compact laser battery dropped from each forearm in readiness.

Claire tensed at the act.

As the double doors burst open, Jenner hurried towards the princess. His lungs heaved, and he sucked air to regain his breath.

Tay-lore and Claire both relaxed as the young soldier collapsed to his hands and knees.

"Princess Claire... your father..."

"What? What happened to my father?" She leapt to her feet.

"He sent me to tell you that everyone is after the wrong thing. Sam knows where the artifact is and told me that you're all chasing the wrong item. He sent me back for support—he gave me directions and told me to meet him there."

"But everyone is already gone," Claire said. She stepped off the dais. "Let's go, then!"

"Princess," Tay-lore said worriedly. "You can't run off and into battle blindly! What if you are needed here?" He lied, using a convenient truth. Tay-lore had noted Zabe's suspicions of a traitor within the castle—it was why he'd been hovering in the first place.

Claire blinked, and everything within Bithia testified to her royal obligations. Claire nodded, but still looked confused.

"Should I call for Shandra?" the android asked. "Surely she could assist Sam Jones? She's already recommended the planeswalk."

Claire nodded. "Do it." She looked at the soldier, the youngest they'd ever before let into the Guardian Corps without a father or mother to train under as an apprentice. He'd proven capable in the years since entering the company. "Jenner, keep them safe."

Wulftone, guided by Tay-lore's tracking system, led the small force through the darkness. They'd arrived unchallenged to the bottom of the winding stairs and tunnels, which eventually opened into a large chamber. Rows and rows of pylons supported the stone ceiling; each pillar bore intricate tapestries of lore preserved in ancient hieroglyphics which wrapped around the vertical structures.

They skulked through the dark, ignoring the carved plinths and tables adorned with suspicious, potentially valuable relics from the ancient world. As they closed in, the glowing blip on the sensor moved ever nearer the center of the HUD.

Suddenly, a shot rang out, and a grenade exploded, rattling the pylons and shaking millennia-old dust from where it caked the stonework ahead. Shouts echoed in the distance and bursts of light from both muzzle flashes and chemical flares illuminated the cavern. Chaos erupted.

"There it is!" Wulftone shouted to his forces. The enemy's flares backlit a central stand where a half-moon curved blade rested in a place of honor.

"I've got it!" A nearby soldier ducked his head as his support laid several bursts of laser fire as cover. He got three paces from it when a burst of automatic gunfire mowed him down.

The enemy forces ducked around the edges of the pillars, trying to get an angle on the men from the Prime. Casualties fell on both sides to weapons fire.

Jackie turned to face Gita. The girl looked terrified, but she continued pulling the trigger. Adrenaline pulsed through her body and pounded in her ears.

"No—him again!" she yelled as a familiar man walked through the gunfire. She leveled her rifle at the magician and opened fire.

Jacob Sisyphus batted away any energy bursts that came close enough to damage him. Jackie howled with rage as she poured on the intense fire. The former pro wrestler looked even more ominous than in their last encounter in Nebraska, half a world away.

Her high rate of fire finally snuck a shot through, sizzling through his defenses and blackening the flesh of his shoulder.

Sisyphus snarled and locked eyes with her. He seemed even more empowered by his rage and he snapped up the artifact amid the chaos of the battle.

"Finally, it's mine," he roared as his fingers closed around the handle of the wicked khopesh. He whirled the ancient sword around in a few practiced motions and batted the bursts of deadly energy from the air with the weapon's keen, alien edge. He laughed as the khopesh glowed with an arcane light, which his eyes mirrored.

"The power is finally mine!" Sisyphus waved his arms and a telekinetic burst knocked back the entire remaining cadre from the Prime. Only Wulftone was unaffected. He felt a surge of defiant power as Zahaben's bracer protected him from the darquematter artifact's abilities.

Jackie crawled to her feet even as Wulftone's shape blurred and grew into his lycan form.

Wulftone snarled and shrugged off the bullets fired by the Heptobscurantum grave robbers. He leapt towards Sisyphus and traded blows. A group of cultists threw themselves at the werewolf as the muscular wizard sidestepped the battle and used an outstretched arm to mentally grab hold of the very foundations of the ancient, buried structure.

It trembled and then shook violently as the support pillars on the Prime's side of the engagement began to crumble and break.

Harken sprinted towards the magician where he stood, momentarily concentrating. The cult leader reacted too quickly and kicked the soldier in the face, sending him sprawling to the ground even as Wulftone finished off his remaining attackers.

Sisyphus telekinetically grabbed the structure again, but this time directly over Jackie's head. He howled with rage and ripped the ceiling free, collapsing swaths of rubble all around the musty burial chamber.

Jackie screamed as stone and dust rained down from overhead.

Harken and Wulftone both charged back to rescue her, searching frantically among the debris and billowing clouds of grime. All gunfire suddenly ceased as the cultists retreated with their prize and the interdimensional troops were left alone to search for their dead and wounded.

Zabe signaled three of his men to circle around and watch their flank as he and two others crept closer to their goal. Only a short distance away, a glass enclosure protected the royal scepter of the mad Pharaoh Akroth.

They couldn't see the whisperers in the dark, but could sense their general direction as they shuffled in the shadows. Zabe scratched his head, wondering exactly how these other intruders had accessed the museum. He and his men had scouted for several hours and seen no sign of any others during their watch.

The whispers grew closer—finally close enough to discern. "There it is, Skrom. Grab it and let's go."

An immense figure shambled out of the darkness. Grumbling, a behemoth vyrm walked towards the scepter.

Zabe tensed, poised to spring out and surprise their rivals. The big one paused right in front of the case, less than a pace from where Zabe crouched.

Activating his earpiece, Skrom stared at the glass as his communicator connected. "Yeah. It's team two. Idrakka and I will have it in a second... get ready to grab us."

Zabe nodded to the soldier behind him and just as Skrom reached for the case, Zabe lunged at the huge tarkhūn, spearing him with a tackle like a battering ram. The second guard smashed the case and swiped the scepter. Lights and alarms switched on all across the hall.

Skrom and Idrakka hissed with reptilian ferocity. The smaller of the two ducked below Zabe's men as they pursued and pulled disruptor pistols. Bursts from the weapon caught one and sent the other two diving for cover.

Zabe wrestled the massive warrior to the ground. The vyrm's clawed hands and feet snatched his facemask and pulled it free before hitting him with such force that they flung him aside where he crashed through a preserved limestone wall-sized relief.

Skrom snarled and scrambled to his feet. He sidestepped the other warrior from the Prime and taunted as he tried to get an angle to attack the man protecting the scepter. "Was that the son of Zahaben? I expected so much more!"

Zabe snarled and leapt through the busted and toppled displays in his lycan form. The two massive warriors slashed and clawed at each other, each with his own designs upon the nearby scepter.

Idrakka poured more deadly energy into the stone retaining walls his enemies used as cover while he tapped his earpiece. "What? Good! Then get us out of here!"

Two security guards appeared in the large atrium door. They fired at the wily vyrm, cursing with surprise when they saw his green, scaly face—neither Idrakka nor Skrom had bothered with makeup to disguise their forms. Guns cracked loudly with a report distinct from the zap-blat sounds of the vyrm's disruptors.

The air nearby split open as a triangular shaped wall of energy ripped through existence, pierced by crackling light like unstable laser beams. It grew from a point to a ripple the size of a football before a surge of power opened it wide.

Idrakka turned and snapped five shots off into the archway, killing the officers threatening his flank. "Skrom! Forget the scepter—team one is good already!"

Skrom chuffed an acknowledgment as he disengaged from the battle.

Idrakka fired a barrage of energy into the men he'd pinned down. His battery pack chirped a low-charge signal, and he turned and fled with uncanny speed, leaping through the triangular portal. Skrom jumped through immediately after and the energy gate winked out of existence.

A moment of stark silence reigned in the air as soon as the vyrm escaped—even despite the blaring klaxons. Three of Zabe's men went over and grabbed their fallen comrade as he took Akroth's scepter.

"He's hurt pretty bad, but he's still alive."

Zabe nodded as he turned the artifact over in his hands. "Good. We've got to get out of here immediately. Local police will be here any minute."

*Funny,* he thought as his men grabbed their friend. *I thought it would be heavier.* He turned it over in his hands again as they hurried towards the exit in the rear. His eyes caught a small marking at the base of the unit.

He paused to get a better look and held it close to his eyes. A tiny word had been stamped into the metal at the bottom, along with a company logo. *Replica.*

Zabe shouted a string of curses in a language foreign to any of his troops and he frustratedly beat the fake artifact against the floor until it flew apart in pieces, revealing the cheap interior makeup.

Fuming, he headed towards the door. It would take them nearly two days to get back to the Prime based on the lunar alignment. "Let's get out of here," he muttered in a rare display of ire.

Sam Jones kept glancing at his wristwatch in the dark. "Come on, come on. You should be here by now," he chided the night air, wondering where Jenner was.

He bit his lip and watched another patrol by the bored security guard who made his rounds on a golf cart, which had been outfitted with lights. Holding a bolt-cutter, the illicit archaeologist leaned back onto the grassy berm and blended in with the ground on the outside of the chain-link fence.

The guard's floodlight washed over the area and then passed by as he completed another lazy circuit required by his job. Sam sat back up and noticed a car pulling up on a gravel service road nearby. Recognizing the flashy, pink mustache of the Lyft vehicle, he chuckled, wondering what his other-worldly friends would think of the transport.

As the confused driver shrugged, Shandra and Jenner exited the vehicle in full warrior garb—Jenner from the Guardian Corps and Shandra in the vestments of the Veritas. Her crimson hooded cape, the same material Nitthogr had once worn, trailed after her as they walked through the empty field in search of their friend.

The driver sped away even as Sam's phone buzzed with the alert that Jenner had paid with his credit account as instructed. He popped up and waved his friends over.

They spotted him and moved stealthily through the grassy lot.

"What did you tell him?" Sam laughed.

"Costume party," Shandra said.

"He didn't seem to believe it once we got here," Jenner interjected. "I told him it was a *secret costume party*."

Sam shook his head and started clipping a segment of the fence away. The razor wire at the top of the fence reinforced the severity of the Keep Out signs posted every fifty feet. Rows and rows of warehouse-like storage spread out before them.

"It doesn't look like much," Sam stated, "but there's a facility here where the museum holds potentially valuable, fragile, or hazardous items from antiquity. They keep the real items under guard and use replicas at the museum displays."

"That seems counter-productive," Shandra said.

Sam shrugged. "Not my call. Many of the wealthy pay for private viewings of authentic pieces. It's something that started a century ago when people suspected mummies of being cursed or occult powers bottled inside sacred items. Lots of nonsense, really..."

Shandra locked eyes with him. "Is it really?"

Sam blinked and wordlessly worked his jaw for a moment and then shrugged again. "Maybe not, I suppose." He pointed out the way to the warehouse in question. "We've got a few minutes before the next patrol comes by, but we've got to go through there and there." He pointed to a few rows between outbuildings. "They are the only lanes without any video cameras. As soon as we're inside, I need Jenner to cause a distraction."

Jenner nodded. "I can escape through the front gate, right?"

"You should be able to. Don't get caught—but if you do, say nothing. I'll come get you after a few days... they'll probably go easy as long as you're not armed." He nodded to the soldier's armaments.

Jenner scowled but tossed aside his sword and disruptor pistol.

Sam glanced to Shandra's side where a short hafted warhammer hung from her thick belt, mirroring a pistol on the other side.

She scowled, but also tossed her weapons into the growing pile.

A few moments later, they skulked through the first alleyway. Another golf cart drove by, but the trio remained safely within the shadows between buildings. They sprinted through a fluorescent glow cast by a mounted luminary and then snuck over to the second alley.

They'd just navigated the rest of the way to their target when a hail of gunfire erupted around the corner. Screams from men and women pierced the air. Lights from the golf carts whirled around in the distance as they turned to converge on whatever this threat was.

"Quickly!" Sam snapped the lock off a corrugated access that looked like a security-style garage door. They hopped inside just as the fight spilled into the alleyway where they'd been hiding.

"What are they?" one of the patrollers yelled. "They look like snake men!"

"Aliens!" another yelled just before a disruptor bolt blasted him into a pink mist.

"We should help them fight the vyrm," Jenner said.

"We don't have time for that," Sam yelled, trying to navigate a way through the stacks of boxes blocking their passage deeper into the storage unit. "We've got to get Akroth's scepter before the vyrm do!"

He turned back and spotted a familiar shape through a security window: the glowing triangle invented by Dr. Pietro Walther. It trailed a troupe of vyrm soldiers as they battled the security team.

The glow caught in Jenner's eyes and captivated him.

"No!" Shandra yelled as Jenner's wrath overtook him. She ran after him when the youth charged into the fray.

Howling with rage, the young warrior sprinted into the fray—determined to kill whatever was behind this thing that had taken his father from him three years ago. He reached for his weapons and then stumbled behind the cover of a nearby golf cart which lay in flames; he suddenly remembered his weapons were a hundred meters away—outside the fence!

The security team fled before the overwhelming force, and Shandra was caught in the middle of it. As the last few men tried to flee, another vyrm with a terrifying beast leashed by chains rounded a corner. It lashed out with its tentacle face and eviscerated the men with reckless ease.

Sam ran for the door. "Shandra!" he yelled, but blaster fire cornered him so that he couldn't escape the room.

The handler closed in on the cleric of Veritas, but his animal reacted differently—barking and pointing like a drug dog at a customs waypoint.

Pulling a blaster, the vyrm changed the setting and shot Shandra with a stun blast. The azure stun bolt crackled all over the cleric's body until she fell limp and smoking on the pavement. Laughing, the vyrm turned and fired several blasts at the archaeologist, who dove for cover behind a pile of crates.

Another vyrm joined the beast's master. "What's the holdup, Charobv? I already reported to the other team that we've got it—the real hierophanticus is in our possession."

Charobv pointed at Sam's position and laughed.

Sam poked his head up and saw the lithe vyrm soldier holding the real scepter of Akroth. To his horror, the scepter wielder transformed into Sam's exact doppelganger.

"Come, Jarkara," Charobv hissed. "His woman will make the perfect sacrifice for the next brother—the abyssal auraphage has sensed she's a perfect match for the next darquegate."

"No!" Sam screamed and charged headlong for the assailants. From the corner of his eye he thought he spotted a familiar face on the other side of the triangular portal. "You!" he accused.

Charobv leveled his blaster and shot Sam Jones square in the chest, dropping him cold.

The vyrm scooped up the unconscious Shandra and then escaped through the portal.

Jackie emerged from the underground labyrinth and wiped the soot and dust from her face. It had completely caked her with a fine, ruddy layer.

Gita emerged after her and likewise wiped her eyes clear, too.

With the hot, midday sun beating down on them Wulftone and the Guardian Corps emerged one by one. Harken and his dejected military also spilled out with a speed appropriate for a failed mission.

They crossed the sandy ravines of the short expanse. Despite the blistering heat, Harken and Wulftone jogged to catch up to Jackie.

Two steps back, she turned to give them a stern glare. "Don't even. I'm so mad at you both right now—just don't..."

Wulftone and Harken traded confused glances with each other. "I don't understand. What's wrong?"

With a set jaw and tight lips she stared at them while the rest of the warriors walked past. For a moment the guys thought she might actually refuse to tell them.

"You want to know? Of course—you're too dense to figure it out." She checked her clock and turned to begin walking, mumbling as she went. Her two suitors quickened pace to keep up.

"I'm highly trained, you idiots—you should know: you're the guys who trained me!"

"I'm not tracking," Wulftone admitted.

Jackie exploded. "You guys had the thing! You had that Sisyphus guy—probably the head of the Heptobscurantum by now—you had him dead to rights! He played you and preyed on your weakest links. I'm a big girl who can handle whatever comes my way. You've got to let me deal with my problems. Instead, you both came running to help me the moment you thought I was in any real trouble and you let the mission suffer because you thought I might be a casualty. You can't run a military operation like that!"

"I'm sorry," Harken started. "I just..."

Jackie refused to even look at him. "I said don't talk to me." She quickened her pace and checked her watch again. "Now hurry up. Our gate will only be open for less than ten more minutes and there's no way I want to get stuck here with you two idiots for another week until it opens again."

Caivev stood next to the decaying goatman deep within an ancient tomb lit by battery-powered portable LEDs. The air smelled thick and malodorous with no inflow of fresh oxygen.

A petrified man, bound and gagged, writhed on the altar inside the buried tomb of the pharaohs. Undisturbed mummies lay in gentle repose as they lined the walls of the catacomb-like room.

"Perhaps they were delayed?" Kreephast offered.

A triangle opened moments later and closed after belching a handful of allies through the gate and into the subterranean location. Charobv stepped in with an unconscious woman slung over his shoulder. The abyssal auraphage happily rushed through and hurried to its true master. It gleefully slobbered thick slime all over Akko Soggathoth's legs. The goatman, wearing his oversized oven mitts, rubbed his pet and wiped away the blood and ichor that coated the creature's maw.

Caivev whirled to face Jarkara when he entered the chamber disguised as Sam Jones. He held out the scepter and Akko Soggathoth greedily snatched it from his hands.

Jarkara met his lady's gaze and then quickly reverted to his natural form.

"Where did you learn that face?"

"He was with *her*," Jarkara pointed at Shandra. "We took her for the next sacrifice at the creature's insistence."

"Excellent," Caivev's eyes shone with an intense glimmer of hatred. "That will make killing her so much more rewarding."

The energy gate opened one more time to let in Skrom and Idrakka. Skrom pulled Caivev aside for a second. "We encountered resistance," he informed her. "Zabe and his team of fresh Corpsmen. They were after Akroth's scepter but didn't know it was a fake. It's a good bet that the Prime knows what we're up to. They will resist us at every turn."

Caivev shrugged. "Let them try." She turned to where their Darque ally hovered above his squirming captive with a jagged knife.

"Then, what comes next?" Skrom asked.

"Now, we follow the plan," Akko Soggathoth hissed as he knocked a set of canopic jars off a nearby plinth. He set his opened book upon it—even carrying something with Darquematter gilding seemed to pain the demon, despite the protection of the mittens. "I will release and bind Akko Hormundlyr as I have done before."

# Chapter Ten

Sam's mind awoke before his body did. He felt himself being dragged roughshod across the ground; Sam sensed his heels digging grooves through the dirt, but couldn't open his eyes. He suddenly shuddered and awoke with a start, flailing until whomever dragged him released his or her hold.

"It's me!" Jenner yelled with hands held high and defensively.

Sam relaxed his fists, which he'd tightly balled, ready for hostility. He wiped the slobber from his chin and massaged his sore muscles where the stun blast had scorched his chest. "How long was I out?"

"About twenty minutes or so." Jenner's furrowed brows proved his deep disappointment. "That... thing. The triangle—it's what took my father." The young man's frustration moved him to the verge of tears.

Sam understood completely and nodded with sympathy. "I was taken through that same portal once before—kidnapped like your father. I'm sure that he's out there somewhere and that you'll find and rescue him some day," Sam lied. He'd seen the mechanics of the device—knew how its Heptobscurantum masters bled captives dry in order to power the arcane machine.

Jenner tried to put on an optimistic face and stuffed his rage deep down inside. He would save it all up for later whenever he found the one controlling that evil three-sided portal—if he ever caught them.

The archaeologist retrieved his mobile phone and dialed up a ride before collecting the equipment Shandra left behind. There was no good way to disguise them and so he cradled the futuristic gun and her warhammer in his arms as the same pink-fuzzy-stached Lyft pulled up.

With an awkward shrug, their driver stowed the weapons in his trunk. "Where to? Home or another costume party?" He eyed the burn-mark that had scorched a hole all the way through Sam's shirt.

Sam handed him his credit card. "We have a longer trip planned. One way; I'll pay extra and you can charge us for both directions if it helps."

The driver nodded enthusiastically and took the credit card. "I'm all for it—rent's due tomorrow."

Without another word, the vehicle sped off into the night.

Zabe walked straight from the portal location to the meeting room where his peers had gathered to debrief following the bungled mission to collect the hierophanticus. Sam Jones and Jenner kept pace with him, and they'd met up at the portal location. Both headed for the nearest available nexus point after the vyrm invasion.

Time played crucial in their plans. The returning group from Earth walked into the keep and didn't spare a second.

"Any news on your end?" Zabe looked at Respan, hoping for some kind of breakthrough.

The scientist shook his head sadly.

Zabe nodded grimly and moved on. "We fought a big tarkhūn in the museum—someone by the name of Skrom," he stated plainly. "Either Basilisk is a liar and playing us, or he's had another defector."

Tay-lore piped up. "It is entirely possible that, if Basilisk is telling the truth and the Black and Tarkhūn have allied and are pursuing peace, mixed factions have splintered and could be collecting the darquematter pieces for their own ends."

Tightlipped, Zabe signaled his agreement. That made sense. He wasn't entirely positive who was behind it yet, but he had his suspicions, especially after learning that the Heptobscurantum was involved and that their arcane science department provided assistance. "If Basilisk isn't directly involved, his earlier mission to establish peace—and give us a sign our current problems aren't of his design—make it likely he knows about it, at the very least."

Zabe continued, "Regardless, I'm certain Skrom identified me. It's a sure bet they know we're onto them." He turned to Claire. "Your father has a hunch."

"I believe I saw Vivian, Caivev, on the other side of the energy gate," he said. "It was right as I was being shot with a stun blaster, though. I know that can have an impact on sensory perception, but I am confident I saw her—she looked the same as when she kidnapped me three years ago." He paused. "We've got to hurry and act. They're going to kill Shandra if we don't rescue her right away."

Sam looked at Tay-lore. "Where do we go next? You speculated that the Seven Brothers of the Winnowing had to be awakened in a certain order. Where is the next location?"

"Yes. I did say that. The Sh'logathian heralds, according to the legend I read, needed to be awakened from youngest to eldest and is rooted in an ancient folktale that may predate our own existence." He paused and realized it was not the time for a historical tangent. "Anyway. The next brothers in the birth order are twins. It is impossible for me to tell you what or how that works." He successfully imitated a sorrowful tone.

"Then we have only a fifty-fifty chance of rescuing her?"

Claire stood. All eyes focused on her. "No. We will take the fight to the enemy," she stated. "We know of two locations. We send two teams, and this time I'm coming." She said it with enough force that when she looked around the room, none dared disagree with her—except for Zabe's eyes: they pleaded her not to risk herself. "I've been training under Pollando, the monk who trained Bithia," she said. "I may not yet have her skill or strength, but I'm getting better. Pollando says I've got a raw, natural talent."

Jenner piped up, "But isn't Pollando mute?" everyone looked at the teen and he shrank back sheepishly as he realized that a psychic priest didn't need a voice to communicate.

"We don't always need mouths and ears to say what we need. In fact, we rarely say the things we most mean to speak with our words." She looked at Zabe when she talked.

Zabe slowly nodded his understanding and smiled lopsidedly, replying to her unspoken proclamation of affection.

Tay-lore didn't understand any of that. "You need not go if I make more of the darquematter trackers, though, right? I could make them right away."

She shook her head. "I'm going. I need to go. Plus, I'm confident that I could locate Akko Soggathoth if I was in the same dimension. According to what we've learned from ancient vyrm lore, these heralds cannot touch darquematter. Trenzlr and the Veritas believe that touching him with it will dispel him—banishing him back to the fractured dimension of the Darque." She playfully toyed with the dimensional inversion pendant that hung from her necklace. "Any hierophanticese should also work. If you get a chance to force contact with them, do it. It might be the only way to end this madness."

She looked around the room of committed soldiers, researchers, and family, and saw the dedication on their faces. They each silently signaled their assent and desire to act from a more offensive stance. "Good. Now let's stop this monster—whoever is controlling it—and save Shandra."

Cerci Heiderscheidt knocked on the door to Dr. Pietro Walther's private sanctum within the uppermost, utilitarian floors they'd leased in the Highlight Towers overlooking Munich. They'd gutted the thirty-second and converted it to a workspace while keeping the topmost suites for living space.

Walther's door slid open to reveal the bored pioneer of pseudo-sciences. Pro wrestling memorabilia adorned his walls, indicating the scientist's guilty pleasure. A pile of gold bricks and precious gems lay heaped in the corner. The scientists lacked nothing financially, but much of their freedom to experiment and pursue their research fell aside as they answered the beck and call of their benefactors.

"Yes, Miss Heiderscheidt?"

She waggled a cell phone with a text indicator. "A new transport request."

Walther mumbled something about snapping the energy gate shut on the lot of their demanding allies and simply being done with the whole bunch. Regardless, he performed dutifully.

Caivev stepped through the portal a few minutes later. "Thank you, Doctor," she said, eying a second, newly built version of their portal creation device. She knew they'd needed a backup unit to continue their tests since each failed attempt to reach beyond the thirty-three realms of the Tesseract often resulted in burned out parts and the Black could not suffer a breakdown in their transit system.

Walther bobbed his head to greet her and assumed the reason for her visit. "It's not ready yet. I'm sure I'll manage to break the barriers soon, but we still can't seem able to pierce the veil and into the Darque."

Caivev nodded. "Very good, but that's not the reason for my visit."

Both scientists raised an eyebrow.

"I need your help to stage a diversion. We have a large scale operation coming up soon and will need everyone's participation." Her cell phone chirped.

"We're hardly freedom fighters," Heiderscheidt reminded her. "Our idealism ends with our paychecks."

Caivev looked into her eyes and winked. She recognized the bored, glazed over look of a predator in captivity. "I'm not offering idealism or principles or any kind of purpose," she said. "I'm offering adventure and excitement. Something new that's never been done."

She had Heiderscheidt's attention and knew that the old man craved similar things, but didn't yet know it.

The traitor to the Prime walked over to a communications array and dialed in some information, but she waited to push the call switch. "I think your good friend would invite you to participate." Caivev pressed the connect button and Jacob Sisyphus's face filled the flat panel display.

Walther crowded into the camera's range and waved to the former entertainment athlete.

"Oh, Caivev," Sisyphus said with the invitational, lecherous tone he always used when talking to her. "Glad to see you're with friends."

"You have something of interest to tell me?"

"Just that the Heptobscurantum is nearly rebuilt to its former glory—yet commands more power and influence than ever before. And you certainly held up your end of the deal." Sisyphus held up the pommel of the ancient blade he'd acquired in Egypt via her information. "If our last encounter occurred again, if I got another chance to fight Nitthogr, I'm certain that this time I would emerge victorious—by leaps and bounds." He leaned towards the camera and grinned so wide it dripped with hubris.

Walther merely hovered in the background, smiling like an excited fanboy. But the wrestler's threats were real this time, not a string of singlet-wearing banter meant to ham for a camera.

"And how can you help? What are you offering?"

"An invitation to use us as the need arises. We don't want to be left out when Sh'logath comes into glory." He winked at her, masking their true goals with the gesture; Sisyphus knew that Walther and his team didn't understand the ultimate result of the Awakening. "I know we helped you with the whole Wainsmith thing; we're ready for a bigger role."

Caivev tapped her pursed lips thoughtfully. "I may have something for you. We will discuss it later—I need you in Central America. Plan for an extended stay—you still speak some Spanish?"

"Si lo hablo pasablemente."

She nodded and then turned to gesture towards the scientist. "The Doc's on the fence. Tell him why he should help us with our cause."

Walther took two steps forward. "I'd like a convincing reason to continue helping. I have more money than I could ever need. It's not about riches anymore."

Sisyphus watched his super-fan through the camera for a moment and then leaned closer yet. He knew exactly what buttons to push. The wrestler smiled and put a little gravel into his voice to imitate the carefully honed persona he'd performed for so many years, and which the scientist had religiously followed. "Look at Caivev, Doc. You see her? Just like you believe in me, *I follow her*. If she needed it, I'd bleed for her." He glared down at Walther, waiting for a reaction. "Is that a good enough reason?"

Walther swallowed the lump in his throat and nodded. "I'll do what she asks."

Caivev smiled knowingly and her phone went off. She answered it in a familiar voice.

"It's me. I have something important to tell you—information you will want."

"How are you even calling me? You're supposed to be in the Desolation," she kept her voice low.

"I'm done playing games from Limbus; I fancied a visit to Earth. I'll text you with a time."

"A time for what?"

"For your diversion," the vyrm voice stated plainly.

Using a gnarled and blackened stick, Akko Soggathoth unclasped the lock that sealed the precious tome. He used it to unfurl the cover and flip the reams of blank pages until he came to his next eldest brother, Akko Nuggezeth. Using the end of his rod, a piece of white oak burned to charcoal, he drew an X through the name.

In his human form, the disguised animal paced back and forth as a nervous energy permeated the atmosphere. Mystic power seemed to vibrate the air on a molecular level.

The disguised man leaned over the book and whispered his brother's name aloud. Silvery ink, the lifeblood of Akko Nuggezeth, seemed to evaporate into the air and rematerialize as a black mass even darker than the deep shadows stretching through the room. His sigil—a mark of binding—remained etched on the parchment.

"You are a liar, brother! I gained no energy trapped in your book."

Akko Soggathoth laughed mischievously. "I know—but I did not need you meddling in the plan until now."

"You were always a trickster... I hunger for a body! An avatar."

"I will provide you with one and I will even let you stay out where you can regenerate your mystic powers, brother, but you must first promise to behave."

The writhing darkness pulsed with malfeasant hatred at a command from the younger brother.

Akko Soggathoth chided him. "I have bound you to the pages and until I release the mark, your fealty is to me."

"I know how it works," he snapped. Despite Akko Nuggezeth's incorporeal form, resentment came through loud and clear.

"Excellent," Akko Soggathoth hissed as he donned his oven mitts. "I have a task for you." Very carefully, he tore the spine of his eldritch book; the binding, made of some unknown kind of skin, tore as if it remained alive.

He offered a broken half of the codex to the ethereal Akko Nuggezeth.

"Perhaps we should find you a suitable body first."

A three-dimensional model of planet Earth rotated in Tay-lore's laboratory. Several colored indicators hung off the spherical hologram like digital tabs labeling possible locations of sites where enemy cultists could be delving into the Darque.

Zabe and his team watched the android from nearby as they drew up tactical plans. He and Harken had split up a collection in order to lead successful assaults composed on different fronts. They would be ready to move out as soon as they knew their headings.

Claire entered the room. She walked over and put a hand on Tay-lore's shoulder.

Zabe's heart hung heavy to see her in his younger brother's armor again. He approved of her wearing it, but he wished that circumstances hadn't required her to don it.

"Do you have something for us yet?" Claire asked.

"That gold I asked you for a while ago—I used it to pay a man. He is something of an information broker by the name of Vikrum Wiltshire."

"Vikrum Wiltshire?" Sam scoffed nearby. "He's a crackpot, a self-proclaimed occult investigator. He's tried to buy things from the museum over the years... usually odd things. Artifacts."

Claire gave her father a stern look. "Things like scepters that can open dimensional portals or protect princesses from warlocks?"

Sam closed his mouth and shrugged. He knew he'd stepped in too deep. Maybe Wiltshire was onto something, after all.

"But you may be right to trust your gut," Claire said. "I have met him on a couple of occasions. I do not trust him. He has... certain ties to the heptobscurantum." Claire gave Tay-lore an askew look and a polite order. "Be sparing and be careful with whatever information you share with him. He could be a *very* dangerous man if he decided to make some kind of move.."

"Agreed," said Tay-lore. "Much of my motivation is to ensure that there is none of the forbidden knowledge given to the earth residents. The Architect King had wanted the Earth ream kept separate for reasons of his own, and I am making certain that is the case.

"I had him digitize all the data he'd collected from a paranormal incident," Tay-lore continued. "He found a trove of information at the original site, where I believe Akko Soggathoth was released. A group of cultists had gathered a large body of arcane writings—some of them even vyrmic in nature. Wiltshire will make sure we can know what they did and maybe decipher what they were up to." He indicated the labels on the globe. "These are all places mentioned throughout their collective lore."

"There are dozens of markers," she said. "How will we know which locations are the right ones?"

He keyed in a few commands and overlaid his sensory research to show the places with the greatest concentration of eldritch energies. Most of them had some kind of reading, as indicated by what looked like a weather map overlay—a kind of holographic, colored haze.

"This is energy leaking into our dimension through micro-fissures. Every plane has them. We only recently discovered where they come from: the Darque. And only Earth has them—as if it were somehow connected in some inexplicable way."

Zabe walked closer. "So how do we extrapolate which of these locations are darquegates?"

Tay-lore punched in more commands. "I'm removing the weakest readings and the strongest signal here," he tapped a dark zone on the edge of Russia, "which is likely the final brother. That way, we can find the remaining two locations of the brothers."

"Two," Zabe corrected. "There should be two more brothers after these two."

"Akko Sxkakzacros devoured the youngest of the litter, Akko Quarnyk, when they were still young. He is literally the 'two-in -one.'"

Zabe muttered some curses about losing more ground in the battle and never even knowing it.

"More information we can thank Vikrum Wiltshire for," Tay-lore said. "The lore is really quite fascinating."

Sam, more impatient than ever before, blurted out, "But there're still like sixteen of these godforsaken possible locations!"

"These thirteen readings contain nearly identical amounts of energy, according to my readings. Any could potentially be the location."

Zabe rubbed his chin. "You said weeks ago that these readings were a kind of energy signature and you could see what they looked like because they represented as a kind of pattern, right?"

"Correct—they are quantitatively numerical, but can also display as a pattern—music is also like that."

"Perfect," Zabe said optimistically. "Can you display one for us?"

The display panel on the nearby wall lit up with a spiky pattern that looked like a digitally recorded audio signal.

"Were these twins identical or fraternal... did any of Wiltshire's readings say anything about it?"

"They were identical!" The android ran a quick scan and all the patterns cycled through the display screen until two identical ones remained. Only two locations lit up on the holographic map: one blinked at the bottom of the globe and the other pulsed in Mexico. "I believe that we have our locations."

Jenner walked through the corridor and playfully hip-checked Gita as they moved through the elevated walkways. She caromed off, overreacting for the sake of pleasing his ego, but kept careful not to loosen the grip on her weapon. They were on their way towards a supply cache for the journey to one of the coldest locations on Earth. They still needed to join the others to be outfitted for the extreme climate.

Gita glanced back at him. He was a couple of years younger than she was but still more than a head taller than her. He'd turned his back to watch something happening outside, but she grinned at him regardless, to let him know she wouldn't find his advances altogether unwelcome.

Jenner's body tensed and he recoiled from the trellised window arches as he snapped his disruptor rifle into a ready position. The eruptions from his weapon split the air as he opened fire. "The alarm!" he shouted over his shoulder. "Gita, sound the alarm!"

She rushed to the edge, weapon ready, and saw what he'd spotted. A giant flaming triangle had split the sky open above the central courtyard. Hundreds of vyrm soldiers poured through the opening, repelling on loose cords anchored somewhere beyond the gate. Others sped through the air on a zip line connected to a nearby rooftop.

Jenner's pulse blasts found their marks as he growled with rage for the burning geometric portal. Dead bodies of his targets plummeted to the ground as they fell from the heights.

Gita snapped off a few shots, joining his fire with hers, but they were too many. A second portal opened on the ground of the main yard. It started small and then suddenly yawned open as more vyrm rushed through with reckless abandon. She turned and poured deadly energy into the opening, but the troops ignored the dangers and stepped over their own wounded.

Jenner repeated, "The alarm!"

Gita lowered her weapon and sprinted for the end of the corridor even as the enemy began returning fire. Support pillars that held up the rooftop of the exterior hallway erupted in clouds of shrapnel and debris.

She lunged for the alert system at the edge of the corridor just in time to see Jenner dive for cover. Gita pressed her hand over the palm scanner and hit the attack signal.

Warning sirens wailed across the castle. Still, the vyrm kept coming.

Father Salazar walked to the door, where someone rapped loudly and insistently for a few minutes. The priest and the others at the convent usually ignored the door unless a visitor proved themselves persistent. Despite the rough location, their commune was located within in the poorest part of Mexico City. They felt safe behind their solid stone walls and thick doors—but they did little to discourage mendicants and vagrants from seeking handouts.

He passed through the garden beds where the nuns happily tended their plants in the hours before vespers. Though the nuns subsisted solely on their efforts in the garden cloister, they were not unwilling to share, and the women would often sacrifice their own comfort to feed the destitute.

Sliding the iron peep sight open, Father Salazar found a congenial-looking man in priest's robes. A black town car idled on the street behind and kept the air conditioning circulating. The visitor smiled warmly, and he held a dog's leash, though the animal was too close to be seen through the aperture.

"Hello, Father," Salazar said, assuming the visitor was a guest from their order's headquarters based on the quality of his transportation. "What brings you to our part of the city?"

"Greetings," the stranger said. "I've come on an errand of urgency and I'd hoped to quickly tour your facility. I am on a mercy mission, looking for the right place to yield my district's financial support."

Salazar's brows raised at the unexpected boon. He had friends who were always looking out for him, sending him benefactors to keep his local efforts afloat. "Did Father Gomez send you?"

"The very one. Won't you invite me in?"

"Yes! Please, enter," Father Salazar urged.

The well-manicured man in robes entered, holding his Rottweiler's chain. He scanned the courtyard and looked face to face, from nun to nun, and bent to rub the scruff of his lethargic dog's neck.

"A tour, my friend. We engage in so many community outreach projects that you should know about. First, let me show you the—"

"Is this *everyone* who lives here—all the sisters of the convent?"

Father Salazar narrowed his eyes, getting the impression that the man's intentions might be less than honorable. He'd always been an advocate and defender of women—even prior to answering the holy call. Before Holy Orders, he'd administered the occasional dose of vigilante justice on behalf of wronged women. Salazar had been a long-time Golden Gloves champion before the local gym fell when the gentrification of his home area forced out the dregs. "Where did you say you were from?"

The man ignored him and followed his dog's lead as it sniffed the ground.

Becoming more demanding, Father Salazar growled, "Tell me where you came from and state your business, or I will forcibly remove you."

The man giggled at the premise. "I am looking for someone. My pet knows who I need; he says she is here."

Tires screeched in the distance. Someone near a window shouted "Las Siete Muertes!"

Father Salazar put a hand on the visitor's chest. "It is time for you to leave. You are not welcome here!"

The robbed visitor hissed. His dog's shape suddenly morphed into something horrific and as grotesque as something out of Bosch's horrific triptych paintings that Salazar had seen during his seminary days.

The priest's eyes widened in terror and screams echoed through the courtyard as the beast escaped the leash and pounced on a nearby nun, shredding her to pieces. Salazar shouted with righteous indignation as the doors kicked in; gun wielding cultists from Las Siete Muertes rushed inside.

Balling his fists with rage, Father Salazar spun his hips to throw a right cross that would've knocked the imposter's teeth from his head, but the demonic visitor tapped him on the head first, and broke the priest's neck.

Salazar was in glory before his body even hit the ground.

The alien dog-creature trotted back to its master with fresh, hot blood dripping from its maw. "Find what we came for," he whispered to the abyssal auraphage.

# Chapter Eleven

Harken leveled a pistol towards the scrum and snapped off a few shots as he barked orders into the communicator in his other hand. "I don't care what it takes," he shouted over the clamor. "You've got to get those towers manned again and use the laser batteries to mop up this mess!" He switched the channel closed and turned back to the attack with disgust. The timing was too perfect; somehow these vyrm knew exactly when to attack—when the laser batteries would be unmanned during a shift change—and right before they were set to mobilize against the enemy.

The military commander traded a knowing look with Wulftone, who led a small force across the courtyard where they blocked any enemies from accessing the deeper segments of the royal grounds. He'd had the same thought, and they both knew it. They may have been rivals, but they were allied in their duty and dedication to protecting their home.

Claire, under the lycan Zabe's protection, peeked out at the battle behind Wulftone's barricade line. Tay-lore followed her closely. She pointed at an energy gate. "I thought we could disable these things?" she asked him.

"In theory," Tay-lore replied. "I never actually saw them in the last attack. The Black forced me into a slave camp and made me a glorified cook. I believe that a blast from the turbo lasers can overload the energy gates and close them."

She looked expectantly at Zabe.

"There's no one manning the laser batteries!" he howled and then turned to face his fiancée and Tay-lore. "Get her out of here," he told the robot. "No matter how much she resists—she's too important to lose in the off chance that this is an assassination attempt. If it all goes down the tubes, get her out of here through the highland portals guarded by the Veritas."

Tay-lore nodded and tried to move Claire away from the attack. "But what about you?"

"They haven't stopped coming yet. I've got to go plug a leak."

Claire noted the determination in his eyes and nodded an acknowledgment. "Okay, but I'm not going far!"

Zabe grinned. "I knew you wouldn't." He watched her slip around the corner where she could be safe as she contributed in the ways she was uniquely qualified.

As Claire leaned against a retaining wall in relative safety under Tay-lore's guard, she released her consciousness from her body: less clumsily than "going up the mountain" all those years ago, but also much less adept than Bithia ever was.

Her psionic form walked invisibly through the chaos nearby as bullets and blast beams flashed around, piercing through her invisible energy form. She didn't spot any vyrm lichs; other psychics would have stood out to her astral senses. None of the invaders had any special powers or training. These were only foot soldiers, piling through the portals on their way to certain death.

*What could drive such reckless insanity?* She reached into the mind of one of the attackers and searched for answers.

"Cover me," Zabe ordered into his com. "I'm going to get rid of these things!"

He charged into the nest of vipers and leveled his shoulder, ramming through the crowd of enemies. Vyrm blasters tore seams through his thick, hairy hide, but he kept pushing forward.

Jackie and a few others on the upper deck walkway opened fire with precise shots and opened up a path with their blaster fire. The attrition from overhead drew enough attention away that Zabe could continue moving through the enemy's shots. Between his armor and the healing factor, he could still only absorb so much damage before it overwhelmed him.

The massive lycan tried bolting past the cluster of vyrm huddled near the burning, triangular portal. They barred the entry to the bastion-mounted artillery weapons and leapt on him with a malicious hiss.

Zabe scrambled and shook himself free, kicking one of the scrawny reptiles into a nearby crowd; they flung apart like an arrangement of bowling pins. Some reeled backward and bumped into the jagged lines of the energy gate, which cut through them with uncanny ease. The enemy vyrm fell apart into smoking, lifeless pieces where the portal edges eviscerated flesh with surgical precision.

Not waiting for the next wave, Zabe scrambled inside the access door and sprinted up the spiral staircase until he came out atop the parapet wall. He didn't waste a moment as he slipped into the control console, targeted the floating triangle, and unleashed a hellish, crackling burst of energy. It exploded on contact and flamed briefly before the fiendish geometry winked out of existence with implosive fury.

A group of vyrm intruders caught between ground and sky plunged to their deaths below even as the second triangle on the ground shrank and disappeared, not wanting to risk a similar explosion at the second portal generator. The vyrm took up a battle cry and seemed to surge even more ferocious with any hope of retreat or surrender stricken from them.

Zabe lit up the console and linked the heavy, wall-mounted weaponry to his central controls with a slave circuit. Before the next vyrm could launch any kind of offensive maneuver from the courtyard, he hit his trigger and launched a massive artillery blast from the walls. Intense laser fire scorched every living thing in the yard to slag and dust.

Silence reigned for a few moments, and then a cheer rose up from the men and women of the Royal Military and the Guardian Corps. Zabe crawled down from his perch and met with his soldiers as they filtered into the battlefield, kicking over bones and charred weaponry in a search for anything that might've survived.

Claire rushed to Zabe as he met up with Harken and Wulftone at the edge of the senseless carnage. His face showed how glad he was to see her unharmed.

"I know why they came—their purpose."

She had their attention fixated. "They didn't have one—I saw into one of their minds. They came with no mission and with no intention other than to die—they had no hope."

Zabe stared, looking for more info, and then realized what it all meant and arrived at the same conclusion Claire did. "They were just a distraction meant to slow us down. These lives were thrown away just to give our enemies a head start!"

Shandra startled awake with someone poking her in the forehead. A boy repeatedly tapped on her face until she regained consciousness: not maliciously, but rather playfully.

"What—who are you? Where am I?"

He shrugged. The boy, maybe fourteen years old, said, "The room."

Its walls seemed to spread off in every direction, and the whitewashed bulwarks radiated a dull light. The only identifying marker seemed to be the door which they sat nearby.

Shandra sat up. "They took me—the vyrm! *I've got to get back.*" She leapt to her feet and jerked on the door handle, to no avail. She pounded on the door for what felt like hours before sliding back down to the ground. The boy watched her the whole while—the passage of time didn't seem to bother him one bit.

He skootched over next to her in a show of solidarity. "They took me too. Who got you? Nitthogr?"

Shandra looked at him. "You're from the Prime?"

He nodded.

"Nitthogr has been dead for more than three years now."

His eyes widened. "That can't be. His forces, the Black, they took me just yesterday—the sorcerer was there. I saw him!"

"What's your name—who was your father?" She glanced at his outfit—a smaller suit of Guardian Corps armor; before the huge invasion a few years ago, it was common for new recruits to apprentice under their fathers and continue a proud family tradition.

The boy pointed to his Guardian Corps' armor where his name had been poorly engraved, where his name and rank would've normally been. His brother had scratched it there not so long ago as a point of honor. "My name is Zurrah. My father is Zahaben, the commander of the Corps. He'll come and rescue us any day now. He's coming for me. He just needs time to find us—I've only been gone a day."

Shandra's heart sank, and she realized that time did not pass in this mystic chamber. "Zurrah—you were kidnapped almost ten years ago by one of Nitthogr's failed raids. Your brother killed the sorcerer three years ago after finding the legendary Stone Glaive."

Zurrah looked up at the cleric. His eyes welled up with both intense sorrow and with joy and hope. "Zabe survived the attack? I'm so glad—how is he? How is my father? What is taking them so long—do you think your kidnapping will lead them here?"

She looked down at the teen, not prepared to take away his only hope. Shandra wasn't sure what to say, so she said nothing.

"My father will come for me. I know he will."

Shandra put her arm around him, painfully aware of her impending sacrifice. "I'm sure he will. Hopefully sooner, rather than later."

Sam and Jenner stood in the circle of others and insisted that what they'd seen was the same kind of portal controlled by Caivev's scientists. Both of them brimmed with different shades of rage.

"We've got to assume that they can travel anywhere with these things. They could be prepping Shandra for sacrifice right now! We've got to get moving," Sam insisted.

Claire put a hand on his shoulder and tried to calm her father, but he obviously felt responsible for Shandra's kidnapping. If he hadn't sent Jenner back to the Prime for help, or if he hadn't thought disarming was the wisest course of action, this might not have happened.

Zabe looked over at Harken, who'd just joined the group after a status update from one of his soldiers. "How soon can we get under way?"

"They're reporting minimal casualties," Harken said. "We should be able to move out immediately. I've got confidence in my crew to clean this mess up and hold down the fort in our absence."

Zabe glanced at Wulftone for a second opinion. Both men had been responsible for training their current military force. Wulftone nodded an assent.

"Then we'll move out as soon as possible; the plans haven't changed, they've only been delayed and hopefully by only a small margin."

Walking out among the blackened debris field of the courtyard battle zone, Zabe whistled with a loud, sharp trill. "Get ready to move out as soon as possible, people. We've got a cleric to save and a minor deity to banish."

The crowd of gathered soldiers gave a shout of acknowledgment. "If you are on my team, assemble in the hall of mirrors in half an hour. Secondary team gear up—you're moving out immediately afterwards. Move out!"

They shouted an agreement one more time and then dispersed.

Sam caught Zabe as he tried to leave for one last errand before the planeswalk. "I'm not on a team, Zabe."

Zabe nodded and tried to gently push past him, hoping the short timeline would allow him to move beyond any confrontation. Sam didn't let him by and pushed against his pending son-in-law's chest.

"I'm coming along. It's my fault she was captured!"

"It's not your fault. She would've done the same for you."

"And that's why I'm going. You'd do the same for my daughter."

"I am in love with her—I'd die for her. Duty, honor, love... all demand it if such a thing is required." Zabe looked into Sam's eyes and saw complete agreement echoed in his expression. He could not tell Sam that he had no right to fight for his own love.

Zabe bit his lip, sighed, and relented. "Okay," he whispered, "But Claire cannot know you're in danger. She would be distracted with worry and I already fear for her safety. I can't have her mind compromised by worry and doubt."

Sam nodded his assent. "That's fine. I wanted to go with the other team, anyway; I trust you and Claire to rescue and protect her if you find her." He didn't complete the thought... only a few knew of Zabe's suspicion that his inner circle included a traitor and only family remained beyond suspicion.

"Be safe." The two men shared a brief embrace and headed to their respective positions.

"I really wish he was here right now. I'm sure he'd know what to do," Zabe said as he stared at the statue of his father in Respan's lab.

The scientist removed Claire's Dimension Inversion Pendant from his stony neck. "Obviously it did not have any effect," Respan offered. "I'm still working on a few other ideas, however. The pendant seems to give off the same kind of energy signature that the Seven Brothers do, according to the data gathered by Tay-lore. If it's as the android suspects and contact with the hierophanticese might harm these foul creatures, I would strongly urge the Princess to wear this at all times."

He put the item into Zabe's palm. The soldier agreed enthusiastically; anything that could be done to protect her would be considered.

Respan pointed to the Stone Glaive. "You should take that. I have done all I can with it for now. I don't think it can help me as much as it could benefit you at the moment."

Zabe nodded grimly and shouldered the baldric that held the weapon slung across his back. He took one last look at his father, who'd been encased in such a defiant repose, and then departed for the Hall of Mirrors.

In the time since Zahaben's sacrifice and his tenure as commander of the Guardian Corps and Master at Arms to the princess, the amount of planeswalking from the Prime had increased exponentially. He sincerely hoped that his actions did more good than harm; the ancients had put a moratorium on the practice for many reasons—especially barring anyone against traveling to Earth.

As he walked, Zabe felt certain that his father would've made these same difficult decisions if faced with them. Still, uncertainty riddled his subconscious. Zabe only knew that doing nothing would lead to a quick demise of the universe.

He sighed with the weight of the thirty-three worlds on his shoulders as he climbed the tower stairs to meet his men. The mission must go forward, but there was no way to adequately train and prepare for his tenure in Zahaben's footsteps—nothing could train him for the trials of battling these reptilian zealots, and that fact drug his spirits low. How could he ask his peers to join him in such an impossible task against such steep odds?

Men and women of the Royal Military and of the Guardian Corps lined the hallway. Each person stood at attention, outfitted and ready to go. The resolve on their faces reminded him of their dedication and their grit.

His dour mood lifted when he looked at them, friends and family, each. With every step, Zabe knew that he'd made the right move. Sh'logath had to be stopped and every force that tried to awaken the agod had to be destroyed for the sake of all reality. That was his calling; that was his duty.

Zabe stopped halfway down the hallway. Claire stood at the ready, outfitted in Zurrah's armor.

"How do I look?" she asked coyly.

He motioned for her to turn around. She complied, and Zabe clasped the darquematter pendant behind her back. "Better, now."

She turned and gave him a kiss in front of everyone—something Zabe had always been reluctant to do. He returned it and then they walked towards the mirrors together. Their team followed. They stared at the mirror for a moment and prayed for success, knowing they would need all the help that they could get.

# Chapter Twelve

Claire smeared sunblock on her face and tied her hair back so that it wouldn't drag in her face during her mission. She hugged her best friend. "Be safe," she told Jackie, who wore a heavy parka by contrast.

Zabe handed her a plain looking cloak to cover her armor with. They expected they would run into locals.

"You too... make sure this wedding is still happening."

Claire winked. "I will—you make sure you've still got a plus one."

Jackie smirked and glanced over to Harken and Wulftone. Her ire with the boys had finally died down to minimal levels. Both looked up and caught her looking at them, and offered a smile in response. "I don't think that will be a problem... can I have a plus two?"

Claire laughed and joined Zabe's side. "Don't press your luck—and I mean it. Be careful!" They turned and leapt through the glass, which seemed to melt like liquid silver as they passed through and beyond. Their team followed them.

A moment of silence followed their departure. Wulftone stepped into the middle of the room and reset the portal indicators which would get them to their secret location in Antarctica.

"Listen up," he spoke at the top of his lungs as he worked. "We're going in hot and we're going in big. Zabe and the princess have a long way to travel from their drop site to the darqueportal. We're going to come out only a few hundred meters away from our target."

Wulftone looked over the hallway filled with prepped and ready troops that would soon charge through the breach and into the snowy unknown. They hoped their large show of force would distract from Zabe's smaller team, who would need as much stealth as they could.

"The more eyes that fall on us, means less of them searching for our friends. Are you all ready to do this?"

Shouts arose through the hallway.

Wulftone's Guardian Corps armor stretched at the joints as his body bulged and shifted into its lycan form. He snarled, "Then follow me!"

The werewolf strode confidently to the glass and then put his hand against the mirror to push through. Something stopped him. He pushed harder, but nothing moved.

A ripple of anxiety washed through the troops as the anticlimax took root. Wulftone pushed again. Nothing.

Harken stepped close and pushed against the side of the mirror's frame. It slid across the floor a few centimeters. He sidestepped and then pushed the glass for the same effect: they could not move it.

"Something is blocking us from the other side," he realized.

Wulftone muttered a string of curses at the stroke of luck. "You keep trying!" he shouted at Harken while he turned and began sprinting away.

Harken pulled his hand back from the glass and shook the frosty moisture away. "It's so cold," he shouted back to his comrade.

"I'm going for help," Wulftone shouted back right before he sprinted around the corner and out of sight.

Shandra didn't know if it had been seconds or weeks since being thrown into the chamber. She recalled having many conversations with Zurrah, and yet it still felt like only moments had passed since her incarceration. Those moments also felt like an eternity.

They leaned against the doorway and could occasionally hear the muffled sounds of voices in the room beyond. Something in the tone of those subdued voices reinforced in Shandra's mind that her time had nearly drawn to a close—they would come for her, and soon.

"What do you think, Zurrah? Do you want to get out of here?"

The youth vigorously shook his head.

"I have a plan."

Claire and Zabe burst through a copse of trees, as if emerging from an underwater swim. They rushed through the greenery and let the rest of their fifteen man team catch up. A hundred meters beyond their hiding location, people buzzed enthusiastically and unaware.

The crowd members beyond were as varied in attire as was their skin. People of many stripes meandered around the foot of the ancient structures, pausing to snap photos or purchase trinkets from a vendor.

"Tourists," Claire stated, and then pulled her head back into the dense vegetation that hid them.

Yardi and Spireth, the two soldiers accompanying Claire, Zabe, and Jenner to complete a five-man team, argued under their breath. A geometric pyramid towered in the distance above the canopy.

"What is it?" Zabe demanded.

"Portals are supposed to take us to places of greatness," Spireth whispered. "Why are we in the woods instead of atop the pyramid?"

Claire stepped forward. Years of study with her archeologist father had taught her the answer. "Portals from the Tesseract are places of power and energy; because we don't always understand that energy, indigenous people will often ascribe supernatural, mythological, or theological reasons to explain it and build a legend to suit."

She pointed to the looming structure. "That's the Pyramid of the Sun. The oldest it could have been established is one hundred B.C.E. But the name of the Aztec city, Teotihuacan, translates as 'Birthplace of the Gods,' and gives us an idea of the mythology surrounding the area. I think the ancient people perhaps met planeswalkers—maybe even saw them emerge—and jumped to conclusions about the area and then later built temples to uphold their mythos."

Claire's allies took her explanation at face value. It had a certain bit of logic. She decided not to share that the Teotihuacans practiced human sacrifice and worship a deity called "The Flayed God," amongst others.

"We're about forty klicks from Mexico City," she said, pointing to a wide street barely visible through the foliage. "That's the 'Avenue of the Dead.' We should be able to follow it and get to a parking lot; tour buses, taxis, and personal cars will be parked down that way."

Zabe held the Stone Glaive in one hand. It had been wrapped in burlap to look like a simple package as they walked among the public eye. "You all have the coordinates of the island. Make all speed to the site and be careful. Try to remain as inconspicuous as possible for as long as you are able." The troops received their orders and nodded.

"Then, good luck," Zabe said.

Claire pulled up her hood and led the way through the leaves. Zabe followed closely while Jenner, Yardi, and Spireth followed a little ways behind. She pointed at a tourist walking away from the parking area and towards the Temple of the Moon, the furthest of the three superstructures.

The other two five-man teams each broke through on their own and went different directions.

With an old cell phone in hand, she walked up and greeted him. "Excuse me? Can you snap a quick photo of my fiancé and me in front of the pyramid, please?"

He agreed and took her cellphone. As Claire explained the type of shot she hoped for, Jenner slinked up behind the photographer and unclipped the key and lock fob from his rear belt loop in one fluid motion and then walked away.

As the would-be helper verbally directed them to step further and further back to get the perfect angle, he eyed the mobile device with a well-trained eye. Once he'd positioned Zabe and Claire a reasonable distance away, he broke into a sprint opposite them and through a crowd of others and beyond.

Claire laughed as the man ran closer to the pyramids to hide. "He's probably heading that way with plans of doubling back and then selling or cloning the phone later. I sure feel less bad about stealing his car, now," she said.

Jenner approached them, spinning the keys on his index finger. He tossed them to Claire, who knew best in their party how to drive Earth vehicles.

In the parking lot, they pressed the alarm button on the key fob until a vehicle began honking. The team found a dirty, yellow taxi cab that smelled like old queso and piled in. It was not glamorous, but at least it would get them to the city as quickly as possible.

Claire turned the key, and the vehicle roared to life. The radio had been turned up loud to cover over the fact of the muffler's dire need for repairs.

Zabe reached to turn it off, but Claire stopped him. She cocked her head and listened to the broadcast, decoding foreign words she hadn't used in years.

"They are talking about a kidnapped nun. There's been a huge manhunt looking for her... something about a group of men who took her, religious zealots, they called them. Apparently, they burned down a convent and spray painted seven-pointed stars on everything nearby." She listened for another few moments. "I guess it's some kind of cult that's taken over a huge segment of the local drug trade—they even forced out a majority of the cartel with their brutality, and that's saying something."

"I didn't think any of the Heptobscurantum could've survived Nebraska... it must be a new crop of them. Sounds like they've gotten involved in the drug trade," Zabe scowled. "Let's just hope they don't spot us."

Claire agreed and threw the vehicle into gear.

Ten minutes later, their yellow cab roared down the road and the silhouettes of the Teotihuacan pyramids faded from the skyline. Zabe sat in the front seat with his massive sword balanced between his knees. Their three accomplices managed to squeeze into the backseat; comfort had not been their primary concern.

Zabe reached up and readjusted the rearview mirror so that he could use it. He narrowed his eyes.

"What is it?" Claire asked.

Zabe pointed to an upcoming exit off the highway. "Signal like you're going to go there."

She used her blinker and then got into a turn lane, but pulled out the last second and didn't take the ramp. "Problems?"

"That dark van behind us," he said. "They've been following us since leaving Teotihuacan."

Wulftone ran back towards the mirror room with Tay-lore hot on his heels. They both carried large pieces of equipment. The android carried an immense laser emitter while Wulftone carried a tripod slung across his shoulders and a huge battery in each paw.

As Tay-lore analyzed the mirror while Harken tried to pass through, Wulftone assembled the equipment and connected the batteries to the device. "Your assumptions were correct. There is a physical object blocking entry through the gate. I deduce it is an ice mass of some sort."

Wulftone clipped the last few leads to the laser's circuitry. "We're set up and ready to go."

Anyone near the Earth mirror took a few steps back as the lycan threw the switch. A brilliant vermillion beam cut the air and terminated at the mirror. It shed heat in every direction and the beam seemed to pass through the mirror; it didn't reflect back as they would've otherwise suspected. None had been certain they could send pure energy through the portals at all, but their luck hadn't been all bad.

The heat rose and those closest to the circle of mirrors wiped away, beading sweat from their hairlines before finally shedding their coats. Tay-lore began swiveling the business end of the beam emitter to widen an entry location.

"This may take some time," the android noted as the soldiers watched impatiently.

Harken grimaced, "Yeah, yeah. Hurry up and wait."

Caivev stood on the precipice of the entry to her pyramid and observed the hive of activity as the excavation around the Hidden Temple had grown and expanded, giving the dig-site a moat-like feel around her fortress. She mused that the stepped tiers of the prehistoric building might have given the ancient Aztecs their ideas for building designs all across Central America, and likely inspired the Mayans before even that.

The trenches below crawled with vyrm, mostly members of the Black, but she knew a few Tarkhūn had worked their way into their number. Some had been slaves or prisoners of wars and race riots—but these were mainly all believers in the cause or else dissidents not quite ready for Basilisk's One Vyrm union.

In an act of fealty, the new vyrm tribal leaders had each sent one hundred of their finest fighters. Her lonely jungle hideout had been nearly overrun by the influx of dimensional foreigners.

Additionally, Basilisk had arranged to send her the last of the Black who languished in his dungeons—the worst of the offenders in the race wars—and had them sent as a diversion to slow down the enemy in the Prime. The tarkhūn leader knew far too much about her inner workings to make her comfortable, but she'd assumed an info leak ever since Jarkara the Shade joined her cadre at Basilisk's insistence. She still got the better end of the deal and readily accepted his gift that stalled Claire and Zabe at the starting line.

Nearby, oily smoke from peat fires cooked all manner of earth meats which vyrm hunters had discovered in the jungles. The pungent odors did little to dissuade Caivev. She'd spent enough time shoulder to shoulder with the dregs of humanity and vyrm alike that she'd nearly burned out her olfactory senses.

Caivev instinctually knew it was time. She turned and walked down the corridor of her Hidden Temple while sidestepping vyrm troops as she paced the lengths of the ancient facility. Everywhere she went Caivev had to wave away salutes or nod to bowing servants and scuts.

Arriving at the main antechamber she liked to think of as her "war room," Caivev called for Skrom. The massive tarkhūn proved always ready to do her bidding.

"It's time, boss?"

Caivev nodded. "Very nearly. Call Walther and have him prepare."

Skrom picked up a cell phone that looked minuscule compared to his huge hands and punched in the digits.

A pair of yellow eyes watching from the shadows finally emerged into the light of the narthex. The finely dressed, eleven-fingered man and his dog bowed genteelly. Those glowing, golden orbs fixed on the leader. "A favor before we go, Caivev?" Akko Soggathoth beckoned with a waggling, bony finger.

She followed, and they descended further into the belly of the temple until arriving at the locked door to Koth. Caivev shot him an apprehensive look.

"I've had a premonition—of a sort. Would you please unlock the door for me?"

Caivev eyed him suspiciously for a moment and wondered what he was up to. She locked her wrist and performed the hand motions.

With his intense, yellow eyes, he watched Caivev cut her arm and use the pooling blood like a painter's palate. She painted the arcane sigil and the door unlocked. Caivev pulled it open ever so slightly.

"Excellent," Akko Soggathoth said. He turned and began climbing the stairs back towards the war room.

"That's it?"

The avatar shook his head. "Yes. Something of a safety measure is all."

As soon as they'd crested the steps to the narthex, her war room flew into a flurry of chaos. Skrom had Shandra subdued and wrestled to the ground, but the youngest son of Zahaben had broken free. Three reptilian soldiers lay dead within the timeless chamber.

"Run!" Shandra screamed before Skrom coldcocked her, bouncing her skull off the stone floor with a sickening thud.

Zurrah punched his way free from a trio of Black and spun a roundhouse kick that leveled the fourth would-be subduer. He ducked the next and sprinted away until he stood face to face with Caivev. His face suddenly lit up with hope.

"You! The Guardian Corps have arrived—my father has finally found us!"

A split second passed and Zurrah suddenly understood the guilty look in Caivev's eyes. "You're not with them anymore—you're a traitor?"

Caivev's heart sank at the accusation, however true it might have been. Her conscience ached as the last member of the Prime who might think her a source of hope understood that she'd betrayed her people. In fact, she'd given Nitthogr the very information that led to Zurrah's capture and the destruction of the old outpost.

Zurrah stood tall as Caivev pulled her blaster on him and cranked the dial. He spat his accusing question. "How long have you been betraying my father?"

"Long enough. Oh, and by the way, your father's dead!"

She shot the whelp in the chest just as his eyes widened in despair. Blue energy crackled and wreathed his body; Zurrah crumpled into an unconscious heap.

Akko Soggathoth nearly giggled at the turnabout. He pointed at the nearby vyrm who crawled to his feet, rubbing his face where the teen's foot had dented his face. "You. What is your name?"

"Theera," the vyrm stated, standing straight.

"I have an important task for you, Theera. There is a symbol drawn on the door below: a star with an eye drawn in blood. You must not let that sign dry up. It must stay fresh with blood." He pointed to the unconscious boy. "Use his blood." He pointed at another vyrm, "or use his. I do not care. Just do not let it dry. Do you understand?"

The soldier gulped hard. "Yes." He knew that the penalty for failure would likely be worse than death.

Skrom tucked Shandra's limp body under one arm as Walther's energy gate split the air and opened a passage to a large room and the Berlin skyline. The big tarkhūn ducked his head and stepped through, followed by Caivev, the goatman's avatar, and a small army of vyrm.

Vikrum Wiltshire sat in his office, which was tucked away within the Red Keep, a secret set of floors far beneath a cathedral in New York City. It was a stronghold and a sanctum which was warded against most forms of supernatural incursions. It was also where they kept one of their many archives: vaults in which they stored and catalogued many of the arcane artifacts that the brothers of the Red Order were tasked with removing from access by the general public. They also stored in them thousands and thousands of files on all types of creatures, ranging from Beelzebub, to the Jersey Devil, to Nessie.

They'd not fully caught up yet to the digital age, but they did what they could depending on the level of need. And lately, Wiltshire had been spending his time researching the strange incident from several years prior: when his friend and fellow paranormal detective, Quintin Hall, had gone missing.

Atticus Sexton, Wiltshire's partner, had gotten the files they'd collected safely into the archives of the Red Keep where Wiltshire had digitized them at the first available opportunity. Accessing the archives was always monitored and so Wiltshire could only sneak in a few opportunities at a time when he had cause for other cases.

While there had been an overwhelming glut of high-impact cases running up to the mysterious Black Goat Cult in Texas, they had tapered off in a sharp decline afterwards. It was almost as if the supernatural delinquents had taken an extended nap.

There had still been plenty to do—catching up on paperwork and investigating very minor incidents like alligator men in the sewers, a faerie circle in Central Park, and other intrigues, but the faith-shaking kind, or the apocalypse-level threats, had all but disappeared. That left him with fewer opportunities to access the vault.

Though Wiltshire had remained in contact with the mysterious T, who had initially requested the copies of the data and promised him he would provide some kind of way to decipher their meaning. Wiltshire knew better than to test Praetor Russo by asking too delicate of a question.

"Better to ask forgiveness than permission on this one," Wiltshire muttered to himself as he sent off the latest couple of scans of pages to T.

Sexton mumbled a query from where he entered data into a series of digital forms. He'd been focused on doing a lot of data entry lately. Wiltshire found it tedious, but Sexton seemed to prefer it over the chaos of an active, dangerous case.

The doldrums of paperwork were predictable and ordered, and they always let the detectives go at quitting time, which made Sexton's wife happy. He'd also fathered his first child since Pecos and enjoyed the family time.

"You say something?" Sexton asked.

Wiltshire's gut rumbled. "No. That was just my brain melting and falling out of my ear. You wanna grab some supper?"

"I actually have an appointment with the wife, child, and Paw Patrol," Sexton said.

Wiltshire nodded, noting the time. "Well, who am I to usurp Chase the Pup."

Sexton grinned. "Next time. I'll put something on the calendar," he said.

Wiltshire shrugged and watched his partner head out. A few minutes later, he finished packing up his own set of files and headed for a little restaurant several blocks away. It was an open air kind of joint, casual but not too laid back, and the early evening air was comfortable enough that Wiltshire didn't sweat beneath the suit jacket that concealed his shoulder holster.

He ordered a glass of water and waited for the waitress to return and take his order.

Night sounds in the city kept his attention for several minutes. It was just dark enough for automobiles to begin turning their lights on, but street lights made it bright enough that most still left them off.

Nearby, a house speaker pumped out Neil Diamond and Wiltshire, looked down at his glass and wiped the beads of sweat away. He saw a familiar shape reflected over his shoulder in the glass. Wiltshire cocked his head and studied it.

Time seemed to stretch out infinitely as he recognized the figure he'd seen once before. Pale skinned and with thin hair that fell in washed-out reddish locks past his shoulders. Wiltshire had faced one of these fiends before in the catacombs beneath the praetor's offices, hidden deep under the Vatican.

*It was a strigoi!* But worse than that, it was no regular member of this fiendish psuedo-vampire race. It was one of the Solomanari: the thirteen cursed fiends who collected an account of all human history and worked on behalf of the devil himself.

*Well, twelve...* Wiltshire thought to himself. He'd killed the one he'd captured, despite Praetor Russo's insistence otherwise.

There was no silver in the glass, allowing for the reflection. The image of the strigoi wore a wristwatch that he pointed to insistently, as if to say, "Time's up."

Wiltshire whirled around, kicking his chair back out from under him at the same time. In a flash, his gun was in his hand, pulled from his shoulder holster.

Other patrons screamed and ducked for cover as Wiltshire waved his gun around, searching for the creature, who was suddenly absent.

"Tik tok, Mister Wiltshire," came the strigoi's raspy voice from the other side of the table—now behind him, again. "The time to repay us comes soon."

Wiltshire spun back. But, again, nobody was there except for other diners who sprinted for cover. He took out his wallet and opened it so that it hung. It didn't matter that it wasn't a badge as he brandished his identification. Nobody ever checked closely. "I'm a detective. Nobody worry. I... thought I saw something. APB on a CSI B and E," he rattled off whatever official sounding acronyms came readily to mind.

He looked down at his water glass. Near it, a pocket watch lay open on the bistro table where he'd been sitting. Its arms did not move.

"Holy Hell," Wiltshire whispered.

# Chapter Thirteen

Two soldiers set the next armload of batteries down at the base of the laser. Everyone in the room had broken a sweat except for Tay-lore who was incapable of it. The android worked feverishly on a new device that resembled a disco ball mounted to a bracket.

Something had somehow combated their heat ray from the other side, preventing their clear passage with an intense cold that kept refreezing the gate almost as soon as it melted.

"It is almost ready," Tay-lore said as he affixed the device to a wheeled carriage filled with daisy-chained batteries. "Got it."

Harken bent over the machine and set the timer as Wulftone barked orders. "Everyone, try to wipe down as much as possible—sweat in the frigid climate we're detecting can plunge your body temperature to unsafe levels."

Tay-lore signaled that everything was ready, and Harken kicked the wheeled device below the laser's field and through the portal.

Everyone in the room held their collective breaths and watched the synchronized timer tick down. As soon as it hit zero, Tay-lore's strobe machine would zap a bubble of intense heat lasers and give them enough space to charge through the breach—but it was a one-way ticket until the celestial bodies aligned again.

Harken shouted down the time as the troops prepared for an assault on the unknown. Wulftone slung together as many batteries as he could fit on the heavy cable; the lycan shouldered them as if they were a school of fish caught on a stringer. Both men glanced across at their troops, both gazes lingering on Jackie. She reached across and squeezed Gita's hand, despite the terror so obviously lodged in her own eyes.

"Three! Two! One!"

Wulftone slammed the button on the laser turret and killed the beam so nobody would trip through it and fry themselves.

"Move out," Harken yelled and ran through the mirror with his rifle ready. The troops followed his lead.

Wulftone yanked the alligator clips off the nearly depleted battery cells laying on the floor and scooped up the beam emitter. "Thanks, Tay-lore. I'm gonna take this with me, just in case." He ran to shore up the militia's rear guard.

Tay-lore bowed as the lycan leapt through the mirror. "Do be careful."

Claire tugged at the collar of her outfit, trying to move some air in the stifling heat. She flapped the cloak around her neck and tried the windows of the dilapidated vehicle. They didn't work and barely managed a crack that flooded the interior with a shrill whine.

Zabe flipped the switch labeled Air Conditioning and the engine suddenly lost a third of its power as something under the hood made an ugly, grinding sound. Traffic around them switched lanes and zoomed past. He flipped the AC off and the vehicle resumed its normal power. Zabe shrugged apologetically to the rest of the car.

The black panel van kept pace with them even through the brief slowdown, a sure bet that they were indeed following them. The black automobile finally began to creep closer as Claire peeked at them through the rearview mirror.

"It says something on the front of their van. Can you read that?"

Zane craned his neck but had trouble getting an angle.

"I've got it," said Yardi. "I've always had good eyesight. It says 'How's my driving, call,' and then a bunch of numbers." He read them off as Claire typed them into her cell.

She put the mobile to her ear for a few moments and then looked at Zabe. "Coronado Iron Solutions? Look that up." Claire tossed the phone into her copilot's lap.

Zabe typed info into her phone's browser, glad that she was focusing on driving instead. He didn't want to die before meeting their enemies in battle—and the vehicle's handling was already sketchy without the added distraction in her hand.

"Top two articles," he said, "the first one is a news article about a company merger and buyout by the Heptobscurantum Group, the real estate company. Second one is an old one about the company's stock numbers—it says it was owned by the Wainsmith Holdings, or it was before the sale."

Claire bit her lip. "Go figure." She glanced at the mirror again. "Get down!"

She swerved the car across a couple lanes of traffic as the van's sliding door opened with a man leaning out. He pointed a fully automatic pistol towards them and unloaded a full magazine.

Bullets pierced the upper section of the auto glass as Yardi and Spireth leaned into the swerve, ducking as low as possible. They squished Jenner between them as Claire clipped another car, which spun out of control and forced the black van to decelerate.

Claire floored the gas pedal, and the car groaned and gasped for more speed. The van swerved around the obstacles and lurched forward. From the opening, the gunman leaned out again and fired off several more magazines worth of ammunition as the battered taxi zigged and zagged through the other cars on the highway.

The van closed the distance and the passengers, covered in broken glass, could almost see their attackers' face as he reracked a new mag full of ammo. Claire slammed on her brakes just as the gunner pulled the trigger. A line of bullets ripped through the asphalt where their car would've otherwise been.

Braking to match, the van swerved and sent the spray of lead wide even as Claire punched the throttle again. The bullets tore through the side panels and tires of two vehicles which collided just as the car zipped past, smashing together to form a twisted metal barrier and forcing the black van to skid to a momentary halt.

"We're not out of it yet," Claire muttered, catching sight of the van as it plowed through a ditch and merged back onto the highway. It clawed for speed with every cubic inch of its eight-cylinder engine. "Oh no," she gasped with a glance at the rearview mirror. The edge of Mexico City loomed on the horizon—but it would not come fast enough.

Zabe turned as much as possible and painted a tapestry of curse words. The trio in the backseat turned just in time to see the gunman from the van hoist a rocket launcher over his shoulder.

A missile streaked towards them on a gray trail of spent propellant even as Claire swerved hard and cut off an old pickup. With flaming fury, the explosive round flipped over the truck she swerved in front of.

The interior of the cab became a shrieking cacophony of profanity as everyone gave vent to their fears. Another rocket narrowly missed; it slammed into the hot pavement and erupted with volcanic ferocity.

"There's the exit—up there!" Zabe shouted hopefully. His heart sank as he watched the assassin shoulder the next rocket and draw a careful bead on their car's obvious exit path. He instinctively knew that the next shot would strike true.

A helicopter seemed to zoom out of nowhere, sporting the blue and white of the Mexican Police force. The helicopter cut a strafing line across the highway and a gunner opened fire on the black van.

It careened through the median, cut across traffic, and then got back on course as the other passengers in the dark vehicle opened fire on the aerial with small arms fire.

"I think we're going to make it," Claire shouted as the car climbed the off ramp. She steered through the arcing turn with white knuckles as her passengers watched their pursuit.

A rocket streaked across the sky, barely missing the police chopper, but it seemed to drive it off momentarily. The black van accelerated as the helicopter came around again. It hovered a second as it took aim, and then a rocket of its own shot out and detonated with trained precision.

The Heptobscurantum pursuit ended in a heap of blackened debris and melting rubber on the Mexican highway. Police spotters assessed their handiwork for a few seconds, and then the chopper climbed for air again just as Claire sped the vehicle through the city at unsafe speeds.

"They're coming for us next," Zabe shouted. "They have no idea who or what we are—they probably think we're all warring cartel members and plan to shoot first and sort it out later!"

Claire grinned, keeping an eye on the chopper from the corner of her eye. "With in this fancy car? They should've guessed diplomatic envoy."

The helicopter began an arc around a cluster of tall buildings that would give them a clear shooting lane.

Claire hit the cruise control and balanced the steering wheel as best as she could. "Alright. Everybody out!"

All four doors opened simultaneously and the five warriors abandoned their ride at high speeds. They rolled to a stop and dove for cover as soon as possible.

As soon as the police chopper cleared the high rises, it opened fire with a pair of missiles that streaked to the target with laser precision. The cab exploded with an oily eruption of flame and debris and the husk of Detroit steel skidded to a fiery stop two blocks later; two flaming tires bounced for another two blocks beyond that, but none of the infiltrators from the Prime stuck around to see it—they'd already regrouped in a narrow alley and begun sprinting for their next waypoint on the other side of a run-down ghetto that housed the low-income residents of the north central side of one of the most populous cities in the world.

Frozen winds blasted Wulftone as soon as he crossed over, and the brilliant, hollow light of the sun tainted everything with somber hues. Explosions blasted all around him and screams of man and vyrm alike pierced the frigid air.

He ducked his head and darted behind a giant stone column while he took stock of the odd surroundings. A ring of standing pillars identical to Stonehenge encircled the portal location.

Wulftone flung himself to the ground to avoid the rapid-fire disruptor blasts that peppered the rocky barrier he hid behind. He landed on his back, careful to protect the laser heat emitter and batteries that he carried; glancing up from the frozen earth, he saw the sky from the bottom of a bowl-like basin.

Tay-lore's heat bomb had melted away more than just the ice blockade. It burned the top off of what had been some kind of ice bubble protecting the frozen subterranean cave from satellite discovery.

Ice seemed to grow and fly with blizzard force as Wulftone rolled to his lupine haunches and sprinted towards natural trenches where his friends had dug in. He spotted Harken in a gravelly ravine and he dove for cover even as a trio of laser bursts burned the muscle of his flanks.

"Glad you could make it," Harken said, ignoring the stench of burning flesh and fur rolling off of the werewolf's smoldering hide. "I'm afraid it may be a one-way trip." He pointed.

Wulftone's wounds began stitching themselves up almost immediately, though that fact would do nothing to stop the pain until the nerves fully regenerated. He grunted and grabbed a clawful of ground where ice shards seemed to grow like polar lichen. As the alien forces dug in to assess the surroundings, the portal site began to regrow the ice blockage with supernatural speed and block any further support.

A sudden blast of arctic air bit Wulftone's nose and a storm head blew down the slope at the edge of the frozen basin. "Is that a pyramid?" He ducked his head behind the edge of the trench and warmed his nose.

"It sure looks like it," Jackie said, approaching in a kind of half-crouched run. "It's built into the side of that ice shelf—well, the shelf probably formed around it." She crawled into his arms.

Wulftone glanced down at her in surprise.

"The thing I remember most about lycans is how hot your skin is," she said, trying to downplay how secure his arms made her feel.

Wulftone shrugged. "Okay, but what's causing all this snow? It's certainly not natural."

Harken tossed him a pair of thermal binoculars. "Look at that cloud two thirds up the hill."

He held the device to his eyes and poked his head up over the ridge. Scanning the horizon, he easily spotted the heat signatures from the vyrm forces, who each wore a special suit with hot wires seaming the outfit to provide constant warmth necessary to their reptilian physiology. Wulftone focused on the swirling cloud of cold that emanated from a humanoid figure in the middle; ice and snow churned around him like a freezing tornado. Wulftone dropped the binocs.

"Yeah," Harken joked with a shudder, "I wish we'd have thought up suits like that."

"Its body temperature is sub-zero—is that thing..."

"Yeah," Harken filled in the blanks. "It's a tarkhūn frostmancer!"

"I thought they were extinct following the Syzygyc War?"

"Apparently not," Jackie spat, starting to shiver again. "How are we supposed to get up to that temple with evil Frosty the Snow-vyrm up there?"

Wulftone slapped a man wearing Guardian Corps armor and a thermal facemask on the shoulder. "You got any ideas?"

Sam Jones peeled his mask off, much to Harken and Jackie's surprise. "Not particularly. But at the rate that creature is able to regenerate the ice, I'm afraid that we will all be stuck here permanently, and soon, if we don't act immediately. Every minute that passes," he gazed longingly towards the sloped temple entrance, "and the chances of our success decreases."

The lycan grinned at Harken as he placed the thermal goggles on his head lopsidedly. "You guys make sure you cover us. This involves arcane artifacts and so it falls to the Guardian Corps." He tucked the heat laser under an arm and yelled to his forces, "Let's show these snakes a little revenge for what they did three years ago!"

All corpsmen under his charge took up a shout and Wulftone leapt past the ravine's edge and charged up the slope, howling. Still shouting, the rest of the Guardian Corps followed him at top speed, ignoring the defensive disruptor bursts and the icy winds that bit their faces.

"Attack!" yelled Harken.

The vyrm hidden within drifts along the slope fired recklessly at Wulftone, who shrugged off the burning bolts that hit him. He drew their fire, and Harken's troops pinpointed the enemy who gave away their relatively undefended positions by attacking. Any who held their fire still found themselves targeted by Harken's sniper fire as he picked off unit after unit that his thermal vision located.

Only half a dozen of Wulftone's men fell, though the commander could barely keep his pace as jolt after jolt of energy wracked his body with pain. His corps zigged and zagged up the mountain, avoiding as much fire as possible. "Shoot that frostmancer!" he screamed as he and the troops opened fire while making a line for the shifting white dunes.

The vyrm further up the hillock fell into retreat and headed towards the temple mouth. Harken's forces cheered and crawled over the lip in pursuit. They added their weapons to the corpsmen and charged.

A giant bastion of ice protected the frostmancer who battered the forces with a frigid gale of ice shrapnel that drove them many to their knees and buried others up to their waists in powder. Blaster bolts chipped away at his frozen blockade, sending him further up the hill where he conjured another frosty barrier.

Another column of ice rose from the snow, growing in height and girth. The wind hissed and roared, carrying the rage of the frostmancer even as his massive ice tower shook the frigid basin.

Wulftone suddenly realized what the vyrm intended it for. He snapped the laser up, used the ruby heat beam to slice through its base like a sword through yew. The column tipped and fell, hurtling to the ground like a hammer. He set off the vyrm trap prematurely and the tip of the tower smashed to the slope mere meters from his charging troops.

Swiping the hill with the radiant beam, Wulftone bathed the tarkhūn's ice barrier with heat and weakened it so that his force's blaster fire effortlessly disintegrated the shields.

Another ice wall went up and fell. And then another rose and broke as they beat the villain back far enough that he retreated into the temple.

With the raging winds finally subsiding, both Harken's and Wulftone's troops charged up the slope in pursuit. They halted in front of the yawning entryway to the tiered pyramid-like structure; the aperture had iced over with such an intense temperature that it radiated cold and misted the air, even in the sub-zero climate.

Wulftone dropped his stringer of batteries and unslung the laser's tripod mechanism in order to configure the device as Tay-lore had done earlier. He glanced back down the slope with a grimace and noted the standing stones had been completely iced over again, barring the portal's use. He muttered, "I just hope we'll have enough battery power left over for a return trip."

The five foreigners tried to remain inconspicuous as they walked the backstreets of the run-down inner-city neighborhood of Mexico City. This part was off the visitor guides, hidden beneath the thin veneer of nearby tourist attractions. They passed only blocks from safe places Claire had visited previously with her father.

Claire and her companions didn't fool anyone, and the few people loitering in the streets kept a wide berth of the suspicious strangers. A greedy teen, trying his best to look as if he'd been careless or didn't mind the intruder's presence, walked too close. Claire said to Zabe, "Mira sus manos."

The boy looked her dead in the eye and grinned smugly when she identified him as a pickpocket. Zabe didn't understand, but the pickpocket did, and it was better for him that Zabe didn't speak the tongue; the native followed for half a block, cockily shouting explicit threats at Claire. If Zabe had understood, it might've resulted in a bloody detour.

They kept their heads down and hurried toward their destination. After crossing a street, they walked into an alley that suddenly quieted and grew uncannily empty. Doors affixed to the pocked concrete walls shut and sliding corrugated doors amid the exteriors marred with blistering paint bubbles clicked as they locked.

Zabe growled as the hair on his neck prickled even in his human form. His eyes shifted to the skyline and the windows of the two-story urban canyon; it made a perfect trap. A derelict husk of a Google Maps camera car lay burned out ahead, where it had finally succumbed to the wounds earned in the rough neighborhood.

Skootching towards the edge of a building, Jenner whispered, "I don't like this."

Zabe goose stepped three more paces and sniffed the air. He nodded towards the graffiti on the crumbling stucco; an immense seven-pointed star dribbled stray drippings from the peaks. "When it starts, you all sprint for our waypoint and find the others."

Yardi eyed him hesitantly. "You'll be fine on your own?"

Claire looked at her fiancé and grinned with pride. The others didn't know him as well as she did—they only knew his reputation.

"I'll be fine. Get ready." He peeled the burlap wrapping from his massive sword and gripped the handle. "Go now!" Zabe snarled as his body stretched and sprouted fur just as the doors on either side of the street crashed open. Heptobscurantum cultists poured from the buildings.

Claire and the rest of the crew sprinted down the alleyway as the lycan roared and swung his blade against the crowd of cultists. The tip of the arcane weapon barely grazed his enemies, but that was enough to freeze a swath of them in living stone.

Sounds of the scuffle echoed down the corridor. Screams of man and the howls of beast scared off any interlopers or looky-loos. Gunshots erupted, but Claire and her teammates had nearly cleared the area. She looked back only briefly before rounding the corner and spotted Zabe ripping the hood off the automated mapping car to use as a shield against the gunmen.

Her heart leapt slightly when she spotted a man on the roof propping a shoulder-mounted rocket launcher over the top ledge of the building to target her love. Claire wanted to shout to Zabe to warn him of the powerful sneak attack about to hit him—he was preoccupied with a new wave of attackers popping up behind the line of newly formed stone statues.

She paused and considered turning back, but caught sight of another gunman on the opposite rooftop. The midday sunlight glinted off the lens of his scope as he aimed a sniper rifle at her and the trio of escapees rounding the bend in the alleyway.

"Go!" Claire pushed the others ahead and jumped around the corner just in time to avoid a trio of bullets that tore up the corner of the building that shielded her from harm. A moment later, she *felt* the rumbling before she heard the explosion's noise tumbling down the alley.

She bit her lip and refused to give her emotions creative license. They would otherwise craft some unlikely scenario where Zabe lay dismembered and bleeding in the streets. Claire forced her heart to have more faith in him than her imagination did.

Zabe had to still be alive. She refused to entertain any other assumption as she led the way to their next destination.

# CHAPTER FOURTEEN

Wulftone pointed the heat blaster at the giant heap of ice blocking the entry. As soon as the beam penetrated halfway and they began widening the hole, the tarkhūn frostlord would refreeze everything and undo all their work.

The invading force huddled near the massive stone frame of the ancient door. Given the proximity to the heat beam, it was the warmest place, and they shared their corporate misery in clustered crowds.

Through chattering teeth, Wulftone muttered under his breath. He worried that they would not have enough battery power to melt the glacial barrier at the portal's location if they did not see a breakthrough soon. As the laser's bore neared the midpoint, Harken tapped him on the shoulder.

"I got this," he said cockily. Harken activated the wireless sensors on a cluster of remote detonators. "Just say when."

"Now!" Wulftone flipped off the laser as Harken chucked the fist-sized wad of explosives down the ice-bored pipe. A second later, everything had frozen over again.

Harken wiped away the white effluence on the edge of the frigid block. It had frozen so thick and hard that they could not see more than a few inches through the mass before the murky density obscured all vision. "I can't see it, so it must be in there pretty deep."

"Perfect," Wulftone said. "That means they probably don't know it's in there either." He ducked around the corner of the temple to get clear of the blast radius. He barked commands to the two large groups lined up against either side of the temple's exterior. "Everyone get ready!"

Harken leaned against the ancient wall right next to Jackie. She smiled approvingly at his plan, glad to finally have the opportunity to get out of the frigid air—even if it meant running into gunfire. Harken winked at her and handed her the detonator.

Her smile spread ear to ear. "Really?"

"Yeah. Go ahead, do the honors."

She giggled with excitement—a laugh almost disturbingly macabre, bordering on a menacing cackle. Gita grinned behind her. She glanced at the other side of the blast zone and spotted Wulftone and Sam Jones, whose eyes yearned for her to press the button and let them save Shandra.

Her finger hovered over the wireless ignitor and thought about her friends who weren't there. She sent up a brief prayer on behalf of Claire and Zabe... Jenner too, although he always struck her as a little sketchy, like he might snap under pressure if it meant avenging his family.

Jackie yelled, "Fire in the hole!" and mashed the trigger. The structure rumbled and shook with the blast; a horizontal pillar of fire propelled giant ice chunks out of the doorway where they landed halfway down the slope—they presumed it shot the other way too, frying many of their enemies who'd blockaded themselves within the Antarctic stronghold.

Claire tapped her foot nervously as she hugged her arms to her body despite the sticky heat. She refused to worry... at least she tried to tell herself that. Deep down, she was terrified.

Jenner, Yardi, and Spireth hovered nearby to help offset her nerves as Claire spoke with a tour guide to arrange for aquatic transport. The other two strike teams casually trickled towards the waypoint destination and gradually converged with them.

Claire counted heads as she spoke with the ferryman in her halting, seldom-used Spanish. She turned to the new arrivals and shot them an inquisitive look; only nine of the ten others had arrived.

Chira, one of the other team leaders under Zabe's command, hung his head slightly lower than normal. "We lost one," he said sorrowfully. "Earth's Sh'logath cult—the Heptobscurantum—came at us out of nowhere. They knew we were coming."

Claire nodded to Chira with a frown. She looked around and prayed, hopeful for a glimpse of Zabe's return.

She turned back to Jose and continued haggling over the price. Dirt and sweat stained his brow and clothes. His river skiff could barely hold the travelers from the Prime; it floated nearby, tethered by a fraying cord. Neither boat nor ferryman was anything special—and that's the sort of anonymity they needed. With the well-connected cultists hunting them, stealth was at a premium.

Claire was sure that Jose needed the funds from any charters. She couldn't tell if he just enjoyed arguing over prices or if something else was at work. Her guts churned inside as her mind replayed the sound of the recent rocket blast over and over. Finally, she slapped down a metal tile the size of a compact disc's jewel case.

Jose's eyes widened as he recognized the element: pure gold. The ingot was worth more than he might make in a lifetime working the river.

Claire locked eyes with him. "You know what this is and how much it's worth? Stop playing games with me and take us to the island."

Jose's eyes shifted nervously back and forth. He stammered, "I... I am sorry—but if I take you there, men from Las Siete Muertes will find me and kill my children. They came up and down the river these last two weeks and warned everybody that the island is off limits for the next month."

Claire scowled and turned to ponder the next course of action, understanding that the Las Siete Muertes was the local name for the Heptobscurantum. She hated to force the man if it jeopardized his family, but if it meant the difference between awakening Sh'lo-gath she knew she must do it.

Jose noticed that she didn't react to the name. "You don't know the Las Siete Muertes?"

Claire shrugged.

"They are at war with the city—and have spies everywhere. Everyone knows they kidnapped those nuns and destroyed the convent." He made a brief sign of the cross at the mention of the tragedy. "It's been all over the news.'

"I... uh, haven't listened to the news in a while," she said.

"The police want nothing as badly as they want to destroy this cult—but they've also infiltrated even that office. We thought things were bad when the cartels ruled the city. Las Siete Muertes makes them look like altar boys." He shook his head and clammed up for fear that someone might have overheard him.

Claire knew she couldn't give him a death sentence by forcing him to help. She scowled and turned to leave in search of other options.

"However," Jose called her back as he furiously scribbled on a piece of paper, "I could sell you the boat as long as you know where you are going?"

She nodded and took the bill of sale to sign. Jose walked past her and pulled a large knife from his belt; he used the blade to pry off the name plaque and scrape away any other identifiers that he could readily find.

Taking the slip back from Claire, Jose said very gravely, "Whatever motivates you to visit that haunted place, especially while Las Siete Muertes has forbidden it, is beyond me. Just make sure that no one ever finds this boat when you are done with it."

Claire nodded and looked up to find Zabe limping towards them in his human form. He carried the Stone Glaive wrapped in his bloody and tattered cloak. A huge section of his Guardian Corps' armor had been blasted away over the torso, and the pieces covering his midsection had been ripped and charred by fire.

Zabe wore a pained grin as he walked forward with a brave face. He whistled through the agony as Claire rushed forward to hug him and then pulled away when he winced at her touch.

Jose watched with bewilderment. He wordlessly worked his mouth for a few moments, but had nothing to say—he could only stare at the tortured, bloody man who joined their crew. His eyes fixed on the gaping, bleeding wound over the lowest part of the man's ribcage as it slowly stopped leaking and began to stitch itself back together.

"I'll be just fine in another few minutes," Zabe grunted. His eyes did a brief headcount. "We lost one," he noted solemnly.

"I'm thankful it was *only one*," Claire injected with levity.

Jose looked at them apprehensively and then tossed the boat keys to Claire. He turned and then hurried away with all due speed and a commitment to forget everything that he'd just seen.

Gita screamed as she poured an entire battery's worth of firepower down the hallway. Blood from a fallen comrade splattered her face and return fire zipped over her head. It puckered the stone walls as she charged to the next pillar in the tall passageway.

Jackie dove beneath a swath of enemy disruptor blasts and skidded to a halt near Gita's feet—just in time to pepper a sneaky vyrm soldier who had gotten into flanking position on her friend's blind side. Grenade blasts rattled the walls and shook ice crystals from the ceiling. They floated serenely towards the battle below, oblivious to the chaos.

They cleared the corridor inch by inch, stepping over the bodies of fallen friends and of vyrm—so many vyrm. The maniac worshippers of Sh'logath gladly threw away their lives in pursuit of their nihilistic beliefs.

Jackie glanced back at Sam Jones, who brought up the rear. His face had been fraught with worry over Shandra. Jackie glanced to Harken and to Wulftone, who worked well together, protecting each other's' flanks and tearing through the enemy lines as they worked in tandem. She knew that humans were no different from the enemy: they threw away their lives for causes that they believed in, just as the vyrm did. *Usually, those causes are people*, she mused as she pulled the trigger and then swapped out a chirping, depleted power cell for a fresh one.

Sam ducked his head down and scurried over to Jackie. "I think I know the layout of this temple. At least, I believe I can guess at it. I've been inside pyramids that have such similar designs all around the world that their similarities cannot be mere coincidence. I think I can sneak us around the enemy."

Jackie noticed the helpless look on his face. She had been the same as him only a few years prior: always at the mercy and whim of stronger forces, helpless and powerless to reckon with the world until she'd discovered her own strengths and taken training with soldiers of the Prime. She waived Wulftone and Harken over. It wasn't her call to make.

Bursts of return fire popped only infrequently as the soldiers secured the larger room and its connected hallways, making it safe enough to assess the situation. The two officers met up with them.

"Sam thinks he knows his way around here," Jackie reported.

Harken raised his eyebrows. "I've got scouts that should report back in at any second."

"There will be five tunnels branching off from the next main room," Sam told him. It would've come off matter-of-factly had there not been so much urgency in his voice. "They each go off in different directions, but the middle tunnel will lead the deepest into the heart of the pyramid and will terminate in a kind of priestly, ceremonial room with an altar. That is the most likely location for any sacrifice they would make."

A breathless scout sprinted to their location just as Sam finished speaking. "Big room up ahead," he spat. "It splits off five ways. Each tunnel is crawling with enemies."

"Oh good," Wulftone said with relief. The others looked at him incredulously. He explained, "They wouldn't be here defending anything if they'd already resurrected Akko Thakkanon."

"There is a secret tunnel!" Sam blurted. "Many pyramids have them and we should be able to use it to get to the bottom—it's like a human-sized laundry chute running down at a forty-five degree angle."

"How many men can we get through at once?" Harken asked the tactical questions first.

"It won't be big. One person at a time at most, I should suspect."

Wulftone gave the order for all forces to assault the central tunnel, knowing that the enemy would defend it to the last in order to hold onto their dark agenda. "Lead the way. That diversion will only buy as a little time—if we don't act fast enough, they will speed up their sacrifice in response."

Sam nodded and ran half-way back to the entrance with Harken, Wulftone, Jackie, and Gita in tow. "I'm sure I spotted the access on the way in." He pointed to a stone block at the wall barely larger than a square meter in size. It appeared indistinguishable from the others.

"I don't get it," Harken said. "Where is the door?"

Sam pointed again. "You can tell by the way the texture changes."

"I can see it," Wulftone growled. His heightened eyesight helped him identify it.

The others shrugged and Wulftone pounded on the panel. Its thin, stucco veneer shattered and broke free from the cedar panel as the werewolf ripped it out. He immediately crawled down the hole. Sam dove in excitedly and followed.

Slicked with frost, they slipped and squished into each other as his or her grip gave away momentarily and they made all due haste down the steep chute while trying to remain as quiet as possible. Only Wulftone's powerful grip remained true, and he kept the clandestine crew from sliding all the way to the bottom.

Hand over hand, they worked even as they heard the sounds of the battle vibrating through the stones above them. With blood pounding in their ears, the intruders tried to silence their breathing—and then they came to a hard stop.

"The tunnel ends," Wulftone whispered.

"Lemme see," Sam said. He and Wulftone skootched around some so that Sam could get a look at the wooden panel. He scratched the wooden plank and sniffed. "Cedar. It's probably the exact same construction as the topside door."

Sam fished out his pocket knife and extended the corkscrew. Quickly and methodically he bored a peephole through the thin wood and the porous stone before pressing is face against the spy hole.

"I see her!" he said excitedly. "They have her tied to the altar. He's got a knife—they're going to sacrifice her!"

The tentacles of the abyssal auraphage snapped to attention and looked directly at Sam's peep sight. It snarled and the rotting goatman looked up and at the false wall.

"Intruders!" it snarled, clutching the yellowed, tattered half of a broken book in hands protected by leather gloves.

Before the sentries in the room could turn to react, Wulftone busted through. He ripped into the guards nearest the door with his claws as Sam rolled to the ground and dove behind cover. Jackie, Gita, and Harken all tumbled out after him.

Sam dodged a few bursts of enemy fire and crawled perilously close to the altar—far closer to danger than he'd been yet. Harken rolled under the next wave of blasts and came up on his knees next to the archaeologist, mowing down a crowd of scaly cultists. He laid down suppressive cover-fire, looking frantically for the goatman he knew had to be close, but couldn't find him.

With blaster fire flying all around and bursts of concussive shrapnel punctuating the air, Harken blew Jackie a kiss and winked from the eye of the storm. "Go save her, Sam," Harken nodded to Shandra, who lay only a few meters away, bound and wild-eyed on the profane altar. "I've got you covered." He popped in a fresh power cell and bathed the area beyond the Cleric of Veritas with deadly energy.

Jackie and Gita joined Harken's cover fire as Wulftone protected their flank with his powerful claws. Sam slid across the floor with more than enough protection.

Harken's eyes caught sight of a darquematter carving just on the other side of the pillar he leaned against for cover. He glanced back to Sam, who used his tiny knife to cut feverishly at Shandra's bonds. Harken looked back to the artifact that he intuitively knew was the hierophanticus necessary to open the gate.

He leapt around the edge of the column and hurried towards the arcane carving, while keeping his enemies pinned down with his rifle. He reached out to grab the hierophanticus just as Shandra rolled off the table and into Sam's arms.

Suddenly, the four-legged tentacle beast bound around the corner and leapt towards Harken with unbelievable speed and ferocity. It tore through Harken's midsection before he could react with anything more than a scream. The abyssal monstrosity plunged its head into Harken's torso with bone-crunching power and wrapped the tendrils of its wicked maw around the soldier's spine before shaking with unbelievable violence.

Harken's body snapped and thrashed like a rag doll. Blood splattered everywhere as the beast shook its prey to pieces, slicking the kill zone with gore and effluence.

Jackie stood to her feet, dumbstruck for a split second. Grief and rage suddenly overtook her, and she charged towards the next closest pillar, mowing down her enemies, screaming the whole way.

Sam escorted Shandra towards the escape tunnel and helped push her up the slippery slope. He looked back to find the vyrm forces drawing closer to protect the glowing, eldritch portal that had opened from Harken's sacrifice—the auraphage had keyed in on him, knowing his blood could split the veil.

A tunnel vision of rage—Jackie tried to kill the murderous animal. It proved lightning fast and leapt to safety after she burned its hind legs with a superficial wound.

With everyone else preoccupied, the goatman walked through the darquegate and disappeared from sight. Vyrm forces crowded the room, drawing closer to defend the Sh'logathian Herald.

"Vivian!" Jackie screamed as she caught sight of Caivev in the battle. Splatters of Harken's blood-streaked her unmistakable face.

Caivev sneered and leveled her hand cannon at her.

Jackie dodged back around her cover just in time.

"You know her?" Gita asked, yelling over the loud blasts of their enemies' weapons.

Jackie snarled through the tears in her eyes and sorrow in her heart. "Yes—and it's time for her to die. Cover me!"

Gita leaned over and laid suppressive fire from a half-crouch while Jackie rolled out to the floor and took a shot from a new angle. Her first burst of shots took down the vyrm soldiers at her enemy's sides. The next shot burned a single, smoldering hole through Caivev's forehead.

Caivev's eyes crossed and then rolled back into her skull. Her body collapsed into a heap and a wisp of smoke puffed from the blackened hole through her brain.

"Fall back!" Wulftone howled, retreating slow enough to cover the girls' retreat. His body bore multiple wounds and burn marks from the overwhelming enemy forces. "There are too many!"

More and more vyrm poured into the room from another side-door on the far side of the room. Their only hope was for the diversion team to punch through the main hall and come with enough force to push the enemy back so they could steal the hierophanticus and close the portal before the goatman returned.

The Mexico City waterways were barely more than overgrown canals. Their edges crept closer as they neared their wetland destination in the low parts of Xochimilco. A dread silence crept over Claire and her companions as they drew closer to the Isla de las Muñecas. The warning given by Las Siete Muertes must've been effective—not even birds dared to chirp as they drew closer.

"My map says it's just up here past the Island of the Dead," Jenner scrolled through information on Claire's smartphone as she piloted the aquatic skiff.

She'd turned off the gasoline engine a half mile back and switched to the silent, electric trolling motor Jose must've had installed in order to fish the overgrown canals. Claire merely grimaced.

"An appropriate name," Zabe muttered under his breath.

The only sound they made as they approached were the gentle whirs of the electric prop and the brushing of lily pads and other vegetation against the hull as Claire turned off of the main trunk and onto a smaller, reed-lined waterway which would lead directly to the haunted island. No one on the boat dared utter a sound; each one looked back and forth at each other, not caring to admit that it sounded as if childlike laughter floated on the gentle breeze.

Ahead, a crude sign had been painted on a sheet of corrugated steel. It simply read *Isla de las Muñecas.* "Island of the Dolls," Claire whispered a translation to her companions as they cleared the bushy stalks.

Trees hung over the water, each adorned with hundreds of dolls. Their haunted foliage partly obfuscated the dilapidated buildings surrounding the boat landing. Each structure leaned with various states of disrepair; strings from tree to tree tethered the creepy tourist location with a chain gang of hanging dolls weathered by the elements and blackened by the palsy, which hung over the nest of evil.

A collection of trajinera style tour boats had beached on the banks, not bothering to properly tether at the landing. Below the child-like effigies, a collection of human bodies lay in a heap at the landing. Blood leaked from the pile.

"Las Siete Muertes," Claire muttered.

"Not *everyone* here must've been with the vyrm," Zabe noted.

Claire nodded in agreement. "Probably the boat drivers."

Jenner looked up from the data as he scanned. "Legend says that a young girl drowned here and haunts the island. The caretaker who found her body began leaving out dolls for the spirit of the girl and continued bringing her whatever he could find. People say that..."

Zabe pointed, and Jenner followed his finger. All the dolls and severed plastic or porcelain heads had turned to watch and mark their arrival.

Jenner swallowed the lump in his throat. "People say they do *that.*"

The warriors slid off the boat as quietly as possible and Zabe shifted back into his lycan state. Using his powerful muscles, he tipped the boat up until he could tip the prow below water. He waded in and fully submerged the boat below the murky depths where the muck and invasive vegetation would conceal the craft, for Jose's sake.

He quickly returned and regrouped with his team. Shucking the bloody cloth from his celestial sword, he pulled the cloak around his body to provide any additional camouflage he could get. Zabe's ears perked up; he was sure he could hear the ethereal singsong of dolls whispering dark things to each other in a fiendish, indecipherable language.

Claire drew closer to his side. The worried look on her face and the faces of the others meant he wasn't the only one hearing fell voices.

She pointed and guided them through the silent landing and old buildings. Eyes watched them from everywhere and from every angle. The damp earth silenced their footsteps, but only made the feeling they were being watched that much more agonizing.

"I can feel a palpable wickedness," Claire whispered to Zabe.

Zabe listened and stretched out with his senses. Tens of thousands of dolls blanketed the trees of the overgrown island; creaking cables that tied off in every direction seemed to groan a dire welcome as the breeze pulled the strings and made severed doll limbs and disembodied parts chatter hungrily.

"The island?"

Claire nodded as she picked her footing through the undergrowth and moved deeper into the forest. "But more than that—I feel *him*... Akko Soggathoth—almost as dark as Sh'logath. I can sense him further ahead."

Zabe put a hand on her to halt their progress. "Can *he* sense *you* as well?"

Claire closed her eyes and concentrated. Several moments passed as she stretched out with her astral senses. "I do not think so. I think those parts of me that are so deeply Bithia have been subconsciously masking our presence. Sometimes she does that... covers for my weaknesses."

Zabe gave her an understanding nod, then leaned down and kissed Claire on the cheek. He knew her struggles were wholly different from what any other person faced.

She pointed ahead in the direction of the fiend and his hierophanticus. They took two steps forward and Jenner tripped on an old stump hidden amongst the bent grasses. A cloud of noisy birds leapt into the air, complaining as they fled.

All eyes turned and locked on the youth. Jenner grimaced apologetically, feeling as disappointed in himself as anyone else.

"I think they know we're here now."

Jackie roared and fired the last few rounds from her weapon around the edge of a colonnade where she bunkered for cover. The shrill whine followed by her string of exasperated profanity alerted the nearby vyrm that her power cells had depleted.

She unstrapped a short sword, which all corpsmen wore. A hissing reptilian soldier jumped around the corner before she was ready and she threw her useless rifle at him, bashing his face in. The bleeding enemy recoiled and pounced as she unsheathed her blade and relieved him of both arms.

Jackie snatched up the armless vyrm's disruptor and a fistful of energy cells. Leaning against the pillared entry to the ceremony room, she spotted the twisting, shimmering portal where the goatman had entered the Darque. To her left, allies tried to push through the last hallway to seize control of the room and seal the darquegate.

The pitched battle raged relentlessly and regardless of Jackie, Gita, and Wulftone's attempts to flank the opposition and soften them up enough to aid at all.

"They keep coming!" Gita screamed. She pointed to the tunnel on the far side of the room where the reptilian cultists kept pouring through. "We've got to plug that hole!"

Wulftone growled his assent as he raked his claws across a group of assailants. Another throng tried to gang tackle him; the suicidal maniacs pressed the giant lycan, running headlong for him just to keep him occupied.

Gita launched herself forward, towards a closer support column. She shrieked and toppled as a disruptor blast caught her in the bicep and spun her to the ground.

Jackie roared and darted through an open section. Blaster fire trailed after her. Skidding on her knees, she slid through Harken's eviscerated remains.

Slicked with the blood of her would-be lover, she hardened her heart with stone and grit. Jackie rummaged through Harken's belongs, turning out his pocket. A grenade fell out along with a bloodstained photo of her and him taken shortly after their meeting: when they'd purged the Prime of Nitthogr's followers.

Jackie activated the explosive and chucked it at the far side of the room. Her accuracy had always been good; the bomb landed just inside the door where the vyrm came from.

The temple rumbled and shook as the grenade detonated. Dust rained throughout and the tunnel which defenders came from collapsed in a heap of rubble.

Harken's soldiers and their fellow corpsmen finally began inching down the tunnel without reinforcements to replace the fallen reptile warriors. They'd just begun creeping into the ceremony room when the darqueportal pulsed with bright light and then winked out.

A cadaverous goatman looked across the room and locked gazes with the red-eyed Jackie. He screeched with hellish fury, and the alien tentacle beast loped out to his side from somewhere in the darkness.

Jackie howled with rage at the murderous fiend. Her fellow warriors had just finished beating through the alien defenses; they rushed to her side just in time to see the terrifying enemy standing defiant and successful.

Blackness oozed off of the humanoid creature. The ethereal dark consumed the light around him like an aura of nonexistence which devoured all light and goodness around him. It uttered ancient words heard with their ears but somehow understood in their hearts. "Now you will know the power of Akko Nuggezeth!" The words threatened them with madness as much as terror.

The inky fire flickering around Akko Nuggezeth intensified as he channeled the dark fire into the abyssal auraphage. The tentacled beast writhed and shrieked as Akko Nuggezeth visibly slumped and retreated into the shadows after imbuing the creature with power.

Gita, back on her feet, joined Jackie's side. They and the rest of the warriors from the Prime stared in horror as the demon shook violently and erupted in size. It twisted, seeming to turn itself inside out as it grew into a giant, worm-like form. Gita shrieked and fired a few shots into the monster's thick hide.

It snapped its giant head-like segment towards her. It fixed Gita with its keen, eyeless senses and brayed. Toothy, tentacle-like proboscises flapped in the air as its roar blew hot wind from the jagged, human-sized maw.

The army opened fire, but the thing shrugged off the blaster fire which merely scorched and puckered the creature's skin. It moved for Gita with quicker speed than seemed possible. The thing didn't bother weaving through the support columns; it crashed through pylon after pylon as it pursued its prey.

Gita turned and fled towards the safety of the troops, who poured more fire into it. As it lunged for the soldiers, the ceiling cracked and groaned as if the temple's spine had broken. Overhead stones began to buckle and shift tenuously.

With Gita in full retreat, the rest of the army followed. Their blasts remained ineffective as they charged back up the ramped tunnel. The creature's tentacles snapped onto the entry's colonnades and tore them free, collapsing the hall and sealing the escape route.

An eerie silence followed once the rubble stopped falling. Wulftone gently took Jackie by the arm.

Luckily, the beast stared only at the broken exit, confused by its prey's escape. Wulftone put a finger to his lips to keep Jackie silent as they tiptoed backward slowly. His sensitive lycan ears detected more than just Akko Nuggezeth's dread creature—the Herald remained in the room, too.

Clapping with glee and clutching a tattered half-book, the corptic, rotting goatman staggered from the shadows, followed by the tarkhūn icelord.

Both praised the giant worm as if it were a proud dog returning from a successful hunt.

Nearing the far wall, Jackie's heel struck a broken shard of stone and sent it skittering across the floor. The beast, Akko Nuggezeth, and the remaining vyrm turned their heads as one.

A tentacle rocketed out like a scorpion stinger as the monster leapt forward, guided by impulse. Wulftone snatched Jackie away just in time and darted towards the secret tunnel as fast as his legs would carry them.

He scrambled through the small opening, pushing the bewildered Jackie up the tunnel. The giant smashed against the secret aperture. Wulftone didn't wait to assess the situation as he clambered up the tunnel, following Sam Jones's voice as he shouted from the mouth of the tunnel.

Behind them, the crunching sounds of breaking stone rattled the air and set his teeth on edge as the last remaining exit crumbled. Suddenly, the floor beneath them heaved momentarily and then settled as something deep within the temple collapsed—and then everything went quiet.

# Chapter Fifteen

Zabe directed the other two teams with hand signals, silently sending them off to flanking positions as they crept through the lush vegetation. A thick, green canopy hung high above them, enclosing the jungle-like habitat on all sides.

The other teams disappeared into the misty darkness. Dense foliage blotted out most of the sunlight and significantly cooled the Mexican midday heat.

Even though the island was barely more than an oversized city block, finding their enemy within the slough would prove difficult. Trees grew in thick copses and made a convoluted maze filled with shifting shadows and stringers of doll parts.

Barely functioning peekaboo eyes on decaying dolls followed their movements into the grey and green landscape. Laughter floated in the mist—as if some child's disembodied spirit giggled, expecting new playmates that would dwell with it for eternity.

Zabe laid a hand on Claire's shoulder.

She leaned against him. "I can sense him." She pointed towards the heart of the wild growth. "It's an evil like I've never felt before... not like Sh'logath's raging hunger... it's more palpable—malicious."

He nodded and took point, making sure he could defend her from any unexpected surprises. Zabe walked forward, holding the Stone Glaive at the ready.

The island air fell silent—too silent. More than merely muffled and stymied air trapped in a greenhouse effect: the wildlife felt the tension of Akko Soggathoth's malfeasance.

Zabe's crew stopped mid-step as shouts erupted from the nearby team. Gunfire rang through the trees and birds which had been hunkering down for safety sprang skyward, squawking in terror. The brush shuddered and shook as the team scattered; Zabe hoped it was defensive. He didn't dare call out and give away their position.

The lycan beckoned his team forward, and they tiptoed around a macabre circle of trees, brandishing long ruddy streaks where rusty spikes stained the limbs of crucified dolls. Ahead and off to the side, more screams and movement as something attacked the other team. An other-worldly roar echoed through the deadened air and the bushes shook.

Claire followed closely on Zabe's footsteps, which quickened as they hurried through the natural corridors of thorns and doll parts. Stretching out his senses, he could feel a presence watching them—hungry and primal.

Something snarled and shook the bushes behind them. Yardi screamed as some kind of beast charged from the undergrowth with lightning speed. It tore his leg off cleanly as it rushed past, sending him reeling to the ground.

The others barely had time to react to their friend, whose stump spurted blood across the path. By the time they'd turned, they only caught sight of the creature's tentacles wrapping around Yardi's other leg as it yanked him into the thick underbrush.

Yardi shrieked and left ten deep furrows through the soil as his fingers clawed the ground in protest.

Vyrm dropped to the soft soil like wraiths in the jungle. They were barely visible beneath camouflaged outfits similar to the cloaks the intruders wore.

Claire yelped and turned to fire her weapon. Jenner already had his rifle shouldered; his rapid-fire burned through the foliage and scattered the nearly invisible enemies. In the thick growth, they couldn't be found without help.

Pointing to a nearby green patch, Claire reached out with her senses and detected their thoughts. She could barely find their attackers' minds through the overwhelming evil of Akko Soggathoth's presence. "In there!"

Jenner blasted the area while Zabe concentrated his lycan senses on the trail ahead of them. Something ahead stalked them. The youth's blasts flushed the invisible vyrm out of hiding.

Spireth snap-fired a trio of pulse bursts and a scaly body slid to a permanent stop on the path. "At least they're not shades," he muttered. "We'd never find them."

Like a flash, the snarling abyssal auraphage cut across the trail. It lashed out with the vicious barbs retracted within the powerful mandibular tentacles; the spurs sliced through Zabe's torso as if his thick hide were made of paper.

Zabe roared in pain—the beast disappeared so quickly that he couldn't react. Flesh hung from his pectoral muscle and exposed the bones of his ribcage. He was uncertain that his armor, damaged by the earlier rocket explosion, could have withstood the insanely sharp claw even if it was intact.

Claire wheezed as she felt his pain on the psychic plane. She stepped forward to try to help but he warned her back. She was too important to let the alien beast near her.

He whistled through his teeth and stretched his muscle back into place. Sensing the predator's opportunistic hunger, Zabe stepped back just in time to avoid its next lunge even as his muscle fibers began to stitch together solidly enough to hold the wound closed and cover his ribcage.

Jenner fired another burst into a vyrm that Spireth drew into the open. He oozed satisfaction when the attacker crashed into a heap against a tree, ripping a collection of dolls from their age-old perches.

Something hissed all around them as if the dolls' spirit grew angry at his irreverence.

Zabe keyed in on something with his instincts and slashed the Stone Glaive just in time to catch the bestial predator and turn it to stone, stopping it in its tracks. But it wasn't the source of the hissing.

A vyrm dropped from a high branch, driving a spear through Jenner's midsection, lancing through him, shoulder to hip. The polearm pinned the young corpsman to the ground, where he howled in agony.

The hissing assailant cackled. His laugh ceased immediately as Spireth's short sword flashed from behind the sneaky enemy and severed head from neck.

Jenner's teammates rushed to his side and provided medical attention. Unbelievably, the weapon missed his vital organs. While he would survive, the torment he would endure until they removed the spear remained almost intolerable—and it was too risky to do it in the wild.

He downplayed his anguish and spoke in a halting, breathless speech. "Go on. You've got to complete the mission," he urged them. "Just don't leave me here too long!"

Zabe nodded and dosed him with a powerful painkiller that helped the wounded soldier relax slightly. "We'll be back for you," he promised, turning to move towards their goal. Zabe glanced at Claire. "Still going the right way?"

She nodded dizzily after stretching her mind into the ether. "Yes. He is close."

A radio clipped to the headless vyrm's belt rumbled with a squelchy voice. Spireth snatched the device and turned it up. Only Claire cocked her head with understanding at the vyrm dialect they spoke. Bithia had been well-versed in linguistics—including those used by the enemies.

Claire took the communicator and spoke with raspy, hissing words and in as gravelly a voice as possible. The other end responded and signed off.

"They think we've all been neutralized." She grimaced. "All other targets are down, they said."

Zabe's face darkened. "Then we're all that's left. We must succeed or all is lost."

Idrakka staggered through the darkened belly of the frozen temple. He dusted the frosty detritus from his scaled face and activated the chemical light sticks which burned brilliantly. Using so much of his power had grossly overexerted him—even though the climate had helped sustain his abilities for longer than he'd ever thought possible. The vyrm warrior badly needed rest.

Lifeless bodies lay strewn across the chamber, stretched out upon the floor or heaped in mounds with blaster wounds still smoldering. He shook his head at the wastefulness of it all but could merely shrug—his kinsmen had died for their beliefs... yet he believed there was a better way: a better leader. But for now, he obeyed his orders, and they came only from Caivev until he was instructed otherwise.

The icelord grimaced at the rotting Fifth-Son of the Winnowing. The cadaverous man-goat monstrosity sneered at the vyrm who assessed the damage. Akko Nuggezeth hovered around the fallen, worm-like atrocity that had caused the cave-in. He dotingly checked it for life signs, appearing to care more for the vile creature than for the ranks of fallen devotees.

Satisfied that the fallen creature had surpassed his ability to resuscitate, Akko Nuggezeth joined Idrakka near the fallen body of Caivev. The timeless denizen of the Darque stretched out his hand

and forced the corpse to relax. Its skin sagged momentarily and then tightened back into the visage of Jarkara. Only the blackened hole in the shade's head remained the same as the shapeshifter regained its true form.

"Pity," Akko Nuggezeth hissed. "I was beginning to find him intriguing. Then again, I always find traitors so interesting." He fixed Idrakka with a knowing gaze.

Idrakka frowned sorrowfully at Jarkara but held his emotions in check—he could mourn for him later, in private. He thumbed the communicator on his shoulder and the LED flashed as it reached out to establish contact with their support team. He didn't bother to verify or ignore the goatman's accusation. "Do you have the book?" Idrakka reached out his empty hand and beckoned for the second half of the empty, blank tome just as Akko Soggathoth had instructed him.

Akko Nuggezeth gave him a wry smile and held it up teasingly. He showed the vyrm Akko Thakkanon's sigil where he'd made his mark, but he did not surrender the book. "It was difficult to force him into the book. The eldest will resist even further."

Idrakka flexed his hand and beckoned for it.

The goat man curled his lips contemptuously. "I know what lies in your heart, *tarkhūn*."

Idrakka shrugged as the collapsing superstructure rumbled. "I don't care what you may or may not know." He pulled a folded paper from his hip pouch and grinned. "And I don't have time for your trickery."

Akko Nuggezeth's eyes widened in unexpected fury when Idrakka produced the page where his name had been bound. Before he could say anything—either use his wicked magics or beg and barter, Idrakka licked the charcoal cleanly from the seal.

The beast burst into a cloud of thick black mist with no discernable form. Like a cloud of frenzied carrion beetles, he faded into a thin mist which the mystic page inhaled. Ripped away from his avatar, he left behind a scared Central American teenager to stand in the frigid Antarctic cold. Naked and shivering, the boy held the book—unsure of how he'd gotten here. His last memory was a strong hand clamping over his mouth and a blindfold hobbling his senses.

Idrakka plucked the book from his grasp. Laying the loose leaf of parchment in place upon the codex, the binding reached up from the spine and knitted the missing page back into the larger volume.

He slipped away into the blackness, picking his way through the rubble that led him back to the huddled members of the Black as they gathered, ready to rejoin their larger assembly. A burning triangle split the darkness a moment later and allowed him to slip away to a warmer climate, leaving the lost and confused avatar for Akko Nuggezeth to freeze to death in the heart of a pyramid buried at the South Pole.

Tay-lore slid out of the carriage seat of an anti-grav sled. His transport sat amongst a small fleet of others that waited for the return of the Antarctic expedition.

The android directed traffic and made sure that medical attention was easily accessible and prepped nearby to treat frostbite. He let his robotic eyes record every detail; this had been the largest inter-planar operation since the Syzygyc War.

Like strobes of lightning, the gate flashed and sizzled as his friends winked into existence in the Prime. They exited the platform single-file. Tay-lore long ago proved he was no genius when it came to body language, but even he could sense the dour mood and somber quiet that indicated a failed mission.

He watched with rapt interest as his shivering friends headed for treatment. The flashes began to slow in frequency, and he hadn't seen his closest friends yet return.

The android equivalent of relief washed over him when Sam Jones staggered off the teleport area; Shandra walked beside him, leaning heavily on the archaeologist's strength. Finally, the last few flashes came; Wulftone followed Jackie away from the ancient dimensional-gate.

Tay-lore shifted nervously. He desperately wanted to know what had happened but felt wrong to ask if the information hadn't been volunteered.

Despite her flushed cheeks, Jackie didn't stop at the medical area. A nurse called after her for a check, but the stubborn, distraught girl muttered, "It's not much worse than Minnesota in January—and I walked to school."

She stormed off under a gray mood. As Jackie drew close, Tay-lore gently put a hand on her shoulder. "What happened? Where is Harken?"

Jackie looked at him with such pain and grief in her eyes that the android regretted the question. He had no idea how to process the emotion he read in her. He only wished he hadn't asked.

Exhaling in tight measures, she shook her head almost imperceptibly. She shot a look back at her peers. Wulftone stood with Gita as the doctors dressed her arm; the superior officer stood diligently with his wounded troops, who'd obeyed their duty at great cost.

Jackie grimaced while her heart broke—it was as brave of a face as she could muster. She only wished that Wulftone could be with her through the pain tearing her up inside. But she knew she couldn't let him inside that world of pain and grief... maybe if she'd made a choice between the two suitors prior to Antarctica, but not now. Fate had decided... and *it* had eliminated Harken—*not Jackie.* She instinctively knew Wulftone would always resent her for that.

Her stone façade began to crack as she noticed Harken's dried blood splattered on her forearms. A deep sense of shame burned through her veins: a great man had just lost his life and here she was wallowing in self-pity because of her love life?

If she could've cried, Jackie would have—but she'd run out of tears. She turned away from Wulftone and laid a hand back on Tay-lore while nodding to the auto pool. "Get me out of here... back home... wherever. I don't care. Let's just go."

The android wasn't quite sure how to proceed. He didn't have enough data or experience with grief, and so he followed her lead and walked her to a transport, activated the hover mode, and took her away.

Wulftone watched Jackie leave with Tay-lore. Part of him approved, the other part urged him to chase her. He gave it serious consideration and then he looked over the chaos of the triage area. Responsibility weighed him down and he knew his presence was needed here.

With a stressed sigh, he ran his fingers through his hair, trying to squeeze out whatever tension he could. He desperately wished for someone else to share his burden with in that dark moment—Zabe, Zahaben, Shardai—even Harken. Wulftone relaxed his grip and released his hair, suddenly wondering if, of all things, he might make himself go bald from the stress... *would my lycan form be bald, too?*

At this rate, he assumed he might find out.

Zurrah lay slumped in a heap against the stone wall. The musty air tickled his nose, and he did his best to pretend he'd slipped into unconsciousness while the two vyrm argued nearby.

He slowly, methodically, used a small piece of metal wire he'd snagged during his attempted escape to pick the lock on his gyves, just like his father had taught him. The mechanisms were tricky, but he felt certain he'd figured out how to trip the internal tumblers and free himself—as long as his captors didn't pay too much attention.

"See! Look at this, Theera... the blood is congealing, and it's dried at the edges."

"Not yet!" Theera argued. It had been his life that the ancient demon threatened if the Koth gate closed. "It can wait a few minutes before we bleed him again."

The vyrm accomplice glared at him suspiciously.

Theera explained, "If the doors shut, Akko Soggathoth will kill us..."

"He'll kill *you*. I'm fine."

Theera continued. "If the boy dies, *Caivev* will kill *us*."

"You don't know that."

"Don't you know who that is?" Theera pointed at the boy.

Zurrah held his breath and made sure not to even twitch.

"It's the other son of General Zahaben."

Zurrah's wrists hurt as he wriggled the wire through the keyhole, praying that it wouldn't break. He felt suddenly old and bone-weary as his captors argued over who was a more reviled warrior, his brother Zabe who had killed Nitthogr but not prevented the Black from scattering to diaspora throughout the multiverse, or his father who'd kept their kind so vigilantly in check, but barely turned back the old sorcerer so many times.

They kept arguing even as they walked towards the teen. Zurrah froze at their approach, feigning unconsciousness. He clasped his hands over the lock to hide the wire pick hanging out from it and hoped they wouldn't notice.

He groaned as if being woken from slumber as they manhandled his limp body and unsheathed a dagger. Zurrah made sure not to resist as they cut him and drained a cup full of blood to keep the arcane darquegate open.

Working the knife, Theera's friend grumbled, "We should just cut his neck and take all of it right now. One less son of Zahaben to worry about."

Theera clucked his tongue condescendingly and then retreated to the door with a vessel full of blood.

Grimacing through the raw pain of his wound, he concentrated all of his energies on the lock. The wire slowly twisted, bound tightly against the mechanisms, and halted. Zurrah gave it a slight jiggle, and it clicked free.

He breathed a sigh of relief. Zurrah felt rage rise up within him as he tried to silently slip out of the chains, keeping a vengeful eye on his captors.

The lengths of chain rattled louder than he liked and Theera's companion turned and locked eyes with him while the other vyrm freshened up the door's "paint."

Zurrah, the other brother trained by the great Zahaben, leapt towards the soldier who reached for the dagger sheathed at his hip. They locked into a grapple. The vyrm snarled and bared his fangs; Zurrah head-butted him and busted the sharp teeth inward.

As the bleeding vyrm reeled from the feisty captive, Zurrah snatched up the dagger and slashed Theera across the chest. He turned and sprinted into the only hallway leading to the gate-room in the bowels of the ancient facility.

Blaster-toting vyrm were already rushing towards the deep chamber at Theera's shrieks. They drew their weapons, but Zurrah backpedaled before any of them could get a shot off. A siren rang out as the sentries scrambled and sent up the alarm.

Zurrah sprinted back into the room and rushed towards the Gates of Koth. Theera lay strewn on the ground, trying to keep pressure on the wound. The other guard tried to prevent the youth from entering the gate, but Zurrah's hands flashed like lightning.

The sinister vyrm trooper who'd wanted him dead fell to his knees, holding the fatal cut across his throat as he gurgled a curse upon the teen. Zurrah stared into the condemned one's eyes for just a second—his gaze let the captor know he'd heard the creature's murderous threats which had now come back to roost.

Footsteps echoed in the corridor and Zurrah leapt through the gate, not knowing what to expect. He charged ahead through the darkness, plunging into the Darque.

Tay-lore led Jackie by the hand as they entered the restaurant in the rebuilt commercial district of the Royal City. She sat down as if she was a ghost.

The android cocked his head and watched her. She didn't do anything. She merely was. And she was not well.

A waiter came out from the back and Tay-lore waved him off. The man nodded and watched from a distance so he could get an order whenever they were ready. With all the recent military commotion, there were no other customers.

Finally, Tay-lore broke the silence. "You are an outsider. You do not really belong here, Jackie."

That got her attention. Jackie glared balefully at her host.

"Perhaps that came out wrong," Tay-ore shifted defensively. "You are an outsider, like me. Do you know the history of my kind—the *homo diurnus*?"

She shook her head, but he had her attention.

"'Men of the Day,' they called us when we first came into sapience... we were the next step in evolution, said the Technites who created us. But even among *them*, I was an outcast. I was weak and flawed—different.

"The Diurnans took control of their own destiny. They killed the Technites and began reproducing until they were capable of waging a war against Bithia's grandfather during his reign. My brothers were strong, cold, unfeeling. They were monsters—but they were family." His automated voice sounded almost pained.

"Unlike them, I suffered from indecision. I saw value and beauty in organic life and in emotion. They cast me out because I was weak—and I was alone."

Jackie reached across the table. "You weren't weak," she insisted.

"Weakness is a matter of perspective," Tay-lore countered. "I have long struggled with my identity as an almost-person and that will probably continue long after today."

He stopped talking. Jackie waited for more. Finally, he continued.

"In the end, I am here and they are not. I still exist while they have been extinguished. My brothers, flawed as they were, are all dead... Sometimes, when it boils down to it, what really matters is enduring—surviving the hardships. At times, simply 'being here' is what matters in the face of all the could-have and should-have possibilities."

Jackie looked at her friend and determined to pull herself out of the pit she'd fallen into. If the android could grapple with such deep emotions, perhaps it was not beyond her ability. "I just don't know what to do next."

"We cannot ever go back," he said, "but we can choose to embrace what we have. Begin there."

Jackie bit her lip. She had a lot to think about—but first, her appetite had returned.

Zabe, Claire, and Spireth paid extra attention to their feet. Their footsteps landed on soft earth, clear of dry reeds or bracken.

They approached the nearby clearing as silently as hungry predators and hunkered down below a stringer full of doll heads. All of their lifeless, yet eager eyes seemed to stare either at them or at the grisly scene playing out fifty meters away where a huge tarkhūn tore the nun's habit from her head and laid the bound woman upon an altar made of piled rocks and sticks.

"Skrom," Zabe hissed, recognizing the massive reptile warrior from their last encounter. A team of scout vyrm returned from where they'd gone to dispatch a team of invading Corpsmen.

Caivev walked through the middle of the company. "Where are those two other teams?" she complained as she walked, digging into her sack for the ancient artifact that would unlock the gate when combined with the nun's blood.

A lithe man dressed as a priest stepped around the odd stone that protruded from the earth at the clearing in the island's center. He grinned at the imprisoned nun who struggled below Skrom's mighty paw and a tall Rottweiler flanked him obediently.

"There's something wrong about that dog," Claire whispered to the others, rubbing her temples.

Spireth looked at her inquisitively.

"Don't you feel this heat? Why isn't the dog panting to keep cool?"

Zabe pointed to two sets of eyes watching them from across the clearing. He signaled the two corpsmen silently, telling them to stay put until he gave the word. "It's Murdo and Tahnak. They were with Chira. At least we're not totally alone."

The nun seemed to recognize the priest as he approached her. When he reached up and tore his collar off, terror overtook the woman. His facial features melted away, and he stretched taller as a horrific half-goat-half-man. The dog likewise shifted into the abyssal auraphage: the tentacle-faced tracking beasts they'd encountered on the trail.

Akko Soggathoth stroked the cheek of the nun with mock compassion. He wiped away a tear that rolled down her face.

Claire bristled at the sight. She could identify with the woman's terror—Nitthogr and the Heptobscurantum had been equally villainous.

Caivev turned and walked to the eldritch plinth. The oddly smooth, leaning obelisk wore etchings of arcane runes that had a distinctly vyrm flair to the well-trained eye. After placing the hierophanticus into a hollow in the stone, the engraved glyphs seemed to glow with a strange light.

"We've got to go now," Spireth urged. "We have to stop them before it's too late."

Zabe held up a hand and looked into the distant sky. "Wait. Don't you hear that?"

Claire and Spireth searched the horizon. The abyssal auraphage also turned, pointing its face to the tree line's canopy. Suddenly they all heard it: the distinct thumping sounds of a helicopter—*and it was close.*

"Do it!" Akko Soggathoth screamed at Skrom.

"No!" Spireth rushed out from the trees and rushed directly for the sacrifice. Zabe snarled and followed after.

Skrom grinned at the Prime's warriors and raked his claws lengthwise down her body, spilling her blood and shredding her bonds. The portal ripped open near the hierophanticus as the chopper broke past the edge of the clearing.

Zabe charged for Akko Soggathoth like a feral hunter. He glanced quickly at Murdo and Tahnak, who leapt from the foliage and joined the mad dash.

The rotting goatman sneered. He used one talon to cut his palm and then held out the bleeding hand, commanding him to stop.

Zabe staggered at the sensation that rocked his body, knocking all power out of him as if Akko Soggathoth had been capable of splitting body, spirit, and mind. Taking two more staggering steps, he lost his focus and the ability to hold the lycan form. His body melted into the softer, pink human form and he collapsed just as the helicopter opened fire.

Bullets ripped through the sky above him. Dirt scatted and pandemonium erupted in a hail of gunfire.

"Foolish darquechild," Akko Soggathoth growled at Zabe. "Where do you think that power comes from? You might certainly use it to honor your Architect King—but who do you think is lord of the realm from which it was birthed?" He hissed and seethed with both amusement and rage. "There, I am a god—and you cannot conquer me."

Barely discernible voices from the police helicopter screamed at them in two languages not to flee; both voices came warbled through the loudspeaker. A bracket-mounted fifty caliber gun opened fire again. The guns refused to stop firing on them even as they demanded surrender.

Spireth leapt forward and pulled the wounded nun into his arms. The helicopter pivoted towards them and opened fire, cutting them both down in a hail of indiscriminate lead.

The darquegate split even wider with the nun's death.

Clutching half a book in a mittened hand, Akko Soggathoth jumped through the portal. Skrom ducked his head and escorted Caivev through as well. Half of the vyrm under her command leapt into the unknown after them; the other half, those nearer to the cursed-doll forest routed for the cover of the woods.

Zabe, still bewildered, stumbled to his feet with Claire's help.

A rocket streaked overhead and the edge of the clearing exploded. Flames chucked shrieking and charred vyrm through the air. The next explosive round loaded into place and fired as the chopper systematically destroyed the eldritch site.

Claire put her arm around Zabe and guided him towards the portal. Chira's remaining two warriors each grabbed him on either side, relieving the princess of the task. Zabe stumbled as he ran the first few steps like a drunkard.

Another rocket clicked into place to launch and the chopper turned its nose to aim for those fleeing targets headed for the shimmering portal.

Zabe and Claire leapt through the unfamiliar portal even as an explosion behind them flung them through the breach and into the unknown. Ballistic fire melted the site to slag, severing any chance of a return trip.

# CHAPTER SIXTEEN

W ulftone balked at his haggard reflection in the restaurant's window. He frowned and tried to smooth away the stress lines from around his eyes, hoping Zabe, Claire, and their crew would return soon. Wulftone didn't fear that they'd fallen to the enemy—he knew his cousin could handle that—but he struggled to carry the weight of leadership. In Zabe's absence, everything seemed to fall on his shoulders instead.

From outside, he watched Jackie through the glass for a few moments longer. She looked confused; her face remained placid, but there was pain in her eyes. Wulftone knew that the kind of turmoil she dealt with might eat her alive if she didn't deal with the pain. He'd felt much the same after his parents died, before General Zahaben took him in.

Wulftone meandered through the restaurant with his eyes glued to her. He'd pursued her ever since their meeting three years prior—during the vyrm occupation when his cousin pulled the vivacious earth girl through a portal. She'd demanded that the scattered remnants of the Guardian Corps and any under the care of the Veritas help rescue her friend before the attempted Awakening. That internal fire had been what he loved most about her.

He slid into a seat opposite her, but she did not look up. That somber look on her face made him worry that the fire within her had died. Then she looked up, and he saw how brightly that pain burned behind her eyes.

"I'm sorry," he said sincerely.

She gave him a wounded smile as she struggled through the pain.

"No. *I'm* sorry," she said. "I should've made a choice between you two a long while ago."

He took her hand. "Shh. Don't worry about that or feel like you've got to carry the pain of his death all on your own. I know how bad it must hurt—we may have had our conflicts, but Harken and I were also friends."

Wulftone looked into Jackie's eyes as they glistened. He regretted how timidly he'd acted with her before. It was for fear of what Jackie endured right now: that he could love someone who would be taken from him, just like his family had been. He never wanted to feel that pain again, but as he looked at Jackie, he wanted nothing more than to risk that for her—and so he opened himself to sharing her pain for Harken.

Jackie squeezed his hand. "I know. I see that now, and that's why it was always going to be you that I chose."

Something in the way she said it convinced him that it was true. He held her hand until a waiter approached, looking at Jackie.

"The same as before, ma'am?"

She nodded. "Make it a double."

The attendant nodded and retreated as Wulftone glanced at her dubiously. "I'd been trying to take you here for a long time," he whispered. "You've been coming here all along?"

She shook her head. "No. And Harken tried to bring me as well." Fancy dining hadn't returned to the royal city since the vyrm had laid siege to so much of it in recent history. While it wasn't swanky, the modest bistro made a passable attempt at the finest place in the areas hit hardest by Nitthogr's invasion. "I came here last night with Tay-lore."

Wulftone smiled and sat back. "How did that go?"

Jackie smiled—maybe the first genuine smile since Antarctica. "It was interesting. I wanted something that nobody in the Prime could make—it's kind of comfort food for me: the thing I always ate whenever I felt sad or confused or hungry... basically, one of the best things ever."

"That Krispy Kream you talk about?"

Jackie shook her head. "Buffalo wings."

Wulftone looked at her confusedly. "I've seen that animal. They don't have wings."

Jackie chuckled. "It's just a name for the food. It's a long story, but it's actually a spicy chicken recipe. We actually ended up in the kitchen with the chefs," she laughed. "He used all that fancy processing power to come up with a pretty close recipe. He insisted that they make it special for me."

He smiled as a waiter arrived with two plates of the foreign food. "I knew the android would figure people out, yet." Wulftone felt happy that the android succeeded in demonstrating compassion—he knew Tay-lore was compassionate, but the automaton struggled to mimic humanity sometimes.

She picked up a wing and bit into the drumstick before sitting back, watching as Wulftone picked up a wing. He'd never eaten wings before and mimicked her.

Jackie laughed as Wulftone immediately guzzled a big gulp of water after eating the first wing. She smirked knowingly; food in the Prime didn't tend to lean towards a spicy palette.

He coughed and turned the tables on her laughter. "You know we don't have chickens in the prime?" Wulftone held up a fried drumstick. "These actually come from a large insect they raise in the rural areas."

Jackie merely grinned. She reached for another and took a bite. "I actually knew that already," she smiled unflappably, "and I don't even care because they taste right."

The waiter returned a few moments later with another bowl and set it down. "Apologies. I forgot the other part."

She dipped her next hot wing in the speckled white substance while Wulftone watched her, impressed with her gastrointestinal fortitude. "He also got them to facsimilate ranch dressing, as well. It helps."

Despite the apprehensive look on his face, he trusted her enough to try it again and found it more tolerable. He looked into her eyes. A moment passed between them. "Are we... good?"

She returned his gaze and nodded. "We might be better than good. Just give me a few days... I'm still not quite right, if you know what I mean."

He understood grief—probably better than he'd let on. Wulftone smiled warmly, but pledged to himself that he wouldn't be timid with her. "I have a question to ask you, then... in a few days."

She looked at him coyly—and then they both turned as a messenger rushed through the entry to the restaurant. Both could tell by the urgent way he moved that it must've been something important.

The pile of fighters tumbled into a heap inside the blazing gateway. Flames shot through the darquegate and the doorway quickly winked out of existence; the rockets must've either destroyed or dislodged the hierophanticus.

A stark silence ruled the atmosphere as soon as the raging thunder of explosions disappeared with the portal. Murdo and Tahnak jumped into a ready position, and Claire rolled to her feet. Zabe staggered to his hind legs, only to discover that he had somehow assumed his lycan form without intending to.

Standing a short distance from them stood Caivev, Skrom, and two dozen armed vyrm of the Black. Akko Soggathoth, wearing his ridiculous mittens, returned from behind the vyrm troops where he'd retrieved the spirit of his brother and bound him to the cursed book. Sneering, he paced wistfully near his minions, and the loyal, tentacled creature followed him faithfully.

Zabe and his men cloistered around the princess in order to protect her. They couldn't, however, sense or hear anything except the stark nothingness. Caivev and Skrom obviously shouted commands to their troops who took careful aim with their disruptor cannons, but those orders were muted.

The intruders from the prime looked around, desperate for suitable cover, but nothing lay nearby except blasted ground and shards of glass, not unlike the parched landscape of the post-Syzygyc War in the Vyrm's home realm. Skrom's lips were not hard to read as he shouted, "Open fire!"

Flashes of light erupted as the blasts from the impromptu firing squad lit up the creeping darkness. The bolts hit some kind of invisible wall. It either absorbed them with a kinetic ripple or deflected entirely. Two blasts ricocheted back; one zipped past Skrom's head as he screamed for them to cease fire—the other caught a gunman in the chest and dropped the enemy with a smoking hole in his torso.

Claire approached the breach with a sense of wonder. Somewhere in the distance rumbled a cracking, splintering sound as if the galaxy were encapsulated inside a crystal and some cosmic fissure had just split open in the distance.

"Princess," Tahnak cautioned.

She waved his concerns away and moved closer. Several vyrm did likewise on the opposite side. The barrier looked like a pane of glass, barely prismatic until looked at closely.

The cracking noise suddenly ripped the sky with a peal like sharp thunder. A jagged line of splintered reality shot through the barrier as Claire's companions jumped in surprise.

"We are in the Darque," Claire said plainly. Her company joined her at her side. "This whole realm is fractured and broken, fissured into compartments." She pointed at the black vyrm who seethed and hissed at her as if only centimeters separated them. "They are not really so close. The rules of distance between us aren't real anymore. You cannot feel him, but I should be able to sense Akko Soggathoth easily—like a sewer stink on a clear day... but I barely feel him, as if he was very far off."

As if in response, two of the snarling vyrm pounded on the glass. When they touched the crack, one of them burst into dust—the dust-vyrm held his form for a split second before disintegrating into a heap. The other enemy flashed with a burst of light and his body immediately rearranged itself in grotesque ways; an arm protruded from his head and the other from his belly where his surprised face also moved, except for his teeth, which replaced his eyebrows. Its eyes rolled back and its chest heaved desperately for air, suggesting that its lungs no longer connected to an airway. The creature collapsed pitifully before them.

Akko Soggathoth watched gleefully. Everything about their situation amused them.

"Stay away from the cracks," Claire stated. The warning in her voice indicated that she knew more about the cracks than from mere observation.

A wave of energy like a fell wind washed over the vyrm on the other side. Caivev glowered at them from beyond and a trio of her soldiers clutched their skulls and began screaming as madness took them. Two of them ran screaming, and a third turned on them like a rabid dog.

Skrom blasted the immediate threat in the face. One ran off into the distance, and the third charged for the crack. He hit it like a bird against a window and knocked himself senseless before regaining his composure and his mind to no other effect.

"This place is dangerous and unstable," Claire insisted. The pulse of energy that had afflicted their enemies suddenly rushed towards them. "Get together! Quickly!" she shouted at them. "Everyone jump!"

They looked at her apprehensively.

"Do it!"

Murdo stumbled, as the chain of lightning crawled across the wasteland below. The others timed it correctly, but the energy burned the life from Murdo in the span of a heartbeat.

They watched the distant ground lightning crawl away in the distance. Murdo's smoldering corpse lay upon the burned and barren ground.

"How did you..."

"I read some of the forbidden books long ago," Claire confessed. "Bithia was intensely curious about all things."

"And this was in here?" Tahnak asked.

Claire shrugged. "Some of it. Snippets of conversations from the early age with kidnapped vyrm heretics contained references to things like this... it's difficult, however. I know these things from Bithia's experiences, so I remember them more as a feeling than like a memory. Does that make sense?"

Zabe nodded. "You can keep us safe—guide us home?"

"I hope so," she said, turning just as Akko Soggathoth and his pet approached. The goatman reached out and stuck his hand into the fissure; he and his abyssal auraphage disappeared.

A young soldier rushed over to the table once Wulftone beckoned him. Wulftone didn't recognize the recruit, meaning he must've been either fresh from training or still in it.

"What is it—urgent news?"

Nodding, he said, "You should head for the hospital right away, sir!"

Wulftone looked to Jackie, beckoning an invitation with his eyes in case she wanted to join him. They both stood and considered boxing the food while the messenger continued.

"Survivors just came back from the other expedition. Just the three survivors."

"Zabe, Claire, and who else?"

The soldier looked at him coldly. "No, sir. Neither Zabe nor Claire were with them."

Wulftone and Jackie ran out and headed directly to the hospital. They burst through the emergency unit's doors. The nurses, recognizing one of the more well-known officers under Zabe, pointed the way.

He peeled back the curtain and found the doctors working on the soldiers—all men who he'd been proud to have trained.

Wulftone's face fell at the sight of the severe injuries; something had gone gravely wrong for the Mexico City team. As informed, Claire and Zabe were not among them.

Chira sat back in a chair, charred and singed; despite his bubbled and peeling skin, Chira's injuries looked the least severe. Nearby, a group of doctors worked to remove the spear that had impaled Jenner. At the adjacent bed, a nurse finished bandaging the stump leg of a soldier who'd been nearly mummified with wraps that still soaked through with blood.

Wulftone looked at the bandaged soldier and then at Chira, who briefed him. "It's Yardi under all that gauze. He was attacked by some kind of beast before they got to the portal. I found him bleeding out in the trees next to Jenner."

He looked at the youngest of the survivors who had been skewered. "Is he..."

"They've sedated Jenner, but he was alive when I found him," Chira informed him. "They promise he'll pull through as long as they don't find any surprises. I think he'll be fine given what we went through to get back to the portal—he's a tough kid."

"Zabe and Claire?" he asked.

Chira shrugged. He had no knowledge.

Jackie could only stare at the trio incredulously. Wulftone noticed the pain welling up in her eyes and knew that she couldn't take the loss of her best friend right now. He squeezed her hand. "I'm sure they're fine," he reassured her.

Chira stood on uneasy legs and walked with them to clear the room and let the doctors work. More importantly, they could speak more openly and not risk outing confidential information. He accompanied Wulftone and Jackie to a conference room where Tay-lore waited with Claire's father, Shandra, Respan, and Trenzlr.

Wulftone eyed the last two suspiciously since he knew that they had some kind of security breach. He shook off his initial suspicion. At this point, he didn't care—they'd have to deal with the information leak later when there was time to dedicate to the problem.

Sam Jones paced the room anxiously while Chira gave his account of the events. He'd made up lost time too late as he drew off an abyssal auraphage from his strike team and not been able to get close enough by the time the rockets had begun tearing apart the Island of the Dolls. Chira suspected that Zabe and Claire lived because he had arrived in time to watch Murdo and Tahnak charge towards the enemy. He also guessed that Caivev might've perished in the destruction; Chira hadn't been able to spot any sign of escapees from the island and didn't see any energy gates, but admitted his report might be mere wishful thinking.

"I don't know what else would inspire Murdo and Tahnak with enough courage to throw themselves into such a battle except for defense of our Princess." He explained that he stumbled upon the others while doubling back the way they'd come. And dragged them to safety.

Shandra, who looked only a little worse for wear, thumbed her chin as she listened. "You didn't actually see them, though?"

Chira frowned, admitting he had not.

"I have run some scans," Tay-lore said. "Princess Claire's, uh, uniquely dualistic makeup makes her something I am able to search for. She possesses a specific energy signature. I can confirm that she is not on earth."

Sam turned to his robotic friend hopefully. "Is she maybe in some other dimension—maybe she planeswalked?"

"I am sorry. I too had hoped. She is not... anywhere."

A long, uncomfortable silence hung between them.

"Are you telling me that she is... dead?" Sam nearly puked the offending words as they fell from his lips. "No. That simply can't be." He looked around the room, but nobody would meet his gaze.

Shandra stood and tried to slip away.

"Where are you going?" Wulftone asked. Everyone perked up optimistically, hoping she had good news.

"I have a theory about why we cannot detect her, but I must consult with the head of the Veritas on it."

"You think she might live?"

Shandra measuredly nodded, wanting to give them hope—but not unrealistically so. She slipped past the doors and Trenzlr caught up with her in the hall.

"I know what you suspect," he claimed. "But if you think she's in the Darque, then we should pray to Maetha that death has found her instead."

"What do you know of the Darque?" They spoke in hushed tones.

"More than the average follower of the Devourer—the rovers still follow the old ways. We don't know all, but we still remember some things about the land that spawned us."

Shandra raised an eyebrow. "Go on."

"An ancient myth, long forgotten by most of our people, tells of the exodus to Edenya—what is now Basilisk's Desolation. The Darquelands were our ancient home before they became so broken by the unleashing of the seven demigods who became known as the Brothers of the Winnowing after the post-exilic renaissance of old vyrm lore. My people forgot that they initially *fled* to Edenya because of them and their building of the Nihil Bridge, an engine to open a door into the vast nothingness. The Tesseract may have accepted we vyrm and bound us to the fate of its dwellers, but I would not enter the Darque for any reason."

The cleric clapped Trenzlr on the shoulder. "The line of the Architect King cannot go unbroken, such has been prophesied," she said. "So, for all our sakes, I hope that you are wrong."

Trenzlr bobbed his scaly head. "I will pray that it is so."

Shandra bid him farewell and left for the Order's monastery with as much speed as she could muster.

The guards at the monastery gate stepped aside and let Shandra pass when they recognized her. She walked with purpose and nobility that defied the wounds her face bore after her recent kidnapping.

Shandra passed the outer cloister where a collection of battered tents remained. Even after several years, many of those who sought protection from the Order of the Veritas during the vyrm invasion had chosen to remain. The tranquility offered within their grounds brought an inner peace that so many yearned for. But Shandra's heart brimmed with anything but.

Beyond the public cloister of the old grounds, she went through the postern where another set of sentries stood—these ones kept out all but members of the Veritas. They nodded and granted her access.

Hurrying past the barracks wing, Shandra entertained returning to her cell and changing into something more clean and proper—but decided against it. Time was imperative; she turned back to the main path and made for the Chamber Superior, where the head of the Order would be found.

Shandra walked past the silent monk Pollando who smiled at her, himself likely returning from a meeting with him. She arrived at the door and removed her weapon, which Sam Jones had been kind enough to return. Shandra rested the battle hammer on the floor near the doorjamb and then stepped through the entry.

The High Cleric turned and greeted her as she entered. "Shandra! Good to see that you have returned safely from your trials."

She bowed. "Shjikara," she stated tensely. Their relationship had not been entanglement free, and they disagreed frequently. "I've come on an errand of some urgency."

Shjikara cocked his head with intrigue, bulging up one of his jowls. While not yet corpulent, The High Cleric exercised less self-control than the rest of the Order—a general point of contention Shandra had battled him over before. Two decades her superior, he'd never actually entertained her concerns and merely written her off as a divisive trouble-maker.

"What exactly are you looking for?"

"I need help to locate the Princess and her protector."

Shjikara's smile gleamed with pride. "I thought that surely the android's science could find your lost princess?" He spoke almost disdainfully of Tay-lore; the last of his kind, the machine race once threatened the Prime almost as much as the vyrm and Shjikara grew up in the aftermath of that conflict.

Shandra bit her lip. "He tried. We even know Claire's unique energy print, but we could not locate her or Zabe on any plane of the Tesseract."

The High Cleric leaned forward. His eyes bulged slightly and then rolled with disappointment. Shjikara muttered something under his breath about Zabe's recklessness and the potential danger of a lycan running around with such a powerful artifact weapon. "I certainly hope it has not been lost to us forever," he murmured to himself, and then reiterated his position to Shandra. "All artifacts ought to be locked within the Chamber of Secrets—especially the Stone Glaive."

She kept a straight face and stuffed her desire to slap the man deep down. He was a trained psychic, after all.

"Did you seek Pollando's assistance?"

"I came to you straight away. I needed to bring this to the top of command... I fear that the Princess is no longer bound by our existence."

Shjikara glanced at her and then quickly hid the expression that crept onto his face; Shandra didn't have to be a psychic to read his mind. His ambition was unmistakable and Shandra had long suspected that Shjikara would readily assume the throne if it vacated without an heir—prophecy aside. She had to trust that he still abided by principles that bound the Veritas and would serve and honor the daughter of the Architect King enough to lend his skills to her aid.

He grimaced slightly, guessing that she'd noticed his covetous transgression. "Let me reach out to her." Shjikara sat on a plush stool and stretched out with his astral senses. He stood a few moments later and frowned.

"Did you find her?"

"You know when there is a scent on the wind that you can't quite identify?"

Shandra nodded, and her superior rummaged in a nearby alcove. He took out an ornate box which shimmered with gilded craftsmanship and returned to his seat.

"It's like that. She must be alive—but she exists *nowhere*. This artifact will amplify my power."

He went silent and stretched out again while holding the box. Shandra watched him, trying not to acknowledge his hypocrisy concerning the artifacts lest he pick those thoughts up in the astral realm while he searched for Claire.

Shjikara's eyes opened, and he put the box away. "She lives, but is definitely outside the purview of the Tesseract. I can sense her aura like a shadow—like a trickle of water leaking in through a crack from somewhere beyond."

Shandra looked at him one last time. "She is in the Darque?"

Shjikara nodded. "I know not how she can return—especially with Zabe's presence—the line of Vangandra is tied to the Darque and it will not easily relinquish its own. The land itself will try to keep them." He looked into Shandra's eyes and instantly knew all about the struggle against Akko Soggathoth. Shjikara blanched. "You must stop this next great evil from awakening at all costs!"

Slinking down into his seat, his thoughts were suddenly flung far off. "The brothers and sisters of the Veritas will pray for your success. If you fail, it will be the last time we ever do."

The terror in his eyes shook Shandra to her core. She'd never seen him like that before. Gone was his posturing and ambition—something genuinely rattled the High Priest to his core.

Shandra nodded and then turned and left with all haste.

# CHAPTER SEVENTEEN

"Your brother Vylar has served me well," Basilisk said as he wandered through his statue garden. Like all of the evolved tarkhūn, the vyrm with special powers, his conversation partner was related to a specific bloodline. "And don't think that I have forgotten the time you served in my garden here, as all shades do for a time."

Seykarr nodded vigorously. He knew of his brother's extreme sacrifice for the sake of such deep cover, and without the promise of ever gaining release from his commission. "I live and die in your service," he hissed.

Basilisk smiled a broad, toothy grin. The shades were perhaps the most loyal amongst all his vyrm.

"There is an earth-man who has long since been asleep. His spirit was broken when my brother tried to awaken the master long ago." He handed Seykarr a ceremonial knife. "Study him. Learn to be who he was before his injury—and then replace him. You know what to do. There may come a time when I need you—but for now, you will *be* Andrew Thornton."

Seykarr grinned. He'd always wanted such a high appointment. The shade bowed low. "It will be done, my lord."

Caivev and Skrom stared hatefully at their enemies opposite them. Such a seemingly insignificant distance and only a thin pane of crystal separated them. The deaths of the troops that touched the crack left them momentarily surprised.

Akko Soggathoth returned from a nearby black monolith, which had been his earlier priority. The cosmic fissure had belched him out a hundred meters away, where it passed by the ebon spire.

He seemed amused as he approached the barrier. For a moment, Caivev thought that the goatman might either break the wall down or pass right through it. She felt certain that he could've done either, and the demon seemed somehow more powerful in this realm.

"My brother is almost as ambitious as myself," he said, beckoning for his pet. The abyssal creature trotted over to him, not seeming to sense the enemies opposite the clear wall. "I must not allow him any space to entertain thoughts of usurping my authority in matters of the Awakening."

"Let us kill the princess and be done with it," Skrom called out.

Akko Soggathoth shot her a sidelong look. "And be done with the game so soon?"

"Then where do we go from here?" Caivev asked.

The beast grinned. "Don't you humans have a saying, 'the journey is half the fun,' or something like that?"

She glared daggers at him.

"There's always a back door. I'm sure you'll figure one out." He made a show of counting the lesser beings he'd allied with. "I'm sure that at least *some* of you will survive. I only know how *I'm* leaving." Akko Soggathoth reached into the crack again and winked out of existence with his pet and broken tome.

Skrom stared. This time, the beasts did not pop back into existence nearest the dark obelisk where Akko Soggathoth's brother had been bound. "Did... did he?"

"No," Caivev guessed his thoughts—that the insane beast might've been self-destructive. "He's somehow using the crack to teleport, or maybe squeezed through it like it was some kind of travel conduit."

Three scouts returned, out of breath from their sprints. Caivev had dispatched them immediately after entering the Darque.

"You were right," the first reported. "It looks like we are in an identical version of the Earth realm... just one fallen and broken by the madness—and somehow mirrored. Everything is in reverse."

Caivev tapped her chin thoughtfully. "Then it stands to reason that we know exactly where our exit points will be."

"Other Darquegates?" Skrom asked. "How will they open from the other side? We don't have any way to force a portal open from here."

She bit her lip. "No. But we know where doors must open next, don't we?" The knowledge didn't make the route any easier, and she wished Walther's machine had proven capable of tearing a hole through the fabric of the Darque.

Skrom nodded his understanding. He dispatched half of their number to head for their Central American lair. From within the Darque, it would be the Temple of Kith, which would have to open sometime in the future.

Splitting their number meant the best odds of finding someone who could dispatch a rescue party. He turned back to find his lady staring at the ten-foot-tall, black obelisk where Akko Soggathoth had retrieved his prize.

Obsidian shackles hung from their eyelets where they'd bound Akko Skoldagrath for unknown millennia.

"One more obelisk remains," Caivev said. "We've got to make it to Akko Sxkakzacros before the gate is closed, trapping us here forever."

She glanced at the sky. The sun moved across it at a brisk pace, but in the wrong direction. "If such a thing as time even exists in this dimension," she muttered.

Zabe put a hand on Claire's shoulder. Tahnak joined them and they watched the vyrm party split ranks, heading in opposite directions.

"They must know something," Tahnak said.

"Or they *think they do*," Zabe corrected. He looked at Claire, hoping Bithia's knowledge would help them find a way out.

Claire shrugged when both men looked at her. "Let's start heading that way." She picked a random direction, and they walked. Before long, they realized that the layout was similar to that of Earth, except reversed. Odd spirit creatures meandered of their own accord—they appeared like shadowy smudges in the air—similar to a pulsing swarm of gnats in the heat. She couldn't determine if the things were alive, dead, or something entirely other.

Time didn't seem to have any meaning as they traveled. They found a number of cracks as they made their way back to the portal location by the pyramids. A spiraling web of fractures surrounded the site.

As they navigated the network of deadly, glassine splinters that seemed to hover in mid-air, another cosmic wave flashed through the realm, but to seemingly little effect. Then an ill mood seemed to settle over the three, and each shivered in terror. The pall seemed to weigh most heavily upon Claire.

"It must be some kind of psychic attack," Zabe growled, the least affected by it.

Claire suddenly collapsed, on the verge of fainting. She trembled, "I... I can feel him... his thoughts..."

"Who's thoughts?"

"Sh'logath's," she whispered. "His mind is a real thing, here—even though he may not exist."

She groaned as Zabe set her down and stood to his full lycan height. Tahnak followed Zabe's eyes and turned his head.

Someone approached in the distance: another lycan. The corporeal creature approached them from just beyond the thorny helicoid. The creature appeared every bit of a smaller copy of Zabe, right down to the Guardian Corps' armor.

Zabe's jaw dropped. Even if he couldn't recognize his brother, who was similarly transformed, there was no missing the mark scraped into the chest piece of the uniform. *Zurrah*. He'd etched the name so long ago—but he would never forget it.

"Zurrah? Zurrah!" he shouted.

"Father?" Zurrah responded. "No—Zabe?" The excited brother recognized the younger version of their father. "Zabe! It's you!"

He barreled headlong towards the three, where they remained entangled by the jagged whorl of reality fissures.

"No! Zurrah—no—don't touch it!" Zabe howled as his long-lost brother grabbed the outermost edge and ducked under it.

The three stared in complete disbelief. They'd witnessed a different action each time someone had come in contact with a fracture—and each seemed totally random.

Zurrah shrugged off their concern when they relaxed after his initial contact. They calmed down, and he stepped under the next rung. Only a few feet away from a grand reunion, he touched the next fissure.

His eyes widened with surprise and the cochlear shape flashed with brilliant violet light. In a burst of ozone, Zurrah's body wreathed in glowing purple fire. and he blinked out of existence.

Jacob Sisyphus exited the private jet and deplaned on the rolling staircase. He strolled a little way down the tarmac until he arrived at his private car. Those three minutes in the sun were plenty warm enough to make him break into a sweat. Luckily, the interior of the black sedan was frosty with the air conditioning turned to maximum.

He crawled in where Charobv and General Nyagittari sat. Sisyphus would've preferred two scantily clad females, but he'd gone to Chiriquí on business, not on pleasure. As the leader of The Seven, the Heptobscurantum cult's ruling body, he greeted them each with a nod as the car pulled away; he knew that both were vyrm plants and worked with Caivev, the commander of the Black. He also knew that General Nyagittari's real name was Kreephast.

Sisyphus grinned as he sat back and enjoyed the AC. The first time he'd met the hopeful Dunnischktet, a powerful hybrid with both human and vyrm forms, he'd shamelessly flirted with her. Now, he saw her as more of a coworker in service of Sh'logath—that is, unless she suddenly desired he let his lecherous mood take over.

The city gave way to the lush and verdant landscape as the car pulled away. Watching through the window, the wizard commented, "Almost a shame that it's all gonna be devoured... but that's the breaks," he chuckled.

Both of Caivev's generals shot him unfavorable glances. They didn't appreciate how he seemingly trivialized their faith—even if he shared their core doctrines.

"So she left you two in charge while she is gone?"

Charobv nodded. "We really expect her to arrive at any moment."

The former pro-wrestler turned-occultist smiled. "Good. I'm looking forward to working with her again." His phone got service again and chirped with a bunch of incoming messages. "I'm getting detailed reports right now about how my Mexican Heptobscurantum slowed down the enemy."

Kreephast nodded and moved on to the more important matters of business. "A new awakening is at hand. Wainsmith is ready?"

Sisyphus bobbed his head vigorously. "He is already on his way. He is one of the faithful. Percival Wainsmith knows what to do."

"Zabe? Zabe?" His hearing finally came back to him amid the shock of rediscovering his brother—only to lose him again just as quickly. He rubbed his eyes and tried to determine whether or not the whole thing had just been a hallucination.

"Did you all see him?"

Claire and Tahnak agreed with him. In this place, though, shared dreams might have been possible.

They coaxed the bewildered lycan back on task, however reluctantly. None of them were sure of their ability to think straight within the muddled madness tugging at the edges of their thoughts.

Zabe wrung his powerful hands with worry and doubt. They would have to return to the mystery of Zurrah once they were free of the Darque and its sanity draining effects.

Slipping between petrified and desiccated husks of long-dead trees, the team navigated the last few strands of the broken helix which ensconced the portal location. Zabe raked a talon across his hand and they activated the portal as normal and set it for the Prime, the only location they could be certain of on the confusing runes engraved upon a flagstone-like clearing.

The portal burbled and pulsed like a swampy ichor. Claire looked at the gateway apprehensively. In the distance, another wave rushed towards them and she launched herself into the void; her two companions likewise followed, just before the next random plague wave struck.

An acrid stench like burning hair hung in the heat that clung to the blackened version of the Prime they arrived within. Seams of magmic fire burned just below the hot surface. Puddles of tar hissed nearby and cracks opened in the crust where they zigzagged across the surface in streams of fire and crunchy, igneous embankments.

"This is not what I imagined," Claire confessed.

Tahnak pointed towards the ruins of the Royal castle and capital city. "Nothing's left," he said, awestruck.

Few of the sky-stretching monoliths that shored up the foundation remained. Most of the outer wall had been turned to slag. Old damage from some ancient war had strewn rubble from the castle for as far as the eye could see.

Zabe tried to melt his form back into a human one, but still could not. He stepped away from the portal site and his foot ground against something chitinous.

Claire joined him and untangled his foot from the threadbare scraps of cloth that bound a bleached-bone skeleton. Zabe's foot had punctured the chest cavity and caught between the bones like a Chinese finger-trap. She snapped the strapping and pulled away an old satchel that was still wrapped around the desiccated body.

The worm-eaten purse burst and a collection of darquematter trinkets poured from the bag. An old journal also tumbled out amidst the collection. Before anyone could reach for it, the sky flashed with a pulse of energy.

A new wave of psychic terror gripped them with an intense dread that neither had ever experienced. Claire screamed and collapsed, panicking as if her chest were squeezed by a vise.

"I hear him again! His mind... it's as if we're trapped within his belly!"

Zabe was least affected by it. He scooped Claire up into his arms. She shuddered as if a seizure had taken hold.

Tahnak groaned and pushed his fingers against his temples, trying to resist the madness creeping about between the lobes of his brain. Finally, he broke. Tahnak howled like an animal and ran off, screaming with lunatic ravings.

Zabe held Claire for a few moments longer, until he felt certain Tahnak wouldn't return and injure them. He crouched and leafed through the journal. The letters were nonsense and unlike anything he'd ever seen before and so he tossed it aside.

He scooped up two of the metallic baubles in case they held some significance, and then took Claire back to the portal site. He wasn't certain it would even work, but he felt sure that whatever dark machinations were in operation had been amplified in that realm.

Zabe breathed a sigh of relief when the portal opened back to the same location they'd come from. He gently lifted Claire into his arms and walked through.

Akko Soggathoth zapped into existence at the end of the crack, where it terminated near the Temple of Koth. Despite the steep incline, he could see its crown of obelisks where the tall spires raked the sky. Above them turned a gigantic, fiendish device, the Nihil Bridge—it hung in the sky like a thorny halo—an ancient machine of hellish purpose.

He and his pet strode up the incline of the blasted landscape until he came to the tunnel that led through the superstructure and into its bowels. Akko Soggathoth paused at the sealed door which led upwards and to the rooftop. He grinned and then descended by the main hall, the mirror of Kith's narthex, and then walked to where the doorway remained open, but barely.

The goatman strolled through the aperture. His pet followed him through the breach.

Akko Soggathoth gazed around the room and locked eyes upon Theera, the vyrm he'd tasked with keeping the gate alive. He paid no attention to the vyrm corpse on the floor that had obviously been harvested to keep the door active.

Terrified, Theera backpedaled when the tentacle animal began sniffing him. He didn't know what to do except submit. As the auraphage fondled the vyrm with its facial appendages, Akko Soggathoth leaned in and whispered.

"He likes you. You need not ever be afraid again—you served me well and so you will continue to serve, evermore... Theera." He breathed on the terrified sentry who suddenly calmed—never more fearless and never as dedicated to a cause as before. "Theera the Undying," Akko Soggathoth whispered into his ear.

The congealed blood on the gateway finished drying, and the door clicked shut with a subtle rumble. Eldritch locks held it fast.

Theera stood straight and postured himself at his master's service. He bowed, altogether changed.

The abyssal tentacle creature suddenly stopped and looked up as if it sensed some other, more interesting thing approaching. Akko Soggathoth turned his gaze as well; in a blur of stygian mist, he transformed into the handsome visage of his human acolyte.

Footsteps clacked in the nearby hall. Charobv, Kreephast, and a large human descended the stair. Their voices reverberated and announced their presence as they approached; the human insisted how eager he was to see the fabled door.

Charobv and Kreephast merely stared at the beast's human form. Sisyphus looked back and forth from the door to the man, equally impressed with both.

"You are the Herald?" Sisyphus beamed with glee as the wizard identified him.

Akko Soggathoth nodded with slow deliberation. "I sense power in you—both learned and... innate." His eyes fixed on the jacket pockets of the large man.

Sisyphus withdrew a medical bag from his pocket. It appeared dull and ruddy in the low light of the interior chamber, but it was obviously a device used to hold the blood of his Prime doppelganger. "You are correct," he grinned and brandished his false vampiric tooth implants, which were a holdover gimmick from his wrestling days.

The shapeshifter immediately understood that the human thaumaturge siphoned power off of his own variant from the Prime. Akko Soggathoth grinned mischievously at the thought.

"Where are Caivev and the others?" Charobv asked.

Akko Soggathoth shrugged. "They are lost in the Darque and the way is shut. Perhaps we will see them again yet before the Awakening of Sh'logath."

Charobv and Kreephast looked towards each other apprehensively. In her absence, they were instructed to carry out her detailed plans. She'd given them her wishes in the time-locked chamber to keep them private—fearing that the demon might not remain entirely trustworthy.

"Will she return," Kreephast asked directly, "or must we make other arrangements?"

Akko Soggathoth shrugged again. "We shall see." He eyed Jacob Sisyphus with optimistic scrutiny. "Do you know the signs required to open the hidden doors?"

Sisyphus smiled confidently. He perfectly performed the series of hand gestures required. "Now if you'd have marked that door with fresh reagents, it would have unlocked."

"Excellent," Akko Soggathoth stated. "You will accompany us to retrieve my final brother," he hissed. "Theera—is Akko Nuggezeth returned?"

Theera bowed. "Yes. He returned with Idrakka some time ago and was returned to the codex."

He carefully handed his servant his half of the book of names and tossed the colorful oven mitt aside. "Excellent. Carry this—we must go and retrieve the other half before someone meddles with the astral plane."

Again Theera bowed and then led the way.

Sisyphus asked, "And then to Romania?"

Akko Soggathoth looked at the cultist with dead, hollow eyes. He flashed a mischievous grin that did not align with those hard, dead eyes and then nodded.

Zabe carried Claire through the widening spiral of jagged, glassine edges. She'd only gotten worse since warping back from the forsaken version of the Prime. His normally strong and resilient fiancée trembled with frailty.

She opened her eyes and gasped a ragged breath. He saw Bithia in her pupils, trying to keep the dual-mind stitched together.

"Where are we going?" she asked weakly.

"I don't know—I just know I've got to get us out of here!"

She reached up and stroked the fur of his face. "I'm falling." Her voice trailed off as if she lost consciousness and her pupils dilated until the blackness overtook the entire eye, as if some foreign invader finally succeeded in hollowing her out.

Zabe shut her eyelids and finally burst out of the winding spiral. A flash of light zapped behind them—at the portal.

"Zabe! Stop," a voice yelled.

He crooked his head back and spotted Tahnak. The man waved as he hollered, holding a book in his hands—the journal.

Zabe didn't respond—he thought it too risky to stop for a man whose mind might've been overtaken by the will of the Devourer. Claire was too important to him to risk her further harm, even if that meant leaving behind one of his soldiers. His highest duty was due to the crown.

The long, jagged line of broken reality flashed amaranthine and Tahnak suddenly stood next to them. His grizzled face and torn up clothes seemed to have aged far longer than the fifteen minutes or so that it must've been since parting.

"Zabe! Claire!" he exclaimed with relief. "How long has it been? It must've been ages. I'm so glad I found you so soon."

Zabe crouched low so that he could set Claire down gently and respond to any attack should Tahnak's disposition suddenly change again. "How did you do that?" Zabe demanded. "How did you get over here?"

Tahnak held up his hands. He grasped the old journal in his fist. One of the darquematter trinkets hung from his neck attached by a leather thong.

"Less than half an hour ago you ran off, struck by madness."

Tahnak tilted his head in confusion. "I remember that. It happened years ago. I don't think this place affects us all the same, but I think I know a way out."

Zabe cocked his snout towards Claire. "She is not alright," he said, not taking his eyes off of Tahnak. "We've got to get her out of here. Now. You've only got a few seconds to tell me why I should listen to you."

"I remember roaming the burning hills for years as my mind slowly came back to me—like I said—time must've been different for me. The madness, dark voices with no discernible language. They consumed me for so long that I began to make sense of them. Once I'd finally regained my mind, I hurried back to the gate. On my way, I found this journal and this," he fidgeted with the necklace.

"The journal is gibberish."

Tahnak agreed. "But somehow, those voices that plagued me taught me the language. This book talks about how those with ties to the Darque can travel the cracks like energy conduits or rivers. A note in the margin suggested a shard of darquematter could create that bond."

Zabe stared at him for a long moment, weighing the options. He looked into Tahnak's eyes and judged him quite lucid—plus he'd already seen the man translated through the crack once already.

He took out the two shards from his pocket and put one into Claire's grasp, just in case it was somehow different from the pendant that she always wore. The trio walked over to the craggy seam through reality, reached out, and grabbed a hold.

With a burst of ozone and a flash of energy, they disappeared.

# Chapter Eighteen

Caivev ran ahead of the pack of Black vyrm and even her Tarkhūn general. Her rage sustained her as she pulled away from the group. Skrom finally called out to her.

The large, muscled reptilian hunched over as if he might puke. *Even he* needed a break.

"How long have we been traveling?" she demanded.

Skrom shrugged through his labored breaths. "Hours... days? Maybe years—I don't know. Time doesn't feel real here... especially after that last pulse wave washed over us."

The leader offered a tight-lipped smile: neither a frown nor a pleased gesture. Caivev felt deep down that she knew what those pulses were—the heartbeat of Sh'logath—waves of terror and madness birthed by the coming annihilation.

"We're never going to make it," she spat at a derelict vehicle nearby. It had long ago succumbed to age and atrophy; her vyrm had tried already to fix a few others, but the technology proved too foreign to be an expedient use of their time.

One of the Black hissed nearby. "What does it matter? If the glorious Awakening occurs as planned, then this is an exercise in futility. We will have already played our roles. We can lie down, die, and be done with it"

Caivev shot the soldier a piercing glare. His eyes suddenly lit up as he understood her motivation: she didn't fully trust the goat-demon. The mouthy warrior wilted beneath her gaze... she meant to be present at the unshackling of the last obelisk to ensure that the Brothers of the Winnowing kept their promises.

She paused while the overexerted minions tried to regain whatever energy they could, and mulled over a jumbled cluster of thoughts in her mind. Akko Soggathoth had left them with a riddle before he departed—had he teased them with the possibility of riding through the craggy lines of the cracks just as he had done?

The panting soldier who'd spoken up caught her eye again. He seemed to know her thoughts and see the same possibilities she'd pondered. "You want to travel through the jagged breach—even though you don't know who might die and who would live? And if we did either, would it even matter as long as it eventually served Sh'logath's purposes?"

Caivev nodded resolutely. There was no point in denying it.

The Black vyrm shrugged and walked towards the nearest crack. "Then let us test if it is even possible. I volunteer. Who is with me?"

Three others joined him at the crack. "We shall discover the odds of success—let's hope the ratio is consistent."

Caivev didn't say a word. She merely watched as her troops performed an act of service to their deity and for their peers' education. If they succeeded, perhaps some of them could still make it to the releasing of Akko Sxkakzacros.

The brave instigator looked back to Caivev. "Are you really committed to the Mighty Agod? If your faith falters—are you worthy of Dunnischktet?" While looking at her, he reached out and grabbed the crack.

Immediately, his body turned inside out from his center, crushing him from within and liquefying him into a puddle of shrieking flesh and fluids. The reward for such faith in a terrible deity proved harsh.

His three peers grabbed on at the same time. One of them burst into flames and crumbled into blackened heaps of ash; another turned to face his peers as he staggered towards them—his eyeballs sank away and he melted down with each step as if he'd turned into wax and his belly were a furnace. The final vyrm disappeared with a puff of ozone and seemed to wink into nothingness.

Skrom toed the twitching mass of waxy flesh that had puddled a step away. "Twenty-five percent chance? I expected worse."

"Closer to fifteen if you count the others from earlier," Caivev growled.

Her general shrugged his bulging shoulders nonchalantly. "Do we continue on foot or risk glory for Sh'logath?"

"A twenty-five percent chance is far better than our odds of beating Walther's travel machine to the haunted circle on foot."

Uncomfortable glances rippled through the party. Then they turned to risk everything on Caivev's whim—their faith overrode every self-preservation instinct within the vyrm. Even if none of them survived, there still remained the other group trying to reach Earth through the Temple gates.

Skrom winked at Caivev as she and his leader approached the same segment of the crack and lined up alongside it. "See you on the other side—I hope."

The outspoken vyrm's words rang in her ears. *Are you worthy of Dunnischktet?* In tandem with all of her scaly counterparts, Caivev stretched out her hands. As one unit they laid hold of the reality fissure, and then nothing remained of her.

"I don't know what to say except that we must act—and it must be swift!"

Wulftone glowered at Shandra, who insisted on action. She stood nearby with a half dozen other clerics of her order within the Veritas—The Merciful Hammer, though Master Druen wouldn't join them. The four leaders were far too important to risk in battle.

Shandra's clerics had equipped for battle; their war hammers hung at their sides, each imbued with a fragment of a rare element they claimed could disrupt the powers of the Darque forces: an ingot forged of darquematter.

"You've criticized Zabe in the past for rushing to act," he spat. Wulftone fully agreed with her call to arms—but he resented the implications of it: that Zabe and Claire might be incapable of returning.

Very seriously, Shandra lowered her voice with fear and reverence. "I have consulted the head of our order. Even Shjikara is shaken to the core at the thought of a full release of Akko Soggathoth's kin... this is the same man who remained within the cloister during Nitthogr's assault, yet he has pledged support now."

Wulftone nodded diplomatically and scanned the room. Besides their inner circle, it contained only Shandra's clerics and Chira, who had become an interim replacement leader for the Royal Military following Harken's death.

"I have still been unable to locate the princess," Tay-lore stated woefully. "Have your clerics had any success?"

Shandra scowled and bit her lip, refusing to glance at the two people on her right. All eyes avoided the blank stares of Sam Jones and Jackie. They sat together at the head of the long table—where Claire would have normally presided—and listened to discussions that presumed Claire and Zabe were lost.

The cleric sighed and put a hand on Sam's shoulder. "Yes. But she hasn't been truly located. With a little help, Shjikara was able to feel a glimmer, but nothing resolute. She is beyond the Tesseract, though he believes that she lives."

Wulftone leaned over the table. "I know this whole thing sucks," he said. "But we need everyone focused on this one problem—we've got to stop Caivev's plans, no matter the cost." He looked over at the android. "Tay-lore knows the location of the last darquegate and we're sure the enemy is on the move even now—plus they can travel incredibly fast because of her alliance with those same forces that aided Nitthogr and killed Jenner's father three years ago."

Tay-lore projected a map onto the table. A visual plan grabbed Sam and Jackie's attention as they leaned forward to assess the strategy. Glowing like a star, their entry point on the north side of the satellite map pulsed with hope.

In his robotic voice, he said, "There is an ancient monastery near the old forest. We can use the mirrors to enter and remain fairly close; we must only traverse the woods, which locals believe is cursed, in order to reach the location."

Jackie spluttered with laughter. "Of course it's cursed. Where is this haunted woods at?"

"Romania."

Sam's ears perked up. "What part of Romania—specifically, Tay-lore?"

"Transylvania," he said. "This is the Hoia Baciu Forest."

The archaeologist exhaled a terse sigh. "It's been called the 'most haunted forest in the world.'"

Chira shuddered. "If it's anything like the Island of the Dolls, I might recommend some liquid courage before departure."

Shandra squeezed Sam's hand. "I thought you didn't believe in that sort of nonsense?"

"I didn't believe because I hadn't yet seen. I've been through enough to convince me in these last couple of years... heck in the last week."

Wulftone shrugged. "Haunted or not, this is our line in the sand. We cannot allow the vyrm forces to release Akko Sxkakzacros. If all brothers are revived, we might not stand a chance."

Trenzlr, the defector from the scaly race, interjected a thought. "Once the last brother is awakened, they will possess unspeakable power, though they will be fixated on the Nihil Bridge if they are in league with Caivev. If the secret histories of my people are right, the release of Sh'logath might be a merciful end better than allowing the Brothers of the Winnowing to remain at large."

A ripple of assent circulated the room.

"You all know what must be done. Gather your troops, gear, or prepare accordingly. We roll out as soon as possible."

Respan piped up at the far end of the table. "If you're going into the woods, I've been working on something that might help prevent the kind of sneak attacks encountered during the last missions at the Island of the Dolls and Antarctica." The scientist glanced sheepishly towards Tay-lore. "Well, *we* worked on it."

Akko Soggathoth fingered the fresh bindings of his mystic book. Flesh had regrown and wrapped around the spine and covers, healing itself. Rolling his eyes back into his head, the eldritch beast connected his sight to that of his minion, his acolyte Theera. He looked *through* his eyes and experienced everything that Theera did, as if he was a passenger in the man's head.

Theera waited at the chamber door in the lobby of the secret society's meeting room. He knew that the Heptobscurantum's Seven met inside.

Finally, the doors parted, and they invited the cleverly disguised vyrm within. With his concealment makeup, Theera looked as passable as any human. He didn't need it in the company of the Seven, but everywhere else in New York City necessitated a certain level of obfuscation.

The Seven each pulled back their ceremonial hoods to reveal their faces. Theera didn't care—he wouldn't have recognized any of them, no matter how famous they were, and he knew some of them were just that. Akko Soggathoth was no respecter of fame, and neither would Theera be now that his heart and mind were touched by the beast.

Theera nodded and acknowledged the introductions and small talk, but paid little attention to the rest of their banter. His visit was not for pleasure; he made certain that everything followed his master's plan to the letter.

The vyrm glanced at the cloaked man with salt and pepper hair and a million-dollar smile. He recognized Percival Wainsmith because of the man's importance, rather than his notoriety.

Wainsmith and Sisyphus stood next to each other.

"You are ready for the great sacrifice, Mister Wainsmith?" Theera asked.

The magnate nodded unflinchingly. He almost seemed happy for his part in the great game Akko Soggathoth had engineered.

"I have noticed such sorrow and indecision in humans when so much is required," Theera said.

"Then you've not known many powerful humans," Wainsmith stated with a hint of threat in his voice. "My dedication to the Awakening remains unwavering. Didn't I deliver up my daughter, just as promised?"

Theera smiled diplomatically and bowed.

Sisyphus quelled the tension and redirected the rest of the Seven to take their seats.

Andrew Thornton, finally brought out of hiding, leaned over the carved table and cocked an eyebrow. "We were heavily involved in the last attempted Awakening—as per described in the Grimmorium Nitthogr," he referenced the weathered tome that now lay at the center of the table. "What part will we play in *this*?"

Theera looked right through Thornton and sneered with needle-sharp teeth. He didn't give away the man's secret, but the two locked eyes and both of them knew that the other knew something was hidden from the rest.

"We are only there to observe the arrival of our glorious agod," Sisyphus stated. "The Awakening will be unleashed by the Brothers of the Winnowing from within the Darque at the gates of Koth. Theera, Percival, and I will leave shortly to collect Mrs. Wainsmith, who is vacationing in Romania. You may join us briefly in Chiriquí, but will celebrate in the usual manner from a remote location."

The table rumbled with murmured blessings. They understood their roles.

A triangular energy gate tore itself open and invited the threesome to enter the waypoint in Germany before it could send them to their next destination.

"Gentlemen, and lady," Sisyphus greeted his illuminati once more and then departed.

Claire, Zabe, and Tahnak tumbled to a stop as they hit the end of the line for the crack they traveled along. They'd zipped along like a current through a circuit, but fell out and back into existence, such as it was in the Darque, when the conduit tapered to an end.

They rolled to their feet and faced their destination. The reverse image of Mullen Nebraska spread out before them, except the houses and buildings they'd once seen on Earth weren't made of wood and brick here. Rather, they towered as crystalline formations of varying translucency.

Cracks terminated all over in the distance surrounding the town as if it were some kind of central hub. A jagged spider web of craggy fissures coiled all throughout the town. More menacing than that, however, was the towering crown of obsidian spikes that broke through the middle part of town where the Heptobscurantum had once tried to sacrifice Claire on the Earth version of this place.

Twelve curving obelisks curved like claws that scraped the sky and clutched the central nexus location. Curling, jagged lines wreathed the spires like vines. They pulsed with a toxic kind of light.

"I don't think we should touch these ones," Tahnak said of the different kind of cracks.

Claire had barely come back to consciousness, though wearied greatly. She and Zabe nodded their assent.

The trio moved as quickly as possible and weaved their way over, under, and around the serrated obstacles. Those same ethereal creatures they encountered previously floated through the cracks and the crystalline structures.

At the center of the winding helicoid throbbed an ill light. It pulsed with a kind of dread heartbeat. The unnatural vibrations made the shimmering spirit creatures act differently as the intruders grew closer.

Swarming aggressively close to Tahnak, the ghostly creatures buzzed as close as they dare. They snarled and postured as much as they could in the eerie silence.

Tahnak drew his pistol and fired through a flurry of the things. The laser burst burned through the air and passed through the creatures with no result, except to make them angrier.

A small phalanx of the shadowy things swooped around and dove towards Claire. Zabe growled and stepped between them, drawing the Stone Glaive from its scabbard. The swarm split and peeled off into different directions as if terrified at the sight of the arcane weapon; they even seemed to make an audible noise—like a yelp of terror.

Navigating the spiral took only a few more moments, but the floating ghost-things kept a wide berth. Their hollow eyes remained fixed upon the ancient blade.

Suddenly, the ethereal things turned their heads towards something in the distance, as if they heard some call, only they were attuned too. With muted hissing and screeching, they slowly descended towards the ground and migrated towards the nearest cracks, their empty sockets never departing from the edged bane within Zabe's grip.

Only a few steps away from the center, Zabe, Claire, and Tahnak watched as the creatures filtered through the fissure and bled into the bright core nearby the inverse Nebraska site. The eerie glow intensified as it absorbed the disembodied things, and then the core flashed and darkened.

Claire looked at the site with a mix of worry and skepticism. She met the eyes of her companions, who shared the same look.

"Well... that was something different," Tahnak quipped.

"This whole place is different," Zabe commented, standing in the shadow of the curved, talon-like obelisks.

"And yet," Claire stepped into the center. She opened out her hands and closed her eyes—stretching out her senses into the astral plane. "It feels all so familiar, too... like that same feeling I've gotten in every place I ever believed was truly haunted."

She opened her eyes, and they all traded glances. The intensity in her eyes convinced the others. "We've got to get out of here—and soon—if we're going to stop Caivev."

Respan finished handing each person an awkward looking headband. He put one on his head where it fit snugly and rotated the small arm with a viewing lens in front of his eye. "It has two modes," the inventor said loudly enough to hear. "Tap the button to switch between heat sensing, Darque mode, and off. It should help you pierce the heavy camouflage of the enemy."

He turned to the leaders as he cycled the settings and then paused. He spoke so only Wulftone's inner circle could hear him. "You have a glow, Wulftone."

"What?"

"The scanner, it's in Darque mode and registers your aura... faintly, but you register."

The some-times lycan merely nodded. "Must be from what we learned in the Book of Vangandra."

Respan nodded and then stepped back. He'd been one of the first to help read the book with Sam Jones and learned about the mysterious origins of when their ancestor was exposed to Darque artifacts.

Wulftone placed the scanner on his brow and then cut his hand to awaken the mirror's power. He wrapped a bandage around his hand and looked at Jackie as the mirror portal opened; the wound would heal quickly—fully—as soon as he switched forms.

Jackie gave him one final, tender look before steeling her face for the battle they expected.

Wulftone nodded to Chira, who stood at the head of the military lined up in the hallway stretching away from the mirror room. Shandra stood nearby with a dozen members of the warrior faction from the Order of the Veritas.

All of Shandra's clerics stood as nonchalant as possible, but Wulftone recognized the fear in their eyes. They were shaken to their core—all soldiers from the Order trained with the Guardian Corps before choosing the holy path, but none of them had ever seen actual battle.

The de facto leader swallowed hard and turned to face those men and women about to follow him through the mirror again. He hadn't wanted this role—leader of the Guardian Corps; fidgeting with Zahaben's leather cuff, he prayed to the Architect King that he wouldn't be the last in the line of Vangandra.

"I'm not much on inspirational speeches," he shouted. "Just remember one thing. Everything is at stake—your lives, your families. We cannot fail!"

"We will not fail!" responded the troops in echoed unison.

With stiff legs, a young man approached from down the hall, bypassing the two lanes of soldiers and corpsmen. Jenner walked with his head held high. A bright red patch of skin was held together by staples; the inflamed area spread to the neck exposed around his collarbone. "Permission to come along?"

"Shouldn't you be in the hospital?" Wulftone barked.

"It didn't take. Please, let me come."

"You were just impaled days ago."

"The doc says it missed everything vital—lucky me. I'll hold together... but I've got a bone to pick with the vyrm. They skewered me and killed my friends."

Respan handed the young corpsman a scanning device as Wulftone nodded. "As long as you don't fall apart on me, soldier."

He turned back to the troops and gazed at them for one more second. Finally, he saluted. Wulftone, still in his human form, turned around and rushed through the mystic glass and translated beyond the Prime.

A split second later, he shook off the rushing pain that shocked his system with a kind of cold, electric energy. Warm light poured onto his face through the open door.

The tiny room's walls threatened to squish him as Jackie suddenly burst into existence with a crackle of power. He stepped backward through the door, still looking at the old stonework which boasted holy scrawling text etched upon every brick.

Jackie accompanied him as Shandra and then Chira planeswalked to Earth. "It's a monastic prayer room," she recognized as she joined Wulftone on the steps outside to make room.

They descended the short stair from the cell. It rested upon a dais at the center of the inner cloister. A trio of very bewildered monks watched their approach; the youngest of them ran off to retrieve their elder.

One of the others asked them a question, and Jackie cocked her head.

"You understand them?" Wulftone asked.

"Some," she said. "I speak a little Italian, and many of the words are the same as Romanian." She hedged a little. "But honestly, even my Italian is pretty bad."

"What is he saying?" Wulftone asked as a few others approached them down the stairs.

She scrunched up her face as she tried to parse the words. "Something about a prophecy and us coming from the sacred prayer room to defeat a great evil."

"Well, tell them yes!" he said.

An old, wizened monk approached with cautious steps, unsure of the weight placed upon each footing. The younger monk held his master's arm for support. The aged leader's eyes belied the rest of his condition and remained bright and vibrant with the light of life.

In all the excitement, he began speaking as he approached. Jackie struggled to keep up with his flurry of words.

"He says something about a growing evil in the black woods." They all caught the annunciation of the Hoia Baciu.

Even though Jackie was the only one who could converse with the headmaster, they could each sense the disappointment in his voice. "He says the evil is very great—large—and wants to know if this is all the soldiers we brought."

Jackie shook her head and smiled as a few more soldiers finally descended the steps. "No."

The old man grinned. "Nu," he restated with a thick accent and smiled as the soldiers kept coming.

"You didn't think I'd miss such an important trip, did you?" Percival Wainsmith asked his wife, Theresa, as they left the cathedral.

"It was one of Holly's favorite places and there was no way I was going to let you light a candle in her honor all by yourself."

Theresa leaned against her husband. "I'm just so amazed that you got here so quickly. I was sure you would miss it. I'm sorry for what I said when you told me you had business to conduct—I was just so sure that you wouldn't make it."

Percival kissed her forehead and opened the car door for her. "Forget that. And, of course, this was important. But all is forgotten—we are both grieving, after all."

He joined her in the back and signaled the driver. Theresa's fingers intertwined with Percival's and she squinted away the grief in her eyes and sobbed only slightly.

Pouring her a chilled glass of wine, he handed it to her by the stem and then poured a scotch for himself.

"Whatever will we do without her?" Pain cracked her voice, and she drank the red liquid in gulps before resting her head on her husband's shoulder. She waved a finger over the glass and signaled for another.

"We will live our lives with a higher purpose," he stated as he poured. "You've always been so compassionate and selfless," Percival told her. "Surely you saw how much Holly was just like you in that regard."

Theresa offered a sad, flat smile and acknowledged that fact. She took the refill and sipped it—still draining it quickly. "But what kind of mission and purpose? We've been so involved in charity work for so long it seems we have done it all..."

"There is more we can do," Percival said—perhaps speaking more transparently with his wife than he ever had before. Her eyes widened as she recognized his newfound sense of vulnerability. Some renewed purpose had finally found him. "We can do more than give money to fund organizations!"

"Like... actual volunteerism? Working with lepers or feeding children in India? There are so many good church works we could partner with." She knocked back the rest of her glass and her words began to slur.

He drained the expensive glass of scotch. "So much more," Percival said with a smile. "But the church is not the only one with a grand mission and purpose."

"Like what?" She fluttered her eyes groggily and laid her head back on Percival's shoulders—heavy with sleep.

Percival patted her hair and set the errant glass aside, replacing it near the drugged bottle of wine. "I will show you." He said as their car went around a turn and left the city. "I will show you *everything*."

# Chapter Nineteen

Claire hunched over and shuddered as the core emanated a powerful, astral aura. The disembodied creatures poured their energy into the sickly crystalline root at the heart of the Darque and attacked her through her psychic senses.

"How do we get out of here?" Zabe asked, worried that this fallen realm took far too great a toll on his beloved.

"I don't know," Claire stammered breathlessly. "But I'm certain that it must be through here." She cried out again and groaned as the crack glowed. It looked more like a jagged, spewed igneous formation—or a carving of some microscopic organism blown up on a giant scale.

The black spires surrounding the malfeasant dimensional gate crackled with mystic energy as the core powered up. Zabe howled, fed up with the psychic attacks he had no power over, and swung the Stone Glaive. It severed the reality crack, shattering it into millions of glassine pieces which rained to the ground. The shards were obviously made up of the same stuff as the darquematter they'd seen before.

Shrieking with defiance, the central helix thrummed with anger. A host of the ethereal spirit beings swarmed Zabe, gnashing and slashing at their attacker; their attacks did nothing but blind his vision as they dove through his head and chest trying to assault him on the psychic plane—he was somehow immune to their touch, either by his nature or the fact that he held the weapon of the

Architect King. Zabe didn't care whichever the case might have been; he slashed through the cloud with the blade and the things burst into pieces, bleeding vapor that might have been their insides.

The horde of enemies rushed towards the glowing obelisks and melted inside of them. Seconds later, they whined with a shrill tone and then a burst of power exploded out from the black towers—the same kind of pulses they'd experienced before.

Claire cried out and fell to her knees as the wave slammed through her—tearing through her psychic self and flipping astral switches that few could've ever known about. Zabe bent over and vomited, gripped by intense nausea. Tahnak stared into the distant sky as if he'd been turned into a vegetable.

Standing on her feet again, Claire pushed her shoulders back with a more regal stance. "What... where am I. How in the name of my father did I get here?"

Zabe wiped his chin and stared at her, wild-eyed. He recognized Bithia immediately—something deeply wrong had happened to Claire. He could only stare at her for a long moment, not knowing what to say or do.

"Tahnak?" Bithia asked for an outside opinion.

Tahnak's head snapped to the side, and he caught her in his empty, feral gaze. Frothy saliva spilled from the edges of his mouth and he snarled before hissing one word in the wake of the eldritch wave. "Sh'logath."

Completely emptied of his humanity, he shrieked with murderous rage and sprinted with uncanny speed. Tahnak leapt for Bithia, baring his teeth like a wild animal.

Akko Soggathoth, in his human form, approached Idrakka and Sisyphus. His shapeshifted Rottweiler trotted happily at his side. "Restrain me," he stated.

The men responded with confused looks.

"I'm about to temporarily abandoning this form," he said. "Don't let my prisoner escape. I've grown comfortable in him."

Idrakka looked at the demon with suspicion. "Where are you going?" He looked about inside the well-known forest circle where nothing grew but choked, ragged weeds. The vyrm looked for any threats to their well-being.

"I've grown more powerful every moment I've walked this plane and I can feel a growing presence that threatens our power. Forces of the Architect King are mustering nearby. I am finally strong enough to hex their entry point and block them—if I don't deal with them soon, they might arrive before the sacrifice and with overwhelming numbers."

Idrakka still looked at him distrustfully, but Sisyphus nodded. The former pro wrestler grappled the smaller man in a chokehold, ready to lock it in as soon as the human began to struggle.

The avatar's eyes rolled back into his head and he wheezed with a death rattle. From the corner of their eyes, they caught a glimpse of the vile spirit departing—like a cloud of volcanic ash escaping on super-heated eddies.

Barely visible, the roiling black bubble of inky, tentacle mist shot away through the shadows of the haunted Hoia Baciu forest.

Jolting suddenly awake and lucid, the restrained man screamed. "I am Quintin Hall! I am Quintin Hall. Please, somebody help me before it takes my mind again!" He sobbed uncontrollably and begged them for help.

Idrakka looked on while Sisyphus sneered and flexed his powerful grip, squeezing the breath out of the man. After a few short moments, Quintin relaxed and stopped struggling while the Heptobscurantum's wizard switched between relaxing and tensing the chokehold to keep their guest conscious but compliant.

The desolate ring in the south-west section of the forest remained quiet. Members of both the Heptobscurantum and The Black milled about, waiting for the return of Percival Wainsmith and Theera, the goatman's slave. No insects chirped; the wind did not rustle the leaves. Every sense, natural and otherwise, reeked of death and horror as they guarded a hierophanticus they'd placed at the center: a carved figurine in the form of a goat with four horns and covered in eyes.

Idrakka cocked his head. "I hear someone coming." A moment later, the rest heard it too: the approach of an off-road vehicle.

Percival Wainsmith and Theera sat in the UTV as they transported the cultist's wife, who remained unconscious. They drove cautiously so as not to damage the sacrifice.

The abyssal auraphage, still looking like a large dog, lifted its snout and eagerly watched their approach. Sisyphus chuckled and his hostage stared with bewildered, panicked eyes. "Things are about to get real interesting."

Tay-lore stood watch from the center of the room in the Hall of Mirrors. The high-strung android's circuits burned with worry; if he'd had a stomach, he felt certain he'd have an ulcer by now.

Soldiers of the Royal Military and members of the Guardian Corps still lined the corridor, ready to make the journey. The last of the Veritas that accompanied them had just finished planeswalking.

"Hey, um, Mister Tay-lore," a soldier called.

The android turned to face him. "Just Tay-lore. What is it?"

Putting his hand on the mirror, he said, "It won't let me through. The glass is solid."

Tay-lore scanned the activation points on the eldritch device's frame—the places that had to be touched with blood to power the artifact. They seemed fine.

"Yow—ouch!" the soldier said as he yanked his hand away from the glass. "It's hot!"

Suddenly, the mirror burst into black flames that flickered with supernatural power. The mirror warped and then began to melt as the arcane fire jumped to the other twenty-nine mirrors. Each one melted into a puddle of warped slag before their eyes.

The automaton stepped into the chamber a few minutes later. Nothing else had been damaged by the fire; no smoke damage or charring touched the room, but the Hall of Mirrors had been reduced to an empty room with no power or purpose.

Tay-lore suddenly wished he could turn off the emotion sub-routines in his programming. His internal systems suddenly experienced a very real sense of panic—the soldiers on Earth were on their own and the central gate could not be properly aligned to open a portal anywhere near the Hoia Baciu forest for quite some time.

He turned and fled from the room. Tay-lore had to find Shjikara immediately. With no military commanders and no royalty, only the head of the Veritas would know how to proceed.

Jackie stood with Wulftone and Chira as Shandra approached with Sam Jones and her contingent of clerics. Jenner and Gita descended the steps and waited. They'd come in teams and groups of individuals, just in case they met opposition immediately, as they had in Antarctica.

The two corpsmen waited for the next group of people to exit the old cell, but none came. "I don't get it," Jenner said as Gita shot her friends a worried look. "They were right behind us."

Leaning heavily on the young monk at his side, the monastery leader asked Jackie again if this was all she brought. Jackie shot him a worried look, which required no translation.

After another five minutes of silence from the portal, Wulftone, Chira, and Shandra called their respective subordinates over to form up. "Something is amiss. Whatever it is, we'll have to trust that Tay-lore can handle it in our absence." He fired a disappointed look at Sam, who he'd asked to stay back in the Prime to keep an eye on things. Sam refused to be apart from Shandra again—even though her combat training far exceeded his. "It looks like this is all of us." He mentally calculated their number at about sixty—barely a fifth of what he'd intended to muster before sending that first wave into the woods and then reinforce them with a second wave.

Wulftone scowled. The Royal family used to keep cells of soldiers on the different planes that they could call on for help in times of need—but that practice ended during the Syzygyc war. He pushed the regret from his mind and focused on the mission. It wouldn't have mattered, anyway; Earth had always been off-limits and never boasted an emergency reserve of secret soldiers.

He opened his mouth to speak, but the old man interrupted him with his raspy, aged baritone. With outspread arms and closed eyes, he pronounced a blessing over the planeswalking invaders.

When he finally ended his prayer, the soldiers echoed his "amin" in chorus unison.

Wulftone stood and faced the forest. A looming cloud of supernatural darkness had gathered over the top of the trees. He made a show of setting the coordinates on his wrist monitor. The troops of the three factions followed suit.

He yelled a simple charge. "We must not let the beast free Akko Sxkakzacros. You know what to do. Roll out!"

Under the watchful gaze of the monastery, the sixty outlanders rushed into the forest as darkness fell at midday.

From the black heart of the evil forest, Akko Soggathoth felt the seeds of old curses: ancient, eldritch ties to the Darque—a foundation of hexes and incantations laid down over generations by wicked arcanists. The demigod sent his will through the micro-fractures in the Tesseract and beyond, calling to the wraiths that lived in the fallen realm he once called home.

Summoning any and all incorporeal creatures capable of answering his appeal, the herald drew them into the darkness that blanketed the woods. They leaked through the leylines and into whatever vessels would take them: gnarled trees, malignant shadows, and corpses abandoned by time.

Akko Soggathoth squealed with delight. His laughter reverberated through the trees as he watched his plans unfold. As his crowing mirth caught his own ear, the demon's thoughts turned inward. How he would miss the games once Sh'logath finally arrived.

A scream pierced the air and filled his heart with perverse glee. It would all prove worth it once the master arrived—he hoped.

Jackie dashed through the woods and ducked behind the strange, S-curved trunks of the trees the Hoia Baciu was known for. She poked around the corner and fired a burst of rounds into the chest of a vyrm warrior.

Pulling back behind her cover, she spotted Wulftone tearing through a group of enemies in his lycan form. He dashed the enemies into submission with a growl and then went to all four, charging into a team of flanking vyrm.

Gita hurried over to her tree and skidded to her knees opposite of her friend. She snapped off a few rounds of her own and dropped a pair of human cultists harassing her from thirty meters away.

In the distance, Wulftone's voice rose above the din. "We've got to break through and get to the circle!"

Jackie nodded to her friend, thanking her for the assist. Pockets of dirt erupted around them and fragments of the tree they hunkered behind blasted away under the force of the line of enemy blasters hidden in the trees. Suddenly, the cultist's assault stopped, and they retreated.

The surrounding trees groaned and howled as some kind of haunted ethereal monster stepped out from it. Jackie heard her companions panic behind her. Soldiers of the Prime and fellow corpsmen opened fire on the spirit creatures.

More screams went up as stray blaster fire caught friendly troops. A shimmering humanoid shape reached out from the inside of the tree where the girls hid. Jackie screeched and fell backward, banging her head against the ground and switching on Respan's Darque scanner. The demon took clear shape through the scope as the fallen soul tried to grab her.

Jackie opened fire, but the bullets passed right through the supernatural being. She howled and poured on more fire as it grabbed her—its hands phased right through her, doing no damage except increasing her terror and giving her a fell chill worse than any she'd had in Antarctica. Its frigid tentacles tried to take root in her mind and control her.

She staggered back and reached down to find her inner grit. Jackie latched on to all of that pain and loss; she refused to let this apparition have any power over her. The spirit retreated, snarling.

Nearby, Gita wailed with horror, battling her own demon. The supernatural darkness that clouded the forest intensified and deepened.

"My parents! My family—they're killing my family, even though they promised! They promised!"

"It's not real!" Jackie screamed. "They can't hurt you!"

She glanced backward to see the Clerics wielding their hammers. Each fiend they smashed burst into fragments like glass and evaporated into the ether. Still, soldiers screamed in very real pain from attritionary fire and a tentacle beast that sprinted through their forces on all four legs.

Jackie could only see it through her scanner as it eviscerated her comrades. "No!" she screamed—recognizing the enemies' trap—it was after the clerics, the only ones who could damage these ghostly creatures.

Gita recoiled as she struggled against the demon that tried to crawl inside of her again. Steeling herself against the spirit that tried to possess her, she resisted the nameless thing. It finally fled the strong-willed girl.

As soon as Gita drove it away, she stood and shot Jackie a relieved look. Fired from nearby, a blaster bolt caught her directly in the chest, burning a hole through her armor. Gita's eyes rolled back in her head and she collapsed in a heap.

Jackie shrieked as her friend went down. The smoldering hole burned brightly as she looked up to see Jenner holding a blaster. His eyes had turned black and his face went gray and emotionless.

She snapped her pulse rifle up to take aim. Jenner's body glowed with a faint corona indicating the Darque being controlling him.

Behind the possessed, young corpsman, a beast glowed as it attacked even more of her friends and turned to pursue a cleric whose hammer also glowed with a faint shimmer, radiating an aura from the ingot.

*The mission! We must not fail!* Her inner voice shrieked, demanding she pull the trigger. *Please don't be him. Please don't be him!* Jackie bit her lip and chose between the animal and the target in her sights—her friend.

In the confusion, she could not tell if the animal on her scanner was the tentacle beast or Wulftone. If it was Wulftone and his mind had been consumed by the shadows, she had no choice but to shoot.

Shandra charged ahead and smashed Jenner in the chest with her hammer, even as Jackie squeezed the trigger. The lethal burst of energy flew through the shimmering debris of the disrupted spirit and pierced the skull of the abyssal auraphage that had been wreaking havoc in their forces.

Looking back, Shandra spotted the clean kill and nodded her thanks. A thunderhead rumbled in the darkness, but the light began to return as the remaining two clerics finished banishing the foul creatures. Besides the hammers, only Wulftone's aura remained aglow on the scanner.

"You must have known that Wulftone could resist the dark lure of the spirits. I'm glad you have found such a deep connection with someone," Shandra said as she glanced at Sam, who helped Jenner to his feet.

"Yeah. I knew it couldn't be him taking out our soldiers," she lied.

Jenner dashed over to Gita in a panic. "What have I done? What have I done?" He wailed with distraught.

Jackie could only tearfully watch.

Sam slid to his knees as he and Jenner began first aid. The archaeologist wasn't a medic, but had more training than anyone else who'd made it through the portal.

"Will she make it?" Jenner's voice broke.

Sam shook his head. "I do not know."

Jenner sank back to his butt and sobbed. "Please save her... please. She and I... we were kind of... it can't end like this!"

Wulftone sprinted over and dropped to a knee, assessing the situation and checking for a pulse. "Can you help her, Sam?"

The archaeologist grimaced and shrugged.

"We've got a mission that cannot fail," he insisted. "There's barely more than half of us left. We've got to move right away!"

Jackie hardened her heart and hoped Sam could pull off a miracle. She turned to form up with the ranks. Jenner didn't move.

"Hey!" she spat, getting his attention. "What did Wulftone tell you before we planeswalked?"

"Don't fall apart on him."

She blinked back a tear of her own and hissed a threat. "And don't you dare go back on your word, now."

# CHAPTER TWENTY

Akko Soggathoth fumed when the enemy forces finally killed his pet, but the abyssal creature had served its purpose, and he could always find another if necessary. He drew his presence back together and concentrated himself into the inky mass that housed his consciousness.

Taking ahold of his victim once again, Quintin Hall ceased to be. The fiend tapped Sisyphus and signaled he'd taken possession of his toy once more. The wrestler released his body.

"Greetings," he called to Percival Wainsmith. Akko Soggathoth walked over and touched the faithful man's face. "So glad you could make it." He reverently stroked Theresa's face next.

"Bring her," he commanded.

Theera obediently scooped up the unconscious woman and followed.

"There is no altar here," Idrakka noted.

Akko Soggathoth sneered. "No. Only *this* place is strong enough to hold my brother."

Theera laid the sleeping woman down next to the goat figurine, the hierophanticus which would unlock Akko Sxkakzacros's prison, and began tying her wrists and ankles. He hooked two lengths of rope to each end of the woman's body, looping it around her waist and torso.

Wainsmith leaned low and kissed his wife one last time. She groggily began to wake.

"What... where?"

"Shh," he put a finger to her lips. "You are exactly where you need to be to unlock your destiny." Wainsmith grabbed one of the ropes.

Akko Soggathoth's fair features shrank back and revealed his horrific visage. He pointed to the rope ends affixed to his prey.

Several vyrm hopped into action and grabbed sections of the tether and pulled, stretching the woman in the air above the dimensional key. Akko Soggathoth glared at the humans of the Heptobscurantum, who'd turned pale at the notion of pulling a woman in two rather than mercifully bleeding her with a knife. Even Sisyphus blanched and hesitated before following through on his orders.

Placing a hand on the hilt of his ancient khopesh, the wizard tapped into the mystic blade's power and telekinetically yanked his minions into position where they could grasp the lash.

Amid the pain, Theresa snapped back to consciousness and yelped. She screamed for help from her husband until she realized *he* held the first length of rope. Her eyes went gray, and she fell catatonic. All hope had left her.

Akko Soggathoth snarled, urging his minions to pull harder as the braided line cut into Theresa Wainsmith's armpits and hips. A tear fell from her eyes and her spine cracked under the tension.

Finally, the pain was too much for her and she shrieked with a blood-curdling yell. The goatman watched, cackling gleefully.

An ear-splitting screech split the air and stopped Wulftone and his team in their tracks. They paused only long enough to share their concern over the seriousness of the situation with a worried glance.

"We're running out of time!" Shandra insisted.

"Let's move!" Wulftone shouted, sensing their enemies were only a short distance away.

"For the Prime!" Chira yelled his battle cry. The rest of the soldiers took it up, and they sprinted ahead at full speed, howling at the top of their lungs and with fingers on the triggers.

"For the Prime!" Jackie yelled. "And for Gita!"

A bubble of pure evil burst into existence around the gore-soaked hierophanticus, crackling with negative energy and filling the breadth of the haunted Hoia Baciu forest circle. A greenish murk obscured everything within the bubble, and a low rumble growled in the mist. The space shared a presence between both worlds: the Darque and the Tesseract's Earth realm.

Akko Soggathoth glanced at Theera, and the acolyte retrieved his master's arcane book. The goatman focused his energies and snapped his fingers; they lit with an eerie black flame. Suddenly, the sickly vapors caught fire and burned off with a flash. The trees at the edge of the clearing peeled away in purple flames to reveal a circle of curved obelisks which angled towards them like claws clutching the area caught between the Tesseract and the Darque.

A second, rotting man-goat—a behemoth of one—stood only a little way away, chained to an obsidian spire by engraved, silvery shackles. A twisted face moved around the belly of Akko Sxkakza-cros as if some creature tried to push itself free from within. Standing taller than a minotaur, the bellowing creature roared when he recognized his brother.

"Akko Soggathoth!" he hissed. "Traitor!" Akko Sxkakzacros shook his mighty hands and rattled the chains.

All eyes of the vyrm and heptobscurantum locked onto the younger brother. Akko Soggathoth merely shrugged and grinned playfully. He approached the monster, who stood nearly twice his height and poked him in the belly. "What was I supposed to do? Let you devour me, too, and steal my power as you did to Akko Quarnyk?"

"Free me or I will destroy you!"

The younger laughed. His minion held out his book and indicated the brother should make his mark.

Akko Quarnyk squirmed in his belly and Akko Sxkakzacros spat in the brother's face. A howl went up in the distance, and blaster bolts began flying all around. Akko Soggathoth never broke his spittle-soaked gaze with his older, more powerful brother.

"Sign it."

The vyrm and heptobscurantum snapped into position, trying to protect the bubble for as long as possible against the opposition hiding amongst the trees. A trio of disruptor blasts hit Akko Sxkakzacros in rapid succession; they barely managed to scratch his hide and made him leak a trickle of metallic blood. The beast grinned and glared at his ambitious brother.

"Sign it!" Akko Soggathoth shouted again.

Akko Sxkakzacros growled in response.

Sisyphus watched with rapt interest at the exchange between the brothers when he caught sight of the enemies' new tactic; blaster fire tore up the ground around the hierophanticus. The wizard tightened his hand on the khopesh and, channeling its power through his mind, lifted Wainsmith's UTV. He slammed it down into the dirt on its side to make a shield. Bullets and blaster fire deflected off of the vehicle as the opposition tried to burn through it.

Jackie watched Wulftone absorbing damage on the far side of their line as he smashed the enemy ranks. They'd arrived just in time to watch the enemy open the dimensional locks that sealed Akko Sxkakzacros within the Darque. She pushed her anxiety deep down and trusted him enough to stay safe.

The enemy threw all of its disposable troops at them—both lower caste vyrm and Heptobscurantum zealots. They kept coming, and they kept dying. The enemy had no cover against the better-protected forces of the Prime, who hid in the dense foliage and wore body armor.

Vyrm and cultist bodies piled up, but they continued the charge in order to buy their masters time.

"We've got to close that portal and seal the gate," Chira yelled.

Jackie turned and fired, trying to get an angle on the distant hierophanticus, a tiny target only a few square centimeters in size. It lay amid a pile of revolting gore where some poor woman had been torn in half.

Her first few shots landed all around the target. She cursed and retrained her aim down the weapon's sights.

Suddenly, an invisible, supernatural force lifted the nearby sport utility vehicle and smashed it down as a barrier to shield the arcane key from her bullets.

She growled and opened fire, pouring on an onslaught from her pulse rifle. Jackie aimed for where she knew the fuel tank was and pulled the trigger over and over.

Nothing. Apparently, it wouldn't work like that. Jackie cursed every movie she'd ever seen for lying to her about bullets and vehicular explosions.

She howled with feral rage and took out another wave of enemies who crawled too close.

"What would Mother and Father say?" Akko Soggathoth spat. "Now make your mark! I'm carrying us all to the chamber for a family meeting."

Akko Sxkakzacros glowered at the whelp. He curled a defiant lip.

"You know the rules and our purpose. It is time for the Winnowing. Now, *write your name—make your mark!*" He turned and batted away a hail of blaster charges that would've otherwise struck him. "Don't do it because you are obligated to by law and relation. Do it because you are answering destiny's call."

Another trio of blasts cut down Theera, and he toppled dead. A few seconds later, the undying vyrm gasped for air, collected the book, stood, and regained his composure as if nothing had happened. Sisyphus merely stared at the sight.

With a glower, the enormous fiend pressed his finger to the page and drew his sign on the parchment. He snarled in his brother's face as he did so.

Akko Soggathoth glanced back and cocked a suspicious eyebrow at the ambitious wizard, who watched every moment of the transaction, taking careful note of every detail of the binding process.

As if he turned to smoke, Akko Sxkakzacros evaporated. The sigil he'd penned upon the page consumed him like a vacuum devouring a mist. Micro-explosions burst against the obelisk where the empty shackles hung in the place of the demon who'd been fettered there.

The clever demon smiled with more mischief and malevolence than Sisyphus had ever seen. He looked up and spotted a glowing triangle of energy piercing the air just beyond the bubble zone of Darqueness that overlapped with Earth's space. The science team hadn't yet cracked through the dimensional boundaries in order to pierce beyond the veil of the Tesseract's thirty-three dimensions and access the Darque.

"Let's get out of here," Sisyphus yelled as he spotted Percival Wainsmith and a few other key members of their cadre leaping through Walther's transport portal.

Theera, holding the book, waited dutifully for his master at the edge of the energy gate, unwilling to leave him behind as the nameless members of The Black and low ranking cultists threw their final few numbers at the armies of the Prime.

Sisyphus paused mid-step and locked eyes with one young man at the edge of the woods—he recognized him from the memories that had leeched off his prisoner, the blood donor he regularly victimized. He'd chained this boy's father deep within his inner sanctum and siphoned the primal energies off of him. "Jenner," he hissed at his son from another dimension.

The boy narrowed his eyes to slits and opened fire, standing recklessly amid the vyrm's final volleys of hot death.

Sisyphus smirked, ducked his head. He sprinted towards the escape portal with supernatural speed.

Caivev, Skrom, and two other vyrm popped out of the crack where it terminated within the parched wasteland of the Darque. Despite the puff of ozone, the stink of their peers' incinerated flesh clung to them stronger.

After taking a brief headcount, Caivev looked ahead and spotted what looked like a black dome in the distance. She squinted to try to get a better view.

"Skrom. What do you see?"

The tall tarkhūn shaded his eyes. "It looks like a ring of black towers... curved pillars like an arena, maybe?"

Suddenly, it burst open with an ethereal purple light. The quartet immediately sprinted for the landmark.

"It's the prison of Akko Sxkakzacros!"

The barren ground shifted beneath their feet as they pumped their legs against the sand and sediment. Darque gates only opened with a purpose—and once that purpose expired, it was sure to close and leave them trapped.

Brilliant lines of blaster fire crossed through the shared space between dimensions and they watched the battle unfold as they ran headlong into the chaos. A crackling triangle of light opened in the distance, visible just beyond the Darque; it glowed like a light below murky water.

"Walther's portal!" Skrom howled, continuing his mad dash.

They dared not spare a glance at the hierophanticus which fell under attack in the corner of their eyes. Their chests tightened and breaths came in ragged gasps as they hurried—they couldn't miss their window of opportunity or they would be trapped—possibly forever!

Jenner locked eyes with the man he'd seen once before—a muscular version of his father who'd kidnapped his real parent and then murdered his family. His eyes glazed over with red and he jolted to his feet, screaming with rage and pouring all malice into his trigger finger.

His father's doppelganger sprinted for that same triangular portal he'd used to attack his home three years previous. Jenner fired over and over, ignoring the fatigue in his hand.

The weapon cycled and then chirped a low energy warning. He ignored it, even as his armor deflected a few glancing blows from flanking enemies. Jenner struck down the enemies and felt a hot trickle of blood as their blasts tore free the staples at his neck. The energy magazines depleted and sounded a shrill whine while he ignored the pain and hot leakage melting down his chest from his neck wound.

Jenner reached for a replacement magazine but had none. He cursed and watched his nemesis flee towards the escape.

A tunnel vision of rage overtook his vision as he reached for his last round: the explosive bullet Harken had given him during the academy. He remained so fixated on his enemy as he chambered the round that he didn't see the small group of new intruders breach the circle and break through the Darque and into the Earth realm beyond.

Jenner rammed the action shut and sighted down his barrel. He screamed and pulled the trigger on the UTV. The machine exploded in a ball of fire, destroying both the machine and the hierophanticus that anchored the fiendish bubble in reality.

A wave of purple energy blasted out from the key and snuffed the dimensional link out of existence. The forest circle fell suddenly silent.

Jenner touched the gaping hole at his neck and then looked at the blood. His head swam with dizziness and heat. The soldier's eyes rolled back, and he collapsed.

Zabe leapt in front of the princess and swung his powerful fist, catching Tahnak in the jaw, cold-cocking him with a single blow. The soldier laid out on the ground, sprawled prone like a dead man.

"Are you okay?" Zabe felt for Tahnak's pulse and verified that he was fine, albeit unconscious.

She nodded. "Just... very confused."

Zabe stood and put his hands on her shoulders and looked into her eyes. He searched for confirmation. "What is your name?"

"Bithia," she said, fully convinced of it.

"Tell me the last thing you remember?"

Bithia frowned. "It is difficult to tell. Every part of Claire's memories seem as if they were recent—but my most intense memory is facing off against Regorik in the Royal castle... and... I..."

Zabe cupped her hands in his. He didn't need her to continue. Claire had already explained Bithia's sacrifice—a memory both minds had to endure. "Where is Claire, now?"

Her eyes moved back and forth as she searched her subconscious for some trace of her other half, which had suddenly gone missing—the half that owned her body. "I... I don't know."

The spires in the circle around them began to crackle with energy again. In a few moments, they might discharge another wave of chaotic energy with random effects. Tahnak groaned in the dirt below.

Zabe looked from each danger and then to the princess—not quite sure what to call her. The lycan bit his lower lip with consternation as the wicked obelisks charged up. Finally, with a shout of anger and defiance, he stabbed the Stone Glaive into the center of the core. The organic looking growth that bubbled from the ground cracked and darkened as the mystic blade plunged deep into the heart of the Nebraska Worldgate.

The core seemed to implode as the blade cut a gash through the very fabric of the Darque. A black void tore open, not unlike the rip through which Sh'logath tried to enter via Claire's blood a few years ago.

Zabe scooped up Tahnak's limp body and turned to leap through the hole before the next eldritch wave hit.

Bithia grabbed Zabe by the wrist. "I'm scared!" she said.

Zabe cocked his head.

"Something in this realm brought me back to the surface—something foul and worrisome. What if that goes away, assuming this door leads back to reality?" Panic struck her face. "What if I disappear and Claire is gone, too? Will the line of the Architect King end forever? Will I be nothing but an empty husk?"

Zabe glanced at the nearby threats. He knew they didn't have time to entertain a philosophic debate. "Sometimes you just need to have faith," he said, shouldering Tahnak's body.

"But... but..."

Zabe grabbed the princess and leaned down, and gave her a passionate kiss. As she leaned into his embrace, he tipped over. Tahnak, Bithia, and Zabe plunged through the dimensional breach just as the next blast of arcane power exploded off of the cursed ring of towers.

# CHAPTER TWENTY-ONE

Caivev screamed a string of profanities into Akko Soggathoth's smug face. Flecks of spittle streamed down the human form of the man's face. "How dare you leave us trapped in the Darque like that? I lost many soldiers and I could've died!"

"You did not," the shapeshifter stated with a calm inhumanness.

The vyrm leader rattled off another stream of expletives. "I have half a mind to just banish you and be done with it!"

Akko Soggathoth chirped with a slight giggle.

"Do you think this is some sort of game? I'll show you how serious I am!" Caivev brandished one of the earlier hierophanticese and held it centimeters from his face. "I'm not stupid!" she screamed. "I know that if this touches you, you'll be locked back in the Darque!"

Akko Soggathoth startled at the proximity of the artifact. He recoiled as she shoved it in his face and he switched forms into his true visage, the horrific goat-man shape.

Caivev seethed and glowered at him. The gruesome visage of his presence had been reduced to mere novelty; the ranking vyrm had become familiar with it.

Theera rushed towards Caivev in order to protect his master. With lightning quick reflexes, Caivev drew her pistol and put a jolt of hot laser through the vyrm's face.

As Theera's corpse tumbled at their feet, Caivev fixed her trickster ally with a stern gaze. "*Don't you dare* mess me again," she seethed. "I mean it when I say I will cast you out of our reality once and for all."

Akko Soggathoth met Caivev's gaze, but neither apologized nor wilted beneath the heat of her glare. The two scowled at each other for another few seconds before Caivev turned and left in a huff. Skrom followed, glancing menacingly at him.

Resuming his human form, Akko Soggathoth shrugged and chuckled quietly. He would not change his nature—and he refused to acknowledge any true peril from a mortal.

Touching his minion's wound, Akko Soggathoth poured energy into Theera's lifeless body to speed up his regeneration. The wound stitched itself back together and after a few more seconds, Theera gasped for air and resumed consciousness.

"Master?" Theera looked relieved that Akko Soggathoth remained unharmed.

"I am more than that, my dear friend. *I am your god*."

Theera's eyes twinkled as his heart burst with joy. "Forever and ever!"

Jackie returned to the edge of the desolate glade with Shandra and a handful of other soldiers. They couldn't find a trace of the enemy—not even a blade of singed grass. The piles of dead vyrm and even the destroyed UTV had all been sucked into the Darque when the hierophanticus deactivated.

"Did we stop it?" Jackie asked Shandra. Her voice contained more hope than her heart did.

Shandra didn't respond as they returned to the cover of the forest. She knew that Jackie wouldn't really want false hope, anyway.

They nearly stepped on Chira, who squeezed Jenner's bleeding gash between pinched fingers. He sprayed an adhesive patch over the wound to keep it together and then jammed an injector into the young soldier's neck, administering a dose of stimulant.

Jenner jolted awake with a gasp. The startled youth looked around for a second and then crawled to his knees, and finally, onto uneasy feet.

Wulftone joined them moments later as the party regrouped and counted heads while he let his lycan form melt away. They hadn't suffered any serious casualties in the final skirmish, thanks to their dense cover.

"Did we stop them?" the Corps' leader asked. "Did anyone see evidence that we sealed them inside?"

Chira shook his head. "I saw them escape with seconds to spare," he reported. "That glowing energy portal they've been using to move so quickly appeared on the far side of the clearing... there's more."

Everyone stared at Chira. Their eyes beckoned for more information.

"I saw Caivev and her general, Skrom, come out of the Darque. They are still alive after Mexico City."

Wulftone hissed a curse below his breath. "I'd really hoped this was it." He ran his fingers through his hair and tried to hide his exasperation. "Everyone double check yourselves and your neighbor for injuries. We've got to get back to the Prime ASAP. We move out in two minutes!"

He pulled Chira and Shandra aside as he took out an electronic handheld. Wulftone keyed in a password and dialed up the astrological charts to find out how soon it would be before they could return through the portal. Only the team leaders had access to such sensitive data. Despite that, he knew that the old royalty would be rolling in their graves if they knew how many people had access to the forbidden travel charts from the Grimmorium Nitthogr.

Shandra asked, "What are we doing, Wulftone?"

He sighed dejectedly. "I'm not sure. Stalling? I honestly don't know—but I'm open to suggestions." Wulftone cursed when the program, written by Tay-lore, showed they didn't have any way back to the Prime for at least a day.

Chira looked over his shoulder. "We don't have a day," he muttered. "They could begin their Sh'logathian rituals any moment now."

"Yeah, yeah," Wulftone muttered, wracking his brain for a plan.

"Don't panic," Shandra said, trying to keep anxiety from overwhelming her heart, even though she felt an internal burning as a stress ulcer formed. "We don't know how long their rituals take to perform or if they have any other specific conditions, such as solar or lunar alignment."

"Trenzlr might know those details," Wulftone said, setting his eyes towards the monastery. "We've got to get back and come up with a new plan. The closest route is to wait a day and go back the way we came."

Shandra and Chira both nodded.

Wulftone yelled and got everyone's attention. "Everybody move out!"

Bithia watched Zabe drag Tahnak behind a piece of construction equipment. He'd transformed back to a man immediately after their return from the Darque and without his lycan strength, he struggled to haul the dead weight of their friend. She'd forgotten exactly how much she admired his tenacity.

Her cheeks flushed at the suddenly real senses that she'd repossessed in Claire's human body. While her spirit and consciousness remained in the kind of half-life she shared with Claire, Bithia wasn't connected the same way as she'd been before her sacrifice. *This is everything she'd wanted*, her conscience told her.

Bithia pushed the guilty feelings down deep where she wouldn't have to confront them. Her inner demons—the creeping resentment she sometimes felt when Claire was at her happiest—were a monster for another day.

She looked around. Most of the streetlights worked and shed light on the small community's downtown area. Mullen looked much as it had when she'd first seen it through Claire's eyes. The town had undergone extensive construction to repair the damage caused during the Heptobscurantum's attempted Awakening. Only the central area at the center of the town remained to be finished; it had been the epicenter of the interdimensional chaos. Craters and carbon scoring still scarred the land where the worst of the fighting occurred.

Ducking behind a bulldozer, Bithia avoided a flashlight and motioned for Zabe to stay down. He tucked Tahnak's body behind a heavy loader and hid behind the wheels, holding his breath and keeping silent until the flashlight passed and its owner meandered away.

"It's very late, here," Zabe said a minute later. "That should help us. I don't think we want anybody watching as we try to activate the portal back to the Prime." He was surprised at the security presence in such a small town—but it made sense, given what had happened in the recent history.

Bithia nodded. "Have you found the world-gate's controls?"

Zabe shook his head. Everything had been torn up during the construction and he feared the mystic guidance system had been either buried or destroyed. The portal location couldn't be destroyed—by its nature, the location's power was immutable, but they couldn't tap into that source without them.

He dug with his hands, frantically searching for any of the activators. Time was so sensitive that he hadn't even stopped to discuss what had happened with Bithia. The threat of a revived Sh'logath was perhaps the only danger menacing enough to supersede his deep worry for her.

"I think I can find it," Bithia said, reaching out with her senses. The eldritch rune stones, carved millennia ago, glowed on the astral plane as if they'd been covered with luminescent paint. "They are below us, buried in the dirt."

The flashlight returned in the distance. Something about the way it swung seemed to indicate that its owner walked with purpose. He'd be there any moment. Even if Zabe shapeshifted and risked terrorizing any observers, it remained unlikely that even *he* could dig it up in time.

A swath of light washed over the area as the officer scanned the construction zone. Bithia and Zabe hunkered down behind pallets of building supplies. The beam paused near the loader, where Tahnak's legs peeked out from behind a tire. Audio static sizzled as the guard called for assistance.

"I don't know what I've got," he said into his radio. "Maybe an out-or-town drunk, or maybe another one of those weirdo cultists, but I've got an unconscious man laying behind the Bobcat and dressed for comic con."

"We're on our way," a reply crackled.

Bithia stepped out boldly into the light. Their time window would expire momentarily, and they could not delay another moment. She reached out again with her senses and found what she was looking for.

Zabe reached for her, hissing with stern disagreement. The light caught him as well, and the officer yanked his gun with the sound of steel on leather.

"Don't move a muscle!" the guard howled in surprise.

"Bithia?" Zabe asked. "I hope you have a plan?" He suddenly noticed the stark difference between Claire and Bithia—Claire would not have taken this risk. Zabe didn't like it—not with so much on the line.

Bithia smiled when Zabe called her by name. It helped reinforce her unspoken decision made in the Darque—it validated her on a fundamental level. She grimaced only momentarily and then knelt to touch Tahnak's foot while reaching up for Zabe's hand.

"I said don't move," the nervous officer shouted, gun hand wavering.

"Easy," Zabe said calmly, trying to dispel the tension and keep from getting shot.

Bithia used her mind and felt for the runes—penetrated their defenses and reached deep inside them. Her mind fell for what seemed like an eternity and entered a deep place.

She dared not embrace her own hubris, but Bithia knew that Claire could never have achieved the level of communion she'd gained with the foundations of reality as she palavered with the mildly sentient rune stones. Her pride very nearly threatened to knock her out of the sacred psychic grounds she'd intruded within, but she held fast.

Without words, without arguments, she convinced the eldritch stones they needed to activate, even without the requisite sacrifice—the Prime was in danger if they did not. The Tesseract would suffer if these stones did not open the portal immediately!

Claire's eyes opened suddenly and reality spun back into motion as if it never missed a beat. Her gaze locked with their captor's and she smiled.

With a flash of light, the three traveler's bodies disintegrated. A jolt of cold rippled through the planeswalkers as the Tesseract tore them apart and knit them back together in a different dimension. The Princess had managed to psychically activate the portal, astrally flipping switches and sending them back to the Prime.

Tahnak groaned groggily as he sat up next to his friends who kneeled, looking awestruck at what they'd found. "What happened, guys?" His head pounded with pain, but at least he'd returned to his right mind since the Darque.

He did a double-take at the sight arrayed around the Prime's main gate, just outside the castle, and then stared slack-jawed by a sight he never thought he'd see. Then, all around them, another brilliant flash momentarily blinded those still standing on the portal site.

Basilisk sat in the uppermost chamber of his mansion perched atop Limbus. He focused on the black void hanging in the distant sky and communed with the Great Devourer, which lurked on the threshold between reality and not.

The Dunnischktet's eyes had clouded over and the two became one in essence—sharing a bond in the ways of the Mae'le-ggath, nearly forgotten by all save the highest priestly caste since their flight to Edenya... long before the Desolation.

Emptying himself, the hybrid let his mind fill with the thoughts and will of the Hungerer. Basilisk drank from the mind of Sh'logath, who guided him to the few actions he'd actually taken in service of his cause since the Syzygyc War, including the assassination of Princess Bithia's father.

The dark one spoke to him in urges, communicated with impulses and visions that Basilisk didn't always understand in the moment. He learned what he must do and his body groaned with acknowledgment as the painful emptiness filled him... Basilisk knew he must act again for his master.

He looked away from the creeping doom that filled the sky and shook his head clear. Basilisk opened a tray and removed a flat, egg-sized stone and his engraving tools. The master commanded a rune be made and delivered—a rune of return.

Basilisk grinned. He did not need to understand in order to obey—but he didn't also need to obey in order to be obedient. Even though he remained true thus far, he teetered on the cusp of the same sins as his brother Nitthogr. Yet Basilisk played the game more expertly than the former, fallen darling of the Veritas.

Besides—the rune would not work, anyway. He hadn't lied when he said he could not return those made of stone. He didn't understand why, but some component of power was missing; he'd already tried to engineer such a reversal of the stone-form curse many times in the past.

The tarkhūn leader avoided looking directly at the horror in his sky. Ever since claiming the Architect King as his trophy, he'd become something else... since that day he'd never *fully* surrendered to communion with Sh'logath. *Perhaps that was the root of division between us brothers*, he mused. Basilisk never truly emptied himself to an outside master—there was always a little sip of Basilisk remaining at the bottom of the cup... and less and less it seemed with each filling.

He grinned at how his sins had not been found out over all those years. He'd not been indecisive—he'd been patient, waiting for *his* time to come, and he would play *his* hand better than Nitthogr had.

Basilisk was an expert at the game—one that he'd finally chosen to play again. He would obey Sh'logath in all things and bend the outcomes to conclusions *he* decided would yield his best outcome. For now, that meant applying Sh'logath's will to the information collected by his spies—contacts embedded deep in the Guardian Corps, who were due any day now with a report.

The hybrid grinned. He was Dunnischktet in all things—but he was Basilisk in will.

The combined forces of the Guardian Corps, the Royal Military, and the Veritas burst out of the forest near the monastery. Between the stimulant injectors and a goodly dose of internal grit, most of the wounded casualties came out of the forest under their own power.

Wulftone and Sam carried Gita between them. As the most petite member of the Corps, it had been painfully un-difficult, almost like carrying an injured child.

The full roster of the monastery waited inside the gates for the return of the outland warriors. Leaning heavily on his support staff, the old man watched them approach with his keen eyes.

He rattled off a string of words in his native tongue as Jackie approached. Her sluggish footsteps moved heavily from battle fatigue.

It was obvious that the old man deduced their mission had been unsuccessful. The elder spoke with passion and insistence, as he and Jackie communicated in halting phrases.

Wulftone caught up to Jackie. "What is he saying?"

"He insists that we must 'catch the devil before it's too late.'"

Wulftone nodded in full agreement as Jackie tried to explain through the language barrier that they were trapped. "If only we could," he muttered at the patriarch's request.

The old man pointed at the prayer room where they'd entered from the prime and insisted. "Intoarcere. Intoarcere." He paused and shifted to a word he knew Jackie could translate. "Ritorno."

"He wants us to go back."

Wulftone nodded at the obvious and pointed at the sky. "Tell him we cannot until the heavens let us."

Jackie and the man struggled through the linguistic hurdles.

The old man pointed at Jackie, then Wulftone, and finally waved at them all. "Destin." He jabbed his finger back at the prayer room.

"Destino?" Jackie asked.

He nodded. "Destin. Destino." Putting his fist in the pockets of his robe, the elderly patriarch removed a very old spool. A brilliant crimson thread had been coiled around the bobbin carved of darquematter. He placed it in Jackie's hand and hobbled excitedly to the prayer chamber and beckoned them over.

"He wants you to go first," Jackie told Shandra.

The cleric approached the monk, and he tied the end of the red thread around her left ring finger. He pointed to the room and urged her, "Destin."

"This is a man of sincere faith," she said, looking into his eyes. "He would be most welcome amongst the Veritas." Shandra nodded to him, turned and entered the room trailing a thin line of vermillion and stepped through, crossing the line between realms of the tesseract, floating in the void and tethered by the red cord.

He repeated the act quickly with each of the warriors, including Gita and her escort. At the end, only Jackie remained with a small amount of thread tied around the spool. The old man fixed her with a confident look and looped the last length around her finger.

"Destin," he insisted.

"Destin," she replied and then entered the room, breaking through the veil between worlds.

As one solid unit, the entangled group of planeswalkers burst back into existence in the Prime. They stood dumbfounded on the main platform outside of the castle, nearly stumbling over the Princess, Zabe, and Tahnak who had just appeared at the portal location.

An entire battalion of mixed forces surrounded the stone platform where they rested. At their head, Shjikara and Pollando stood surrounded by an array of clerics, each dressed for war in their version of the Guardian Corps' armor.

Shandra watched Pollando move the arms on his golden armillary sphere by several clicks. He used it to calculate which gates should be passable and which were blocked. Raising an eyebrow at the cleric and her team, which should not have been able to plansewalk, he put the device back within his cloaks.

Pollando fixed Shjikara with a gaze that Shandra knew meant the mute psychic was speaking to him directly. She could hardly take in the sight of the army arrayed nearby.

As a matter of protocol, there had never been more than a handful of Veritas permitted beyond the abbey at any time: it housed the largest stockpile of arcane artifacts second only to the Chamber of Mysteries. That collection needed protection at all times—the overwhelming presence of the Veritas proved exactly how dire the situation had become.

For the first time since Nitthogr fell from their ranks, the Veritas had prepared to go to war.

As Jackie helped the medics transfer Gita to a hospital, a cargo shuttle landed to house the leadership team as they tried to concoct a frenzied battle plan. The team needed to depart as soon as the portal would allow them entry to the location nearest the Hidden Temple in Earth's Central America. According to Pollando's calculations, the astronomical alignment would allow them passage in about an hour.

The reverse thrusters on the shuttle fired and kicked up a gust of sandy air as it landed. Bithia looked away to protect her eyes and spotted Sam Jones, who made a beeline for her.

"Father?" she gushed with emotion. Bithia had lost her own father years before Nitthogr's conquest and Sam was his spitting image. She leapt into his arms as Sam embraced her. The princess couldn't rein in her heart even though she knew that this was not her father, the king... this was her father, Sam Jones.

"Claire!" He clapped her into a bear hug and squeezed her tightly. Sam released her and looked into her eyes. "Claire?" He noticed the change like only a parent could.

She bit the corner of her lip and slowly shook her head.

He whispered, understanding he'd unraveled a royal secret. "Bithia?"

"Yes," she admitted. "I… I'm sorry. I don't know where Claire has gone," she said honestly. She only knew the reasons why, but refused to acknowledge the dark truth: that she'd flexed her psychic muscle in the Darque when a wave of energy pulsed through her and it forced Bithia's will to the surface.

Sam stared blankly at the woman who was, but was not, his daughter. The doors to their makeshift operations center opened, and they both knew time remained too short to ask those difficult questions that demanded hard answers.

Yardi stood in the doorway, propped up on a cybernetic leg. His face still bore the horrible marks from the wounds he'd gotten so recently. Pink flesh puckered around stitches and fresh cuts.

Zabe asked, "We have you to thank for this?"

Yardi nodded. "As soon as the Hall of Mirrors burned, Tay-lore knew we had to prepare for the worst." His voice rasped hoarse and gravelly from his damaged voice-box.

Bithia took a seat alongside Zabe and Wulftone. Chira, Yardi, Sam, and a host of others organized themselves. A digital clock at the head of the transport ticked down with a timer indicating when the portal would allow them access.

Shjikara stood at the front of the room and called up a slide of several ancient glyphs recovered from old texts in the Veritas's records. "We do not know exactly where the enemy has gone," he stated. "These writings from the pre-Sh'logathian Mae'le-ggath reference a 'Hidden Temple' of the vyrm."

The Veritas's leader turned to Trenzlr, who they hoped could guide them. "Do you know the location of this temple?" Shjikara's voice didn't try to mask his usual suspicion of the turncoat vyrm.

"No," he said woefully. "By Maetha, I would certainly tell you if I knew."

Sam stared at the ancient scribbles while Shjikara explained that they would have to send troops through every portal on Earth to try to ascertain the location and such a division of their forces would almost certainly result in failure—as if he could somehow guilt Trenzlr into somehow procuring an answer. The vyrm could only shake his head with regret—he truthfully didn't have the knowledge they needed.

"I recognize that writing," the archaeologist stated. "I've seen it before—three years ago... right before Caivev's team captured me. I know exactly where this temple is hiding."

# CHAPTER TWENTY-TWO

Shjikara spoke as if he was struck by genuine fear. "I had a vision—and that is why I brought the Veritas *here...* to this portal at the Prime's Worldgate. In my vision, the statue of the Architect King stood upon this site and the ground shook so violently that his stone form crumbled to dust. I knew then that all would be lost if we did not come down from our hill. And so we came down, and when we arrived, the android and the cripple had already gathered the military."

If Tay-lore could have glared, he would have. Yardi resented being called a cripple and glowered enough for both of them.

Bithia stood to take over the meeting at the same time as Zabe. She looked at him for a second and then quickly sat, deferring to him as Claire would have done while trying not to draw attention to her change. The last thing they needed was further distraction.

Zabe glanced at the trickling clock and continued as if nothing had happened. "Trenzlr doesn't know anything about the nature of the Awakening that the Brothers of the Winnowing will perform. As long as we remain alive, there is a chance we might still prevent it, but we'll have to throw everything that we've got at it. Akko Soggathoth is as devious as he is deadly."

Shjikara frowned. He'd never approved of Zabe's elevation to his father's position. "So your plan is to run straight into the home of an enemy that you've been unable to defeat thus far and try to figure it out?"

"I'll hit him with my sword," Zabe spat.

"How do you know that will work?"

"Have you seen it? It's a really *big* sword."

Shjikara glared at him while they turned to the commotion at the doorway as Tahnak tried pushing his way past the guards at the door. They'd tried to keep as much confidential as they could, still under the suspicion that they had a mole in their company, and they kept the circle small.

"I know how to banish the Brothers of the Winnowing," he yelled.

Zabe waved the guards off. "You're supposed to be getting medical help."

Tahnak waved his concern away and tossed a small bulging sack into his hands. "Darquematter shards. They can't touch these things without experiencing a violent shift back into the Darque."

Zabe ran his fingers through the collected hunks of twisted metal. They varied in size and shape.

"The ones you got from inside the Darque Prime?"

He nodded. "When I wandered for all those years, I felt compelled to gather as many as I could find. There's about sixty of them."

"How do you know all that?" Shjikara squinted at him suspiciously.

Tahnak tossed him the old journal he'd found during his wanderings in the fallen dimension, even though nobody they knew could decode it. "It's all in there."

Zabe nodded. He trusted Tahnak—even though he'd recently tried to kill him. "So we have a plan." He passed out handfuls of the metallic shards to those in the room. "Make sure you distribute these to your best troops. We only need to stop *one* of the seven in order to succeed... now we just need to get to them." He turned to Tay-lore, hoping the android had an idea of the location.

Tay-lore shook his head. "I am sorry, but I have been unable to..."

Sam Jones interrupted him. "I know where they'll be." He typed some coordinates into the display and pressed a button. The digital map overlaid on the wall panned to center on the recently emancipated country of Chiriquí. It zoomed in to focus on the excavation site where he'd been stationed several years prior during his daughter's first engagement. He glanced momentarily at Bithia and his gut twisted with heartache. "This satellite imagery is old," he stated, "but below this stone formation here is a buried pyramid similar to the one we found Shandra in at Antarctica. We should assume it has been at least partially excavated since the time the rebels chased us out and Caivev kidnapped me."

Tay-lore interfaced with the image and a glowing dot pulsed a few kilometers to the north. "The gate will open up here and allow travel to this site in approximately twenty-nine minutes," he stated. "It is as close as we can go and is as soon as we can go."

Sam recognized the location. "That's where the rebels were headquartered during all the political unrest. The secessionist statists who are in power now formerly operated from that region."

"Then we should have every reason to believe they are working with Caivev and will bring their full force to bear in order to prevent us from getting to that temple in time," Zabe deduced.

"The portal is a choke point," Wulftone pointed out. "How will we be able to get through without them mowing us down as we arrive?"

Tay-lore piped up, "I may have an idea about that."

Alberto wiped the sweat off of his mustache and stared at the Crag, a supposedly mystical ravine that split the earth near the old rebel outpost. "I'm telling you, Carlos—I heard General Nyagittari has lost his mind. I have a friend who works for him in the capital. She saw him one morning and said it looked like his face was melting off. Maybe he's on drugs or something."

Carlos looked at his friend and adjusted his weapon. He shrugged. "Maybe, but Nyagittari has been right all along up until now." He looked into the jagged pit where generations of Brujería had amounted to piles of bleached bones, half-filling the deep maw of the Crag. The ancient washout had hosted many years' worth of witchcraft since the days of Cortés and his secret cabal of conquistadores that flirted with dark powers.

Alberto shuddered. "Still... he's got to be a madman, to commit almost one hundred percent of his military to guarding a pit in the middle of the jungle."

A few of the other nationals surrounding Alberto and Carlos murmured their assents.

"What if he's right?" one of them asked. Two days ago Nyagittari had redirected the soldiers here—a wildly unpopular political move with the Chiriquí's borders still ill-defined amongst its neighbors. "What if the devil and his demonic legions are really trying to break through a portal from hell?"

Alberto glanced sidelong at him and noticed the tattoos covering the man. He was typical of the naïve, native countrymen whose superstitious streaks ran a mile wide. Alberto frowned; he'd been to university. As such, most of such fantasy had been ground out of him by academia. However, he understood why his kinsmen obeyed the order—but Alberto couldn't understand how someone so tactically brilliant as General Nyagittari, the freer of his people, could possess such a frail mind.

"Correction," said Carlos smugly. "One hundred percent *or more*."

Alberto scrunched up his face and looked over his shoulder at the billowing clouds of dust kicked up by Nyagittari's motorcade. His entourage led a huge crew of their remaining forces that piled out of the transports. They began setting up heavy artillery equipment and arranging troops to surround the Crag.

Cursing, Alberto ran his fingers through his oily, slicked hair in disbelief. He lit a cigarette and laughed incredulously. "Why doesn't he just set off one of those nukes they say he smuggled out of Korea and be done with it!"

A man in the distance pulled the tarp off a giant flatbed truck and exposed a missile on the vehicular mounted launch system. It might not have been nuclear, but it was impressive, nonetheless.

"You were saying," Carlos laughed at the irony.

Alberto's cigarette dropped from his mouth in disbelief. "We're all going to die today because of a madman," he moaned.

"He's only a madman if he's wrong," the tattooed soldier commented, pointing to the Crag as a flash of light flared in the distance. "What the heck is that thing?"

Wulftone caught up with Trenzlr and Tay-lore as Zabe released them to make their final preparations and give any farewells that were due. They discussed an encrypted message that some unknown party had been able to send to the vyrm by name. It had been broadcast into the Prime on all frequencies. The android had just intercepted the message and held it for decoding and safekeeping—though it paled in priority to this conflict.

"Can I speak with you, Trenzlr?"

The vyrm heretic nodded, and they stepped aside. "How can I help you?"

Tay-lore bowed. "Pardon my leaving, but I have a weapon to prepare."

They nodded and watched him hurry away.

"Recently, I caught some snippets of conversation between Akko Soggathoth and his brother, Akko Sxkakzacros—talk of brothers and mothers and fathers. Is it important?"

Trenzlr shrugged. "Not from a military standpoint. The legend of Akko Sxkakzacros might be important because it informs us how dangerous he is. In their early years, he devoured his youngest brother, Akko Quarnyk... Akko Soggathoth is not actually the youngest, but Akko Sxkakzacros ate the youngest and gained all of his brother's power, becoming much more powerful than the rest. How did you hear about it?"

He pointed to his ears. "Really good hearing, at least when I'm in my lycan shape."

The vyrm nodded. "As for mothers and fathers, you need not worry about some even more powerful threat. Their primary purpose is to summon Sh'logath after they've paved his way through the chaos they've created in nature."

"They have no origins, then?"

"Yes and no. They were not birthed like you or me. There is a kind of family structure—remember that these are creatures of pure evil—and so they must abide by law rather than love, which is foreign to them."

"Law?"

Trenzlr shrugged. "As much as they are denizens of ultimate chaos, they are bound by rules which only they obey—and maybe only *they* know. I believe Akko Soggathoth is in charge only because he was the first to be released from his prison by a foolhardy band of cultists."

"And the 'Mother' and 'Father?'"

"The original high priest and priestess of Mae'le-ggath... the original cult of Sh'logath worship that formed when the vyrm walked away from Maetha. It's more of an honorific than anything else."

Wulftone's hopes perked up. "Will they have to listen to them—is there a chance that we could somehow kidnap or impersonate someone they must obey?"

Trenzlr grimaced and shook his head. "No. Mother and Father were sacrificed long ago—centuries before my people discovered the breach and entered Edenya... back when we, too, were creatures of the Darque. Even if that line continued, it would've ended generations ago with the Thousand Elders of Neggath."

Shjikara walked past them as the rest of the Veritas prepared to head into war with the Guardian Corps and the military. Four clerics followed on his heels.

Wulftone called out, "Where are you going?"

The leader of the Order paused and looked at him as if deciding whether he owed him an explanation. "The Veritas fight with you. I cannot. There are reasons that I must remain inside our halls—things I've been away from for too long, even now. I must return and maintain a skeleton crew to protect the sacred monastery grounds."

Wulftone watched the leader go. True, the Veritas had helped his family during the last invasion of the Prime, but he'd never been fond of Shjikara who seemed to loathe fighting for the things that were truly important—and it was always Wulftone and Zabe's family who ended up paying the price for his reluctance.

Jackie leaned over the rail of the hospital bed and clutched Gita's hand as the doctors tested the tissue around the blaster wound. The young girl's breathing came in ragged gasps.

"I'm sorry this happened to you, Gita," Jackie said. With a final squeeze, she set her friend's hand down.

She asked the doctor, "Is she going to make it?"

With a tight-lipped shrug, the doctor treaded between cold practicality and positive bedside manner. "I really have no idea. The tissue damage is deep. I'm most worried about electrical damage to the central nervous system—she might seem to be in relatively good health and then experience total organ failure out of the blue." He tsk-tsked and then shook his head. "Things were simpler before these blaster weapons became the norm—I might actually miss the good old days of swords and arrows."

Jackie nodded and thanked the doctor. She stood and took two steps from the door when Gita spoke.

"Hey. Where do you think you're going?" she rasped groggily.

Jackie turned around and took Gita's hand again. "I'm heading back to the battle. We have one final chance to stop him—to shut down whatever this demon Akko Soggathoth is."

"Hold on," Gita said with heavily lidded eyes. "Lemme grab my stuff. I'm coming, too."

Jackie shook her head. "No. Stay and rest."

"Rest? Pfft. If *you're* going, *I'm* going."

"You just got shot!"

With a chuckle, she lamented, "How come I always hafta be the one who gets shot?" She opened her eyes and tried to angle her head enough to look at her chest. "No wonder I feel so awful... wait. *Who the heck shot me?* We weren't fighting anything with guns."

Jackie looked away sheepishly. "Jenner."

Gita groaned. "Crap. Here I thought he might've been sweet on me... hashtag relationship goals, right? Did he at least make it out alive so that I can return the favor?"

Jackie laughed through a few tears of joy, even though her friend butchered the usage of the earth phrase. "Yeah. He's just down the hall. He would've sealed the Darquegate on his own—had we arrived thirty seconds sooner. But he's in pretty rough shape, too."

"Great. If you come back and learn someone smothered him in his hospital bed, I may ask you to be my alibi."

Jackie smiled. "I've really got to go now. In twenty minutes, every soldier we can muster is going to charge against that monster and burn him to the ground. Sh'logath will never rise while we live."

Groggily, Gita growled, "Well, not *every* soldier. Gita, Jenner, and the Veritas will stay back and mind the fort." She spat the last one.

"Actually, no. Even the Veritas have finally turned out against the enemy."

Gita blinked with surprise and even perked up for a second. "Well... that's a shocker."

Jackie almost had to push her back down. She didn't want her friend to overexert herself and she'd heard more than enough times about the girl's resentment of the Order; she felt they had abandoned the Prime during Nitthogr's invasion.

"You know, my parents would still be alive if they'd acted during the last battle."

"I know." Jackie kissed her forehead in order to plant her back into her pillow. "But I've still got to get back. The battle won't wait for me. I'll be back soon."

"You'd better be," Gita warned her. "You're the only family I've got left."

Charobv's thoughts went out to his son, Chartarra. He hadn't heard from him in a long while and could only assume he had died in battle. With the alliance formed between The Black and the Tarkhūn forces, he wouldn't have been under deep cover or on any sensitive mission against Basilisk's agents any longer. He frowned.

General Nyagittari slapped his lieutenant on the shoulder. Charobv was the only other one in the vehicle with Kreephast, so they could talk freely. Together, they'd invented Nyagittari and engineered a revolution out of the preexisting civil unrest. "What's the matter?"

Charobv shook off the dour mood. "Nothing—I'm excited that the Awakening is finally at hand... it's just that I had hoped others would be with to watch it come to pass."

Kreephast feigned a wounded ego. "I see. If the great General Nyagittari is not good enough company for you, then I don't know how I'll be able to cope."

His longtime friend and accomplice punched him back with a laugh. Suddenly, everyone near the Crag began moving forward as if something had happened.

Kreephast put binoculars to his face and stared across the distance. The two vyrm had the advantage of height from their place inside the cab of the missile truck, and he was able to catch a glimpse of a metallic, egg-like device as it crackled with lightning-like energy. Suddenly, amidst the crawling arcs of electricity, a second egg appeared alongside the first.

"What in the thirty-three worlds?"

# Chapter Twenty-Three

"Please, stay back," Tay-lore begged the humans. They gave the synthetic man a wide berth as he finished assembling the large, elongated silver orb upon the portal location. "I would hate to make a mistake and have others pay the price." He twisted a few loose wires together and replaced the control panel; even though his origins were mechanical in nature, he was not immune to error—in that regard, he was just like everybody else.

The input controls lit up and Tay-lore set a count-down timer. Hurrying, he took the second, similar orb and did likewise—offering up a brief prayer for his own safety as he activated weapon number two. Tay-lore synchronized the timers and waved to Yardi, who began walking towards the edge of the mustered troops.

Zabe caught his one-legged officer in a firm grasp. "Be careful. Be safe."

Yardi winced as he winked, despite the pain in his mangled face. "I volunteered for this because I'm probably the least likely to have any significant impact on the coming fight," he said, limping towards the Worldgate on a cybernetic leg he'd barely gotten the feel of.

Zabe nodded, understanding his meaning. If something went wrong—Yardi knew he was more expendable than the next able body in this important fight. "That's unlikely, but I agree with risk mitigation—even if it should be me at the front."

Yardi stumbled as he walked backward towards the set of bombs as nonchalantly as possible. He used a dagger to cut his palm. "That's where we disagree. You're too important to take the risk—even if it is only minimal."

Zabe knew Yardi was right. He'd told Bithia and Claire that exact same thing countless times... and yet she stood beside him, prepared to rush into battle even now.

Tay-lore returned to his spot at the edge of the battle line next to Bithia and Jackie. "The timer is set on both devices. The bio-EMP should detonate twenty seconds after arrival."

His species had specifically designed a weapon capable of disrupting the electrical signals traveling through the nervous systems of biological creatures. It was the machines' answer to the electromagnetic pulse devices the humans had built to use against Tay-lore's brethren. Because the humans had finished their design first, the bio-EMP had never seen the light of day. "Weapon number two will go off half a minute later.

Bithia gave a cold nod. "If this works, you may have saved us all, Tay-lore."

"I merely gave you a fighting chance," he stated, trying to keep his voice devoid of any emotion. In truth, Tay-lore hated violence, and it bothered him to play even this part in the conflict. He glanced at Bithia and felt an internal pain that convinced him he had a soul; he would violate every part of his emotional programming if it meant keeping his princess safe.

At the edge of the portal platform, Yardi walked to the ancient stone plinths and touched his bloody hand to a set of runes etched upon it. A second later, the egg-shaped devices shimmered and disappeared.

With a host of supporters at her back, Caivev made the arcane hand gestures in front of the blood-painted door at the heart of her buried temple. The musty smell of the deep intermingled with the tang of the fresh blood.

A drained body lay discarded and blanched in the corner; it hadn't been necessary to drench the door with so much that it killed the victim, but it brought pleasure to Akko Soggathoth. Six more local men and women, kidnapped from the nearest village, cowered nearby, where they'd been shackled into a chain gang by heavy leg irons.

Andrew Thornton gasped with pleasure as the mystically sealed Gates of Koth opened. The oil baron joined Percival Wainsmith and Jacob Sisyphus as representatives from the Heptobscurantum. The rest of the Illuminati met to privately celebrate the Awakening on their own.

Sisyphus pressed a small talisman into his two peers' palms. "An insurance policy to protect you," he mumbled, keeping his voice low, but not really caring if he'd been overheard or not.

The other two members of the Seven tied the leather thong around their neck and let the twisted hunk of darquematter dangle just below their neckline. They were well-versed enough in arcane mechanics to predict that the alien metal would help prevent possession by the spirits of the Darque. Sisyphus clearly had contingencies covered and didn't want his core team pressed into service alongside those other six souls clad in chains.

Akko Soggathoth led the way into the Darque with his minion, Theera, in tow. The undead vyrm toted the book with the darquematter seal and carried a large, gilded reliquary box upon his back like a Sherpa.

They entered the Darque Temple of Koth. A macabre collection of vyrm soldiers greeted them at the door; part of Caivev's earlier team that had been abandoned at the Island of the Dolls, they had been trapped in tortured poses where they'd tried to escape through the locked door of Kith. One of the chaotic waves of energy had transmuted them into living crystal, much like the Stone Glaive's ability which Basilisk had commandeered.

The goatman walked past and pushed one over with a snicker. It tipped and then shattered against the stone floor, releasing a kind of ghostly form into the air. It shifted transparently like a reflection in a smudged window. The thing faded away and wandered towards the Darquelands as if drawn by an unseen river's current.

"This way," Akko Soggathoth said, guiding them through the winding tunnels. He seemed intimately familiar with the layout. The party followed him through corridors lit by a faint glow emanating from patches of bioluminescent moss.

As the ground lilted upwards, they turned several corners until they came to a central chamber where various ancient religious artifacts and writings laid. Doors to either side mirrored the time-locked cells in the Kith temple. Nobody turned aside to see if they worked—who knew what might lurk inside?

Akko Soggathoth paused momentarily and glanced down the long hallway, which led to the surface of the Darque. Violet lightning flashed at the end of the tunnel and flashes of crimson burned the sky as a fiery hailstorm dropped molten chunks of slag beyond the aperture. He turned and went through the other door behind the party and continued the ascent through a set of winding stairs.

At the flat peak of the pyramid, their door opened to reveal a crown of obsidian spires. They glowed with deeply etched sigils. A slow, churning ring of stone hung in the sky overhead; black eldritch chains hung in the upper firmament and locked the shimmering portal in the fell heavens where the rips of energy zigged and zagged in the shape of the seven-pointed star. The Nihil Bridge.

"It's beautiful," Thornton whispered as the party approached the circle carved into the stone pavement. Seven blank, circular spaces were drawn outside the main etching—each one awaited a Brother of the Winnowing.

Theera ran on ahead, leading the chain gang to the center of the zone where they cowered beneath the twisting circle of chains and ether. He met his master's gaze and set down a package he'd been lugging on his back. The ark-style golden box boasted a mount for the book; he cracked open the heavy tome and rested it on the crook before silently slinking away.

"It is time to begin the rituals of the Winnowing," Akko Soggathoth howled to the sky which responded with a peal of thunder. He signaled to Theera, who traced a symbol over the heart of the lead captive on the tether and then unlocked his cuffs.

"Akko Nuggezeth," the goatman called forth as the freed man tried to bolt. The sigil on the opened page of the codex burst into a black cloud. It struck the man like a viper and consumed him, making him into the avatar of Akko Nuggezeth. He turned and sneered at the others with empty, ebon eyes. In his human form, he caught Idrakka with his baleful gaze and scowled.

Idrakka allowed himself a grin of his own. He hadn't forgotten the creature's threats in the Antarctic tomb where he'd bested the demigod.

Akko Nuggezeth turned away from the vyrm and walked purposefully across the seven-pointed stage. He transformed into a rotting goat form hybrid similar to his brother's and he took his place in the center of one of the tertiary rings.

Jacob Sisyphus watched with rapt interest as the demigod used his own blood to draw his sigil at the base of his circular post. Gleaming, mystic chains snapped up from the seal and latched onto the daemon like squid taking prey.

Nothing would stop the Awakening this time.

Kreephast and Charobv watched their men stationed just below on the ridge. They reacted to the sudden appearance of the two odd items. Suddenly, one of the devices erupted in a brilliant burst of crackling energy. The white shockwave washed over the mustered troops, knocking any biological creatures unconscious. Any persons caught in the surge crumpled like a bundle of sticks. Countless birds fell from the sky and fell to the ground seconds later like a rain of avian corpses, smacking the ground with a steady rhythm.

As soon as the bio-EMP detonation erupted, it seemed to fade, knocking out the bulk of Nyagittari's front line. "What just happened?" Charobv screamed, glancing at the clock and noting the time. Both vyrm knew their enemy was to blame and so they activated the electronic locks on the missile truck. "The cab is bullet and blaster proof, right?"

Kreephast nodded confidently.

The phony General Nyagittari grabbed the mouthpiece for his loudspeaker. "All troops—stand by for enemy incursion." He could see the sudden panic in the eyes of his faux countrymen who suddenly realized their General had not lost his mind: demons were about to invade from some hellish dimension! "Prepare to use the high-tech weapons my scientists developed," he lied about the vyrm technology he'd smuggled in from the Black's caches.

Kreephast snapped the binoculars up to his face and spotted a lone figure standing upon the portal site in the Crag. A massive werewolf who hefted an unmistakable stone blade taunted the enemy and took a lay of the land. "It's Zabe—the Royal protector."

Charobv snatched the missile control unit and prepped the weapon on the mobile launching rail. "All troops, prepare for battle as soon as I launch the first assault!" He watched eagerly with his finger on the launch button, just waiting for a group of people to enter the earth realm so he could obliterate as many as possible with their opening salvo.

Suddenly, the second egg erupted in a crackling blue bubble of energy, larger than the first—and with a bigger radius. Charobv gasped and smashed the launch button just as the electromagnetic pulse rushed for them and with Kreephast screaming, "No!" He tried to bat the launch system away before the ignition could be initiated—but too late.

The launch sequence fired up just as the enemies began pouring in from the Prime and the distinctive EMP blast washed over their vehicle. Charobv pushed his fellow vyrm off of him.

"What have you done?" Kreephast demanded with alarm in his voice.

Charobv looked at his ally, nodding towards the growing group of enemies as they began pouring through the planeswalking gate. He grinned wickedly as he thought he spotted Claire Jones breach the rift and stand within the Crag. "The missiles are shielded against EMP countermeasures."

Kreephast turned to look over his back at the rocket as the boosters rumbled and began to power up. "Yeah! But the rest of the truck isn't—including the transport lock mechanisms!"

Charobv whirled around within the darkened cab of the dead vehicle and squinted at the missile's lock systems. They firmly held the massive explosive to the launching rail, which was supposed to guide the ballistic device to its target.

Panic gripped Kreephast, and he yanked on the door handle—it held fast, locked by the truck's burned out electronics. He pulled his blaster pistol, which had also been drained, but worked as a club and he beat the window in vain, trying to break the bulletproof glass as the boosters fired. Thrusters spat fire and the missile tried to launch.

Charobv and Kreephast howled in terror as the weapon's fiery plume pushed the truck across the road fifteen feet, groaning against the locked rail which twisted and bent under the force and suddenly the missile reached the end of the sequence.

The truck's cab could withstand repeated gunfire, but it was not rocket proof.

Shjikara glanced at his timepiece as the hovering anti-grav sled settled to the ground just outside of the Veritas' walled grounds. He exited the shuttle flanked by four of his guards, who had detailed knowledge of the monastery's advanced security systems. Few knew it, but aside from the Royal castle and its Chamber of Secrets, guarded by the line of the Architect King, the Veritas possessed the second largest store of eldritch artifacts and those powerful items could not remain unguarded for long.

He reached into his pockets as he walked through the outer cloister and grasped the carved spool and its skein of red thread; it would soon find its way into the high priest's vault. Shjikara gave friendly, albeit less sincere, smiles to the refugees who had re-homed to his highlands beyond the once verdant plains surrounding the main castle grounds of the Royal City. The lush geography had nearly recovered from the horrors Nitthogr had unleashed upon it.

Once within the quiet hallways of the abbey where only the Veritas were allowed, his guards fell back and went about their business of maintaining security. Shjikara wandered towards his private chantry knowing that the other four heads of the disciplines would find their way back to the priory after supervising the departure of the planeswalkers. Besides the sparse crew he kept in reserve, Shjikara had sent everyone else to help curb the threat of Akko Soggathoth.

The leader turned the darquematter spool over in his grip and felt its power. It was potent enough to allow its wielders to use gates that were closed by the celestial phases, making it one of the more powerful and dangerous items, as it could alter the expected nature of reality.

Shjikara arrived at a heavy, unassuming door built into the side of the mountain. Only he could open the sacristy vault alone—in his absence, it took the four combined heads of the different orders within the Veritas. With nobody else on the monastery grounds, he left the door ajar.

The door unlocked with his key and swung open to reveal shelves of artifacts. Shjikara allowed himself a little pride in his collection, which rivaled that of the Chamber of Secrets, and placed the spool upon a numbered, blank space on a shelf. He took a seat and opened a heavy codex, which he used to catalog the sacristy's artifacts.

Engrossed in the writing, Shjikara jotted notes about how it came into his possession, the item's abilities, and a brief description. Finally, he closed the tome with a meaty thud and looked up.

Startled, Shjikara yelled out, "You!" The priest leapt backward even as the door slammed shut, locking out any help that might have been nearby. He staggered onto feet that had gone rigid and unfeeling; they slid on the polished ground like skates on ice and he shrieked as his legs and then his waist turned to stone.

"My master bids you welcome. He sent me here on this mission, which even I don't fully understand," the trespasser hissed.

As Shjikara's arms and shoulders began solidifying, his terrified face locked in horror, but his eyes and hands were the last to turn. The intruder jammed a burnished runestone into the priest's hand and then shut it into a fist so that it solidified inside.

"This will allow one stone figure freedom—but it will not be you," he laughed.

Basilisk watched the transformation take hold as Shjikara fully solidified. His spy had continued to pay off with critical information.

The tarkhūn took nothing from the room, though several items caught his eye to tempt him. The Dunnischktet—a herald of

Sh'logath—had made it into the very heart of the Architect King's most ardent religious caste, but he made no move against them except what his master had instructed of him.

Basilisk slipped out of the door silently, knowing that Shjikara's mind would remain fully conscious, but his body locked in an ageless prison. He grinned and closed the door to the sacristy vault, sealing Shjikara within for who knew how long—he only knew that he had obeyed the command of Sh'logath.

Immediately after the first combined wave of clerics, military, and elite corpsmen planeswalked, Bithia and Sam Jones crossed into Earth. Jackie already stood at the edge of the Crag with her pulse rifle shouldered and pouring lethal energy into the enemy. Caivev's forces had not been able to mount any kind of effective counterattack after the surprise wave of crippling EMPs.

Startled by the violence of its noise, Bithia recoiled at the detonation up the hill where a truck-mounted missile erupted with lethal fury. Its mushroom cloud painted the nearby vyrm with a swath of fire that melted flesh and scale.

Jackie grabbed the princess her by the arm and pulled her towards cover. Vyrm enemies caught between the short range of Tay-lore's bio-EMP and the further reach of the standard electromagnetic pulse threw aside their deactivated laser tech weapons and changed tactics.

The enemy scrambled to snatch up the mechanical firearms dropped by General Nyagittari's troops. Bullets would provide similarly effective force if pressed.

"Come on, Claire," Jackie pulled her towards the steep edge of the Crag where they'd have cover. She still didn't know about her friend's change—though she suspected something was amiss.

The Prime's troops continued bursting through the gate. They rushed up the edge of a nearby washout and into the fray with weapons blazing. They didn't pause or hesitate.

Suddenly, Zabe dropped over the edge of the overhang, almost as if he fell. He leaned against the embankment and caught his breath while blood leaked from fresh bullet wounds.

"Zabe, you're hurt," Bithia fretted.

He shook his head. "I'll be fine in a moment. I just need a second to heal up." The tears in his flesh slowly stitched themselves together as he took the blaster pistol from Sam, who'd carried it for him knowing the EMP would drain the device unless it came with the second wave. "I'm sure that, based on the resistance up top, we must be in the right place. Sam, where's the old dig site?"

The archaeologist pointed.

Zabe looked at Bithia. "Do you sense him? Is Akko Soggathoth there? We've only got one chance."

The princess closed her eyes momentarily. She opened them and fixed her allies with a fiery look. "He is there—and more—all of his brothers have been awakened and taken shape. We must hurry."

# Chapter Twenty-Four

"Vikrum?" Sexton called from the larger operations desk in their section of the Red Keep. They shared the venue with another team that handled more localized threats, but that B team wasn't currently in. "You'd better check this out."

Wiltshire came over and found his partner standing by an old-style telephone. A light on it flashed. Neither had ever answered the line before. It hadn't been used.

"The local line?" Wiltshire asked. It was a security feature, but the cathedral's priests seldom interacted with the brothers of the Order, and that was by design.

Sexton nodded and answered. He chatted in brief words and then hung up.

"It was Father Stotemeyer from upstairs," Sexton said. He pulled up a few CCTV feeds and found one focusing on a young man in a uniform meandering through the cathedral. "Package delivery... *for you.*"

Wiltshire raised an eyebrow and then hurried upstairs, finding a lost delivery courier. The man, an obvious college student who'd probably never been in a catholic church before, judging from his reactions to his surroundings, met the detective. He signed over a package and gave Wiltshire possession.

The detective watched him leave and then tore open the bubble mailer. Inside was a small, circular chunk of darquematter. Wiltshire recognized the otherworldly material immediately.

It was about the size and shape of a medium-sized carrot and the outside had a few rotating tumblers that moved in a circular motion. "It's a cipher wheel?"

He stuck his hand in the bag again and fished out a note. It had apparently been printed on an old dot matrix printer, which Wiltshire thought was peculiar.

*Communication difficult. Apologies for delays. Had a contact send you this—I don't need to tell you how rare or valuable it is. Info has been helpful. Keep sending. First thirty pages not relevant to me, but of concern to you. This will help you understand the texts, as agreed upon. T.*

"What's up?" asked Sexton from behind him.

Wiltshire nearly jumped out of his skin. He got his pulse back under control and then showed the cipher to Sexton. "The letter's from a contact of mine," he said without showing it to his partner. "I've, uh, been looking into translating those texts we pulled out of Pecos, Texas."

Sexton narrowed his gaze slightly. "Russo didn't want us looking into that."

"I'm just looking for information that might lead me back to Quintin," Wiltshire said. "And he didn't explicitly tell us not to translate those texts."

"Well, he said, 'We're going to shelve it until I want to greenlight this one,'" Sexton said. "If he was going to greenlight us for the Black Goat case, he would've—God knows it's been comparatively quiet the last couple years."

Wiltshire shrugged, but defended himself with logic. "Russo had to know that I'd look into it, eventually. If he really wanted me to leave it alone, he'd know that he should have stored the files in a different keep, or had them transported to Rome."

Sexton opened his mouth to argue with him, and then wilted. "Yeah. I guess you've got a point there."

"My contact thinks that the information in some of those pages has some dire consequences for us," Wiltshire noted.

"Sixteen sixteen?" Sexton asked, invoking the Order's code for apocalyptic level consequences.

Wiltshire nodded. "I think we need an independent expert, though."

Sexton pulled out his smartphone and thumbed the screen. "I recently read about one of the foremost linguists on the planet. He actually decoded the Voynich manuscript. Guy by the name of Miles Jecima."

"Where does this Professor Miles Jecima live?" Wiltshire asked.

Sexton showed him.

"Damn it. Of course it had to be in Duluth."

Sexton scanned the details again. "Oh, wait. He's coming to New York soon for some kind of convention."

Wiltshire glanced over Sexton's shoulder and past his partner. The door where the courier had exited remained open and Wiltshire saw him standing there: one of the Solomonari.

Snarling, Wiltshire yanked his gun free again. Since the day at the bistro, he'd made sure the belt around his waist was equipped with bullets that could actually harm a strigoi. Several magazines, each loaded with different types of bullets, were holstered in the belt wrapped around his waist and ready to be swapped into his handgun at a moment's notice.

Sexton reeled and turned to address the threat with him. But there was nobody there. Only an old mantle clock rested on the sidewalk.

"What the hell, man?" Sexton asked. "What was that about?" He retrieved the antique old clock.

"Just dealing with some of my demons," Wiltshire responded.

"Are we talking metaphorical or literal?" Sexton joked, knowing that, in their line of work, it could be either.

Wiltshire sighed. "Both, I think."

"It's not working," Sexton noted, turning it over and finding a maker's stamp. "It was made the year I was built," he commented.

Wiltshire scowled and hissed. "Shit."

"Where have *you been*?" Sisyphus glared at Theera. He slinked back to the group just in time to watch his master break the final seal that bound Akko Sxkakzacros. He released him from its pages and his presence shifted and burbled like a malevolent ball of hovering ink.

"Not your concern," Theera hissed. The minion shot his master a sagacious look and received a nod of approval in response. Theera beamed like a happy puppy.

Growling an insult, the Heptobscurantum's high wizard let it go—he only knew *he* wouldn't want to miss a second of the ceremony.

The trembling captive nearby screamed and scrambled away from the cultists before pitching headlong as the carnivorous spirit of Akko Sxkakzacros seized him. He trembled on the ground for a moment before rising to his feet with a snarl.

"Our purpose is fulfilled, then," the man frowned as if he'd hoped there would be more. "Let us get on with it." He pushed down the churning lump of flesh that pushed out from his abdomen as if another creature lived beneath his skin. Akko Sxkakzacros turned and walked towards the giant etching from the Rasthakkan writings.

"Hold a moment," Akko Soggathoth stated. "I sense a powerful enemy approaching who threatens the circle."

Akko Sxkakzacros bared his teeth as he took his spot and drew his sigil on the floor, snarling at the bonds as they took hold. Two empty spots stood at the bottom, two points of the star.

"I will take care of it," Caivev said as she reached for her holstered blaster.

"No," Akko Soggathoth snapped. "I will do it."

"Join the circle and be done with this," roared Akko Sxkakzacros, shaking his chains. He looked skyward where a roiling cloud framed a clear patch of sky. The center seemed to open into a wholly different realm which writhed with annelid-like appendages. Beyond the chains, the lens cleared to reveal a giant, lidless eye that peered yearningly towards the Temple of Koth.

"I must do this."

"You must do nothing! *This* is your purpose. Now come and fulfill it."

Akko Soggathoth smirked. "Eldest brother... always trying to tell me what to do." He began walking away while Akko Sxkakzacros growled at his backside.

"Enough of these games, trickster!" Akko Sxkakzacros dug his fingers into his own flesh and, with a horrendous sucking sound, ripped free the gurgling lump of flesh at his belly. He hurled the hunk of corpuscle and sinew into one of the two empty circles. A bloody tendril flailed about on the floor as it maneuvered about the area. The grotesque proboscis messily made the mark of Akko Quarnyk.

Akko Soggathoth ignored his brother, whose organs began tumbling out of the opened cavity wound, slapping the floor with wet sounds; the giant eye above, which shimmered with anticipation. Only the last brother needed to take his place for the ritual to continue. "Caivev, you have a shade amongst your forces in Kith?"

Confused, she nodded. "There is one within the temple."

"Excellent. I will need to borrow his shapeshifting abilities." He turned to Skrom. "Hold my vessel—I will need it when I return, so we may continue here."

Akko Sxkakzacros scoffed at his brother, who could fulfill their dark purposes in an instant if he only chose. The tarkhūn general didn't seem to notice; Skrom grabbed Akko Soggathoth, and the man expelled the black mist, which quickly dissipated, leaving the ceremony on hold.

The Guardian Corps and allied forces easily drove the enemy armies back into the thick jungles. With the smoking wreckage of the burned up and derelict vehicles well behind them, the EMP wave hadn't affected the vyrm weapons this far out.

"I can sense the Brothers' power growing—like a bright light coming through a tunnel," Bithia stated. "They must be through the temple gates and deep inside Koth. That's where they'd hold such a wicked ceremony—we've got to go faster."

"I don't think that's likely to happen, Princess," Wulftone called over his shoulder, firing his blaster into the trees.

They were only a couple of klicks from the old dig site where the temple lay, but the road that led to it was a corridor of death. So far they'd managed to move down the line, but slowly and only with the help of the giant tower shields brought in from the royal armory which they used to make a series of makeshift, mobile walls to protect against the intense barrage of blaster fire.

"It's a freaking gauntlet," Chira called over his shoulder as he tried to target a few enemies while he peeked around a rectangular shield. The high-tech frames crackled with energy as the microscopically thin force-wall shimmered and sizzled as it blocked the incoming fire he drew. "We will get there—but it's gonna take time. We're gonna have to pray it's soon enough."

Zabe scowled. He didn't need Bithia psychically projecting her thoughts into his mind for him to know what she was thinking. She wore them plainly on her face, and he agreed completely. *They did not have any more time.*

"We will take a round-about way and sneak in if you can cause a diversion... and here comes one now," Bithia said.

The others shot her a skeptical look, and then the trail ahead of them became a tunnel of fire that burned their forward team of shield holders and scorched the leaves and bracken that upheld the lush, green canopy. Soldiers quickly took their places and reset the shield wall, but they had to hunker together in a tight overlap to hold the line against the napalm-like heat that licked fiery tongues around the edges of the barrier. They couldn't move the line without scorching the front half of the soldiers, including the princess's cadre.

"At least they stopped shooting at us while they're trying to start this barbecue," Jackie muttered.

Bithia shrugged off the others' incredulous looks. "A tarkhūn firelord. I could sense him coming... those vyrm possessing gifts seem to burn brighter on the astral plane. Caivev must've been able to get one from Basilisk and his supposedly peaceful vyrm alliance."

Jackie's eyebrows raised, and she racked the action on her sniper rifle. "I've got an idea. I'll take him out as soon as you get out of here."

Bithia turned to Zabe. They had to go—and right away. Sam grabbed her arm and looked into her face.

The princess felt a pang of sorrow—she should've thought of him—surely Bithia's rash course of actions must weigh on him.

"Listen," he said. "I know you're Bithia—but you're also my Claire-bear. Be careful; you're my daughter, regardless." Sam pulled her into a hug for a few quick seconds, squeezing a few tears out of Bithia.

"I'll be okay," she promised.

Sam turned to Zabe. "They're obviously expecting us to come from the main approach where the door is. If you can, get around the backside and to the top of the pyramid. There should be an access chute that will lead all the way down to the heart of the temple. We always thought they were ventilation shafts—and it's not important, now, whatever they were—but you can use them to get inside undetected. You know what they look like?"

Zabe bobbed his snout. Wulftone had shared his experiences from Antarctica.

"Good. We're all counting on you, son."

Zabe nodded again. He scooped up Bithia and dashed into the trees, sprinting through the trees with uncanny speed and using his animal senses to guide him through the dense growth.

"Alright," Jackie said as soon as they were gone. She grabbed a fistful of Wulftone's fur as she adjusted the fit on Respan's visual scanner and pulled him close. "Give me a boost, big guy. I've got him in my scope." Even through the blanket of roiling black and orange flame, the tarkhūn's presence made a solid blip on the brow-mounted reticle.

The lycan crouched and let her crawl into a seated position on his shoulders. She shifted her butt and leaned over his furry head.

Jackie planted a kiss on the top of his snouted. "Alright—go!"

Wulftone stood tall and let Jackie see over the fray. She grimaced through the heat, snapped her sights up to her eyes, and pulled the trigger. Her single shot rang out and the fire suddenly stopped.

Zabe and Bithia could hear the violence erupting in the forest as they looped around the area. It had been mostly excavated, and they scrambled over trenches and obstacles that would deter and bottleneck the army on the road, but the lycan passed them easily.

Finally, they reached a massive trench which had been dug out to reveal the sprawling girth of the ancient site. Wooden walkways, bridges, and stairs eased movement for the diggers.

The intruders avoided those easy paths and stuck to the cover of the foliage until they'd arrived at the rear of the pyramid. They crept over the lip of the trench and kept well away from prying eyes as they worked their way through the heavy machinery used to clear away the soil.

"There it is," Zabe said, pointing towards a kind of stone stairway carved into the backside of the pyramid. It would lead them all the way to the top of the pyramid and it was tucked away from the prying eyes of the defending forces.

Suddenly, Zabe staggered and fell to his knees under the weight of some unseen force. His body shifted back to its human shape. He couldn't seem to differentiate between the waves of emotion that suddenly overcame him: despair, fear, nausea. A horrendous buzzing rose up in his ears and shot his heart into overdrive, as if his insides suddenly filled with a million writhing cicadas.

"We can sense you!" The chorus of voices echoed through his mind; they dripped with condescension and villainy. "Every thought is laid bare before us!"

Zabe's mind replayed a million thoughts and all in an instant: every inadequacy, every embarrassment, each regret and sorrow. His mind crippled his body as the vyrm psychics toyed with him.

Warmness flooded his body, and Zabe grinned. "I don't think you are prepared for who I brought: someone who knows all that stuff already and loves me, anyway."

The vyrm hissed and Bithia stepped into the light. "You three think you can challenge *me*?" She blasted a ripple of psionic energy and the trio of Lichs staggered out of their hiding places between the heavy equipment.

Anger radiated off of her like a corona as Bithia walked unafraid towards the three scaly clerics. Zabe could feel their hold weaken as she pumped them full of her willpower, the astral equivalent of her flexing psychic muscles. She easily over-matched them and they fell to their knees, swaying inconsolably. Their eyes rolled back in their skulls and blood trickled down their noses as she burned their essence away.

As Zabe scrambled back to his feet, the psychics collapsed into the dust with brains reduced to pudding. She hadn't given them an option for surrender; there was no time for that.

Bithia's eyes burned as intense as he'd ever seen them. "They should've sent at least four times as many if they wanted to stop us."

Zabe grimaced. "They don't need to stop us—just slow us down enough to unleash Sh'logath."

Theera walked into the circle, drawing the eyes of all six of the horrendous creatures, and retrieved the blank book from atop the golden box where it had rested. He returned to his station near the doorway at the temple's apex and waited.

Sisyphus watched him the whole way. His eyes narrowed to accusatory slits. "Why did you do that?"

"What do you mean?"

"Why did you take the book?"

"The master willed it," Theera spat, as if the question was beneath him.

Caivev cocked her ear towards the conversation, suddenly curious at such a simple thing. "Answer him."

"I only know what I know—that the master wanted me to hold his book."

"I am your master," Caivev glared at him. "You are a Blackborne vyrm."

"I *was* a vyrm of the Black. But now I am more. I belong to Akko Soggathoth." He spoke matter-of-factly and with no fear.

"Why do you hold the useless book?" Sisyphus stretched tall and put a growl into his voice—but intimidation was useless against the undying minion. "Why would he need that? Protecting the book is irrelevant once the Devourer is unleashed."

Theera bared his teeth. "You know nothing of the ceremony, human. My master is in charge here, not you, and if he wants a sacred ark dedicated to Mae'le-ggath, then he shall have it! If he wants me to hold his book, then I will." He hugged the tome to his chest. "You may speak about it once you know the rituals and the old ways, preserved by the Followers of Krakkath."

Sisyphus traded skeptical looks with Caivev but kept his mouth shut. He wasn't aware of many specific ordinances or rites to be performed by the Brothers of the Winnowing. The wizard only knew that some of the lore survived through time and was considered holy by the modern vyrm rovers who called themselves the Followers of Krakkath. Their major pieces came from the collected scribblings of Rasthakka.

In a huff, Jacob Sisyphus stepped back slightly and turned a cold shoulder to the indignant minion. He pulled out his smartphone and began scrolling. He didn't get any signal in the Darque but possessed scans of all the known works of Rasthakka, complete with translations courtesy of his occult contacts.

He scowled at Theera's backside. He couldn't quite place it, but something didn't feel right... and he knew that, given a few minutes, he would be able to understand why.

# CHAPTER TWENTY-FIVE

"**P**sst!" a familiar voice called out. Shandra waved at Zabe and Bithia from around a stack of clay-mired pallets.

Zabe caught up to Bithia, where she stood among the three drooling vegetables. He grabbed her hand. "Wait. How do we know it's her? It could be a trap."

Shandra cocked her head. "I ran ahead to try to sneak in from the back."

Zabe ignored anything she said and focused on the princess. He sniffed the air with his lycan nose, but had never thought to memorize her scent. The lycan kept his voice down. "Can you sense her... I mean, psychically?"

Bithia shook her head and whispered, "I barely have any energy left right now—I can't tell—it might be a standard Veritas psychic shield, or something else entirely. I may have overdone it with these three, after all. I need a few minutes to regather my strength."

"Who else could hide from you—another psychic... Akko Sogathoth?"

Bithia bit her lip anxiously.

"Then we've got to do it the old-fashioned way," Zabe whispered as Shandra slinked closer to them, retaining the group's cover from any enemies on the perimeter.

"Prove who you are. Tell me something that only *you and I* would know," Bithia said.

They were close enough to talk openly now and Shandra walked forward normally, though with measured steps. "I know that you wouldn't approve of me replacing your mother—and I would never try, but you and I both know how your father looks at me... that might be a conversation we need to have soon. You know, if we survive today."

Bithia sifted through Claire's memories. She'd been training with Pollando and had grown in her abilities, but Claire hadn't always shared everything with Bithia—she'd grown increasingly guarded of her time, especially intimate moments, and keeping the other half of her psyche in the dark. Any of Claire's memories involving close family, her love life, or personal insecurities felt like looking in a mirror with the lights off: it was there, but difficult to see.

"I... I can see that is very likely," she said haltingly as she crawled through Claire's now unguarded thoughts. Bithia marked a few to come back to later... Claire secretly wondered if Bithia might ever vie with her for control of their joint person—she was scared of maintaining such a struggle to retain herself if that ever came to pass. It's the main reason why she'd begun training with Pollando in the first place.

Shandra kept her voice low. "You have to know I would never do that—take your mother's place. And I would never hurt your father." Her face twisted with rage, "But *I would!*" Shandra's shape morphed into one identical to the Princess's and she leapt for her, tackling Bithia.

Zabe snatched his blaster and leveled it at the girls, but they'd already rolled across the ground with such violence and fury that he didn't know which was which. Every detail was identical, right down to the clothing.

They traded blows, growling with feminine fury, baring tooth and claw with primal rage. Crashing through a survey tent, the girls nearly brought the whole thing down as they tumbled through, busting through the support poles.

Zabe resumed his animal form and stretched out his lycan senses, but the two even smelled the same. It had to be a talented shade too, so fully complete the disguise.

The girls held each other firmly in a grapple, snarling. They each looked at Zabe, begging him for help in subduing the other.

"You're good," he muttered, catching a glimpse of the tiny, identifying mark behind the copy's ear, "but not good enough!" He snapped his pistol to aim for her, but the shade rolled to the ground with Bithia atop of her as a human shield.

The shade roared and touched Bithia's neck and she screamed as they rolled across the ground again confusing the two. Each rolled to their haunches in a fighting stance, facing off against each other.

At the same time, they looked at Zabe, touching their necks. Each bore the mark, now. "It must be some kind of magic!" Their voices and mannerisms had synced completely, and they spoke in chorus. The girls stared each other down as Zabe shifted his aim from one to the other.

"My psionic senses are returning," they said. "It's Akko Soggathoth!"

Suddenly, they both went mute, even though their lips still moved. They each looked at him, beckoning with their eyes—more dark magic, some kind of silent bubble! Bithia also lost her voice.

Jenner stood in Respan's lab and rubbed the soreness from his shoulder. The scientist puttered away in the background, still tinkering and trying and reverse the statue's stone-form state. The work undoubtedly kept his mind off the fact that all reality might meet a Sh'logathian fate at any second.

The young soldier stared at the petrified body of General Za-haben. Anger boiled in his belly: the feeling of inadequacy, the desire to fight and overcome his enemies, sorrow for accidentally shooting Gita, resentment for his overall lot in life.

He wished he'd had even *this much* of his father left. Jenner's mother and siblings were in the ground and his father was some-where unknown; the young soldier promised himself he'd contin-ue believing his father still lived, but each passing day chiseled that hope away.

Jenner stared at Zahaben's living monument. He memorized every detail of his face. Every ripple of the great commander's clothing. His heart similarly hardened as he watched the frozen figure.

Seconds, minutes, hours ticked by as the young man stared out-ward and inward. He scowled at the pus leaking down his chest. The world had made enemies of him by taking away something important—and this stupid wound had cost him his ability for revenge!

*What if that big man—Earth's version of my father who is not my father—is there? I'm missing my chance to beat him and recover my father.*

His face darkened and the rage in his heart took root like a seed. Jenner was convinced the world would forget Professor Jarfig and pledged to become as great of a warrior as Jarfig had been an intellect. He vowed to do whatever it took to bring him justice.

*Someone will pay, someday. I will either find my family or I will have revenge... better yet, to have both!*

"Where did you get that?" Caivev asked Sisyphus as he scrolled down the pages and pages of scans overlaid with text translations.

"Vikrum Wiltshire," he mumbled absentmindedly as he read. "Well... indirectly. He could use a stronger password on his computer."

Akko Soggathoth's avatar struggled against Skrom's grip. He tried to turn his head as if he heard a familiar name.

"An earth man who's been playing at a game he knows nothing of." Sisyphus looked up from the screen and meandered slowly around the carved circle, glancing from screen to floor and back again. Caivev followed him nonchalantly.

"I understand enough to translate those writings," he smirked and pointed to the alien etchings written on the floor in the thick, straight lines of the seven-pointed star.

The man in Skrom's grip squirmed and writhed. Squeezing him tighter, the behemoth tarkhūn settled him down, but his impatience grated against his nerves. Skrom scowled at Theera. "What is taking your master so long, worm?" He rattled off a bunch of curse words in the high-speech vyrm dialect. Theera ignored him.

"This mirrors what it says on one of the Tablets of Rasthakka," Sisyphus stated. He scrolled to a new image of a carbon rubbing. Key phrases repeated, allowing them to make sense of the floor's text. "Through the deaths of the demigods, their progenitor will rise, rebirthed in Darque, snuffing the light of life, unmaking creation."

The five goat-like heads turned to stare at Sisyphus as he read the English translation. Unnerved, he angled his shoulders away from them. He followed his notes and tracked a finger across the rubbing before summarizing the text.

"Each of the Brothers of the Winnowing must sacrifice themselves. Through the surrendering of *their flesh*, the portal will open and Sh'logath will be released to devour. In his consumption, all reality will be unmade. These... beasts... are creatures of pure void."

Akko Sxkakzacros grimaced at Caivev and Sisyphus. "You are being played, mortals. Tricked by the deceiver."

Sisyphus turned to Theera. "Why does Akko Soggathoth need a book—why won't he just finish this?"

Theera sneered and refused to look at the man.

Sisyphus snarled a string of profanity and then yanked a chrome plated 1911 from his waistband. "I've had enough of your smug attitude!" He snapped off a trio of forty-five caliber rounds that slammed into the vyrm's chest, spraying blood and effluence across the temple floor. The gunshots echoed across the parched landscape of the Darque and distant thunder grumbled in response.

Everyone stared at the spectacle. The Brothers watched as if it entertained.

Theera lay sprawled out on his back. The blank tome he held in trust laid near his feet. A moment later, Theera gasped and jolted back to life. He cackled with glee. "Fools! My master has made me undying!"

Akko Soggathoth's minion stood and dusted himself off. He bent to retrieve the book when Sisyphus shoved him back.

"You don't know what you're meddling with, *human*," Theera hissed. "You cannot kill me."

The former pro wrestler punched Theera in the scaly snout and rocked him backward. "Well, I'll enjoy all the trying, then. I'll show you what power I *do* wield!" He grabbed his hooked, patinaed sword by its darquematter hilt and telekinetically lifted the insolent minion. With a roar, he smashed Theera into the ground over and over with his unseen hand before dropping him back down onto the stone.

Theera staggered to his feet on grinding, broken bones, barely conscious. He opened his mouth to speak, but Sisyphus had already made his hand motions and muttered a string of words to complete his incantation.

Sisyphus blasted Theera with a jolt of eldritch fire like a laser cannon. He funneled his rage and pride into it, pouring on the fire and melting his enemy's skin. Chunks of flesh blasted away from blackened, slagged bone. Finally, the burst blew Theera clear of the pyramid's ledge where and he tumbled into the darkened distance, barely more than a ragged piece of scorched meat.

"Was that entirely necessary?" Caivev asked as Sisyphus hunched over with a touch of fatigue. "What if we needed your magic energies for something else?"

Sisyphus winked and pulled a vial from his pocket. The lines of chemical coolant glowed faintly, making the container look like a chemical glow stick. He broke the top off and drained the ampoule of Jarfig's blood into his mouth. "I've got that covered," he smirked as he stole the energies from the Prime version of himself that he'd held as a hostage for years. "I don't make the same mistakes over and over again." He rubbed the long scar on his neck from where he'd lost a fight against Nitthogr several years ago when his power ran dry. "I always keep spares."

Zabe kept his pistol trained on the two women as they rolled through a grapple, beating on each other at every opportunity. They both looked at him and silently shouted for him to shoot the other one.

They struggled against each other's arms and hands, each locking hands around the other's throats to choke out their opponent like some twisted kind of mirror. The girl on the bottom looked pleadingly into Zabe's eyes and dropped one hand to her attacker's chest.

Zabe realized she was holding onto her enemy's pendant. That gift from her father had been made out of darquematter and Akko Soggathoth could not touch it—it had to be fake! He snapped his barrel to attention and fired a jolt of burning energy through the imposter's cranium.

Bithia coughed and gasped for air as she regained her voice. The dead shade toppled limply to the ground. Black ether rose from the corpse and seemed to evaporate as their true enemy escaped.

"Come on," Zabe hauled her to her feet. "We've got to hurry even more, now—they know we're coming." He slung her across his back and she wrapped her fists in his fur for a grip, sandwiching the Stone Glaive between them. "Hang on!"

He surged forward on all fours and shot up the hidden stairway in a matter of seconds. The climb barely winded him.

Cresting the peak, they slowed at the top, deferring to the side of stealth. After a moment of searching, they spotted a discolored panel where the builders had mortared a veneer over the access hatch.

Zabe shrank into his human figure. The two intruders crawled across the roofline and kicked in the hidden entry. They glanced down the slope, finding their army advancing down the trail; brilliant flashes of color lit up the jagged seam, which cut through the greenery as the trail meandered. The army advanced at a better pace than expected—but still slower than needed to stop the Awakening.

"I'll go first." Zabe cleared away the broken debris and laid his immense weapon down on the lip of the steep slide.

"That doesn't look safe," Bithia groaned as Zabe sat on the broad blade like some kind of deadly, narrow toboggan.

He winked at her. "Good thing I heal fast."

She kissed him. "Just don't get killed before you have the chance."

Zabe kissed her back. "Don't worry about it—you just worry about your own ride down." He grinned at her and then launched himself into the dark and narrow chimney like a luge rider. The grating sounds echoed into the distance as screeching stone on stone noise faded away.

Bithia steeled herself and then slid in after him, albeit at a slower pace than Zabe. She popped out and landed on her rump in the big room.

A number of vyrm wore surprised looks that had been preserved in stone. Zabe, again in his lycan form, had neatly dispatched the lot of them; his newly earned wounds healed before her eyes, though he winced slightly to her touch.

He sheathed the ancient weapon and pointed the way. A massive set of double doors towered before them and opened to an identical looking room, which radiated an ill kind of light. The air made their skin crawl, and they knew they were in the Darque.

"Koth," Bithia whispered, wondering aloud, "Those shards of darquematter in your pouch are supposed to stop them—but how can they banish them *back to the Darque* dimension if we're already *in the Darque?*" Bithia fixed her eyes on her champion. "Will they have any effect here—can we stop the Awakening?"

Zabe did his best to flash a confident grin. "I guess if they don't work, then it's back to my original plan."

"Use your 'really big sword?'"

"That's the one." He sighed, bit his lip, and then pressed on until they arrived at a central narthex. A few corridors split off, one terminated in an opening that allowed them to see the sky outside.

"Shall we take the direct route and not risk getting lost in the tunnels?"

Zabe nodded, and they hurried for the door.

Jackie snapped a few rounds off and into the trees, knocking the vyrm snipers out of the branches. A bomb exploded on their left and exposed their flank to a shrieking band of blade-wielding zealots. The vyrm madmen burst out of the foliage on a suicide mission.

Metallic packages strapped to their backs looped around their bodies with gnarled conduit. Mechanical, sharp edges cut through their scaled flesh, but they paid their burdens no mind as they focused on their singular purpose.

With eyes narrowed to pinpricks, they charged into the fray, hacking at soldiers and clerics with jagged cleavers. They shrugged off bullets and blasters with a snarl of drug-fueled rage that promised to burn the Sh'logathian zealots out from the inside.

One of them laughed maniacally and threw himself into a group of soldiers. He detonated his pack, erupting in a fireball that further collapsed the shield wall.

Jackie stood bravely and fired round after round into the zealot who charged directly at her, barely stumbling as each lethal dose seared through his body. She growled and kept pulling the trigger. "Just die already!"

Her battery pack chirped as it emptied. Jackie's eyes suddenly went wide.

The suicidal warrior cackled and charged at her.

Wulftone leapt over her shoulder and turned his back to face the bomber, who detonated the explosives. He shielded her from its fire with his thick lycan hide. The blast threw him forward and on top of her, and the two collapsed to the dirt. His backside smoked where his pelt had burnt and chunks of flesh had been blasted away.

Jackie's protector whined like a beat dog as he rolled off her, grinding gravel into his black and bubbled skin. He barely remained conscious, and Jackie couldn't reach a replacement battery pack in time: another team of zealots charged for them.

"I got you," Chira yelled, stepping over to them. A battery pack hung on a sling over his shoulder. It whinnied through its rapid recycle rate, powering the minigun the soldier had commandeered elsewhere. The rapid fire cut a swath of chaos through the line of doomed vyrm. Bolts cleaved limbs and chopped them down like a hedge mower.

Still, the zealots crawled towards them on bloody stumps and snarled through their blackened burns, moving ever forward.

Chira cocked his head and adjusted his aim upwards slightly. He targeted the munition packs they wore instead and detonated them with his stream of deadly energy. They exploded in a chain-reaction, like dominos, leaving nothing behind but charred wreckage and smoldering bones.

"Thanks for the assist," Jackie said, crawling to her knees.

Another group of soldiers ran ahead and retrieved the tower shields. They reactivated them and restored their section of the protective wall.

Jackie slapped her lycan friend's exposed rump where the detonation had blasted it away. It had already healed significantly, even though it smelled like burnt hair.

Wulftone groaned and slowly pushed himself up on all fours.

Jackie rubbed his back affectionately. "Come on, ya big baby. We've got more reptiles to kill!"

# Chapter Twenty-Six

B ithia curled her nose at the stench. The air reeked of fresh sulfur from a recent firestorm but they quickly went nose-blind to it as they crawled up the outside of the pyramid. They reached the ledge just in time to peek over and watch Akko Soggathoth take hold of his puppet once again. Skrom released the man, and the gathered crowd of humans and vyrm shouted at him.

Akko Soggathoth blinked and looked around. "I see you have my book. Where is Theera?"

Jacob Sisyphus jabbed a finger into his chest and screamed a mouthful of threats. The wizard waved the empty codex in his face. "I threw your little pet over the side after burning him to a crisp—and you're not getting this thing back."

Akko Soggathoth looked neither surprised nor worried by him. He shrugged. "As you wish."

Zabe made a motion for Bithia to cover him from behind the base of the nearby obelisk. He skulked around the side as their enemies argued and commanded Akko Soggathoth to complete the ritual.

"Now!" Zabe howled, jumping out from behind a different spire. He leapt into the circle while Bithia laid down a canopy of blaster fire.

The mortals leapt for cover while the Darque Heralds sneered and deflected the laser bursts away. Zabe snatched a fistful of shards from his pouch and chucked them at Akko Soggathoth; the shrapnel bounced off of his skin as the beast assumed his goatman form. The mystic ingots clattered to the floor, no more threatening than common gravel.

"It is too late," he taunted. "Six of them are already chained to the eldritch fetters. Only a few forces in existence can stop what has begun here." He pointed skyward with his six-fingered hand. The stone ring rotated like a funnel cloud overhead, draped in arcane hooks and chains.

Zabe stole a glance upward. His stomach panged when his sensitive eyes realized it wasn't made of stone... but of a massive collection of bones. Zabe roared and lashed out with the Stone Glaive.

Akko Soggathoth recoiled from the cleaving blow and ducked the second. The beast whirled around and grew a set of long, razor-like claws from his hand.

Caivev popped up and screamed, dumping a barrage of lasers in Zabe's direction. The werewolf ducked and rolled behind the body of Akko Nuggezeth, who appeared altogether disinterested. The monster's body absorbed the brunt of the damage and Akko Soggathoth stepped wide in order to get an angle on his prey.

Suddenly, everyone stopped at the distinct *clink* sound of a grenade landing on the stone floor. Akko Soggathoth looked down and leapt back; the explosive round rolled past his feet, right next to the bloody heap that was Akko Quarnyk.

The device erupted in a ball of napalm fire that rocketed the tumorous creature from its spot. Eldritch chains tethering the creature held it fast in the fire. With a dreadful "skreee!" the caustic flame ate up the flesh, reducing it to ash and burning away the bloody sigil, launching the inky, cloud-like spirit from beyond its prison.

Akko Quarnyk dissipated in a puff of smoke, eluding his celestial chains. The churning, hellish halo overhead cracked and groaned in the sky.

"Where did he go?" Percival Wainsmith shrieked like a child. "I've sacrificed so much—this can't be happening!"

"Calm your whelp," Akko Soggathoth snapped to Sisyphus. "He merely needs a new pile of flesh to house his spirit. I will find him as soon as we kill these interlopers."

Suddenly the whole pyramid shifted beneath their feet with a micro-quake... as if something inside it had exploded. Zabe and Caivev locked gazes: neither was sure whose side caused it—but hopefully, it meant reinforcements would arrive at any moment.

Shandra roared and smashed her way up the stairwell with her battle hammer. She shrugged off a glancing blow to her armor and offered a more precise one in return. It sprayed vyrm blood against the wall.

Fighting had gone mostly hand to hand inside the narrow, winding halls of the Kith Temple where the vyrm defenders had retreated to. Hers and Tahnak's teams had been the first to make it through the gauntlet and charge through the pyramid, entering the Darque.

As soon as they'd breached it, the vyrm marshaled their forces back inside the Lost Temples of Kith and Koth. They dug in to make a defensible last stand, preventing any others from reaching Koth.

The room ahead sprawled wider and Tahnak cleared it with concussive charges that momentarily shook the entire pyramid. He charged through the smoke and fired a quick burst of blaster fire before his team secured the perimeter. The cleric's team joined them a few seconds later.

The doors on either side were meaningless to the crew—they only knew that they needed to go up. "Didjee," Shandra barked to one of her clerics who'd been trained with psychic abilities. "Where are they—can you sense the princess?"

Didjee pointed up. "I can sense her, but barely through all of that evil... it's... it's difficult to cope, but she burns like a candle in the night."

Shandra clapped the bald woman on her shoulder as a sign of gratitude. "Two paths up, Tahnak. Which one do you want?"

He jerked his thumb over his shoulder. "We've got the stairs—you take the other way up."

Shandra nodded and muttered. "Race you to the top." She hurried towards the mouth of the long hallway Zabe and the Princess had used. Her team followed hot on her trail.

Exiting the mouth, she swallowed her trepidation as she looked skyward to see the turning portal that threatened to loose the Great Annihilator if they delayed. The sounds of battle echoed behind her, but she didn't dare look back or consider helping Tahnak—her destiny was at the top. Shandra couldn't spare time enough for a backwards glance.

Idrakka hissed as his soldiers pushed their way down the stairs towards the lower chamber. They'd clogged up the passage so perfectly that neither side could move. Neither vyrm nor human could get in or out of the passage that had become a clogged maze where warriors used whatever was at hand—including the fallen—as barricades.

He halted his group of warriors and sent them back to the next landing and to the rooms above before sending down a final soldier who mowed the hallway clear with a rapid-fire minigun. In the first three seconds, he cut down his own men, burning hot fire through their backs before razing a line of intruders.

A grenade rolled over the floor, blowing the artillery gunner to pieces. Seconds later, the landing filled with the advance team from the Prime as they pressed forward.

Their exit at the rear suddenly iced over and the temperature plummeted, trapping them within the ice-box. Then, the front of the tunnel froze over as well.

Idrakka taunted them from behind a clear pane of ice. The glacial wall resisted the blaster bolts and the scorch marks refilled almost immediately.

The frostmancer smiled wickedly as the rear hall's ice floe grew to envelop Tahnak's men like some kind of giant single-cell organism. The ice wall crept closer and closer to him, leaving only Tahnak remaining in his tiny ice prison.

"Oh," Idrakka promised, "this will be fun."

Akko Soggathoth ducked under the werewolf's weapon with uncanny speed, almost playfully. Zabe kept moving and angling his position so that he kept the monstrous goatman between himself and the shots Caivev tried to target him with.

Behind Zabe, Bithia continued looking for an angle to either take out their enemy's mortal forces or suppress their attacks against her fiancé. The Stone Glaive had to work—*it had to!* The way Akko Soggathoth avoided it suggested the weapon might actually wound the creature. Some kind of force field within the circles where the others were stationed, however, protected the heralds from the blade.

Zabe looked back, catching an impulse that Bithia had sent him psychically. He could feel her mental thumbprint all over it—something he'd experienced before, but wanted to verify before attempting such a dangerous maneuver.

Bithia winked at him from behind her cover and Zabe threw himself to the ground, tucking and rolling just over Akko Soggathoth's thigh and exposing himself to the full brunt of Caivev and her elite forces. They lit him up even as Akko Soggathoth whirled to deliver a massive blow to the foolish, careless lycan.

Suddenly, Shandra leapt over the lip of the flat-topped structure and brought her mystic hammer to bear with a ferocious scream. She smashed the monstrous beast in the spine with her weapon, hitting him so hard that it knocked the ethereal spirit from the man's body like stuffing from a rag doll.

Akko Soggathoth's disrupted spirit shimmered and shuddered like a writhing ball of blackened vibrissae. The man screamed when he collapsed in pain, crippled by the spinal injury.

Shandra turned and panicked momentarily, caught in the open with nowhere to go for cover as Caivev screamed, "Open fire!"

Zabe jumped to his feet and snatched Shandra up in a huge embrace, protecting her from the deadly blasts and yanking her to safety. They scrambled behind the nearest obelisk and Zabe shot Bithia a fatigued smile as he rested for a few moments to let his body heal the damage his hide had taken.

"Did we do it?" Shandra buzzed with adrenaline. "Did we stop the Awakening."

"We've only just delayed it, for now," Zabe wheezed. "But you did good."

The rest of Shandra's team caught up with her and peeked over the ledge, returning fire shot for shot.

Caivev's voice screeched above the din. "You're just delaying the inevitable!" She mashed a button on a remote and the pyramid rumbled slightly. "My reinforcements will be here momentarily."

The tunnel had no light—it barely had air—but that's where they found each other, and neither creature needed those things, anyway. Wordlessly they communicated—in the same manner they used to... before the mortal denizens of the Darque crawled up from the primordial muck.

*I'm glad I found you here, brother—I'm glad you did not return immediately.*

Akko Quarnyk didn't respond immediately. Like his brothers, he did not experience fear—but that did not mean he couldn't be reluctant.

*Tell me brother Quarnyk, do you want to play a game?*

The spirit shimmered. *The last time we played, brother Soggathoth, I was eaten. Why should I play with you again?*

*That was so many millennia ago. Come, now. I miss our fun. And I've had so many opportunities to mature since then.*

*I do miss our games,* Quarnyk said. *What kind of game is it?*

*A game of revenge... and of mischief.*

*I do like those things.*

*Excellent.*

Akko Quarnyk had never been very bright, but Akko Soggathoth found himself in need of an accomplice he could control in Theera's absence.

*Excellent. I will tell you exactly what to do, brother Quarnyk.* If he could have giggled in this form, he would have.

Zabe and Shandra hid behind an obelisk. It crackled under the intense barrage that had them pinned down. They looked over to Bithia. She experienced the same—with their locations flagged, they were sitting ducks. Only their crack marksmanship kept the vyrm from rushing them.

"They are down two heralds," Zabe muttered. "They can't complete the ritual without them." He scowled at the opposition. "We've got to regroup."

"Agreed," Shandra said.

Zabe gave a retreat signal to Bithia, who nodded.

The two access points on opposite sides of the temple suddenly swarmed with vyrm reinforcements that intensified the assault on Shandra's team. "Fall back," she ordered, sliding over the edge.

Zabe tossed a tiny disk near their obelisk as they fled. He answered Shandra's questioning look. "One of Respan's new gadgets—an AV spy device so we will have eyes and ears on top."

The remote detonators blew the doors off the time-locked stasis chamber and Caivev's army poured out from it as fresh as if they had just entered. They found the stair upwards blocked by ice and they fled deeper into the pyramid, back towards the Kith gate, and found a second stairwell that led upwards on the opposite side of the structure.

Her army burst through the roof access at the same time as the remains of Idrakka's, and they peppered the ridgeline with lethal doses of energy. Caivev gloated as the intruders turned and fled down the side of the pyramid and she congratulated herself on the foresight to stash a group of forces within for emergency contingencies.

She ran across the cleared platform to join the Black and arrived in time to see a few Guardian Corps casualties slide down the side of the building. The rest escaped through one of the four access points leading back inside the facility.

"Don't just stand there! Pursue them." A large force charged over the side; the rest stayed at the top to protect their mission—and the vyrm continued coming from their hidden cell.

Caivev sneered. She'd nearly forgotten how big the army was.

Jackie and Wulftone pushed their troops ahead even harder and split a wedge through the vyrm troops. A well-placed grenade cleared a room and widened the gap just long enough that they had a shot at reaching the darquegate.

"Let's go," she screamed, leading the charge.

Wulftone and the troops sprinted after her and down a small, turning hall that descended into the heart of the temple. Right behind them, an explosion blew a door off its hinges and a new wave of scaly reinforcements flowed from deep inside the base, filling in the gap. Wulftone spat a curse—Chira and his group had been following just behind them. There wasn't likely to be anyone watching their backside for a while now.

They paused inside the innermost chamber where the giant doors between worlds remained open, dripping with wet blood. A badly burned vyrm walked out from them, shambling on dead legs and dragging a long, crusty string of entrails that had gathered mud and dust from dragging them through the soot and dirt of the floor. His hollow eyes didn't even look at them, and they let him pass. Theera collapsed atop a pile of corpses lying in the corner and breathed in ragged gasps.

Jackie aimed her gun at him. "I've got him." She pulled the trigger, thinking she'd put him out of his misery, and then she followed Wulftone and the rest into the Darque.

Skrom watched the broken human who had been the avatar struggle to his feet and wondered if he ought to grab the wailing man. If nothing else, he was tempted to end Quintin Hall's pained moans with a quick stomp. But the doomed man stood and looked directly at him and his eyes turned black as coals. The tarkhūn knew their missing herald had returned, following the cleric's meddling.

He groaned slightly and shook all of his appendages back into place. The cultists kept a distance, but their eyes waited with reluctant expectation. Finally, he said, "The Awakening begins... Akko Quarnyk has found a new body and our final member shall be here shortly."

A few seconds later, dripping with melted frost, the possessed body of Tahnak walked onto the rooftop.

"No more games, Akko Soggathoth," Sisyphus spat. He clenched the handle of his khopesh in one fist, and a backup vial in the other. "Finish this and fulfill your destiny."

The herald within Tahnak easily overrode the man's will. He opened a vein with his own teeth and then made the binding sigil of Akko Quarnyk on the sooty floor.

Sisyphus oversaw the action to make sure that it was done properly. He nodded. "Now you, Akko Soggathoth."

"Gladly," the form of Quintin Hall giggled and almost skipped over to his station where the bloody mass had been incinerated earlier. The beast dragged a jagged fingernail across his wrist and slicked his hand with the pulsing stuff of life—the required sacrifice of his dark king and lord. He bent down and made his sign—the only one that Sisyphus had never seen before, though he no longer had cause to commit it to memory. Soon, nothing of reality would remain.

# Chapter Twenty-Seven

P rofessor Miles Jecima got up from the chair in the hotel lobby where the professional convention for language scholars was occurring. He savored every bite of the cheeseburger and french fries. He only seldom ate such low quality food; usually, he did so while travelling and this was his second trip to New York City this year—uncommon for him.

Millie had broken him of his fast food habit a decade prior in an effort to preserve the linguist's health. And then *she* had been the one to go on and die. As a force of nature, irony was a real bastard.

The elderly professor stood up and tossed his rubbish into the proper receptacle and then headed for the room in the convention hall where he was supposed to give the night's opening keynote speech. He rummaged in his suit pocket, looking for the note cards where he'd jotted enough thoughts and anecdotes to satisfy the attendees.

He paused when he found two men barring his path near the rear entry to the assembly hall. He looked up and blinked at them.

"Excuse me," said the taller of the two men. "Are you Professor Miles Jecima?"

"I am," he confirmed.

"We are with the Red Order. Perhaps you have—"

"Yes, yes. I am aware of your organization. I was in contact with one of your praetors over the whole Grimmorium Nitthogr situation."

The tall one reached out and shook his hand, introducing himself as Wiltshire and his partner as Sexton. Wiltshire turned over a small artifact.

Jecima held it up to the light for a better view and then turned the cipher wheel's dial. His eyes bulged with wonder as he looked over the sigils engraved on the rare metal.

"Professor, we need your help," Sexton said.

Wiltshire followed up with, "There are some documents in our possession which match the language on that artifact and we would like very much if we could decipher the text."

Jecima turned away from the hall where a crowd had assembled to hear him speak. He started shuffling away from the entrance with his eyes still locked on the cipher.

"Professor, aren't you going to do your speech?" Sexton asked.

He waved the thought away. "Listen, when you're my age, you won't ever know how much time you have left. So let's make the most of it... I never found these sorts of gatherings to be useful or particularly interesting... but *this*?" He flashed them an excited look. "Do you have a space where I can work out of?"

Shandra's team took heavy losses as the overwhelming vyrm numbers threw themselves at the intruding force with reckless abandon. The situation drew bleak enough that the clerics used the bodies of their fallen comrades to build a slight wall for cover.

Blazing blaster fire sizzled over the top of their despairing crew as Wulftone and Jackie surged ahead to catch up, evening their numbers. Zabe breathed a sigh of relief as they momentarily beat back the oppressors with their reinforcements' momentum, and the vyrm yielded a few meters.

"We thought you might like some help up here," Jackie shouted, and picked off a few scaly warriors.

The enemy suddenly grew a waist-high ice wall for protection of their own.

"Their frostmancer is here," Wulftone spat. They'd met in Antarctica the day Harken lost his life.

Jackie fired a bunch of burning holes through their defenses. They sealed back up shortly after. "Two can play that game," she growled as four of their troops activated their tower shields and laid them horizontally to provide a similar measure of cover.

Zabe, Shandra, and Bithia breathed with relief when allies took over their protection and bought a few more precious moments. Zabe flipped on the handheld screen and connected a wireless signal to the spy device, which relayed visual and audio data. His paws were too big for the touchscreen controls, so he passed it off to Shandra, who navigated Respan's infiltrator droid.

His face fell when he spotted two of the heralds who had peeled back their veils of flesh, holding them open as if they were shrouds for miniature black holes. The screen's image shimmered and shuddered as the void they'd called forth from deep within sucked away all light and visual data from the machine.

Zabe cried out, "They've started it! They are waking Sh'logath!" He stood tall and looked back towards the peak, drawing a barrage of laser fire that made him instinctually duck.

"There's no way we can get there in time," Shandra cried. She looked to Bithia. "You're supposed to be super powerful in the astral plane—can't you do something? It's now or never!"

Bithia's eyes turned milky white as she projected her power towards the mighty evil that was Sh'logath and tried to impose her will, just as she'd done with the vyrm psychics earlier. She suddenly convulsed and screamed; her eyes turned black like coals. Bithia babbled repeatedly. "It was me. It was my fault. I did it. I'm sorry. I didn't mean too—but it was me."

Jackie grabbed her so she wouldn't harm herself under the dark spell. "I've got you. It's okay."

Zabe grabbed his cousin, Wulftone. The two had been a formidable duo ever since the loss of Zurrah so many years prior. They glanced at the line of weapons arrayed against them on the steep climb. "This is the end. Are you with me, brother?"

Wulftone nodded. "Of course. Always."

As Zabe turned to Shandra, Wulftone leaned down and kissed Jackie on the mouth. Wulftone pulled away. "No regrets. If I live, I'm going to marry you... just so you understand my intentions."

Jackie raised her eyebrows and blinked with shock, though she was hardly surprised. "Well, get out there and save the world then—I expect a proper proposal. You can't do that if you let the world get eaten."

"Shandra, give us as much cover fire as we can get," Zabe ordered.

She turned from Zabe and barked the order.

Howling their charge, Zabe and Wulftone sprinted up the steep pyramid slope. Their bodies absorbed blast after blast. Shandra's troops picked up their shields and charged towards the icy line on the uneven terrain, diverting attention and drawing as much fire as possible from the lupine warriors.

The air screeched as Akko Skoldagrath peeled open his skin and revealed the great nothingness within. Tattered flesh ripped and flapped as the abyss consumed it during the macabre ritual. Pure force of will held his body together despite its center transmuting into a tunnel linked with the agod—it wound and churned like a vortex, connected to the twisting portal overhead.

Akko Sxkakzacros glared at the next two brothers. They would follow after him and then Sh'logath would devour them and make himself tangible through their sacrifice. The eldest's midsection was already destroyed, but he completed the ritual by dragging a claw through the remainder of his sternum and becoming one with the gate.

"You will honor your obligation, this time," Akko Sxkakzacros spat across the mystic circle.

Sisyphus stepped forward as if to ask for clarification. "This has been done before?"

The familiar man with the slicked-back hair, Quintin Hall, who Skrom had restrained so often, giggled and pointed to his chest playfully. "Who, me?" He reached into his jacket pocket and withdrew a simple audio recorder. He activated the playback feature, cranking the volume to the maximum.

A horrid screeching, wailing, and clicking language played a vile message that made skin and scale crawl for any who heard the darquespeech. Despite that, the cultists drew curiously closer to the circle.

Akko Sxkakzacros roared so violently that it shook the bone halo in the sky, rattling its chains. His void suddenly stitched itself back together with naked flesh. "How long? You had a prerecorded message... so how long have you planned this whole charade?" He glanced at Akko Quarnyk and Akko Soggathoth; neither of them wore eldritch chains.

The rest of the heralds solidified as well, and the sky-bound portal cracked with an ominous grating sound. Akko Sxkakzacros tried to leave his circle of binding but his ethereal chains held fast; he jerked and struggled, shaking the black obelisk where the chains drew their power from.

"What is it?" Caivev demanded an interpretation. "What was on that recording?"

The beast within Tahnak's body uttered more of the black speech and named the remaining brothers by name. a different sort of fetter lashed out from each of the obelisks and snared their spirit forms to prevent them from being freed if their bodies died—the same kind of chains that bound them originally.

Akko Sxkakzacros locked eyes on Caivev as he leaned against his unbreakable bonds. The floor suddenly gave out beneath Tahnak's body and the possessed man fell through the breach just as Akko Sxkakzacros hissed one word. "Betrayal."

The gilded box in the center of the formation detonated in a caustic blaze far more intense than any grenade. Quintin Hall's body flew backward, well beyond the mushrooming cloud of chemical fire. The other five heralds were flung back and held firm in their chains. Intense flames incinerated the flesh and bone to dust, rendering it unusable for sacrifice.

Overhead, the circle of bone split. A massive fissure spread like a spider web. The breaking filled the sky with thunder.

Within the ring, the portal lens cracked as it stretched. Sh'logath beat upon the door with his flailing tendrils. He glared at the scene below, beaming with hatred, willing himself through the cracks, but only succeeding with one inky, black splotch of ether—almost microscopic in size. The filthy drop fell like vile rain and shot through the air like a bullet, searching for its dark destination.

Sh'logath's ebon bullet pierced the wounded body of the traitor in Quintin Hall's body as it shot away. Its exit wound blasted a fist-sized puncture through the man's chest as the escaping herald tried to outrun the bombs he'd had Theera plant within the golden ark, and elsewhere. He collapsed but kept crawling on his hands and knees, trying to flee back towards the Kith Gate.

Shaking violently, the ground became unstable and threatened to throw everyone off their feet as a string of explosives buried within the pyramid blossomed with kinetic energy. Caivev screamed a curse and staggered to keep her balance—the trickster had played them all along! Another bomb rattled the stones as the foundation far below them broke into unstable pieces.

Zabe and Wulftone ascended the climb just in time to see Caivev and her crew panicking at the chaos of the ritual gone awry.

Quixotic chains bound most of the heralds, but they no longer had bodies, and the Sh'logathian gate to nihil had fractured.

They looked at each other and each knew the other's thoughts. Something else had intervened; the Awakening had become impossible at this point.

Another bomb erupted and quaked the pyramid. A vent of fire blew hot ash upwards nearby, and the two lycans threw themselves over the edge of the structure and slid back down its side.

Percival Wainsmith scrambled through the corridors; with his face covered in soot and ancient dust, he bounced from wall to wall. His fine clothes had torn, and the flames had burnt away much of his hair and rashed his face. Every breath he exhaled came with a curse.

He looked from door to door, trying to decide which archway to take as he frantically searched for Sisyphus or Thornton to guide him. Wainsmith knew they'd be heading for the gate back to Earth—but he did not know the way.

Another explosion rocked the structure, nearly knocking Wainsmith off his feet and covering him with a fresh coat of dirt. He chose the left path.

Twenty meters deep, the trail turned completely dark. The billionaire tried to feel his way through it and suddenly saw light. A fist clubbed him in the jaw; Wainsmith reeled backward, landing on his butt while his attacker leapt out from the shadows.

Tahnak snarled and hit the cultist again.

"Akko Quarnyk! Why?"

The beast within him laughed as he drew a dagger, pinning his prey down. "Everyone is still fooled? Excellent." Another bomb rumbled violently, and Tahnak looked off wistfully. "Good Theera—you've done well."

Wainsmith squinted at him. "Akko Soggathoth?"

Tahnak sneered and used his knife to cut the leather strap around Wainsmith's neck before batting the charm away. He hissed and expelled the murky cloud that was his essence. Akko Soggathoth took the rich man as his trophy.

He pushed the confused Tahnak off of him. Before the soldier could get his bearings, Wainsmith pulled out a handgun and shot the corpsman in his face, ending him in the dark. Akko Soggathoth chortled gleefully as he recovered the amulet Sisyphus had given Wainsmith.

Shaking one end of the leather thong, he pulled it free and let the amulet clatter to the ground. A broken stone potsherd lay nearby and Akko Soggathoth snatched it up and used his magic to change its shape to a near perfect replica from the clay. He threaded the leather through and tied the fake artifact around his head.

A wide smile spread across his face when he spotted Jacob Sisyphus fleeing past the door Percival Wainsmith had come from. Copying his host's mannerisms, he fixed the man in his sights and gave chase.

"It's all coming down," Jackie said, still cradling Bithia in her arms. High overhead, the ring of nihil sundered and split. Lightning flashed across the sky as if rage personified.

The princess shook as the giant halo began falling, its power broken. She opened her eyes. "It was so... so evil!"

"We've got to get out of here," Jackie yelled against the howling buffets of wind and the explosions that blasted hunks of the pyramid away. "Our boys must've done it!"

"Praise the Architect King," Shandra yelled, and they formed up just as Zabe and Wulftone slid to a stop at their perimeter. Their enemies had already broken ranks and scattered.

Jackie hauled Bithia to her feet. "Can you walk?"

Bithia nodded and brushed herself off. "I'm fine."

"Now is our chance," Zabe barked. "If we can beat them to the door and seal them in, we can finally put an end to all of Caivev's plans!"

They all looked to Bithia for the final word. She curtly bobbed her head in assent. "If we can do this, we will finally end the corruption and influence that began with Nitthogr."

The invaders couldn't spare another moment. They turned and made for the door even as broken, smaller fragments of white-washed bone and links of broken chain rained down from the collapsing Nihil Bridge.

# Chapter Twenty-Eight

The smells of sulfur and ancient soot-caked his nose as Sisyphus dashed through the dark halls. More reverberations from the collapsing superstructure shook him through the hallway. The exits collapsed in heaps of rubble, blocking off the hallways.

He cursed and whirled around, looking for Thornton. Sisyphus had gotten turned around in the dark—and all because of one cursed creature's antics. The conjurer screamed a string of expletives at Akko Soggathoth.

Wainsmith stepped out of the shadows. "Sisyphus? I have found the way down."

"Oh, good—I thought I'd lost you—but we have to hurry." He scanned his friend closely, looking for signs that he still wore the darquematter trinket he'd placed on him earlier. The spell caster howled, a final call for the last member of his trio. "Thornton? Thornton!"

"Here," he called back. The trio reformed seconds later. Sisyphus discretely checked him for his protection talisman as well. The oil baron had located the bloody, barely functioning body of Akko Soggathoth's favorite form, Quintin Hall.

They joined him and Sisyphus towered over Hall, grinning. He met the coal-eyed gaze of the possessed man and recognized the opportunity. "I did not become the magus I am today without skills and resources," he spat. He scrolled to a spell on his smartphone and read a binding spell that locked the wicked spirit within the body of Quintin Hall.

They were alone in the tunnel and the herald had nowhere to go—no way to escape. Even if he could abandon this form, options would have been limited.

The wizard opened the blank tome and held it out to his prisoner. "You've played your last trick. Make your mark—it's your only way out of here."

With blood spurting from his mouth from all the internal bleeding, he looked at the three men. His eyes lingered on Wainsmith. Finally, he reached up and drew a symbol on the book, freeing his spirit from the host, but locking it within the pages.

Sisyphus cackled and snapped it shut, gloating to himself about how clever he was to have tricked the ultimate prankster any world had ever seen. "We may have cause to press him into service in the future," he said, winking at his peers, "though, it is a wonderful trophy to hold—even if I decide to lock it away or drop it into the ocean."

Thornton hissed, "Sh'logath will not rise today, but at least we've gained a powerful boon, should we ever decide how to best use it."

Wainsmith nodded. "Now let's get out of here before we lose that chance! I don't trust Caivev to hold the door for us and this place will come down at any moment."

Grabbing his khopesh, Sisyphus used its telekinetic abilities to move the fallen stones that blocked an exit tunnel.

Wainsmith pointed the fastest way down. "Quickly!"

Zabe and Wulftone brought up the rear. Their friends moved as fast as possible back towards the large antechamber where the door to Kith had been located. Intermittent bombs rocked the structure still but did not shake as violently in the center, nearer the foundation.

Suddenly everything shook so fiercely that most everyone was thrown from his or her feet. It sounded like they were inside a cracking egg—the ring of nihil had finally crashed into the pyramid and the impact crushed the temple's upper levels.

Vyrm of the Black tumbled down the stairwells on either side of them as they all rushed for the same exit portal. It was a race for survival.

Zabe looked back in time to brace against a blaster beam that caught him square in the back. He growled in response and leapt to his feet, yanking his blaster from the thigh holster and firing a quick burst into the mass of scrambling vyrm behind him.

Wulftone's weapon whined and went dark with depleted batteries. "I'm out," he shouted and turned back to the escape. His cousin joined him, likewise firing blindly to his rear as he ran.

Zabe's weapon echoed the empty signal and Zabe turned in a spinning motion, flinging his pistol at their pursuit. The pistol-whipped a vyrm in the face and he crumpled while the Prime's men and women ran ahead.

The last room opened up before them and the two lycans tried to buy any necessary time for their friends to reach the doors. Many of the injured or those carrying others needed the extra few seconds.

Snarling at the entry point to the room, the two werewolves held the chokepoint and roared their success at claiming the room. They warned their enemies against approach, but it went unheeded as they fired a barrage at them.

Zabe looked back and saw the doors begin to close as their forces made it through the gate. On the other side of the door, Chira and his men used flamethrowers to burn away the wet blood that kept the door activated.

The pyramid rumbled again as the other half of the ring impacted. A massive section of wall collapsed, exposing the doors to a small army of vyrm—Caivev was with them.

She screamed, "Kill them—take the room!"

Scaly enemies poured in with weapons blazing, shooting at the lycans and any of the Prime's forces who had barely cleared the door. Chira and his men hid behind the closing gates and returned fire while the lycans made a mad dash for the exit.

Another section of wall collapsed close to the door, revealing Skrom and more Black. At Caivev's side, Idrakka raised a rocket-propelled grenade launcher and aimed for the gate.

Wulftone, nearly through the door, turned his head just in time to scc him.

Jackie screamed, "RPG! RPG!"

He reacted instinctively and leapt into the air as the explosive round shot like a missile. Wulftone spun and shin-kicked the round like a soccer defenseman saving the day. The eruption detonated like a powder keg and blasted flesh from bone and knocked him to the floor, unconscious.

"Wulftone!" Zabe and Jackie screamed in unison.

Skrom and his soldiers snarled as they rushed towards the fallen hero whose leg barely hung from the socket. His lower half bled upon the floor, where tattered and torn muscle and ligament hung from ragged tibia, fibula, and metatarsals.

Zabe, already scorched from the glancing firebrands, leapt to his cousin's defense. He swung the Stone Glaive and barely nicked a group of pouncing vyrm with a spinning whirl, freezing their surprised looks as they turned to stone. The other enemies stepped back and gave him wide berth.

Skrom snatched up one of the stone soldiers and wielded it as a club. Zabe and Skrom traded blows as more vyrm rushed towards them; the door had nearly closed behind them. Jackie and Bithia screamed for his retreat.

Zabe glanced at the horde of vyrm pouring towards him and didn't see Skrom's windup with the club. He smashed the lycan and knocked the Stone Glaive free. The mythic blade clattered towards the Kith Gate.

Howling in response, Zabe slashed the tarkhūn behemoth with his claws, staggering him backward. The lycan snatched up Wulftone's body and chucked his friend through the gate. Zabe slashed at the other vyrm as they tried to grab a hold and then sprinted for the gate, snatching the Stone Glaive as he passed.

The lycan turned his body and squeezed through just in time. He turned and glared, meeting Caivev's gaze as she burned the closing door with her hateful scowl and the air echoed with the sounds of the pyramid's collapse.

With a resounding thud, the Darque gate of Koth closed and entombed Caivev and her forces in the dimension cut off from the multiverse.

At insurmountable speeds, the inky splotch flew through the air. It instinctively knew its host, instructed by the Master.

Squeezing through keyhole and crack, the thing slammed through any objects in its way and rolled over anything that did not yield like an inanimate object fluent in parkour. It rolled itself in human blood and skidded across ancient runes, bridging arcane connections, and activating sigils that allowed it to pass into realms beyond—to where its destiny called.

Soil and grass were of no interest to the fleshless blob as it passed over the splendor of the Prime. Beauty did not move it and compassion would not deter its dark purpose: conceived of nihil, ether, and rage.

There was no way it could breach the ultimate object of its desire—the Chamber of Secrets was beyond even *its* ability. It searched for the host, finding a petrified soldier in Respan's lab. The insolent child of Jarfig, filled with fury and bitterness, paced nearby.

If the thing could have laughed, the onyx smear would have. As it hovered high above the castle and looked across the land, it saw all, and it pulsed with expectant, hideous glee. It knew who to possess by sheer impulse.

It moved quickly and took its host with no resistance. Burrowing its way in, it felt the warmth of human flesh as it regained a body and senses. Overcoming the host's mind, he seized control and inhaled a deep breath. He had forgotten what it was like to be human—the creature had not been human for a long time.

With returning senses, so too did memories and emotions. Hate burned like a fiery star in his heart. He turned to face the Royal City and its gleaming castle.

The long game had resumed for the hidden enemy. Nobody would know he even existed until it was too late.

Wiltshire steepled his fingers as he read over the translation of the documents Professor Jecima had provided him with. The cipher had been made during the era when Latin had been the prevailing language and so Jecima's revised document had three lines. Under the original was a transliteration that looked like it may have come from the Vulgate. Below that was Jecima's English conversion.

Not all the pages were relevant to whatever had worried T. Some pages detailed foul occult rituals related to something called The Seven Brothers of the Winnowing, plus information about them.

Wiltshire recognized at least one of the symbols as coming from the site in Pecos where it had been engraved into the stone plinth.

The texts detailing the seven brothers were on the latter pages. They seemed the most pressing to Wiltshire, but T had been specific that the earlier pages would be the most troublesome. But they read more like a short story. The earlier pages appeared to be note pages that were older than the ones scribed for use by the goat cult. In fact, they appeared to be unrelated except that they seemed to be in the same handwriting as the latter pages. Whomever had been the vessel for an auto-writing spirit, he or she had played host to more than one source.

T's pages told the tragic story of the maiden Vivianne, who was the princess of Dyfed. Distraught and lonely, confined to a convent, she was visited by a being named Suranvyn who was some kind of incubus demon. He seduced her and fathered a being of immense power: a man with six fingers and touched by destiny despite his heritage as a cambion, a half-demon scion.

Wiltshire scanned the name and read it aloud. "Myrddin... this is a very early Merlin tale. It's Arthurian?"

Before he could delve in again, the door banged open loudly and Praetor Russo entered. He stormed over and snatched the copies from Wiltshire's hands. "Do not meddle where you do not belong!"

"What? How did you—"

"I put two and two together," the praetor hissed.

Wiltshire shot Sexton a glance, but his partner shook his head. Sexton and Wiltshire had differing opinions, but he was no rat.

"We have cameras and logs for a reason," Russo said. "And you've skated a thin line for a long while, Brother Wiltshire."

"What's so damned important in these files that you're trying to keep me away from it?" Wiltshire asked.

"It should be enough to let it lie because I told you to leave the files alone," Russo said, his Italian became more and more pronounced. "The Order does not share its dirty laundry, or their history, with *anyone.*"

Wiltshire worked it out. "This is what you were protecting in the vaults below the Vatican. The Solomonari—they were looking for this?"

Russo looked Wiltshire dead in the eye and spat, "Vai a fart fottere."

Wiltshire gave the praetor a look of mild disapproval and held up a finger. He typed in his best approximation of the insult into an online translator. He got the result and then upgraded his frowny face to an offended one. "How dare you—you're a man of the cloth!"

Russo's vulgar response had practically been a thumbs up as far as Wiltshire was concerned.

"This is your final warning, *Vikrum.*" Russo used his name as a threat—no honorifics, not even a last name. If he pressed the issue, he'd be out of a job. "Pursue this further at your own peril."

The Italian praetor tucked the pages under his arm and turned to make an exit.

"I have copies of it," he called after Russo. "It's the digital age, Praetor. We've got backups."

Before stepping out and closing the door behind him, Russo gave him a dark look. "Do not test me on this." And then Praetor Russo was gone.

It felt like he'd sucked all the air out of the room when he went, and it was several seconds before either Wiltshire or Sexton could speak.

"Did he really come all the way from Rome just to yoink those papers from your hands?" Sexton asked.

"Evidently," Wiltshire said. Little ever frazzled the detective, but threats from on high did put him on uneasy footing.

"They can't fire me," Wiltshire said, his voice a few decibels quieter. He turned to Sexton. "Without us, this whole planet would fall apart."

Three days after Russo left, the Praetor sent them a follow-up message.

*I may have spoken hastily. The Order has dirty laundry and requires someone—someone lower ranked than Praetor—to clean it up. Meet me in Rome.*

# Chapter Twenty-Nine

Mere days had passed since returning to the Prime, though the campaign felt nothing like a victory. Too few had come back, but the casualties seemed low compared to the last two attempts at awakening the Agod Devourer.

Even throughout the wake of Caivev's campaign, the royal military had kept busy training the next class of soldiers, who were ready to step into the shoes of their predecessors. Luckily, with fighting subsided, they were readily employed in whirlwind cleanup efforts and they kept earth-side evidence of any alien forces to a minimum.

Tay-lore even sent out false signals to sidetrack paranormal researchers and occult experts like Vikrum Wiltshire to keep them from stumbling upon fresh truths while the Prime's forces buried the incident in layers of fresh dirt. He'd gone so far as directly hiring Wiltshire for a wild goose chase. The Veritas had long insisted that the Architect King's special Earth dimension remain as undisturbed as possible—they had to make a renewed attempt at the mandate, at least. At the top of that list was the destruction of the Koth Gate.

Other than the missing faces, things appeared to have nearly resumed normalcy. Changes were subtle. The Veritas were found more readily in the palace hallways—especially Shandra, who often accompanied Sam Jones.

"Please, call me Princess," became a common request. Only select people knew about Bithia's reemergence and Claire's traumatized catatonia from the Darque.

The fallback to formality helped obscure that fact, and such a request did not strike anyone as odd. It was difficult only for Sam, Jackie, and Zabe.

The archaeologist was able to fling himself into his work or his new relationship with the attractive cleric. Jackie and Wulftone were disgustingly in love and focused on each other. Zabe... took the change with difficulty.

Popping his head into Bithia's room, Zabe rapped gently on the door frame. "Princess?"

Bithia waved him in. "Come in, please."

He looked around uneasily. Perhaps the most awkward change had been her relocation back to her old room. It was a stark contrast to the one Claire had kept in her father's apartment. That room had been free of royal vestments and pretense... it allowed Claire to be freer and escape the shadow of the crown. It was not necessarily better... just different.

Perhaps for the first time in the days since their return, Zabe had been capable of putting everything back in order and finding some personal time. Nothing required his immediate attention, and he could take a shower and relax.

Zabe remembered how he and Bithia connected—it was different from his and Claire's connection. The internal struggle between the two eroded his gut with emotional tension. He wasn't sure he knew how to be alone, though—Bithia or Claire, he couldn't imagine a life without her.

"Would you like to accompany me to supper? It's probably good to be seen in public after all the recent turmoil." Zabe almost blushed. He didn't know why he felt the need to excuse the invitation.

"I would like that," Bithia said. Her eyes sparkled a little more vibrantly than they had since her reemergence.

Zabe escorted her to the bistro that had come on such high recommendation from his cousin. Through the front window, they spotted Jackie and Wulftone sitting as they arrived. He'd just begun walking again with his leg finally healing thanks to his altered forms incredible regenerative abilities. Despite that, however, he retained a slight limp whenever he took his lycan shape.

"Should we sit with them?" Bithia asked—she desperately yearned to spend time with Jackie. Bithia never had a female friend as close as her, but she knew from Claire's memories that it was something she greatly desired.

"No," Zabe said. "Let's stay incognito and not steal his thunder. I think he's got something special planned tonight."

Pollando stood with Minas, Perribelle, and Druen outside the door. They'd been knocking for hours, trying to ascertain that Shjikara would not—or could not—open the door to the Sacristy. None of the faction leaders had seen him in days.

Though Pollando could not speak, it was clear that he agreed with the other leaders of the four disciplines: they should open the door. Such an act was considered an extreme measure within the halls of the Veritas.

Perribelle, the studious bookworm and head monk of the Wax Order, reinforced the gravity of their decision. "Only once previously has the four heads agreed to open the doors without the High Priest's lead."

Minas rolled his eyes. The leader of the Order of the Flame had heard his peer tell this story countless times. "Yes, yes... Master Tangellaf was so diligent that he died while executing his duties and had to be retrieved by the four heads."

Perribelle frowned at the more brazen head of the arcane branch of studies. It was probably that trait which had helped propel him to his current rank... but it would likely never allow him to take Shjikara's seat... in the event that he'd met a similar fate. The Veritas had remained conservative ever since a previous head of the Order of the Flame grew too zealous and fell: Nitthogr.

Druen, with a silence almost as stoic as the mute Pollando, thrust his fist into the lock of the door. His surprised peers did likewise on their specific ports, each one engraved with the crest of their discipline.

The door warmed and vibrated momentarily. Finally, it unlatched and yielded before them.

Drawn and haggard, with a thick growth of stubble on his face, Shjikara looked up from his seat at the long table. Books upon books lay open and a variety of artifacts had been pulled from shelves. The sight made Perribelle glow with camaraderie.

All at once, they noticed their leader's fist. From forearm to fist, his left arm had been turned to stone—the same kind of living stone that resulted from the Stone Glaive's power. They stared at Shjikara in awe.

His lips were cracked and his voice sounded raspy and weak from fasting. "My research has taken a serious turn." He held up a stone chip that they all knew had come from the Stone Glaive, though it had never before demonstrated the ability to cause a transmutation. It had been on the Sacristy shelves since losing the weapon during the Syzygyc War.

Shjikara looked at them with both fear and excitement in his tired eyes. "I've been at this for days, and can find no answer to my predicament," he tapped his solid fist on the table, "but I do believe that I have learned the secret of turning stone back to flesh and reversing Basilisk's curse—that is, for anyone else." He met Minas's gaze, "Of course, we all know the basic tenants of the arcane arts. 'For every spell, there is a cost.' I think this may be just that for me."

"To what end?" Druen asked.

"There are so many," he rasped as his friends helped him to his feet so they could guide him to his bedchamber for some much-needed rest. "Chiefly among them is compassion," he said. "And I know exactly who to release first... as soon as I've perfected the technique."

Pollando caught Shjikara with an askew look. A freed and restored General Zahaben would have several implications.

"No, my friend," Shjikara defended. "It's not because of any particular disdain for Zabe—though I've made no attempts to hide my dislike of Zahaben's son—we *all want this*, it matters not whether it deposes his command of the Guardian Corps."

The others let the topic rest between the two psychics. It could be discussed later, *after* Shjikara had gotten some rest and sustenance.

As soon as the others left the High Priest on his cot and closed the door, Shjikara looked at his hand and smiled with a broad, mischievous grin. He'd always had plans, and crippled or not, they'd become easier with this new development.

Shjikara grinned again. He might earn a nickname out of it, too. "Shjikara the Stonefist," he whispered aloud... or even just *Stonefist*. He liked the sound of that.

Wulftone pushed Jackie's chair in for her.

"Ooh, fancy," she quipped.

He sat opposite of her and smiled. "You have no idea. I researched some of your Earth customs and came up with your perfect night."

She leaned forward, intrigued, and playfully tapped on his foot with hers. "You better be careful and not tip your hand *too early*."

Wulftone smiled and poured two glasses of sweet wine. He signaled the waiter, who disappeared through the kitchen. "We haven't yet revisited that last thing I told you in the Darque."

Jackie blushed. "I've been waiting for you to get around to that."

He smiled. "It is apparently a custom for you to receive a ring—and I know your favorite kind."

Their waiter appeared with a pale pink box that he set on the table. It was far too large to be a diamond ring. She raised her brows inquisitively.

"Tay-lore helped me locate a recipe from Earth," he noted as she lifted the lid.

A dozen warm and glazed imitation Krispy Kremes rested neatly in two rows. She looked up at him with eyes that twinkled like gems.

"I hope these rings make you happy."

She sniffed the box as Wulftone bent onto one knee. "Jackie..."

"Oh dear Lord, yes!" she exclaimed as she began stuffing her face with pastry.

He took a ring from his pocket—he'd had it specially made from a fragment of darquematter. "Will you—"

"I already said yes," she said, stuffing a doughnut into his mouth and smashing most of it against his face.

He ignored the sticky mess and put the ring on her finger anyhow as they laughed together.

"I haven't eaten this many in a long time—so be warned that you're going to have to help me work off some calories later," Jackie said playfully.

Shandra walked down the hallway with a hip swagger that indicated she was on a mission. Her footfalls stopped clacking for a moment as she glanced into one of the research pods. She knew Trenzlr had made friends with Respan and Tay-lore and hoped to find the vyrm turncoat in the area. Only Jenner was in the research pod.

She stared at him for a few long seconds, frowned, and departed. Jenner had never struck her as someone prone to research, but he was an incredibly driven young man and it wasn't out of the question that some task had inspired him to pour so deeply over data. Truth be told, the recent incidents had touched every person in different ways. No person involved in the fight against Caivev escaped the battle unchanged.

The cleric poked her head in on the scientist-inventor Respan, who appeared totally engrossed in some kind of test he'd undertaken upon the statue of Zahaben. He didn't even look up.

"Definitely alive," he mumbled aloud. "So it can't be some kind of fake or ploy that Basilisk is undertaking for nefarious purposes."

She asked, "Have you seen Trenzlr?"

He jumped, startled at her presence. Slightly embarrassed at his gaffe, he smoothed his shirt and shook his head while pretending that he'd seen her all along. "No. Not since… before."

Shandra knew what he meant. She nodded and walked further down the hall to Tay-lore's lab. The android sat on the edge of the workshop with a number of machines hooked up to opened ports on his animatronic body.

"Greetings. Pardon my state," he said, "But I'm in the middle of some routine diagnostics. I hope you're not offended by my… nakedness." He tried his hand at humor again, but it dripped with over-the-top lewdness, complete with eyebrow-raising.

It was all that Shandra could do to keep from laughing. She merely shook her head with amused disdain.

"Too much?"

She nodded.

"What brings you here so late?"

"I've been sent on a mission that I do not fully understand," she said. "Shjikara has always been cagey, but he's been even more so lately. He hasn't cared much for Trenzlr, but his regular indifference has given way to something completely different since our return. He sent me to find him but nobody has seen him since that day we all planeswalked to Koth. I know he forged a bond with you—have you seen him?"

Tay-lore seemed reluctant to answer. "Not since that day."

"Well, where did he go?"

The android shrugged but did a bad job concealing that he might know more.

Shandra crossed her arms. "What aren't you telling me?"

Tay-lore grudgingly admitted, "He received a coded transmission that appeared meant for him. It originated from the Plains of Neggath."

The cleric frowned. "You didn't tell anyone?"

"Everyone was... preoccupied."

"But now—after he's gone? I hope you have a copy of the message. Did you read it?"

"No."

"No? Why not—we've had security problems lately. It didn't occur to you that our leak could've come from the only vyrm living on the Prime?"

"You previously vouched so strongly for him. Besides, he is our friend. It would've been *wrong* to go through his messages. I'm certain he couldn't have been the mole."

Shandra crossed her arms and glowered at her synthetic teammate. She fumed for a few long moments. "Shjikara's not going to like your answer. Speculate."

"Thankfully, I only report to the Guardian Corps," he said. "I don't think Shjikara ever cared for me. Regardless, after he read the message, it seemed to give Trenzlr no end to his consternation. He disappeared later that afternoon. I had assumed he returned to the monastery and the Veritas."

Shandra held her severe posture, so Tay-lore continued.

"I did catch one word he kept mumbling to himself. 'Maetha.' There is a high probability that the contents of his letter drove him to flee on some personal errand—probably religious in nature; it may have otherwise been a call home. There is a low probability that Trenzlr is the source of the security problem."

Shandra bit her lip, tempted to curse with frustration. She began her departure and muttered, "I think maybe Trenzlr and Shjikara both know something that no one else does."

Zabe reached across the table and took Bithia's hands. He looked into her face, trying to stay positive, though inside he ached over what Claire's disappearance might mean... was she dead? Was this a split personality thing? Were Claire and Bithia even different?

He pushed down that internal struggle and locked it away in the deepest part of his mind and glanced across the room at the happy couple. Wulftone and Jackie seemed oblivious to the world around them. Zabe didn't know if that was a good thing or not—but he wished he could stop the wheels of his mind and feel like that again.

Bithia smiled. "It is good that they have finally found each other. The worlds can be so dark and hard at times... and life can be so short." Her words hung heavy between them.

"Too short," Zabe agreed.

Bithia glanced around and then stiffened her posture. Zabe followed her eyes; the other diners had recognized the royalty in their midst. Patrons already buzzed with excitement at seeing the engagement of a notable officer of the Guardian Corps—now they were treated to a visit from the most prestigious couple of the realm who had only recently made news of *their own engagement* public prior to Akko Soggathoth's grand joke played out.

The royal couple lowered their voices slightly for privacy's sake. She watched Zabe for a few long moments with hopeful expectation. The perfect time for a hard conversation would never arrive; now would suffice.

Zabe didn't talk. He drew his face together, obviously deep in thought.

Bithia dropped the question on him bluntly and with brute force. "Are we still a thing? Is there hope for us, Zabe?" She scanned the room while wearing a brave face brimming with false bravado. The diners who met her eyes smiled warmly, as if she'd somehow blessed them.

Zabe glanced back and saw the expectation on the faces of the crowd. "The people expect a wedding... and the realm needs an heir to the Architect King."

Bithia did her best to keep her posture erect and pretend that the wind hadn't been knocked out of her emotional sails. "So your intentions are..."

"Still to marry." He didn't meet her gaze.

Bithia's heart tightened. It wounded her to know that she had played some small part in causing Zabe such agony and doubt. "You loved me once... when I was Bithia... before..."

Zabe looked into her eyes and nodded.

"Can you not love me again?" Her eyes glistened with fresh pain.

Zabe's eyes moistened likewise. "Of course. *I never stopped loving you!* It's just... something has changed... I... don't know."

"But you still love me?"

He took her hands in his and nodded vigorously. "Always. We will still marry... I will just... need some time."

Bithia squeezed her fiancé's hand and nodded. "My love burns as passionately as ever—more if such a thing is possible. I have, and always will, love you."

# Chapter Thirty

Caivev didn't need to search the darkness to know that she'd lost a few more troops. She could smell the death within the musty stone tomb. Fewer mouths would help with their rationing, a necessary protocol if any were to survive.

Most of her troops had fallen weak and gaunt in the weeks since the cave-in at darquegate. They'd luckily found a small cistern to draw stagnant, bitter water from in short amounts. They could hold out for far longer than any wanted.

Most of those lacking the will to survive had already put their blasters to their skull and surrendered. At least the random chaos waves they'd experienced before hadn't come since the destruction of the Nihil Bridge.

She glanced to her right. While most of the survivors showed signs of emaciation, Skrom seemed to thrive. He'd proven no aversion to eating the dead if it meant the difference between survival or not, and her devoted general had encouraged Caivev to join him in his feral endeavor. So far, she'd declined, but knew her hunger would return in a handful of days once her body stopped burning fat cells for energy and demanded new sources; she would take him up on the offer, then.

Most of them spoke in hushed whispers. Something about the dark made all humanoids mute their words, but she caught many of them. Some talked mutiny, some pledged even deeper dedication.

Caivev wasn't sure help would come, but she was confident if it did not, the last two survivors would be her and Skrom. The tarkhūn would probably eat her and then kill himself, she figured.

The long, silent wait drew on like a foretaste of an endless hell. Gall burned in her heart—her devotion to Sh'logath only deepened as she identified with his tormented languishment. This sensory-deprived confinement must have been what the agod's existence felt like through the ages.

A blinding light ripped through blackness like a welding arc. Everyone in the entombed structure shielded their eyes as the illumination split into three pieces and opened a familiar, triangular shape directly adjacent to the closed Kith Gate.

Cheering arose from the troops and shouts of accolade and support for Caivev. For her part, she merely stared at the blazing aperture in disbelief. A lone tear rolled down her face, cleaning a rivulet of skin amid the sooty grime that caked her cheeks.

From the other side, the midday light and clean German sky offered an oasis of relief for the prisoners. Walther waved excitedly and beckoned her to jump through.

She strode through first, with Skrom on her heels—and then Idrakka and the three Heptobscurantum leaders. Caivev kept her head high and preserved her dignity. A second portal burned on the other side of the large studio where Cerci Heiderscheidt operated the secondary machine.

"Doctor," Caivev said thankfully. "So glad you were finally able to pierce the veil into the Darque."

He wrung his hands as he spoke. "It was a joint effort, in fact. I had some inside information from an outside source. I really could not have done it without his help. You really must meet... where did he go?" Walther looked around with confusion as the folk trapped in the foreign realm continued pouring through.

Percival Wainsmith stepped back into the Earth realm, right on Idrakka's heels. The billionaire smiled at the Spring-like taint of the fresh air as the icelord drew a renewed bastion of moisture to himself that would reawaken his spectacular tarkhūn abilities.

He walked nonchalantly and straightened his clothes as if it somehow improved his stature. Wainsmith looked past the machinery and laboratory equipment that cluttered the eccentric scientist's workshop and spotted his creature. Theera the Undying slinked away from the commotion of the rescue, knowing that his master would find him later. Wainsmith smiled broadly; everything had gone *exactly* as he guessed it would.

"He was right here," Walther insisted, as if his credibility were on the line.

A booming voice from the other portal sucked the attention out of the room, stealing away all concern over Walther's ramblings. Opposite the other energy gate, Basilisk stood, flanked by two long rows of Tarkhūn behemoths. "Caivev. Daughter of the Prime—*you have an oath to fulfill.*"

She narrowed her eyes at the hybrid ruler of the vyrm and hissed. "I owe you nothing but the same dedication we share to almighty Sh'logath."

"I'd hoped that you wouldn't need any more convincing," Basilisk said with mild disappointment. "But I'd expect nothing less from a prize as lofty as *you*." He tipped his head to signal someone behind her.

Caivev whirled around as the entire room filled with a curtain of ice that separated her, Skrom, and Idrakka from the others. The frostmancer held his pistol out and waved them towards the gate. "I knew you would be more comfortable if you had your pet with," Idrakka said, indicating Skrom.

With uncanny speed, Skrom snatched Idrakka by the throat and growled. "Traitor!" he roared, lifting him off his feet and batting the gun away.

The clacking of hands on weapons on the other side of the gate reinforced the gravity of the situation. "Please put him down," Basilisk requested with undue politeness.

Caivev rested a hand on Skrom's arm. "Do as he says. We must return to the Desolation."

Basilisk's face glowed. "Do not be afraid, Caivev. I think you will be pleasantly surprised by how I plan for you to uphold your oath—it is unlike anything you could have guessed."

Zabe answered the knock on his door. "Wulftone? Come in."

Wulftone entered his cousin's apartment and handed him a celebratory bottle of wine he'd tied with a bow. "Congratulations. The big day is coming up soon."

Zabe nodded placidly and then flipped the fancy bow around playfully and gave his cousin an askew look.

He shrugged. "Jackie insisted it needed to be decorated, otherwise it wouldn't count and I would still owe you a wedding gift."

"Fair enough," he chuckled, searching for a pair of long stem goblets. He uncorked the bottle and poured each of them a glass.

"So how are you *really* doing with this whole Bithia thing?" Wulftone knew him like a brother and could sense he still had things to get off his chest.

Zabe sighed and looked around as if he needed to ensure his apartment remained private. "I confess I'm pretty knotted up inside." He looked at Wulftone, face tight with turmoil. "It just... it sucks," he used the phrase that Claire had taught them.

Wulftone nodded. Zabe didn't need to say anything more; he didn't need a hug or to cry. Presence was all that his friend needed.

They drank in silence for a few minutes.

"I really feel bad for Sam, though," Zabe murmured. "I know he and the Princess were getting together tonight."

Wulftone nodded. "Jackie was meeting her after that."

"She wants them to know that although she is Bithia, she is still Claire, too... just... differently."

They poured another glass each.

"You still feel the wedding is the right thing to do? You know you can always move the date back to give you more time to process this."

Zabe shifted in his chair. "I still feel it's right—I know that much in my bones. It doesn't make it any easier, however." He reached for his communicator as it chirped on the nearby counter.

Respan greeted him on the open line. "Zabe? You should come to my lab—and quick."

"You've had a breakthrough?"

"Just come as soon as you can," he said excitedly. "I have some wonderful news!"

"I'll be right there!" He and Wulftone dashed out the door.

"You owe me your oath, but I would much prefer if you followed my cause from desire rather than duty," Basilisk said as he led the way up the winding path to the peak that overlooked Limbus. His estate broke up the skyline against the backdrop of the unspeakable thing hanging in the sky: the monument to the most ambitious of Basilisk's and Nitthogr's campaigns.

Caivev followed at a footstep behind. Skrom shadowed her closely. Idrakka and twenty other tarkhūn warriors nearly Skrom's equal completed the parade.

Basilisk stood at a fork in the path. One led to his mansion, the other led to the edge of his yard where his game tables and garden were located. "We have ceremonies to attend—but first, we should parley in private." He looked at Skrom, but not with resentment—more like an appreciation for such fierce dedication.

Caivev nudged her protector. "It'll be okay. Stay here." She followed her benefactor towards the house and glanced back to the stone gardens where the mixed vyrm had gathered. Caivev could barely make out a bunch of the game boards that Basilisk had been known for; the "king" playing piece on each of them had been turned over.

Escorting her to his posh inner chamber, he motioned for her to sit on one of the sofas. She'd already resigned herself to whatever fate he'd planned for her, and so she sat.

He paced for a few steps, trying to decide exactly how to begin. Caivev almost grinned at this crack in his otherwise impenetrable bravado.

"You know better than I how my brother acted: how his heart had turned to purely selfish desires. He used Sh'logath for his own purposes."

Caivev nodded.

"I have long struggled with a question that the Architect King had whispered to me during our deal that halted the Syzygyc War. It was unanswerable and led to further questions: my ultimate search. *What did I really want out of life?* I have finally arrived at a conclusion—and it is one that fits into my atheology... in case you fear that I've abandoned my faith or lessened my dedication to the Awakening."

She fixed him with a firm gaze. "Go on."

"Finally, I have ascertained my only true desire and I'm ready to make it known. *It is you.* You will rule at my side as Queen. The repeated failures for Sh'logath's release only prove my belief that his time has not yet arrived—but that means I need a powerful mate ready and able to help pave the way for such a time as will come. I desire a kingdom dedicated to our atheocratic rule."

Caivev's face softened—even if she secretly suspected that he'd fallen into the same trap that had seduced Nitthogr. However, her heart tightened—suddenly awake with carnal vigor. She had certainly desired this same thing from her predecessor.

In his own right, Basilisk was not undesirable; the power and strength that he exuded made him alluring. "But would the tarkhūn race follow my lead, or would they revolt at bringing in an outsider—as they nearly did so many centuries ago?"

"It would solidify the all-vyrm alliance." Basilisk smiled. "But I have a better answer to that. I hold the thing that you have long sought. It will be yours as a wedding present. The oft-fickle Black already follow you, and the tarkhūn have never wavered in support of my rule."

She lifted her eyes and met his gaze. Something regal and un-yielding solidified on her dignified face. The slight tug of a smile indicated she would accept his proposal.

He took her by the hands and lifted Caivev to her feet before escorting her out to the party in the garden. Skrom watched her approach and his posture relaxed when he saw her countenance on the approach. She glanced side to side as they strolled. Every game-table's fallen king only made her heart flutter with glee and reinforced her feeling that this was a good match.

Charsk, a member of the vyrm's Black caste and High Priest of the cult of Sh'logath, stood at the center of the semi-circle at the center of the lawn. A human and a vyrm stood with him. "Con-gratulations on finally finding the final two persons connected to your Dunnischkte.

Caivev paid him little attention. She'd never cared for his foppish cajoling at her inability to secure those necessary for the rite. It didn't matter now, though—she had it all.

Basilisk drew a ceremonial blade and held it out for her. "My wedding gift."

Two women sat on their knees, held down by tarkhūn guards—one was vyrm. Caivev's last human variant wore the leather garb of the woodland people in a far-flung and secretive dimension; she trembled like a leaf.

"Marry me, Caivev. Become my queen and bear my heirs. Even-tually, we will subjugate all thirty-three realms until we succeed in unleashing the Great Devourer, yielding to whatever timing he has divinely appointed."

She tilted her head low enough that he could place a crown upon it and then accepted the knife he offered. "I will."

Caivev stood over the two women as the vyrm priests surrounded them to guide her in the ritual. It would grant her a hybrid form and a life resistant to age and decay. The Dunnischkte blessed her with the favor and power of Sh'logath.

"We have a wedding to perform," Charsk shouted over his shoulders. "Begin the ceremony!"

# EPILOGUE

Zurrah put one foot in front of the other and continued the arduous walk. He had no idea where he was or how long he'd been there. It might've been ages for all he knew. The boy had grown accustomed to time's irregular passage.

Something in the Darque sustained him, fed him. He learned how to avoid the chaos waves—but not after one caught him and sped his age up by nearly a decade, closing the age gap to where it might have been if he hadn't been locked away in stasis by Nitthogr.

Far ahead, something shimmered in the distance, but moved closer at rapid speed. Zurrah braced himself for battle.

The point of light rushed towards him and stopped when it arrived. It expanded into a burning, three-sided portal.

Zurrah stepped back, ready to flee, when a familiar voice called out. "Wait—stop. Are you Zurrah?"

He paused. It was the same voice that he'd heard before—the first voice he'd heard after years of captivity. He looked at his own body and scratched at the stubble that had grown on his face. "I... I think so, yes."

The girl smiled on the other side of the portal and a mischievous glint flashed in her eyes. She stretched out her hand. "We talked when your door was still shut. I am Cerci." She beckoned for him to jump through the portal. "Let's go on an adventure."

Percival Wainsmith flexed his gloved hands as he walked through the Yale University Library. His fine shoes made only a faint noise against the polished floors. The facility remained otherwise quiet. His majordomo, Mr. Theera, followed him closely, carrying a wrapped package.

Rows and rows of books towered and passed by like a blur. Wainsmith turned a corner and headed for the Beinecke Rare Book & Manuscript Library. He knew exactly where he intended to go. His money had gained the kind of privileged access only wealth can secure.

Nobody was around. He operated with impunity as he perused the collection of occult works. He sniggered at some and raised eyebrows at others. Some of the texts, such as the King in Yellow and the Keys of Solomon, were potent and dangerous while others like the Satanic Bible were nearly laughable in their potential for arcane thaumaturgy.

"The book," Wainsmith commanded and slid an oven mitt over his hand.

Theera unwrapped the bound manuscript and placed it on his master's palm.

Masquerading as a billionaire, the extra-dimensional being used his magic to transmute the leather of the spine, embossing it with a gilded, archaic script. He chuckled as he slid the tome between two other volumes and stared at it for a long while.

"What does it say?" Theera asked, unable to translate.

"The Divine Joke of Akko Soggathoth," Wainsmith said. "My lesser brother is free, only bound by the book's clasp," he giggled, shaking his head with a broad smile. "Someday in the distant future, some poor sap will pull this opuscule for one reason or another and then all hell will break loose."

Theera followed him out—faithful, but confused. "But why do it? Isn't the book, and a bound and powerful demigod, a valuable thing?"

"Yes, dear Theera. But I do what pleases me. There is sport in the mayhem, a certain amount of fun." They continued walking as Wainsmith digressed. "Someday I will uphold the call and release the Dark One, as Mother and Father instructed so long ago. But not until I'm ready—once life has lost all pleasure for me and I become bored with my current state of existence, I will choose to trade it in for the next one."

He smirked and spun like a child squeaking his shoes on the floor. "And imagine the mayhem when some little old librarian accidentally opens my cursed book fifty years from now! Woo-hoo!"

Theera the Undying followed Percival Wainsmith out of the library. He did imagine it, and it did amuse him. Given his new, eternal nature, he anticipated he would still be around to see it.

Zabe sprinted ahead as Wulftone rushed to keep step, but lagged by several paces given his limp. He skidded around a corner and pulled into the home stretch.

Jenner poked his head out of the research pod as Wulftone drew closer at a jog. "What's the hurry?" he called.

"News from Respan!" Wulftone shouted as he passed, and then hollered over his shoulder, "Zabe thinks they found a way to restore his father, Zahaben."

Momentary fear flashed across the young man's face and he darted back inside the pod.

Wulftone burst through the door to find Zabe with Respan. Along with them stood the Veritas elders and Shjikara. They stood in a circle around the petrified form of Zahaben. "Weird," he mumbled, glancing over his shoulder, "the kid sure has been reading a lot lately."

The high cleric peeled off a modified glove that hid the fact that his forearm and hand had metamorphed to living stone. Shjikara stared at Zahaben and then at Zabe. "I know how important of a man your father must've been to you," he said. "I offer this as an early wedding present for the royal couple."

Shjikara's fist glowed from the inside, streaking it with a ruddy light as if a fleshy hand tightly held a light in the dark. Mystic energy bled off whatever his arm had become and he touched it to Zahaben.

The general's skin cracked and peeled, flaking off like a crumbling eggshell. Zahaben sucked in a raspy breath and staggered until he found his balance.

Zabe watched the transformation with bleary eyes. "F-father?"

"Zabe? Son! You did it. I'm so proud of you."

Just as he stepped forward to embrace his son, the doors kicked open. Jenner leapt through the air, howling with murderous rage and wielding his sword high. Zahaben turned his head only in time to watch with wide-eyes as the young corpsman slashed the blade down and through his face, torso, and belly, nearly splitting him in twain.

Soldiers and clerics stood in shock. Barely recoiling from the violence, the blood of the fallen general splattered all across the room and mottled the murderer's face.

Jenner towered over the mangled corpse of Zahaben, holding the murder weapon in his trembling hands. Zabe's father, the hero of great renown, lay dead at Jenner's feet, nearly cut into two even halves.

Zabe looked up at him with tear-filled eyes. The sudden anarchy triggered a surge of endorphins. He shifted into his lycan form and brandished his razor claws. Zabe poised to strike and kill the boy at any moment, but shocked unbelief rooted his feet firm, momentarily staying the execution.

He could only stare and ask exasperatedly, "What... what have you done?"

The End.

Whatever happened to Zahaben has massive implications to the Prime and to the Multiverse!
Claire's mind—or is it Bithia's?—is fractured, and murder and mayhem rage across the dimensions in the final, epic conclusion of *Wolves of the Tesseract.*
Old things are new again and vyrm prophesies come to pass. Secret enemies reveal themselves and new powers, millennia in the making, are on the rise—and if Zabe and the company serving the Prime can not stop them, everything will burn.
Go grab your copy of The Architect King NOW!

**https://books2read.com/thearchitectking**

# WHAT'S NEXT?

The interconnected worlds of the multiverse intersect a few different literary universes. There are the Casefiles of Vikrum which quite obviously intersect the books featuring Claire and Zabe, but there is also the time mystic adventure series with an overlap from the Red Order (*The Hidden Rings of Myrddin the Cambion*) and also a fey world briefly seen in book 3, *The Architect King*, where *Curse of the Fey Duelist* occurs.

Keep up to date and stay in touch with the author at this link:
https://www.subscribepage.com/wolvesofthetesseract
and add your email to be added to the newsletter list!

**Glossary**

**A**byssal Auraphage – a kind of monstrous, supernatural bloodhound from the Darque.

**The Architect King** – the Creator God. He is currently in stone form, trapped within Basilisk's stronghold at Limbus until some prophesied day.

**The Awakening** – A ritual dedicated to calling Sh'logath into existence.

**The Black** – common, lowest Caste of the species. Also called Blackborne.

**Chamber of Mysteries** – an impenetrable vault where the arcane artifacts collected by the Royal Family are kept; also home to the Tesseract.

**Darquematter** – lead-like metallic substance with magical properties originating from the Darque dimension.

**Desolation** – a realm of the multiverse; formerly known as Edenya before the Syzygyc War ravaged the landscape.

**Dimensional Inversion Pendant** – a mysterious artifact made from darquematter; it alters the link between a Prime and his or her variants.

**Dunnischkte** - a religious ritual to gain a hybrid status between vyrm and human.

**Dunnischktet** – someone who has completed the Dunnischkte; he or she gains nigh-immortality and the ability to shift between hybrid, vyrm, and human forms.

**Edenya** – the name of the vyrm realm before it was called Desolation.

**Frostmancer** – tarkhūn with special abilities including ice/cold control.

**Grimmorium Nitthogr** – a journal kept by the fallen Veritas cleric Nitthogr; it is an arcane work that is the culmination of all the sorcery he learned in his earlier years before Sh'logath taught him even deeper and viler magics.

**Guardian Corps** – royal guards tasked with protecting the royal line and also the chamber of mysteries; some corpsmen decide to join the Veritas, a secretive monastic order drawn from their numbers.

**Hierophanticus** – a darquematter object imbued with arcane power to do a specific task.

**Heptobscurantum** – human branch of the vyrm's cult of Sh'logath.

**Homo diurnus** – android species created by the Technite people; Tay-lore is their last remaining, known member.

**Lich** – tarkhūn with psychic abilities; they are always identified at a young age and pressed into service of the Sh'logath cult.

**Limbus** – the home to Basilisk, the recognized leader of the Tarkhūn, and the capital of Desolation.

**Lycan** – a werewolf hybrid form which can be assumed by certain members of Zabe's lineage.

**Mae'le-ggath** – the original form of dualistic religion practiced by the vyrm in which Sh'logath was one of two philosophical forces.

**Maetha** – a kind of vyrm savior of prophecy that predates Mae'le-ggath.

**Multiverse** – thirty-three connected dimensions of the Tesseract which can be traveled via pathways that open up based on the astral alignment/calendar.

**Plains of Neggath** - region in Desolation where the Sh'logath cult birthed the great Agod; the area is a veritable wasteland and often the home of Rovers.

**Planeswalk** – traveling to different dimensions of the multiverse via the power of the Tesseract.

**The Prime** – the main realm of the multiverse: the ultimate reality. It also refers to a person who lives within this realm; each Prime has dimensional copies living on the different realms of the multiverse.

**Pyromancer** – tarkhūn with special abilities including fire generation and manipulation.

**Rovers** – unaligned vyrm tribes. They are typically either Seekers of Maetha or Followers of Krakkath, two different theologies that some vyrm adhere to.

**The Seven** – Illuminati-like ruling council of the Heptobscurantum.

**Shade** – tarkhūn with extreme camouflaging ability; some have even gained the ability to completely shapeshift their forms.

**Sh'logath** – the Devourer, Nega-God, Agod of Destruction, the Reality Eater... all are names to describe the terror that lurks on the verge of reality.

**Straruck** – the Holy city in the Neggath region; it has holy significance to the vyrm (their religion's kind of Mecca).

**The Syzygyc War** – the war that waged many years between the Prime and Desolation as they sought to awaken Sh'logath; it was prevented by the Architect King.

**Tarkhūn** – high caste of vyrm that once ruled their race before a schism led by Nitthogr long ago. They are a rarer, but stronger breed. Some, who resemble members of The Black, have developed additional powers.

**Tesseract** – a gem created by the Architect King; it is the key to all power in reality and the embodiment of the multiverse.

**Thousand Elder's Sacrifice** – the sacrificial torpor they entered into in order to make Sh'logath real in a ceremony they called the Birthing.

**TRX718** – a high powered blaster pistol Zabe is fond of.

**Veritas** – the religious order that seamlessly integrates into the Prime culture and is dedicated to the Architect King.

**Voice of the Thousand Elders** – the chief Cleric of the Vyrm's Thousand Elders. He stayed alive and died of old age, although his spirit remains disembodied and tied to the Thousand Elders will.

**Vyrm** – reptilian humanoid race whose home realm is known as the Desolation.

# Dramatis Personae

**Akko Soggathoth** – An ancient and mischievous demigod released from his prison within the Darque by the Texas Black Goat Cult.

**Andrew Thornton** – A member of The Seven who rule the heptobscurantum

**Atticus Sexton** – A paranormal investigator and Red Order brother; Vikrum Wiltshire is his partner

**Basilisk** – Brother to Nitthogr. He rules the dimension known as the Desolation

**Bithia of the Prime** – Princess. Daughter of the Architect King and ruler of the Prime, and by extension, the multiverse

**Bruce Cannon** – A member of The Seven who rule the heptobscurantum. Hired Vikrum Wiltshire to save his life

**Caivev** – Traitor to the Prime, former Guardian Corps member. She has wanted to join Nitthogr and Basilisk as a dunnischktet and is a ranking member of the vyrm's army. Took the form of Vivian on Earth

**Cerci Heiderscheidt** – Walther's head assistant, she is a scientist in her own right and commands three assistants underneath her.

**Charobv** – One of Caivev's generals. He is a skilled sniper and has a warrior son named Chartarra.

**Charles Summers** – A member of The Seven who rule the heptobscurantum

**Charsk** – A vyrm leader

**Chira** – One of Zabe's Corpsmen; he took over the Royal Army after Harken.

**Claire Jones** – Daughter of Sam Jones. Human variant of Princess Bithia

**Druen** – Leader of the Merciful Hammer in the Veritas and Shandra's immediate superior.

**Gita** – A young recruit for the Guardian Corps and friend of Jackie.

**Harken** – A local hero who arose during the Black's occupation; post-Nebraska he rose to lead the Prime's Royal Army.

**Idrakka** – A tarkhūn frostmancer secretly sent to infiltrate Caivev's team over a period of years. Secretly he is the brother of the shade, Jarkara.

**Jackie** – Claire's best friend since her high school days

**Jacob Sisyphus** – Formerly a popular professional wrestler. He is a long time cultist and an arcane practitioner and now a member of The Seven who lead the heptobscurantum

**James Shianan** – A former pro soccer player with worldwide fame. His is a form taken by Nitthogr

**Jarfig** – Museum curator and historian from the prime. He is the Prime variant of Jacob Sisyphus

**Jarkara** -  A shade spy sent by Basilisk. He is one of the more talented shapeshifters and Vivian suspects he was sent as a mole to infiltrate her team. Brother to Idrakka.

**Jenner** – Professor Jarfig's son. He was fifteen when he lost his father and is possessed with the singular purpose: to find and rescue his father or punish those who took him.

**Jonathan Trask** – A member of The Seven who rule the heptobscurantum. Turned out to be a Tarkhūn traitor and spy

**Kreephast** – One of Caivev's generals. He is a member of the Black, but his disguise skills rival those of a shade (he is also General Nyagittari). He is very religious and well versed in history.

**Minas** – The leader of the Order of the Flame within the Veritas.

**Ma Kechewaishke** – A Native American woman who helped Claire access the astral plane

**Miles Jecima** – A linguist with specialty in dead, ancient, and unknown languages. He is good friends and peers with Sam Jones

**Nitthogr** – Sorcerer and leader of both The Black and the heptobscurantum. He and his brother were, long ago, members of the Veritas—a monastic order in the Prime

**Percival Wainsmith** – Independently wealthy man with many influences abroad; he has joined the Heptobscurantum's Seven.

**Perribelle** – Leads the Wax Order of the Veritas.

**Peter Greyson** – A member of The Seven who rule the hepto-bscurantum

**Pietro Walther** – A pseudoscience doctor who was originally recruited and equipped by Bruce Cannon.

**Pollando** – The mute leader of the Order of Mystics within the Veritas. He is a highly trained psychic.

**Praetor Russo** – In charge of a large region of Red Order members

**Quintin Hall** – Formerly with the Red Order. He is still a paranormal investigator but has gone private. Hall remains in touch with Vikrum Wiltshire

**Regorik** – Lead war commander of The Black and second in command after Caivev. He is Tarkhūn

**Respan** – A scientist and R&D expert who works for the Guardian Corps.

**Rob** – Another name for Zabe which he goes by when on Claire's Earth

**Robert Schaeffer** – The Earth version of Zabe. He looks like Zabe... but they are not the same person

**Sam Jones** – Archaeologist and father of Claire Jones

**Shandra** – A Cleric of Veritas and member of the Merciful Hammer. She is responsible for tracking down ancient artifacts with arcane power.

**Shardai** – A former member (retired) of the Guardian Corps

**Shjikara** – High Cleric and leader of the Veritas.

**Skrom** – Caivev's behemoth tarkhūn general; he is perhaps even more devoted to her than Regorik was to Nitthogr.

**Tay-lore** – A quirky android member of Guardian Corps and last member of the technological homo diurnus race. He is fully devoted to Claire/Bithia. He finds killing highly distasteful—but he would make any sacrifice at his queen's request.

**Theera the Undying** – An unkillable servant and personal henchman enthralled and empowered by Akko Soggathoth.

**Thomas Chelish** – A member of The Seven who rule the heptobscurantum

**Trenzlr** – A Blackborne vyrm and Seeker of Maetha who fell through a portal and into the Prime.

**Victor Adams** – A member of The Seven who rule the heptobscurantum

**Vikrum Wiltshire** – A paranormal investigator who works for the mysterious Red Order sect of the Vatican

**Vivian Shianan** – Works for the Special Research Division of the government which looks into paranormal phenomenon and dispels questions. Half sibling to James Shianan.  See Caivev.

**Wulftone** – Cousin to Zabe and second in command of the Guardian Corps; he was raised in the same home as Zabe's brother when his parents died.

**Zabe** – Son of Zahaben. Guardian Corps soldier. Friend and confidant of Princess Bithia

**Zahaben** – Captain of Princess Bithia's personal guard and leader of the Guardian Corps

**Zurrah** – Zabe's brother who was captured and presumed dead at a young age.

# ABOUT THE AUTHOR

Christopher D. Schmitz is an indie author from the fly-over states who dabbles in game design. He has published award winning science fiction, fantasy, and humor. He's written and freelanced for a variety of outlets, including a blog that has helped countless writers on their publishing journey. On any given weekend, he can be found at pop culture and comic conventions across the USA or playing his bagpipes for people. You can look him up at www.authorchristopherdschmitz.com.

# Also by Christopher D. Schmitz